CHRISTMAS WITH HIS CINDERELLA

JESSICA GILMORE

SNOWBOUND WITH THE BROODING BILLIONAIRE

KATE HARDY

MILLS & BOON

by Mills & Boon, an imprint of HarperCollinsPublishers Ltd,
1 London Bridge Street, London, SE1 9GF

www.harpercollins.co.uk

HarperCollins*Publishers*
1st Floor, Watermarque Building,
Ringsend Road, Dublin 4, Ireland

Rotherham MBC				
Rotherham MBC	B54 054 564 5	Askews & Holts	24-Nov-2021	
		AF		£6.99
		RTGRE		

Christmas with His Cinderella © 2021 Jessica Gilmore

Snowbound with the Brooding Billionaire © 2021 Pamela Brooks

ISBN: 978-0-263-30001-7

11/21

CHRISTMAS WITH HIS CINDERELLA

JESSICA GILMORE

MILLS & BOON

For Rufus.

And for all the Good Boys and Girls out there who have brought some happiness, companionship and much-needed exercise to their humans over the last year.

CHAPTER ONE

'So, what exactly *is* the problem?' Alexander Everard Montague, Fifteenth Baron Thornham, eyed the so-called crack PR team he'd hired at great expense coolly, hiding his impatience as he waited for an answer.

The pause stretched, as if the two consultants perched on chairs opposite his three-hundred-year-old desk were playing some kind of game of chicken. The male cracked first. 'The problem, sir...' Hugo hesitated.

Xander steepled his hands and tried not to sigh. 'Yes?' he asked silkily.

Hugo looked at his colleague for support, but clearly none was forthcoming. She stayed silent, the serene half smile gracing her glossy lips unchanging.

'The good news is that the reviews for the hotels are uniformly excellent. The food, the facilities, the service. All five star.'

This wasn't a surprise. Xander worked hard, and expected the same from everyone he employed, ensuring that the hotels under the Baron Thornham brand were a byword for elegant luxury and peerless service. And he and they delivered. But in the last couple of years a certain *cachet* the hotels had effortlessly held for decades had begun to slip. Just a little, but noticeably if you were keeping a close eye on all the data—and Xander was.

To an outsider everything might seem business as usual, the hotels filled with the rich and entitled, every whim catered for. But Xander had crunched the numbers and he knew the truth: the waiting list was months and weeks rather than years and they were no longer the elite's first choice. Although still profitable and successful, the brand had somehow lost the exclusivity that set it apart from bigger, older rivals. And that exclusivity was their USP.

No matter what it took, Xander needed to fix it. Fast.

Healthy profits weren't enough. Xander wanted it all: financial and reputational success. The family name demanded it. The family honour demanded it. 'Do I need to repeat myself? Never mind the *good* news, what is the problem?'

Hugo gulped, straightening his expensive tie. 'It's you, sir.'

The word 'you' echoed around the study and Xander could have sworn he saw the portraits of his ancestors lining the panelled walls smirk in confirmation. He sat back, trying to formulate a response. 'Me?'

You. He could hear his father's frustrated sigh, the same exasperated sigh he'd give when Xander wanted to read rather than hunt, when he slipped away from yet another interminable party, when he struggled to make small talk with guests. No matter he had been a shy, bookish child, as a Montague the ability to command a room had been expected of him, should have come instinctively.

Xander's jaw set as he pushed the memories away. His father had never hidden his belief that Xander had been a disappointment as a son and as an heir. He would not be a disappointment as the newest Baron too. 'Explain.'

'Our research found that guests love your hotels. They love the feeling that they have stepped into the pages of a novel or a television show. The stately home, the Scottish castle, the Mayfair townhouse, the hunting lodge, the chateau, the...'

His mouth tightened. 'There's no need to list them all, thank you.'

He knew them by heart. Of course he did because, after all, the famous stately home in Buckinghamshire, the house in a discreet Mayfair square where he was currently residing, the castle in Scotland, the lodge in Yorkshire, the chateau in the South of France brought to the family by a French great-grandmother, the Rhode Island mansion, the legacy of an American buccaneering great-great-grandmother who had also bequeathed a charming Art Nouveau townhouse on New York's Upper West Side to the family, all belonged to Xander—to Xander and to whoever was prepared to pay handsomely to stay there.

Faced with high taxes and no income after the Second World War, his grandfather had resisted selling his property off, turning each house instead into a hotel where every guest felt personally invited, where dressing for dinner was encouraged and afternoon tea an institution, every day a house party complete with lawn tennis, croquet and lavish meals. And the potential of being personally entertained by a member of the illustrious titled family was the biggest draw of all.

Until now.

Hugo cleared his throat. 'Obviously your father and grandfather couldn't greet every single guest, but guests felt connected to them, even if they never actually met them. However, our research suggests that they find you a little more...remote.'

'Remote?' True Xander didn't have his father's bonhomie, his grandfather's easy patronage, but he had worked hard to overcome his natural shyness, to be welcoming. Or at least he thought he had. Clearly it still wasn't enough. 'In what way?'

'Guests feel as if they don't know you. That they're not personally hosted by you. And without that feeling of connection then the hotels are simply just hotels. Luxurious and exclusive hotels of course, but there's a lot of competition offering the same level of service, especially amongst your target market.'

'Luckily—' finally the woman—Pernilla—spoke '—this is an easy fix. We make sure your guests *get* to know you.'

'How?' Xander's forehead creased. What else would it take? Because if they didn't know him by now...

Xander had grown up travelling from hotel to hotel, never having a bedroom of his own, space that was his alone. His baby photos hung in the drawing room of Thornham Park, the family seat in Buckinghamshire, his graduation photo was displayed on the desk in the library at Glen Thorne in Scotland, his toys sat in the nursery here in London. His whole life had been on display, every meal taken with strangers, no family moment so private it was family alone.

Pernilla held up her tablet. 'Social media.'

'No.' Xander didn't need to think, his response a gut instinct; he didn't need even more of his life on display.

'*You* are the brand, *you* are the Baron, and when people book into your hotel it is as *your* guest. You are inviting them into your ancestral homes, to enjoy your hospitality. They need to feel personally connected to you.'

Much as he wanted to repeat 'no', send the pair of consultants back to their trendy Soho agency and demand a new strategy, Xander made himself absorb their words. Personally, he thought the agency name Milk ridiculous, found the consultants' style too knowingly quirky despite their semblance of formality, and he knew their fees were exorbitant, but he was also aware that their reputation was hard earned. If their research had identified Xander himself as the reason the hotels were losing their identity, then, uncomfortable as it might be, both the cause and the cure needed to be considered.

His grandfather and father might have died, but the need to prove them wrong was still very much alive. Xander had what it took to be Baron Thornham, to be the head of the family, to step into their shoes. It was time to prove it. To step out of his comfort zone, away from the spreadsheets.

'What kind of social media?' He braced himself against his desk, alarmed. 'Not the dancing one?'

'No, no, that wouldn't fit your brand at all. We were thinking visual. After all, you have the perfect backdrop. People want to see beautiful pictures of your hotels, famous guests enjoying the facilities, the food and all the décor, so much of it original. Show people your homes, your life, make them want to be part of it.'

Pictures. That didn't sound *too* awful.

'Let them see that the hotels are not just a short-term destination but a home you wish to share with them.' Hugo picked up the narrative. 'Whether that's through supposedly candid shots of you relaxing in an armchair in the library here, fishing in Scotland, playing tennis in Rhode Island or breakfasting on your personal Parisian terrace. Sell the Baron Thornham lifestyle through you, the actual Baron.'

'Through me. Right.' *That* sounded a little more awful. He wasn't really one for selfies. Not one for photos of him at all. 'I see.'

'We also thought—' Hugo pulled on his tie again '—that you might want to get a dog.'

'A *dog*?' Had he heard correctly? 'What on earth would I do with a dog?' Xander had never had a pet. A life spent moving around, regularly travelling across seas and oceans wasn't exactly conducive to pet owning.

'People love dogs—and, more importantly, they love dog owners. What better way to showcase the hotels and your lifestyle than through a dog? But time is of the essence. It's already the end of November and we recommend you launch the campaign over Christmas. We'll start with you choosing a dog to adopt from the local rescue, then spending Christmas with it as it settles in.'

Pernilla held up her tablet to show him a picture of a dog and its owner walking in a wood—an owner who had more than a passing resemblance to Xander. 'According to our research you usually spend Christmas Eve here in London before going to Thornham Park for Christmas and Scotland for New Year. We tested that itinerary, with shots of a dog sleeping by the library fire, the two of you on wintry walks, the dog's Christmas dinner. Our test audience lapped it up.'

'It all sounds very winsome.' Xander was aware the words didn't sound like a compliment and he hadn't meant them to. The concept actually sounded like the plot of the sort of wholesome film he would immediately turn off. At least they hadn't mentioned matching jumpers. 'However, your research has missed one crucial detail. I don't know anything about dogs. I couldn't possibly manage a rescue dog.'

'We did take that into consideration,' Hugo said, a trifle too smugly. 'That's why we thought you should bring your dog nanny on board to assist you exclusively throughout the whole festive season.'

His *what*?

'Now her social media is really good,' Pernilla said. 'She has a lot of organic followers. The hotel itself plays it safe with its marketing, especially its social media, too safe in our opinion and we have a strategy to remedy that, but the dog nanny's account oozes with personality.'

'I employ a dog nanny?' Maybe he needed an audit of every role in every hotel. Was there a cat masseuse and a hamster chef also lurking on his payroll?

'Three, actually.' Yes, Hugo was definitely verging on smug. 'One here in London, one in Paris and one in New York. Dogs are extremely popular right now with your core clientele, but they can be a hindrance in cities as most restaurants and entertainment venues won't allow them in. The dog nannies walk them, and dog sit if the owners are out for the evening.'

'Here...' Pernilla pushed her tablet onto the desk. 'Take a look for yourself.'

Reluctantly Xander picked it up and scanned the account she had selected. A vivid shot of three fluffy dogs, sitting on a checked blanket in the park, greeted him.

Today's the day the teddy bears have their picnic! Meet Babe, Bear and Belle, contenders for

*the fluffiest dogs of the year award. Spending
the afternoon with these three cuties has been
an utter treat. Now it's time for theirs. Picnic-
time, anyone?*

He swiped onto the next post. This time a handsome, slim dog sat posed before the fire in Thornham
House's library, a book open before him, a tweed ker-
chief around its elegant neck.

*It's raining cats and dogs outside and Austen is
more of a bookworm than a hiker anyway.*

There were plenty more, all showcasing the hotel's
canine guests out and about in the local vicinity or here
in the hotel. There was no sign of the nanny herself, just
the occasional booted foot or mittened hand.

'People like to read this?' He pushed the tablet back
across his desk, unable to keep the scepticism from
his voice.

'They do. She has a high following, excellent inter-
action and a much better organic reach than any other
hotel account. That's why this is the perfect place to
launch your social media and to kick-start the campaign. We suggest that she helps you choose the rescue
dog and works with you while it settles in, chronicling
it all on her account whilst you do the same on the one
we create for you. She and the hotel will cross post you
and we'll work with some influencers to do the same.'

This was really their strategy? A mutt and some pictures? 'But the dog? It would actually live with me?'

'You have plenty of staff to walk it and so on after
the campaign ends, if you didn't want to be bothered

with that side of things. As long as your account still features it regularly.'

For a moment Xander felt pity for the putative dog, condemned to live on show, no real home, no family of its own, a prop and a marketing tool only. He knew what that was like. He opened his mouth, ready to send them back to the drawing board, when his gaze fell onto a portrait of his great-grandmother, dog on her lap, one hand resting fondly on it, and then onto one of a great-great-uncle as a boy, surrounded by spaniels. He'd looked at those pictures as a child and wished for a dog of his own every Christmas. But there had never been a dog under the tree for him; instead he would discover a fancy train set or a huge rocking horse. Expensive toys destined to be shared with any child staying here or at the castle or Thornham Park. His lips curled into a reluctant smile. He'd forgotten that old desire for a dog.

'Okay,' he said, to his own surprise. 'I don't have time to go to the shelter myself so get the dog nanny to select something suitable. Something sleek, a decent size. A Labrador or some kind of hound. Nothing that would wear a bow.'

'Absolutely,' Pernilla said. 'Leave it with us.'

Elfie Townsend walked slowly down the concrete corridor, trying not to let her heart get pulled in a hundred different directions. It was an impossible task. She wanted to give each and every one a good home. The keen one with the bright eyes, wagging its tail enthusiastically. The excited one, barking as it danced around its door. The timid one, lying with its head on its paws, shuffling back as she approached.

But she wasn't looking for her own perfect companion. This was work. She had to find the kind of dog Lord Thornham wanted, a dog as aristocratic as he. Something tall, well-bred and aloof.

Easy.

The dog shelter was now Thornham House's official Christmas charity partner and so Elfie made sure she took plenty of photos of every dog she passed for both her own dog nanny account and the main hotel account. Their goal was that every dog here would find an owner by the end of the Christmas season and so every day she and the hotel's main account would post a picture of a different dog looking for a family.

'Aristocratic…' Elfie murmured as she stopped and took a picture of something small, white and very, very fluffy, imagining walking into Lord Thornham's study with that ball of wool under her arm and seeing his horrified expression. But no, she needed to keep her job until the New Year. She had decided against heading over to the Alps for her usual season working in the mountain resorts of the rich and famous, tempted by a lucrative offer to stewardess for a couple of private yacht charters in January instead. The last thing she wanted was to dip into her precious savings if she was unemployed for a few weeks.

'I'm sure somebody will love to give you a home.' She stooped down and scratched the small dog's ears. 'But you wouldn't want *this* home; it's not exactly cosy and you look like a cosy dog to me. Let me take your picture. I bet we can make sure you get a family for Christmas.'

She straightened, sighing as she did so. Helping re-home these dogs was one thing but, truthfully, Elfie wasn't sure she should be looking for a dog for Lord

Thornham at all. Her one encounter with the Baron had been short, to the point and chilly. Oh, she could see why some of her colleagues swooned over their boss; years of selective breeding had resulted in a face as finely sculpted as a Michelangelo. But although sharp cheekbones, a strong mouth and decisive eyebrows topping a pair of chocolate-brown eyes sounded dreamy in principle, the reality was very different when said eyes were piercing into her as if the owner wasn't really sure why he bothered employing her at all. What kind of dog would enjoy a life that seemed luxurious on the surface, but would potentially be starved of affection? She couldn't see the Baron rubbing tummies and patiently throwing a ball. What she needed was a nice, staid middle-aged dog who looked as if he or she would be at home in the pages of a hunting magazine and required little but a comfortable bed and regular meals.

Reluctantly, Elfie said goodbye to the small fluffy dog, promising again that he would be on the top of her list, and took another look around. The assistant who had welcomed her in had suggested that there might be a suitable dog at the end of the corridor, so Elfie headed in that direction, making slow progress as she stopped to acknowledge each dog with a murmured endearment and photo. She tried not to pause too long but found it hard to walk on when a grey, scruffy-looking dog sat up very nicely, lifting a paw to greet her.

'Why, hello.'

The dog gave the kind of yelp that could be construed as a hello back and Elfie took a step closer. 'Now, what are you?' she asked. 'One of the new design of breeds or a good old-fashioned mutt?'

Not surprisingly, the dog didn't actually answer, but

tilted its head on one side in what she had to admit was a particularly endearing way. 'Oh, well, it doesn't really matter because, cute as you are, I wouldn't call you aristocratic. I'm not being offensive; I'm not aristocratic either. It's a good thing, makes us strong. But I am looking for a well-bred dog for a well-bred gentleman. If I had a flat of my own, a permanent job...' She shook her head regretfully. There was no point wasting time on what-ifs and if-onlys. One day she would be able to afford to buy her own home and then she would have a menagerie of pets. She glanced quickly at the printed nameplate. 'Nice to meet you, Walter,' she said. 'I hope we see each other again soon.'

Walter yelped again, rearing up onto his hind legs.

'You have all the tricks,' Elfie told him, backing away. Okay, maybe he would be top of her list for finding a new owner. It was hard; they all deserved one.

A few steps further and Elfie halted in front of Duke, the dog the assistant had mentioned. 'Hi Duke, you have the perfect name,' she said, holding her hand out to the handsome setter, but, to her consternation, instead of stepping forward, he shrank back, tail between his legs. 'I'm not going to hurt you,' she crooned, but Duke was clearly not reassured, retreating to a corner. Elfie bit her lip as she recalled the brief she'd been given. A hotel dog, a dog to be photographed, to be a social media star, to connect with the guests. 'I don't think you'd like that, would you?' she said softly. 'You need to be an only dog in a small, experienced family, not a publicity dog. I'll find you a good family, I promise. But not the Baron. You're not right for him.' Which was odd because Duke reminded her of Lord Thornham in some ways. She stood there, trying to figure it out. Both had haughty, sleek good looks, but that wasn't it.

Slowly, she went over every word of the very brief meeting she'd had with him in the Thornham House study. He'd asked a few questions about her job, her social media account and then handed her instructions to select him a dog with as little emotion as if he'd asked her to pick up his dry cleaning.

And yet, behind the glacial manner, she had seen a glimpse of something she recognised. Loneliness.

Maybe finding him the right dog wasn't such a crazy task after all. Maybe a companion was something he needed just as much as every one of these dogs did. Or maybe she was just trying to feel better about the task at hand.

Either way, she had a decision to make and there was really only one way it could go. She just hoped she could talk him into agreeing or she'd be looking for a new job after all.

CHAPTER TWO

A TENTATIVE RAP on the door broke the silence and Xander looked up, irritated at the interruption. He knew he'd been on edge for the last few days. Setting up his new social media accounts and deliberately putting himself at the forefront of the hotel's publicity had been an uncomfortable experience. An experience he knew was only going to get worse.

What on earth was he thinking? The hotels were turning a profit. Surely that was the only thing that mattered? He didn't have to try and be his father or grandfather. Didn't have to live up to their expectations, especially now they were gone.

But, at the same time, striving to be the man they had wanted, had expected him to be, was all he knew. There was no other path.

'Come in,' he barked at a second less tentative rap. The door edged open, followed by one of the hotel's porters. Xander repressed a grimace as he recognised Jon. The teenager was part of Xander's flagship apprentice scheme which trained local out-of-work youths in hospitality, but he seemed to be totally intimidated by Xander, which made every encounter excruciating.

Sure enough, Jon shuffled forward and addressed Xander's left shoulder. 'The delivery is here, sir.'

Xander raised his eyebrows. Matters like deliveries were not something that he usually dealt with. 'Shouldn't you be telling the chef?'

'No, sir. A delivery for you. For the new addition, sir.'

'Addition?' Xander frowned and Jon's gaze dropped.

'Yes, sir. I believe the dog is arriving today.'

Xander sat back and rubbed his temples, the nagging feeling of having made a misstep intensifying as the porter's meaning dawned on him. 'Surely you can manage to put away a bowl and a lead without my input?' As part of the PR package around the imminent arrival of the rescue dog, a local upmarket pet brand had agreed to additional sponsorship, supplying Thornham Hotels with all the paraphernalia any canine guest could need as well as donating food, toys and beds to the shelter.

'I think, sir, you'd better come and see for yourself.'

Xander stood up and stretched. 'Fine.'

He followed Jon down the corridor to the receiving bay at the back of the hotel. This was strictly staff only territory but there was no doubt of the season, with cheerful lights strung along the wide passageway. The decorations were nothing compared to the glittering display throughout the main public areas, all in the hotel brand colours of gold, crimson and cream, but they were festive enough.

'Here you are, sir,' Jon said with the air of a man glad to have handed over responsibility.

Xander stopped and looked at the stack of boxes in surprise. How much stuff did one dog need? 'What on earth is all this?'

'There are several dog beds in different sizes, coats, jumpers, toys, treats...'

'Yes, yes, I get the gist,' Xander said. It wasn't so much a dog he was taking on as an entire new lifestyle by the look of it.

'I was just wondering, sir, where to put it all.'

For once Xander didn't have an answer. He'd known that agreeing to taking on a rescue dog would add some complications to his life, but he hadn't realised quite how many. Possessions meant permanence, but how could a man without a permanent residence of his own supply that one basic need?

There were still too many unanswered questions. Where the dog would sleep, for a start. He had a preferred suite of rooms out at Thornham Park, but it was let when he wasn't there and he had no designated space here or at any of the other hotels. He usually took whatever suite was free, happy to move mid stay if needed. He lived on the move, travelling from hotel to hotel, country to country, packing lightly, used to living out of a suitcase, buying what he needed when he needed it. The only space of his own was the study he used here and its counterpart at Thornham Park. His had been no life for a child; it was certainly no life for a dog. The kindest thing he could do was put a stop to the whole idea. Tell—what was her name? Pixie? No, Elfie.

Strange name. It suited her, though, with her pointed chin and big grey eyes.

Eyes that had seemed to see through him.

Tell Elfie to forget the whole idea and charge the PR consultants to come up with a better plan. He didn't need a dog to make him seem human.

'Put it in the back storeroom,' Xander said, turning

on his heel. He'd donate it all to the shelter. That was the kind of PR he preferred. Hands-off and philanthropic.

Xander returned to his study but, try as he might, he found it difficult to lose himself in the work that usually absorbed nearly every waking moment, pushing his laptop away to look across at the painting on the wall opposite—a painting of Thornham Park during the Regency.

Every painting at Thornham House was of an ancestor or of an ancestral home. A constant reminder of all that Xander owned and had to hold together. Not that he needed any reminder. He'd known his destiny and his obligations from the moment he'd first tottered across the ornamental lawn at Thornham Park. His grandfather had told him tales of ancestral heroes hacking their way across battlefields for war prizes and the honour of the Thornham name and every story underlined the same message: every blade of grass, every inch of polished parquet, every antique was entrusted to him to care for, to add to and to pass on.

Sacrifices were demanded of every Baron. He might not have to play political games at court or lead an army, but he did have to safeguard his heritage. Safeguard it and pass it on. His sacred duty.

Eventually, through force of habit and force of will, he managed to return his attention to the ever-pressing inbox and paperwork, losing track of time as he dealt with as many of the never-ending tasks as he could. He had no idea how dark it had become until a more forceful knock than Jon's recalled him to his surroundings.

Straightening his shoulders and flexing his aching wrists, Xander wished, not for the first time, that his life wasn't quite so deskbound and that he had more time to enjoy those acres he spent all his time preserving.

'Come in,' he said, and the door opened. He expected to see one of his managers with a query, or possibly a member of his waiting staff bringing him a coffee or snack. Instead, with a not unwelcome flicker of pleasure, he saw the slim, brown-haired woman whose direct gaze and pointed chin had made such an impression just a few days ago.

'Hello. Elfie, isn't it?'

'That's right. How are you?'

Xander stared at her in some surprise. He couldn't remember the last time anyone had asked him how he was. 'Fine,' he said automatically, without wanting to dwell on whether he really was fine or not. It wasn't the kind of question he'd ever been encouraged *to* dwell on. He had his health and his responsibilities, that was all he needed to know. 'I'm glad you're here,' he added, remembering his decision to cancel the dog.

'Oh?' She looked a little puzzled, and then her face lit up, her smile almost luminous with such infectious delight that Xander could feel his own mouth tugging upwards in a rare genuine response. 'Of course. You must be dying to meet him. It's such a big decision; I can't believe you delegated it to me. I hope you're pleased…' For one moment doubt clouded the glowing grey eyes before clearing, as if it had never been. 'You will be. How could you not?'

How, indeed? Xander had a sense of his legendary control slipping away. 'Pleased?' he queried, although he had a sickening sense that he knew exactly what she was going to say next.

'With your new best friend.'

His *what*? Xander had acquaintances and business rivals, contacts and partners, schoolmates and relatives, old lovers and occasionally new ones, but few friends, just a small close circle from school and university. It was hard to make friends when you were naturally shy and always moving around.

'You've chosen then?' Damn. He should have put a stop to this nonsense immediately. Luckily, it wasn't too late. He would just tell her to take it back where she'd found it and he'd make a nice large donation to the shelter. Everyone would be happy.

Everyone except Elfie maybe. But the happiness of one of his many employees wasn't his priority right now.

Although he would miss that smile.

'You are going to love him,' she said, her smile even brighter if possible, lighting up the room like one of the four huge, professionally decorated Christmas trees in the hotel reception. 'I guarantee it. I fell for him straight away. I can't wait to see your face!' She skipped back to the door and he heard her calling softly to something in the passageway outside. 'Come on, Walter.'

Walter? Like Sir Walter Raleigh? Xander's ancestors had once gone adventuring with the famous explorer. Maybe this was a good sign. Xander half rose expectantly, trying to ignore the unexpected hope fluttering in his chest, only to sink back down again as Elfie stepped back into the room, proudly leading something smaller than expected, knee-high at most, and covered with what could only be described as riotous grey fluff. She stopped a short way away and the mutt sat as she gestured towards Xander. 'Here you go, Walter. Meet your new daddy.'

Xander should have protested that he was certainly

not intending to be known as any animal's *daddy*, but he was too robbed of both breath and words as he took in the medium-sized, at best, dog sitting by Elfie's feet. 'What *is* this?' he asked at last.

Elfie stared at him, a small crease between her perfectly arched eyebrows. 'It's the dog you asked me to get...' She faltered, looking a little less sure of herself. Was that guilt he heard in her voice, colouring her cheeks? He was almost sure it was.

'I asked you to get me something aristocratic, a hound.' He looked pointedly at Walter. 'Has this dog got any kind of pedigree?'

'It's hard to tell nowadays,' Elfie said. 'There are new breeds all the time. I'm sure he's got very distinguished parents on both sides somewhere in his family tree.' She caught Xander's gaze and stopped, swallowing, visibly uncomfortable. 'Look, I know, he's not exactly what you ordered, but I did think about this really carefully, I promise you. It's not just that he's cute, although he is; it's more that he's really good with people and he loves the limelight. Honestly, you should see him playing up to the camera. The one dog they had who fitted the brief you gave me was really shy. He'd be miserable living in a hotel, surrounded by strangers all the time, but Walter will love it.'

Xander had an unexpected pang for the unknown dog. Maybe they were kindred spirits.

'He's lovely, Duke, and deserves a really good home.' Elfie's smile turned reminiscent. 'I hated leaving him, leaving any of them, but it's amazing to know that the partnership between the hotel and shelter can help make the right home happen for him and all the others, maybe even in time for Christmas. I have to admit, I wish I could have adopted every one of them. But, for the kind of life you lead, the kind of life your dog will lead, Walter was the best one. It's working already,' she added, pulling out her phone, touching the screen and holding it out towards him. 'Just look at all those comments. He's only been on the dog nanny account for a couple of hours and already he's a huge hit.'

A hit? Xander wasn't sure he liked the sound of that. Because if the dog was a hit, then how could Xander send him back?

He took another look at the dog, who tilted his head to one side and stared up at him, hopeful query in long-lashed, large brown eyes, and felt a faint tug of recognition, a connection. He pushed it away. He was a serious businessman, the last in a long aristocratic line. House pets in his family were for widows and aunts, or children in the nursery. Dogs lived outside and were trained as gundogs or sheepdogs or something else practical. There was no way he could take something that looked more like a miniature walking shaggy sheepskin rug than a noble beast around with him. He took a deep breath and tried to ignore the two pairs of trusting eyes fixed on him.

'This isn't going to work,' he said decisively. 'You'll have to take it back.'

Elfie stared at her boss, unable to hide her shock. 'Take him back?' she echoed.

The Baron nodded. 'I should never have allowed myself to have been talked into this in the first place. You're right, the life I lead is no life at all for a dog. Besides, I don't even want one.'

'But you can't!'

There was a long icy pause. 'And why not?'

Shuffling from foot to foot, Elfie considered her options. On one hand, she couldn't help but agree with Lord Thornham. If he didn't want a dog, then he certainly shouldn't have one. She spent far too much time looking after pooches who were pampered with exclusive diets and designer accessories but lacked routine and genuine affection. Plus travelling from hotel to hotel, country to country was no life for any animal, and she had heard plenty about how much the owner of Thornham Hotels travelled, how he had no house of his own, no home, his whole life dedicated to the family estate and the family business.

But, on the other hand, what was she to do with Walter? Already her post had been shared multiple times, including a couple of celebrities she had dog nannied for, and had gathered thousands of likes, the comments running into hundreds. The hotel marketing department had thrown a lot of money behind this PR campaign and the charity linkup with the shelter; if she returned the dog the negative press would soon overwhelm them. If she could see that, then surely Lord Thornham must. Which meant he must really, really not want the dog.

She tapped her foot, considering. There was another aspect, a less altruistic aspect to her instinctive refusal. Elfie served the ultra-wealthy simply because those clients tipped well, searching out jobs like her current one looking after the pampered pets of the kind of people who could afford to stay in one of the world's most exclusive hotels. Jobs that meant she could keep saving, helping her close in on her dream of buying her childhood home and finally having a place of her own.

She had a reputation for being diligent, hardworking and discreet. But if she was the one who returned Walter to the shelter then who would trust her with their pets or children or to serve on their yacht? No, she couldn't allow her hard-earned reputation to be devalued. She looked at Xander nervously; she couldn't help but feel he'd never heard the word *no* before.

'I'm just not sure it's a good idea, sir.' Understatement of the century.

Xander's eyebrows shot up; she was right, he *had* never really heard the word *no* before.

'Look,' she said, aware that she was sounding more than a little desperate. 'The adoption is already news. If you send him back, the fallout could be huge. People *like* dogs. And it's Christmas; you'd look like Scrooge sending Tiny Tim to the orphanage.'

But, with a sinking heart, she saw that he still looked determined. 'Scrooge didn't send Tiny Tim to the orphanage,' he said, and Elfie blinked. That was his takeaway from her impassioned plea?

'I know, I just meant if he had...' But she could see he wasn't listening.

'My grandfather told me to always follow my instincts,' he said. 'I should have done so this time. But it's not too late to put things right. We'll make a donation, a larger one. Get me the head of marketing in here and we'll come up with a plan to spin this disaster into something positive.'

Dammit. He meant it. 'I...' She wasn't quite sure what last desperate attempt to change his mind to make, different scenarios and arguments passing through her mind. She thought as fast as she could, letting go of Walter's lead as she clenched her fists and, before she realised what he was doing, the dog padded forward and disappeared behind the huge antique desk.

'Walter!' Elfie said quickly, holding out her hand, but all she heard in response was a deep sigh. 'I'm really sorry,' she added, darting forward to retrieve the errant hound. But as she reached the desk she looked down and stopped, hope returning. Walter had laid down, resting his chin on Lord Thornham's foot, his tail softly beating on the floor. He'd made himself quite at home.

And, miraculously, the Baron hadn't pushed him away. Instead, he was looking down at the dog with surprising softness in the usually hard brown eyes.

Hope filled her. 'Sir, you said yourself, when you sent me to get him, that he would probably only be here over Christmas and New Year, and that after that you'd send him to Thornham Park, where the staff would look after him. It's the beginning of December now, just a month to go. Please reconsider.'

There was a long, long pause, broken only by the thumping of the dog's tail. 'Very well. One month. Then he goes to Thornham Park and becomes someone else's responsibility.'

Elfie just about managed to stop clapping her hands together in gleeful relief. 'That's great, sir. You won't regret it.'

But his handsome face was still set in a frown. 'But I don't have time to look after and train him. You'll need to be looking after him full-time. Will that be an issue?'

Elfie thought regretfully of her lost tips as she shook her head. 'Of course not, sir.'

'Call me Xander,' he said unexpectedly. 'If we're going to be spending the next month together then you'd better call me Xander. And don't worry, you'll be handsomely remunerated for the extra hours. I need you to be on hand twenty-four-seven, living here for the next few weeks and then coming with me to Thornham Park for Christmas—will that be a problem?'

'No, I usually work Christmas,' Elfie said, more than a little dazed. Stay here for Christmas rather than in the tiny shared room she was renting in a hostel three tube lines away? 'It won't be a problem at all.' In fact, it would be very helpful. She'd let slip to her mother that for once she would be in the UK over the festive season and her mother had instantly started pressing her to spend Christmas with her. This way, Elfie had the perfect excuse to get out of it without upsetting her mother or being labelled difficult by her stepfamily.

'Then Scotland for New Year. After that we'll see.'

He nodded in clear dismissal, brows shooting together in query as she didn't move. 'Is there anything else?'

'I just need to go and collect my belongings,' Elfie said. 'But it's an hour's tube journey, so I can't really take the dog. What shall I do with him?'

Lord Thornham—Xander, she reminded herself, his name feeling illicit in her mind—looked down in some surprise as if he'd forgotten Walter was there. 'Take a hotel car,' he said. 'The dog can wait with me. Be as quick as you can.'

'A car, thank you. Yes, of course.' Elfie retreated quickly, holding in her squeal of joy. A car to collect her belongings, a hotel room for the next few weeks. This was turning out to be the best gig she'd had for quite some time. And so she'd have to spend more time with

Xander? He wasn't quite as forbidding as she'd thought, and of course he was very easy on the eye. Maybe this Christmas was going to be a happy one after all.

CHAPTER THREE

ELFIE DELIBERATELY TRAVELLED LIGHT, and it didn't take her long to pack up her belongings from the small hostel room she'd been renting since her return to London. Luckily, the hostel charged by the night which meant she wouldn't be paying for a room she wasn't using.

Her limited wardrobe was functional, layers which took her from balmy summers in the Caribbean to the chill of an Alpine winter, and she had few personal belongings: an old, battered teddy, an e-reader, her beloved camera and the photo that stood on every bedside table, no matter which country she was in. She picked it up and studied it, her heart swelling. Three people standing by a lake, trees reflecting in the blue water. Her dad, young, smiling and so handsome, her mother, bohemian and relaxed, bearing no resemblance to the bustling, polished woman Elfie couldn't connect with, and Elfie herself standing between them, gap-toothed and grinning, no inkling that their idyllic life would ever end.

'Miss you, Papa,' she whispered. What would he think of this job? Would he have laughed and ruffled her hair and reminded her to keep it real? She'd never know. He'd died when she was twelve and she'd missed him every single day since. Missed him and their life together. Sometimes it felt like a dream, one of dappled sunshine, laughter and love. All she wanted to do was recreate that dream.

It was the height of luxury to be chauffeured back across London. December had set in, cold and frosty, sprinkling glittering white decoration on the streets and rooftops, Christmas lights sparkling in shop windows and strung up across streets in varying degrees of tastefulness. As they neared the hotel the decorations upped their game, money no object in these Mayfair streets and squares. And she would be right here in the very heart of it, part of the famous Thornham Christmas celebrations.

Once back at the hotel, Elfie had expected to be directed to one of the staff rooms in the attics but, instead of ushering her through the baize doors which still separated the staff quarters from the guest areas, she found herself led to one of the plush lifts which, like most of the hotel, combined twenty-first century technology and efficiency with a historical glamour that somehow managed to mix hints of Regency, Edwardian and Twenties luxury and still feel authentic. Possibly because the authenticity was real, dating back to when the building had been a family home used for the London Season, generations of redecoration and fashions melding together. During Christmas the Edwardian elements were at the fore, from the Christmas trees in every room to the rich, old-fashioned decorations, holly boughs on every mantel and greenery twisting through wooden banisters. The hotel smelt of spice and oranges, a hint of snow somehow permanently in the air. There was something magical about Christmas at Thornham House.

The lift doors slid open smoothly on the second floor and she stepped out onto the dark gold carpet. The porter took her two bags and carried them along the corridor, passing white panelled doors set into walls papered in cream and gold, heavy gilt-framed oil paintings hung between each door. Elfie followed, her footsteps silent on the thick carpet.

The porter halted outside a door at the very end of the corridor. There was no number, instead the oak nameplate read 'His Lordship's Chambers'. He knocked once, before opening the door with a heavy iron key—and holding the door open for Elfie to precede him into the room.

'Thank you,' she said as he placed the bags just inside the door, wondering if she should tip him when she wasn't a paying guest, and they were on the same staff. The solution came from an unexpected source.

'Yes, thank you, Franz.'

Elfie jumped at the deep masculine tones as Lord Thornham—Xander, she reminded herself—strode in, not through the main suite door but from a discreet door on her left, looking almost relaxed in dark denim jeans and a light grey sweater which clung to what she couldn't help noticing was a perfectly honed torso. She stood stock-still, unable to tear her eyes away for what she knew was at least several noticeable seconds until, to her relief, Walter, who had followed in his wake, spotted Elfie and dashed across the room to hurl himself against her legs.

'Hello there, boy.' She leaned down to stroke his ears, aware that her cheeks were heating up and horribly afraid they had turned red. She wasn't sure what was worse, ogling her boss or being so very obvious about it. 'Did you miss me?' She swallowed, trying to regain her composure, and straightened. 'He seems to have settled.'

'Yes.' Xander crossed the room to slip a folded note into the porter's hand. Franz smiled at Elfie as he discreetly backed out of the room and closed the door behind him, leaving her alone with Xander. And Walter. She was grateful for the dog's chaperonage as she looked around. She was in the sitting room of one of the hotel's famous suites. Two cream sofas faced each other over a low coffee table, a lit fire casting a warm glow over the crimson rug. A dining table set for four sat against the wall and two comfortable-looking reading chairs nestled in the large bay window. The door Xander had entered through was on the far wall, a second door on her right.

Her well-travelled bags looked incongruous amidst all this luxury. As, she suspected, did she. Elfie smoothed her jeans—dirtier, older and much less well cut than Xander's—and unzipped her puffer jacket as she searched for a rejoinder to his curt reply.

'This is nice.' Surely she wasn't staying here. Maybe she was looking after the dog while Xander attended some function and then would be shunted up to her expected place in the attic.

'Yes,' he said again, with as little interest as if she had complimented him on his car's valeting. Less. 'We had a last-minute cancellation which has worked out well. This suite is usually booked up throughout December but it's now free until Christmas Eve, when we leave for Thornham Park. Let me show you to your room.'

He picked up her bags as if they weighed nothing, although Elfie knew the exact opposite was true, and headed towards the nearest door. It led into a large bedroom, heavy curtains already closed against the evening gloom. A sumptuous-looking bed dominated the space. Xander set her bags down and nodded at a door almost hidden in the panelling. 'Your bath and dressing room are in there. Make yourself at home. Get room service if you're hungry, need a drink, anything. The staff know to charge any expenses to my account.'

'I…' She was staying *here*? In an actual *suite*? With food and drink on tap? Just think how much money she'd save. 'Thank you.'

'I've put the dog in with you.' His gaze darted to a large dog bed by the wall. 'I trust that's okay.'

'Of course.' She'd share this room with a dozen dogs if that was what it took. The contrast with her hostel room, where she'd shared with three others, curtains around her bed affording her little privacy, her belongings kept in a locker, was stark. 'This is great.'

'My room is the other side. We share the sitting room but, as I have my office downstairs, I don't think that will be too much of an inconvenience.'

'No.' Hang on, back up a second. He was staying *where*? They were sharing a hotel suite? Calm down, she scolded herself. It was a suite, not a room. In fact, they had separate rooms, separate bathrooms; all they shared was a sitting room bigger than a sizeable flat. She need never see him. At all.

She slowly turned and took in the room. All this space just for her—well, her and Walter. She'd be a fool to pass it up. Besides, just three years ago she'd had to share a tiny cabin with one of the male deckhands when she'd been working on a charter yacht and she'd managed six weeks in a space smaller than this room's walk-in wardrobe without any problems. Of course, despite the deckhand's best attempts, she'd had little interest in him whereas Xander...

Okay. He was attractive. She couldn't deny it. But they had a strictly work relationship and she was a grown woman in control of her hormones. 'No inconvenience at all,' she said firmly.

'Great.' He cast a glance at her bags. 'So why don't I leave you to get settled in and then we can spend the evening planning our next moves?'

'Our next moves?' Either she needed desperately to cough or her throat had somehow swollen because she practically croaked the sentence out as if she were Mae West slinking over to bat her eyes suggestively at him. Elfie took a firm step back and folded her arms. There would be no moves. Xander was her boss. This job was too important to mess up just for the sake of a quick fling.

Not that any fling was in the offing. Look at him and look at her. He was a baron. Polished, sophisticated, aristocratic, and she was staff. She knew how to wait on and bartend, mind children and dogs and change sheets. They came from different worlds.

'With er...Walter.' He said the name reluctantly, as if trying it out for size.

Of course, Walter. The whole reason she was here. 'Yes. A plan. Give me five minutes.'

It was time to show Lord Thornham she was worth every penny of that generous reimbursement he had promised her.

* * *

Xander had no idea why he was so uncharacteristically nervous. This was just a business meeting after all, something he did every day. But Elfie, perched on the sofa opposite his, was nothing like his usual business contacts.

She'd changed into a short red dress teamed with black leggings. The bold colour suited her, warming her pale skin, accenting those extraordinary grey eyes. Eyes he was transfixed by—and that wasn't something that had ever happened before, not in a business meeting, not even on a date. And he didn't know what to make of it, of her. And that niggled away at him far more than he was comfortable with.

What *was* it about Elfie that discombobulated him? That made him want to find out more about her? To know who she was, where she was going, what had brought her to his hotel?

Xander had only dated women from his own background, potential future wives who were interested in his title and heritage as much, if not more than Xander himself. And that was fine with him; he liked the no-nonsense nature of those relationships, knowing he wasn't expected to reveal anything about himself, that he couldn't disappoint or be disappointed. Elfie bore no resemblance to any of his past girlfriends. She suited her name, slim and almost otherworldly, with those huge grey eyes, her heart-shaped face with its sharp cheekbones and pointed chin, make-up free, her chestnut hair pulled back in a casual ponytail. Everything, from the way she dressed, the way she sat curled up in a corner of the sofa, to the smile lurking in the dimples that punctuated her cheeks, seemed so relaxed and devil-may-care. It was alien to him. Exotic.

Alluring.

No. What on earth was he doing, thinking that way? *Alluring?* What was he? A poet? Only one Thornham had ever been a poet and look what had happened to him. A duel, of all ridiculous things.

He straightened, pushing all thoughts of creamy skin and storm-coloured eyes determinedly out of his mind. 'Have you read the PR strategy?'

Elfie nodded. 'Yes, and I have some ideas.' She looked at him in query and he nodded for her to go ahead. The consultants had been impressed with her, that was why they'd wanted her on board; it made sense to hear what she had to say. And both social media and dog owning were as alien to him as, well, actual aliens.

'This is all about your personal profile, so everything we do needs to look as authentic as possible. More, it needs to *be* authentic. Every post, every picture. I thought we could start with a walk around Hyde Park tonight, maybe a couple of shots of the two of you on the sofa...'

'Absolutely not. No pets on the sofas in any hotel.'

'We'll put a throw down,' she said soothingly. 'Then tomorrow a little bit of the same. Walter in your office, sitting at your feet while you work, maybe the two of you taking afternoon tea, sniffing round the gardens. Over the next few days we'll build in some Christmas shopping, sitting by a fire in the library in matching Christmas jumpers.' Her dimple flashed, hopefully to signify she was joking. Xander exchanged a look with Walter, a promise that neither of them would go any-where near Christmas jumpers.

'That all sounds very reasonable.' Nothing too terrifying—or too personal.

'It's a good start, but we don't have long so it's important that we make as much of an impact as possible. After a few days warm-up we need to go all-in. You need to make a statement.'

That didn't sound quite so reasonable. He raised wary brows. 'A statement?' It was the hotels which made the statement, not him. 'In what way?'

Elfie clasped her hands together. 'I was thinking we should hold a Christmas fete—and include a dog show.'

'A *what*?' Xander wasn't sure what he'd been expecting her to suggest, but a dog show was nowhere on the list. 'Where?' Add in a *who* and *why* and he still wasn't sure he'd understand her reasoning.

'Here!'

'Here?' Had he heard her properly? 'The hotel is dog friendly, but only in certain areas and exclusively for dogs belonging to guests. I really don't think...'

'Oh, no, I didn't mean inside, but there is plenty of room in the gardens!'

Thornham House boasted the largest hotel garden in London, true, but she was still missing his point. 'Elfie, this is an exclusive hotel. People come here to get away from everyday life. This isn't a public amenity.' Especially not an amenity for the public's dogs. The lawn would never recover. 'We don't simply open our doors and let anyone in.'

'And you won't. This won't be open to just anyone, just local families and anyone who wants to come will need to register in advance. You'll know exactly who attends. Look, I was thinking this could be a charity event for the dog shelter *and* a way of involving your-

self with the community. I was looking through some of
your family history and when this was a private house,
even in the first few years of it being a hotel, there was
always a Christmas party for the local children. Your
family held one at every property they owned. They
were quite the event, with Father Christmas, presents
for every child and their parents and a huge tea.'

That rang a bell. Xander had heard his grandfather
mention it once or twice. Christmas was a big deal for
all the Baron Thornham hotels, with family traditions
at the heart of the celebrations. But, somewhere along
the line, this particular tradition must have fallen by the
wayside. 'And you want to revive it for *dogs*?'

'For local rescue dogs, yes. And local children too.
Look, not everyone is a fan of the Dog Nanny account;
some of the dogs I look after are really indulged, they
eat better than many families. I know a hotel like this
is aspirational, is supposed to be out of touch, beyond
day-to-day, but there's a limit, and a diamond-encrusted
dog collar is that limit for many people. A revival of
the Christmas party for local children tradition would
be a way of addressing that, especially with a charity
angle. It ties in perfectly with the PR strategy and the
partnership with the shelter.'

'Dogs *and* children? You're sure that's all you want?
It's Christmas, Elfie, winter. It's cold out. How much
would it backfire if we ended up with freezing toddlers?
It would be chaos. Besides, this is Mayfair. Any local
child probably has a social diary busier than mine.'

Why was he even debating this?

But Elfie was clearly not giving up. 'You know as
well as I do that there is poverty in every corner of London, and the joy of a community event is that it's open to

all, whether they live in a mansion or a tiny flat. Invite your staff's families too. We could put a marquee up in the garden, sell those amazing mini mince pies and Yule logs the kitchen do, along with mulled wine, hot chocolate. Look. I know I just sprang this on you and it sounds a little crazy, but Xander, it could be amazing. It'll raise money for the shelter but, just as importantly, it'll show that you care about your hotel and the local community, about the charity you're sponsoring. It'll give you a presence online, yes, but beyond that too. Isn't that what this is about?'

Was it? Xander wasn't even sure why he had started all this any more. But both his father and grandfather had possessed the gift of making anyone and everyone feel welcome, no matter their background.

'When?' he asked warily.

Her eyes were hopeful and he could feel himself weakening, wanting, despite himself, to see that spectacular smile again, to provoke that smile. 'The weekend before Christmas, to give us time to advertise it.'

'I'll think about it.' That was as far as he could go. He got up, wanting to avoid the disappointment in her eyes. 'Did you say something about a walk?'

'Please do. We haven't got long, so if you want to go ahead we need to get started. But I appreciate it's a lot to take in.' Her voice was bright, professional. 'And yes, Walter's first walk is definitely on the itinerary. But first he needs his dinner; would you rather I take him to the kitchens or is he okay to eat up here?'

Xander's first instinct was to say the kitchens, but at the word *dinner* Walter had jumped to his feet and was regarding Xander with a hopeful expectation. He wasn't sure he could bear to be the focus of two disappointed looks in one five-minute period. 'Here will be fine.'

'Excellent.' She uncurled herself from the sofa and, caught off-guard, Xander found his gaze travelling up toned legs which, despite her diminutive size, seemed to go on for ever. The very air stilled, thickened, as his blood heated.

'I'll do it,' he said, needing to do something, be somewhere, to get his mind back in order. 'He is meant to be my dog after all.'

'Why have a dog nanny and feed him yourself?' Her smile wavered as he stared. 'Okay, that was funnier in my head. You know the saying, why have a dog and bark yourself? No? You're right, it makes no sense. Forget I said anything. Please. I'll get his kibble and bowl.' Her smile was flustered as she disappeared back into her room. Xander inhaled, long and slow. What on earth was going on? Why was he reacting to her every move like this? Standing and staring like an adolescent addressed by the girl all his mates fancied.

Not that he would know, having spent his adolescence in an all-male boarding school.

Actually, the why didn't matter. What did matter was how the rest of the month went. He might find Elfie attractive, but he didn't have to think about it, have to act on it. His goal was clear. Ensure the hotels returned to the very top of the most desirable lists, safeguard his legacy and then find a suitable Baroness and father an heir to pass it on to. A suitable Baroness who would understand his commitments, his sacred trust, his need to put the hotels, the land before all else. A woman born and bred to the position, just like his mother, his grandmother and every other woman who had borne the title—and subsequently an heir.

And that meant focusing on the campaign and not his new assistant's legs, quite apart from the inappropriateness, considering that he was, after all, her employer. Right. That was decided. Now he just had to somehow manage it whilst sharing a suite with her for the next few weeks.

It was going to be a very, very long month.

CHAPTER FOUR

ELFIE PULLED ON her gloves and searched for something to say as they exited the hotel out of the discreet side entrance and started along the frost-covered, streetlamp-lit street towards the park. She wasn't usually lost for words; nearly a decade of working in the service industry and travelling meant she was a mistress of small talk, able to make easy conversation with everyone from billionaires to fellow backpackers who only had a few words of English. But Xander Montague, Baron Thornham was the exception proving her rule because she had nothing.

It was partly because he had been so lukewarm—at best—about her dog show idea. Which was disappointing because it wasn't a spur-of-the-moment idea; she had done some research and really thought a Christmas-themed charity fete would work and it had been nice, really nice, to flex her brain for a change.

Her mother always said she was wasting herself on a series of go-nowhere jobs. It wasn't that Elfie really cared what her mother said; after all, in Elfie's opinion her mother was wasting her own artistic talent. But to be told by an actual award-winning media agency how much they loved her social media account and inventiveness had been an ego booster she hadn't even known she'd needed. She was determined to do her best to make a real success of her part in the partnership with the shelter.

She was also reluctant to be the one to start a conversation after her attempt at a joke had fallen so flat. Yes, it had been an appallingly bad joke but the accepted polite response was for Xander to at least smile, not to look at Elfie as if he was about to dissect her, was trying to see inside her.

And that was the third reason for the uncharacteristic silence. Because, as she had got to her feet, she had caught Xander looking at her and if she didn't know better she would have thought that he was checking her out. Checking her out very slowly and thoroughly, those dark eyes moving up her body as if he were trying to learn every line. Her whole body had quivered as if he had actually been touching her. Worse, she had wanted him to be touching her, every nerve suddenly standing to attention. No wonder she had made a stupid joke to try and break the tension.

She must have misinterpreted the look. He was probably wondering what to have for dinner. Because why would a handsome, titled millionaire look twice at Elfie, small, scruffy and currently covered in dog hair?

'I'm really enjoying Hyde Park at Christmas,' she said in the end as they turned the corner and the bright lights of the winter markets became visible. As a conversational gambit it was better than nothing as Xander seemed content to walk beside her in brooding silence. It wasn't that Elfie minded silence, she didn't, but she preferred it to be comfortable, not stretch on and on.

'The lights are so pretty; I think it equals New York and they really know how to celebrate Christmas.'

Nothing. She gripped Walter's lead tightly. Silence it was.

'I like Paris.'

Had she heard right? A reply? More, a conversational gambit. 'Sorry?'

'At Christmas I always think Paris is very beautiful. Vienna too,' he added. 'But I don't own a hotel in Vienna.'

'Maybe you should, think of the afternoon teas. I still dream of the *kaffee und kuchen*.'

'You know Vienna?'

'A little.' She hesitated, not sure how professional to keep this conversation. 'My father was half French and I spent most of my childhood in France. Mum and Papa were both landscape artists, so we spent every holiday travelling around; they were looking for inspiration. A few times they pulled me out of school for a few months to spend time in different places—in Germany and Austria mainly. I remember Vienna really well, but I think that might mostly be because of the cakes.'

'That must have been an unsettling childhood.'

'Oh, no, I loved it. Papa always said home was when we were together, and we were always together. We'd stop the van, get out our cushions and rugs and throws and within an hour we could transform any apartment or cabin or house into a home.' Memories of places lived passed through her mind, different locations, different sizes and styles, but all full of love and laughter and for a moment she was so winded by grief and loss it almost floored her. She carried on hurriedly, pushing the emotion back. 'But there was something special about going back to our cottage again. It wasn't much, a little stone house that Papa always meant to extend and never quite got round to starting, but he and Mum chose it for the location, surrounded by orchards, with a river at the bottom of the garden...' Her voice trailed off and for one moment she could almost smell the blossom.

'I went to boarding school when I was eight, but I travelled a lot too, although always to our hotels, places that have been in the family for generations. The difference, I suppose, was that I didn't have a base to return to. A proper home.' There was a melancholy note in the last word that hit her right in the heart. She didn't have a home now, but she had once. 'Do your parents still travel around?'

'No.' She took a deep breath. The words still hurt. 'My dad died when I was twelve. We came back to England; Mum stopped painting and got a job and a year later she remarried. She only travels for holidays and, even then, mostly to their holiday home in Cornwall. No van required.'

'And you?'

'Me? I'm always on the move. I headed off the summer after I turned eighteen and I've been travelling around ever since. I started off waitressing in the South of France, thanks to my language skills, then headed to the Alps for the ski season. That led to a few seasons working on yachts, with ski seasons in between and backpacking in between.'

'And yet here you are. What brought you back to England?'

Elfie grinned. 'This is just temporary. Last year I was offered a nannying job in New York and did some dog walking on the side; when my visa ran out one of my clients mentioned this role and I applied. I've been here six months, which is a long time for me to be in one place. Originally I was going to head back to the Alps but I got offered a really good charter job in January so decided to stick around until then. This is the first Christmas I've spent in the UK for a long time.'

'Your mother must be pleased to have you around for once.'

She shrugged. 'She has a big family now; she knows I'm busy.' How could she say she deliberately kept away at Christmas, at all family occasions, popping back briefly when she knew her stepfamily would be away? That since her father's death she and her mother had grown so far apart it was as if they were on different planets, not just in different countries?

They stopped to cross the road and Walter automatically sat. She smiled up at Xander. 'He's got excellent manners; whoever trained him did a great job.'

'Do you have any information about where he was before the shelter?'

She shook her head. 'Apparently he was left on the doorstep with a note and his favourite toy. Someone who couldn't cope any more. It's really sad, because he was obviously loved. He seems secure, well trained, in good health. Look, I hope you don't mind me mentioning this, but I wouldn't be doing my job if I *didn't* mention it. I know you won't be looking after him full-time yourself, but he does need security.' She had known that the dog she chose was being offered a home for PR purposes, but she hadn't realised it was *only* for PR, how conflicted Xander was about having the dog at all. Walter had already lost one home; he deserved a place of his own.

'The manager at Thornham Park has one of the estate cottages and is more than happy to look after Walter when I am not there or when I am too busy.' Xander's reply was curt but Elfie was relieved to hear that he was one step ahead of her, that he had had the foresight to anticipate the dog's needs.

'That sounds great. As long as he's happy.' She'd known Walter for less than a day, but she was already falling for his scruffy charms. She didn't want to think about parallels to her equally swift but far more unsettling awareness of Xander, not that his charms were remotely scruffy. She stole a look at him as they crossed the road, tall and straight backed, black wool coat buttoned against the cold, a grey cashmere scarf wrapped around his neck, dark hair just long enough on top to give him a slightly rakish Edwardian air if it hadn't been combed neatly back. No, not scruffy at all, whereas her own coat was the one she used for skiing, a cream puffy affair, her hair pulled back because she hadn't had time to wash it. The two of them must look most incongruous together.

They reached the gate that led into Hyde Park. Ahead bright lights showcased the Christmas markets and the fairground. Instead, Xander turned down a quieter path, away from the noise and crowds, taking Walter's lead from Elfie as he did so. 'Doesn't it get lonely, always being on the move?'

She had thought the topic was over, the question catching her so by surprise that Elfie didn't have an answer ready. 'A little,' she said, surprised into honesty. 'Sometimes. I like seeing the world, though; that's why I first headed off. I wasn't used to staying in one place.

I missed the thrill of discovering a new region, a new city, new customs and food.'

Well, that and her mother's second pregnancy. It had been bad enough living in someone else's house, feeling more than a little like Cinderella with her two newly acquired stepsisters and their father, strangers to her in every way. Her mother's first child with her new husband had only made her feel further estranged from this unwanted new family. A second had cemented her position as outsider. Better to leave.

'But you can't travel for ever, surely? You're what? Twenty-five…six?'

'Twenty-eight.'

'What's next? If you keep moving on, then how do you ever move up?'

'Not everyone wants a corporate future.' This topic reminded her a little of her last conversation with her stepfather. Actually, it reminded her a lot. Defiant, she tilted her chin. 'Not that I don't have ambitions. I have a plan. I take jobs where I can live cheaply or for free and get well remunerated. Stewarding on yachts, chalet girl, dog nanny…'

'Dog nannying pays that well?' Was that a smile lurking on his well-cut mouth?

'It pays okay, I guess,' she allowed and was startled by his laugh. 'But the tips turn it from okay to pretty good. And I do have an end goal. My Papa always said that all anyone needed to be creative was time and place. He wanted to extend our cottage and turn it into a retreat for artists and writers. I want to make his dream come true. We still have the land, at least my mother does. I'm saving to buy it from her, to turn the place into the perfect artists' retreat. That dream makes every long shift, every difficult client, worth it.'

There was a long pause. 'I know something about family dreams. I'm sorry about your father.'

Her sigh was more than a little shaky. 'Thank you. And I know you lost yours earlier this year. It's not something that ever really goes away, is it?'

'No. Although of course I was an adult when mine died, and we weren't close. But I still want to make him proud. Even to the extent of getting a dog and agreeing to put photos of me with said dog all over the internet. Speaking of which, is this a good spot for our first portrait?'

Grateful for the change in topic, Elfie looked around. They were under a tree, a streetlight highlighting its winter-bare branches, in the distance the bright lights of the German Christmas market and funfair, the Ferris wheel silhouetted against the sky.

'This is perfect. Stand under the tree, look that way; that's right.' She was always assured with her camera, even a phone one, had been ever since her father had taught her how to properly look, how to frame a shot. She loved capturing a moment that no one else had witnessed, looking for an unusual angle. She focused more on the low branch and the wheel behind it, letting Xander and Walter almost blur into the background, taking a few in colour before switching to black and white. She then changed focus, zooming in on Walter first, posing like a professional, head held high and slightly tilted in an endearing way, before switching to Xander.

Her mouth dried. He was a photographer's dream, each sharp line, each hollow in his face creating the kind of angles a camera loved. He'd relaxed in the moments she'd been concentrating elsewhere, an almost dreamy expression softening the handsome face. She allowed herself the luxury of zooming in even more so that his face filled her camera, her gaze lingering on his mouth almost longingly, until the chill in the air reminded her she was here to do a job.

'Okay, that's good. Let's go and get some mulled wine and I'll take some less arty shots. It's always good to have a variety; each medium responds to different types of styles.' Speak professionally and she might act professionally. 'Come on, Walter, if you're really good there might be a bratwurst in your future!'

Xander followed Elfie as she almost danced down the path leading to the bright lights of the market and funfair. There had been something disturbingly intimate about posing for her, just the two of them in the dark. He could almost feel her concentrating on him, like a caress. He had stood there, barely able to breathe as she had explored him. Wishing he could explore her in turn.

He stopped, shocked. It was unlike him to lose control, even in his thoughts. And there had been no control in the image that had just flashed through his mind.

This unexpected attraction wasn't ebbing the more time he spent with her; it was growing. Maybe because the lonely child in him recognised something similar in her. Or maybe it was something far more obvious. He was a man who hadn't dated for a while, not since his father's last illness. And Elfie? Well, Elfie was pretty, with extraordinary eyes and a gorgeous smile. Add full, kissable lips and a pair of the best legs he'd ever seen and maybe it wasn't a mystery why she had him in a spin. It was a simple matter of biology, hormones and pheromones.

She was also his employee and that put her firmly out of bounds. Plus, now he'd turned thirty the next item on his to-do list was to look for his Baroness. Someone who understood duty, how to be a hostess, the importance of being custodian of an ancient estate. Love and attraction came a poor second to those requirements. But that was okay. Liking and compatibility was non-negotiable; he wanted a comfortable atmosphere, especially for any children, and desire would be a bonus, but he didn't require love. Maybe the expectation of it had been bred out of him by all those centuries of strategic marriage. Even his parents had married because they were a good match, his mother the daughter of an Earl looking for status and somewhere to use the unique set of skills she'd gained living in one of England's best-known stately home destinations.

No, it was too much to expect love *and* the kind of skills his future wife needed, he knew that—and the woman he eventually married would know that as well. It was a good thing he wasn't a romantic, had never fallen in love. It made duty so much easier.

And he was reconciled to loneliness after all.

But one thing was non-negotiable. No child of his would grow up lonely, always an outsider. Xander would do whatever it would take to make sure that didn't happen. When children came along, he would find a base for them, probably at Thornham Park. Work might keep him on the road but his children would have a home. And no matter their interests and personality, he would always encourage them to be themselves. To know that they were enough, just as they were.

By the time Xander caught up with Elfie and Walter they had reached the path at the edge of the fair. To one side were the rides. Families, young hand-holding couples and groups of shrieking friends thronged around the loud, flashing rides, the smell of candyfloss and excitement permeating the air. Ahead was the ice rink, music blasting, competing with the shrieks of the skaters, most inching gingerly around in the manner of the once-a-year skater, a few, more adept, speeding and spinning in the middle. Everywhere was noise and bustle. Looking down, he noted Walter pressing close to Elfie's calf, his tail down.

'It's too busy for the dog,' he said curtly, and Elfie nodded.

'Agreed.' She glanced over at the wooden shacks that made up the German market, just as busy as the other parts of the fair. 'But the light is good in this corner, gives the illusion of being in the middle of it all; we just need some props. Stay here, I won't be long.' She handed the lead to Xander and, before he could respond, disappeared off in the direction of the stalls. Walter whined, a short, pathetic sound, pulling on his lead and staring at the crowds now hiding Elfie from view.

'She'll be back soon.' Xander said gruffly. He wasn't used to offering comforting words. Commands, yes, questions, yes. But comfort? He wasn't sure where to begin.

Walter quivered, still straining at the leash. 'Come and wait with me,' Xander suggested, and the dog's ears pricked up. 'We'll both be more comfortable if you're not yanking at the lead.' He kept his voice conversational and was surprised at the thrill of accomplishment when Walter backed up until he bumped into Xander and sat. 'That's a good boy.' Crouching, Xander dropped his hand softly onto Walter's head. To his surprise, the wiry curls were soft. There was something soothing about the contact.

They waited there for a short time, breath cloudy in the cold evening gloom, until Elfie reappeared, carefully balancing a cardboard tray. The smell of fried onions wafted enticingly and Walter whined again, this time in hope more than misery, and she grinned, Xander's chest constricting as her face lit up once again.

'I've got a special onion-free one for you,' she said to the dog, setting the tray carefully down on the bench behind them. 'Just let it cool. No onions, raisins or chocolate for dogs, which makes Christmas a dangerous time,' she added, handing Xander a wrapped hot dog. 'Here, we didn't get dinner before we left. You're not vegetarian, are you?'

'Um…no.' He stared at the greasy bundle in his hand. He rarely, if ever, ate street food. But the hot dog did smell good.

'There's fries as well. But you need to earn your dinner.' Her phone was out again and she made Xander pose for a few shots, first sitting on the bench then standing with the fair lights behind him, before crouching and feeding Walter his onion-free hot dog.

'I'm not sure he even tasted that,' he said, stretching back up, and Elfie laughed.

'Me neither. Look at him, making up to you for more. You already had kibble, you greedy dog.'

Xander sat on the bench, unwrapped his hot dog and took a tentative bite. To his surprise, it tasted as delicious as it smelt, spicy and hot, the onions soft and caramelised. 'This is good. Thank you. How much do I owe you?'

Elfie sat down next to him and handed him the cone of fries. 'It's on me. Thanks to you, I am spending tonight in the height of luxury and I intend to make my way through the room service menu, so this is the least I can do. Here.' She reached into the tray and took out a sealed cup. 'Mulled wine. It seemed rude not to; it is a German Christmas market.'

'In that case, cheers.' Xander held his cup up to hers and she reciprocated.

'Cheers. To Walter and to a successful campaign.'

'To Walter,' he echoed. For a moment he had forgotten why he was here, why she had been photographing him. For a moment he had been a guy out at Christmas with a pretty woman and their dog. For a moment he had been utterly content.

CHAPTER FIVE

'MORE TEA?' the waiter murmured.

Elfie sat back and considered her plate. She had rapidly demolished her half of the delicate smoked salmon and cucumber, turkey and cranberry, and brie and grape relish sandwiches, and had eaten both her savoury cheese scone—small, she reminded herself, practically doll-size—served with creamed Stilton, and orange and cranberry scone served with brandy butter.

She eyed the top plate of the three-tiered afternoon tea serving platter where tiny works of sugary art awaited her. Perfect mince pies topped with crumble or pastry, a mouthful of chocolate-covered Yule log, a square of stollen, gingerbread shaped into a Christmas bauble and delicately decorated. It all looked too good to eat. Well, almost.

'Yes, please.' She'd need the tea to wash down the cakes. It wasn't often an afternoon tea of this calibre came her way. She wasn't going to waste a single crumb.

Xander, sitting opposite, was far more measured. So far, he'd eaten merely two sandwiches and half his savoury scone. But, then again, food like this was an everyday occurrence for him, whereas for Elfie... She tried to suppress a sigh but failed and Xander raised his brows in query.

'You're not enjoying your afternoon tea?' he asked, and Elfie sensed the waiter next to her stiffen as if in alarm. No wonder when he was serving said afternoon tea to the man who owned all this luxurious decadence—and who was ultimately in charge of his job.

'No, the tea is delicious. It's all delicious. That's the problem.'

Xander leaned back, his mouth curved in amusement. 'I am struggling to see why.'

'Because I'm realising how easily I could get too used to this,' Elfie said, selecting one of the Yule logs reverently. 'Every morning I am brought a pot of perfect coffee with a miniature Danish, just to keep me going while I walk Walter. Then, after his walk, I come here…' she gestured to the orangery, with its comfortable sofas and crisp white tableclothed tables which doubled as the hotel's dog-friendly dining space '…where I order anything I want for breakfast. Anything. And then I sit in a comfortable armchair in the library and work on one of the social media accounts—did you know Walter is beating us both in terms of followers?—where I am brought lunch. And as for my room? That mattress is heaven. It's a good thing Walter likes a lie-in because getting up gets more difficult every day.'

Now Xander wasn't trying to suppress his amusement, barking out a slightly rusty laugh. It was rare to see him respond with more than a polite, mechanical smile and Elfie couldn't help feeling triumphant whenever she provoked a full-on grin from him, when he stopped being the serious and slightly stuffy Lord Thornham and became simply Xander. 'Are you complaining that the food is too good, or your job is too easy?'

'At some point I will have to go back to real life, and I don't know how I'll survive the shock when I am the one offering tea, not accepting it. Plus, if I carry on like this, I am not sure I'll even fit in my clothes come January, which for someone who has one carefully selected travel wardrobe is a serious issue. And yet I can't stop.'

'Isn't indulging the point of Christmas?' he asked, and she shot a pointed look at his own barely touched tier of treats.

'For some.'

He laughed again as Elfie took a bite of the Yule log, closing her eyes as the intense chocolate hit flooded her taste buds, glad of the distraction. Sombre, work-focused, curt Lord Thornham she could handle, but her unexpected suite mate, the man she enjoyed making laugh, the one she was so aware of she could probably describe every millimetre of his wrists was another thing entirely.

No matter that she had her own bedroom and bathroom, sharing the hotel suite felt a lot more intimate than an anonymous bunkroom.

His laptop left on a coffee table, the book he was reading—he liked vintage crime, apparently—on a sofa arm, a bookmark denoting his spot. She saw him in his socks, in his post work version of casual, with his hair shower-wet and as he took his first coffee of the day. She saw the weariness descend at the end of another long, long day and noted how his schedule was all work and no play. Even his dog walks focused on work as she and her camera shadowed him, capturing as many moments as she could for posts, stories and the popular

Walter blog on the hotel chain's website. She challenged herself to make him smile, and once or twice had found herself being gently teased in turn.

Then there were the charged moments... The times when silence descended and it was far from comfortable. The moments when she was achingly aware of every sinew on his forearms, his deceptively muscled thighs and the smooth planes of his stomach, the way his hair rebelled to fall over his forehead and the darkness of his eyes. The way he looked—or deliberately didn't look—at her. The heated caress of his eyes when he did.

He'd made no move beyond looking and nor had she. Here, she sensed, she was in charge. Xander was too aware of his position, his seniority over her to make a move. The power imbalance between them was all too evident. The bedroom she slept in, the food on her plate, that delicious morning coffee was all at his expense. And she was discovering that he was a man of absolute honour, that although his public image might be remote and austere, his staff loved him, especially those who had known him since he was a child, and he took his responsibilities to them very seriously. So no, he wouldn't make a move, his seniority, his rank, his title too much part of him.

Unless she was imagining the connection between them.

But she wasn't. There was no imagining the tingling sensation she felt whenever that dark hooded gaze was fixed on her, that absolute awareness of his every move, the way the very air stilled and thickened and their hearts started to beat together, a slow steady thrum.

Of course she could be the one to make a move. After

nearly a decade of travelling and short-term jobs, Elfie wasn't shy about letting men know when she was interested. Time was too short in a ski season or a yacht charter to play coy games. What was the worst that could happen? A rejection? It was hardly going to compare with losing her family. She was happy to laugh it off and walk away with no hard feelings if she'd misread the attraction. But she didn't usually, her antennae were good.

But, no matter how good her antennae, she couldn't allow them to twitch in Xander's direction; not only was he her boss but he was also as far from her usual relaxed, easygoing type as a man could get. Quiet, thoughtful, clever and with an unexpected gleam of humour that warmed her through, he was a challenge, one she was increasingly drawn to solving. And that set off alarm bells. Elfie had never really fallen for anyone properly, never had her heart broken—or given it away. She wasn't about to start now, not when she was so close to achieving her dreams. Anyone who unsettled her as much as Xander did came with warning signs. She'd do well to heed them.

'Something wrong?'

With a start Elfie realised that she had fallen into deep thought and pushed all thoughts of attraction and love far away. This was the best job she had ever had. There was no way she was stuffing it up by allowing herself to proposition her boss. 'No, nothing at all. I was just thinking of captions.' She looked down at Walter, who was happily curled up at her feet, enjoying his own afternoon treat, a turkey-flavoured chew. 'I've got some great shots of Walter and you, and the cakes in

CHRISTMAS WITH HIS CINDERELLA

the background look delicious so I'd like to draw attention to them; you can't beat a bit of product placement.'

'You're good at that. Have you ever thought of making a career of it?'

'What? Become an influencer?'

Xander winced. 'No. Do you have any idea how many try and blag free stays from us? I hate the very word.'

'But isn't that what you're trying to do? Influence the right people to come here, the kind of people who will make sure that this is the place to be?'

'In a way, but it's not as if we have a problem with capacity; it's just making sure we attract the right kind of people. It's about *who* wants to stay here, not how many.'

'Snob,' she teased, and that almost-reluctant smile warmed his eyes—and her body.

'I'm a Baron. It comes with the job. No, not an influencer, but a career in marketing. You have a good eye and a way with words. Look at the buzz you've created around Walter—it's way beyond the PR team's expectations and that's down to you.'

'I can't take all the credit; Walter's naturally photogenic.' He wasn't the only one. Xander's photos were also catching more than a little attention and some of the DMs he'd been sent would make a sailor blush. 'But thank you. I'm really glad you're happy and it's working, but I don't want a desk job.'

'Because of your artists' retreat?'

She nodded, oddly touched he'd remembered the casual conversation from over a week before. 'That's right.'

'It's a lot to take on. We both know how tough hospitality is—will you run it single-handedly?'

'I need to build it first,' she pointed out as her phone rang. She pulled it out of her pocket, only to abruptly silence it when she saw her mother's name on the screen.

'Sales call?'

'Hmm? Oh, no, it was my mother. I haven't figured out how to tell her I am still in the UK. She's bound to start making noises about Christmas when she finds out.' She pocketed the phone and sat back in the chair. 'It's always an easier conversation to have when I am a plane ride away.'

'Christmas?' He sat back, face wiped smooth and blank. 'Forgive me, I hadn't thought. Of course you should spend Christmas Day with your family. Walter and I will be fine for one day.'

'They're not my family,' she snapped and then, seeing the surprise on his face, she took a deep breath. 'I'm sorry; I just mean that I'd rather work. Talking of which, photos of delicious cakes aside, the purpose of this meeting was supposed to be to discuss the dog show and we haven't even started. Let me pull up the schedule.' She might have confided her dreams to Xander but there were topics that were strictly off-limits to everyone, and her family—or lack of one—was one of them.

But if she was going to confide in anyone, she couldn't help wish it could be him.

Over the next hour Xander found his mind wandering away from the Christmas dog show and children's party, which was rapidly taking on a life of its own with lots of sign-ups and positive publicity about Thornham House reviving a much-loved tradition. Elfie and the hotel events team had done an excellent job. But the deep sadness that had flashed across Elfie's face as she'd stared at her phone, the bleakness in her voice as she had told him the caller was her mother stayed worrying at his mind.

Xander wasn't close to his mother, just as he hadn't been close to his father. His parents had liked and respected each other but they hadn't been in love. His mother understood land and obligation and the need to turn expensive estates into money-making businesses and his father had needed a wife with those skills. After Xander there were no more children. But the marriage had endured successfully enough until his father's death earlier this year, and if either of them had indulged in affairs they had been discreet enough for Xander to have no knowledge of them. Not all his school friends had been so fortunate.

Since Xander had left university and taken on more and more responsibility for the hotels, his mother had become less involved with the UK and US operations, preferring to spend her time in France, either at the Paris hotel or the villa on the south coast, where she continued to be the consummate hostess, still playing her part for the family business. They weren't close; how could they be? But there was no animosity or dislike between them, quite the opposite; he supposed they were quietly fond of each other. If she had called with no prior arrangement Xander would have been surprised, but he would certainly have taken the call, and he liked to see her when their paths crossed. It wasn't family as some people knew it, wasn't close or warm or loving and it wasn't what he would want for any child of his, but it was theirs.

But Elfie didn't even have that, or so it seemed.

'And so, at the end we'll dress you up as Father

Christmas and arrange for a sleigh pulled by Walter to fly over the garden.' Elfie looked at him expectantly, pen poised.

He nodded on autopilot. 'Okay. Sounds…hang on, what?'

'I knew you weren't listening.' She sat back and folded her arms smugly. 'I should have got you to double my pay.'

'Sorry, my mind was elsewhere for a moment. This all looks good, though. Thank you, Elfie. Restarting the Christmas party is an excellent idea; the Thornham experience is supposed to be about tradition, about a glimpse into an idealised version of family life in times gone by. It's a shame this particular custom died out.'

'I know. Without those traditions Christmas just isn't the same. Don't you think?'

Xander could hear a wistfulness in Elfie's voice, strange for a girl who always spent Christmas working by choice. 'Exactly, tradition is paramount. Christmas is the most popular time of the year because we make every guest feel like they're invited to our family Christmas, whether here, New York or Paris. We're often booked up years in advance, with a lot of repeat guests.'

'The famous Thornham Christmas. I'm looking forward to it.'

'It's pretty full-on,' he warned her. 'Christmas always follows the same pattern. A carol service here on Christmas Eve, followed by a special afternoon tea, then I drive to Thornham Park for the Christmas Eve ball and Christmas Day itself. Boxing Day is spent at Thornham Lodge for a nature walk, followed by a buffet of turkey soup, game pie and cheese and an evening of traditional games—it's the smallest of all the hotels; we usually have just one or two large family groups booking there. Then sometimes I head to New York for the week between Christmas and New Year, but of course New Year is spent in Scotland.'

A realisation he had been resolutely ignoring hit him. His father had been ill for the last two Christmases, battling the cancer that would eventually take his life, but had always rallied in December, his love of playing the consummate host giving him the strength needed for the strenuous two weeks of bonhomie. This year Xander would have no one to hide behind, the success of the season resting on him alone. 'Of course, this year it will be just me for the first time. My mother has chosen to stay in France.'

'You, me and Walter, although we'll have to sit New York out. He doesn't have a passport.'

Elfie's matter-of-fact statement warmed Xander, like unexpected colour in a grey landscape. 'New York is every other year, and I was there last year so no sitting out needed.'

'I hope there will be *some* sitting; you're right, that is full-on! When do you get family time during all that hosting?'

'Christmas was nothing *but* family time. We were all together, my grandparents, parents and me through the whole season. It was probably the only time in the year we were all in the same place.'

'And you got time just for you? For stockings and presents?'

He shook his head. 'Stocking hung in the Great Hall to be opened at breakfast with the guests, presents under the tree in the Sitting Room and handed out after Christmas dinner, also with the guests.' That was life as a Montague. Always on display.

'But…' Xander glanced up to see Elfie's hand half cover her mouth, her eyes huge and filled with unwanted sympathy. 'Even when you were little?'

'Even then. That's the promise, Elfie, a traditional country house Christmas, hosted by the owner. And we have delivered for over fifty years. Why so surprised? You work Christmas too.'

'As an adult. By choice. But as a child? As a child Christmas really was magical.' Her eyes softened, her expression dreamy. 'I told you my father was half French, and of course we lived over there, so we had a combination Anglo-French Christmas. It was chockfull of special family traditions, and we never missed one.'

'That sounds fun.'

'Oh, it was. Fun and lengthy. Christmas is a month of celebration on the Continent, and we took full advantage.'

'In what way?' He really wanted to know. To understand what brought the glitter of memory to her expression, the flush of remembered excitement to her cheeks. Even as a child, Xander had known that Christmas wasn't about him, his presents weren't necessarily for him alone. What *did* a magical Christmas feel like?

Elfie didn't answer for a moment, her gaze soft and faraway. 'We would start by getting out the Advent Calendar, a box with little drawers my father made me, each drawer filled with a little gift—beads, a tiny ornament, a hair slide, chosen with love. Then, on December the sixth St Nick would leave me some sweets and there was usually a party at school or in the village. St

Nicholas Day was so much fun. I was too old for it when we moved back to England, but I missed it anyway.'

'We do a St Nicholas Day celebration in the French hotels. I've only been a couple of times, but they are popular. The French hotels have a tradition of exchanging gifts on Christmas Eve as well, which I could never understand as a child.'

'Oh, yes, we would open family gifts on Christmas Eve, after the most amazing feast, and then I would leave shoes out as well as my stocking. Our presents from Father Christmas would be left in those and sometimes under the tree as well, and then we'd head out for a walk before a traditional English Christmas dinner. We celebrated Epiphany too, with a special cake. It was weeks of happiness and laughter and magic, wonderful food and love. I know it sounds like a cliché, but it really was. Sometimes my grand-mère and grandad would be there, sometimes granny and grandpa, but I think my favourite years were when it was just us.'

'It doesn't sound like a cliché; it sounds wonderful.' Wonderful and alien, and for a moment Xander was hit with a longing so acute for the kind of family who made every occasion special, not because it was their duty but because of love, it hurt. He was greedy for more details, to live vicariously for a few moments. 'Did you have many white Christmases?'

'Oh, yes, not all but most. It was one of the things I hated most about Christmas in Surrey, the disappointment of a grey Christmas when all I wanted was proper snow. I remember heading out after breakfast to go sledging, wearing the new hat and gloves Father Christmas had left in my stocking and knowing that I was the luckiest girl in the world.' She stopped, eyes shining this time not with memory but with tears and, prompted by a need to comfort her that overrode his intention to keep a proper distance between them, Xander reached over and covered her hand with his. Her skin was soft and warm, the feel of her a balm he desperately wanted more of. She didn't move for one long moment before turning her hand and lacing her fingers through his as if searching for anchorage.

'Thank you.' She tried to smile but it was tremulous. 'I don't usually talk about then; I try not to remember. It just hurts too much.'

'I guess it changed after you lost your father?' He kept his voice low, even and saw her start to regain control, the desperately lost look slipping from her face.

'Yes. He was the king of fun, my dad. He loved a party...everything was an occasion. Birthdays...' She shook her head. 'Birthdays were always over-the-top celebrations, starting with breakfast in bed—hot chocolate and pancakes, with flowers in a painted jug. I called it the birthday jug. But Christmas was his favourite time of all. We had so many family traditions—we always went ice skating every weekend in Advent, tried to see a version of *The Nutcracker* the Saturday before Christmas, went on a father-daughter present-buying day for Mum which included tea in a café. And then, after he was gone, all of that went too. It's like he was the heart of the family and without him we carried on, but all the happiness, all the things that made us unique, was gone.'

'He sounds like a wonderful man.'

'He was.' She laughed then, the pain in her eyes fading, replaced with nostalgic amusement. 'Oh, he wasn't perfect. When he was in the middle of a painting he could be really grumpy. And he could be really restless when he felt he needed a change of scenery, like this impending storm building. Mum didn't mind me missing school when I was really small, but she put her foot down when I was ten and said we had to stay put in term time and sometimes you could see his frustration at not being able to just jump in the van and go. But he was mostly full of laughter and so kind. But then one day he was walking along the road in the rain and a car took a bend too soon. And all that talent and love and personality was just gone. In a second. Mum couldn't cope and so we moved back to England, to my grandparents. And everything changed.'

'It must have been hard.' Their fingers were still interlaced, the feel of her pulsing through his skin.

Her eyes were unseeing. She was no longer talking to him but to herself, almost bewildered with hurt. 'It was as if everything I had been, everything we were, was washed away. Mum was an artist as well, not as renowned as Papa was, but she had some success. After Papa died she stopped painting, retrained in graphic design and got a job at a local business. Wore suits, makeup, had perfect hair, was always busy. And then a year later she married her boss. I thought she was joking when she told me. After Papa, how could she ever want to marry anyone else? So soon? But it was no joke.' The hurt intensified, her eyes bright with pain.

'Is he nice?'

She shrugged. 'I guess. We don't really understand each other; we never have. He was a widower with two girls, one my age, one older, and so we moved into their house. Mum didn't want them to feel like we were taking over, so she worked really hard to make sure nothing changed for them, especially at Christmas. No more St Nicholas or Christmas Eve presents; suddenly it was church services on Christmas Eve, their grandparents over for Christmas Day, Boxing Day at their aunt's. All our own special traditions were dropped. I put my shoes out that first year and they all just stared at me as if I was doing something really odd.'

'That's tough.'

'I was fourteen by then. Mum said it was time I grew up, but it felt like a betrayal. There was no time for ice skating or going to the ballet; instead there was a pantomime matinee and a trip out to choose the tree. Nice traditions, but not mine. Then two years later Mum had a baby, and I was really on my own. She was part of their family in every way, but I wasn't. I didn't know how to be. I didn't want to be.'

'Did she know how unhappy you were? Did you tell her?' The need to hold her, to comfort her was almost overwhelming.

'She thought I was jealous. That I didn't want to share her. She told me not to be selfish, that those poor motherless girls needed her too. But I had lost a parent too, and now I was losing the other one. Looking back, I just retreated into myself. I can see they thought I was moody and difficult. And life with Papa wasn't all perfect. If he hadn't sold a painting then we could be pretty broke and he left a lot of the household managing to her. There were a lot of highs and lows and by the time she met James I think she wanted stability, and he gave her that. Gives her it. She has a big house, two children and both my stepsisters settled nearby. It's a solid existence. Papa would have hated it.' She stopped, gently disentangling her hand from his, eyes fixed firmly on her plate. 'I'm sorry, I didn't mean to bore you with my family drama.'

'Don't apologise, and you didn't bore me. I'm sorry you had to experience that.' Maybe it was easier to grow up as he had after all, with distance and disappointment a constant, than having that distance enforced by tragedy and change.

'I know many have it worse. I have my memories, and I still do have Mum, just not in the way I used to. But Christmas is hard. That's the problem with having a perfect childhood. It makes adulthood hard in some ways.'

'You'll just have to recreate the traditions for your children.'

'I don't want children, marriage, any of it. Not when I know what it's like to lose it all. It's safer not to.' Her eyes were bleak. 'What about you?'

'I have to marry and have children. Otherwise, the title goes to a distant cousin who lives in Canada and has no interest in the hotels. He is as keen for me to procreate as my dad was.'

'Well, that's romantic.'

He laughed. 'There's no place for romance in my life. My parents married because my mother was bred to be a baroness and to help run an estate like Thornham, my grandparents too. I need a sensible wife with experience of this world, one who knows that work and the personal are always interlinked, who won't expect me to dance attendance on her, who doesn't mind us spending time apart and who understands the importance of an heir. This is how it is. How it has always been, whether it's my great-grandfather marrying a French heiress or his father marrying a buccaneer or the one before that the daughter of a viscount. The estate and the title have to be preserved at all costs.'

'But why?'

He blinked. He wasn't sure he'd ever been asked that before. 'Why do you want to build your retreat?' he countered. 'It was your father's dream, but why is it yours?'

'To remember him, as a legacy, I suppose.'

'Exactly. This is our legacy, ours and the hundreds of people employed by the hotel and the estates, some from families who have worked for us for hundreds of years. It's bigger than one generation, one man.' Xander wasn't sure why it was so important that Elfie understood his destiny, his intention. But for some reason it was. Maybe it was because he liked her, was attracted to her, maybe it was because she had confided in him and he had seen a little inside her soul. But, whatever the reason, there was no future beyond this month for them and he needed to keep their relationship purely professional. Even if his hand could still feel hers imprinted there.

CHAPTER SIX

'OH, MY GOODNESS!' Elfie clapped her hands together, laughing. 'Look at them! This is the best idea ever. You're a genius.' If she hadn't heard him herself, she would never have believed that Xander had personally suggested a prize for best joint costume for dogs and their owners. The very idea of a dog show seemed incongruous with his usual dignified master-of-all-he-surveyed demeanour. But she knew him better now; ever since the afternoon tea a couple of weeks ago things had shifted between them—and in him.

Elfie still couldn't believe she'd been so open, so honest, had talked so much about herself. But that sense she'd had of a little boy lost somewhere beneath the poise and the command prevailed, even if he'd seemed to brush the label off, to deny any need for sympathy whilst offering it to her. And talking to someone who seemed to really, truly understand her had weakened her barriers, despite her vow to keep them firm.

She couldn't regret it, especially as, since that day, they had seemed to shed any awareness of rank between them and become friends. Elfie felt completely at ease around Xander, happy to pad around the suite in her pyjamas, hair tied back after a long day, to watch a film with him sharing popcorn, to tease him. They were the perfect flatmates.

Well, almost perfect because she couldn't deny the intense alchemy that still simmered between them and it took every bit of self-control she possessed not to act on it, to not react when his gaze lingered on her, intent and heavy and caressing. To see not the forbidding man she had first met but a handsome, desirable man who her fingers ached to touch. Every day it was hard to remember why that was a bad idea.

'I like that little boy's costume over there.' Xander nodded at a small child dressed as a red and gold bauble, his small, rotund dog in a similar costume. Both wore identical expressions of determination, scowling through long fringes.

Elfie laughed again. 'Oh, me too. And I adore what that little girl's wearing, the one dressed as a reindeer. Isn't her lurcher gorgeous? I was chatting to her mum earlier and she said that when they got him he was still so skinny and so wary of people they had to tiptoe and whisper around him for the first few weeks. But now he's so relaxed and secure he doesn't even react to fireworks and he's been as good as gold this afternoon. Oh, and look at that small fluffy white dog, the one dressed as a snowball? I saw her in the shelter; I'm so glad she has a home already.'

'And I'm glad you talked me into this; everyone seems to be having fun,' Xander said. Elfie followed his gaze as he scanned the marquee, usually used for upscale weddings but today filled with the enticingly seasonal scent of mulled wine and hot chocolate. The display area for each round of the dog show took up the centre, ringed by chairs for spectators. Stalls set at one end served drinks or food and the dog shelter had been allocated space at the other end where volunteers were ready to talk to prospective donors and adopters.

A smaller marquee held local craftspeople, jewellers and artists, glad of a chance to pick up some last-minute Christmas sales, and the old stables had been turned into Santa's workshop for the day, complete with Father Christmas and a bag full of wrapped gifts. The air hummed with happy contentment. Upscale neighbourhoods like Mayfair didn't usually go in for community activities but a lot of families lived tucked away in the historic streets and not all of them were well-to-do. Anyone who had recently adopted a dog from the shelter had also received an invitation, as had all the staff's families. Some guests had even elected to come and join in the fun, and those who preferred not to had guaranteed privacy inside the hotel, the dog show and Christmas party a strictly outside affair.

The next couple of hours whirled past. Several journalists had turned up from local papers and from the kind of high-end magazines who liked to feature aristocratic bachelors in their pages and both Walter and Xander were photographed relentlessly. In between, Elfie made sure Xander was ready to judge each competition, award prizes and present the dog shelter with the sponsorship cheque. But in the odd moments when he wasn't needed for photos or presenting duties she watched him walking round the marquee, talking to everyone he met, admiring dogs and babies, quizzing small children on Christmas wishes and making polite conversation with adults of all ages. He was charming hospitality personified and all the chatter around her seemed to agree that he was a lovely man.

Pride filled Elfie as she took it all in. She had done this, had an idea and made it happen. Okay, she had had a lot of help; the hotel's marketing department, the events department, the kitchen, the grounds folk had all swung into well-oiled action the second Xander had sent his first exploratory email. But still. In just over three weeks she had created something wonderful. Maybe her dream of running her own retreat wasn't so farfetched; with this role she'd shown that she was more than a glorified waitress and nanny, that she had creativity and flare. Just like her dad.

'You're looking thoughtful.' Her skin tingled as Xander moved closer, his voice low and intimate, his breath brushing her skin.

'I was just thinking how much fun this is,' she half lied. She didn't want to sound big-headed and tell Xander that she'd been revelling in her own role in the afternoon's success.

'Thanks to you. I wonder how many other traditions have disappeared over the years? There may be other ones we can reinvent.'

'Only if Walter gets a starring role,' Elfie said, leaning down to ruffle the fluffy head. 'He's loved being top dog today.'

'You definitely made the right choice with Walter; he thrives on publicity. I swear he knows his best side and the exact angle he needs to tilt his chin for extra winsome.'

'I wonder if his old owner will see the pictures.' Elfie straightened, that same jolt of sadness hitting her whenever she thought about what it must have taken to have given Walter up. This hadn't been a random thoughtless dumping; there had been a letter, a blanket, his favourite toys. 'What if he or she comes forward?'

'Then we deal with it when it happens. Maybe Walter would be happy if he could go back to his old home; as you said, he was obviously well loved.'

'Maybe...' Elfie squatted down and put an arm around the dog, not sure why Xander's matter-of-fact statement niggled her. He was right, surely. Walter would be happier with his original owner if it were at all possible. But she could have sworn Xander was becoming fond of the dog. He no longer stopped him from jumping on the sofa, sometimes volunteered for the morning walk and the other day she had come into the suite to find Xander in serious conversation with the dog about a planned refurbishment for the Rhode Island hotel. Would he really be happy to hand Walter over to someone who had dumped him, no matter the circumstances?

'Anyway, I wanted to thank you for today,' Xander continued.

'Just doing my job, boss.'

'This was a lot more than that and we both know it. I've asked Julio to dog sit and I wanted to take you out. If that's okay?'

Take her out? What did that mean? Although they had spent a lot of time together over the last three weeks they had always been chaperoned by Walter. Every walk, every meal had a purpose behind it, and was always work-related.

Of course, Xander could always want to discuss the next stage in the social media campaign, how this crucial week before Christmas would go, and start to make plans for winding down the dog-related content after

New Year. He might even want to carry on the discussion about discovering other lost traditions, ask her to be involved. That was probably it. Although she could have sworn she'd heard a tinge of self-consciousness in his voice.

Elfie continued to hug Walter, burying her face in his neck, not sure what her face would reveal if she looked at Xander, whether her inner fluster would be evident. 'Sure,' she said, her voice a little muffled.

'Great. There's a car coming at five-thirty; can you be ready for then?'

'Sure,' she repeated.

'If I don't see you before, I'll meet you in reception then. Good.' And he was gone before Elfie had a chance to ask about where they were going or what she should wear. Slowly, she got to her feet. An evening out. With Xander. Right then.

'It's a thank you,' she said to Walter. 'There's no need for me to go thinking this is any more than that. It's actually very kind of him.'

Walter's silence was, she felt, telling.

'I'm moving on in a few weeks and anything more than friendship would just complicate things. Besides, you heard him the other week. He doesn't do romance. He has a wish list for a wife and, apart from the fact I'm not looking to get married, I am pretty sure I don't tick a single one of those boxes. And that's fine.'

Walter put his head on one side and regarded her in a way that if he had been human she would have said was sceptical.

'Obviously I like him, and obviously I've noticed he's attractive, but I like uncomplicated men and relationships and Xander is definitely complicated. Tall, dark and brooding is all very well in books, but not real life, don't you think? So a nice evening out as friends, as colleagues is perfect. I mean it; don't look at me that way.' With relief she saw Julio, the young Spanish assistant manager, making his way towards them, clearly wondering how he had been unlucky enough to have been picked for dog sitting duties. 'I'll see you later; we'll talk more then.' She handed the lead over and made her way through the now diminishing crowds back to the suite, mentally sorting through her limited wardrobe.

A travel wardrobe meant every piece of clothing had to be multifunctional, so Elfie had a couple of outfits that could be dressed up with some judicious accessorising. It was tricky, not knowing if she was going tenpin bowling or to a five-star restaurant, but Elfie did the best she could, matching her favourite green maxi dress with a pretty gold sparkly cardigan she had picked up in a charity shop earlier that week and her beloved boots. She added a long loop of gold beads and matching earrings before making herself up with more care than usual, frowning with concentration as she applied liquid eyeliner and several layers of mascara, topping the whole with a festively red lipstick. She didn't have time to do much with her hair so, after a liberal application of dry shampoo—the backpacker's best friend—she twisted it up, skewering it with hairpins and allowing a few tendrils to fall onto her face. Right, she was ready. Overdressed for bowling or anything physical, presentable for anything else. She hoped. She pulled a face at herself in the mirror.

'Be careful,' she told herself. 'This one is different.' It wasn't just that he was quieter, more thoughtful, more reserved than the men she usually was attracted to, it was the sheer force of that attraction, of her response to him. It was deeper than anything she had ever experienced before, and that was unsettling. He occupied far too much of her headspace already; she needed to make sure she didn't do anything stupid and let him into her heart as well.

Grabbing her coat, Elfie made her way down to the foyer, where Xander was waiting for her. He was still in the grey suit he had been wearing earlier—so probably not bowling then, she thought in relief—although at some point he had shaved and exchanged his white shirt and tie for an open collar blue floral shirt. He looked up as she walked towards him and his gaze heated. Elfie stopped a few steps away, unaccountably shy.

'You look beautiful,' he said softly.

'You scrub up okay yourself.' Which, as he spent most of his life in suits, was a good thing. Elfie was used to men who wore casual clothes, practical clothing as deckhands or ski coaches; she'd dismissed suits and the men who wore them as stuffy. But living and working with Xander had changed her mind, where one man was concerned at least. 'I'm not overdressed, am I?'

'You're perfect. Come on.'

A car awaited them and Xander held the door open for her before joining her in the back. She was still sure this wasn't a date in the strict meaning of the term, but it felt more like a date than anything she had ever been on before. No one had ever told her she was perfect with that degree of intensity before.

Elfie searched for something to break the silence that had descended over them. 'I hope Walter's okay.'

'Julio loves dogs; I'm sure they'll be fine. And he has my number in case there're any issues.'

'Mine too. I asked him to send me any good photos from the walk.' She giggled, struck by the incongruity of their conversation. 'We sound like two new parents who have just left their baby with the nursery for the first time.'

'If I know that dog, it's Julio who we need to be concerned about. Walter will have him twisted around his paw in less than five minutes.'

'He already has.' Elfie handed Xander her phone so that he could see the photo the assistant manager had just sent her of the two of them in the staff lounge, Walter sprawling on a sofa, a nature documentary on the television. 'I don't think Walter misses us at all. Our baby is growing up!'

Xander was unaccountably nervous as the car deposited them at the small restaurant he had booked, just around the corner from Covent Garden. He'd wanted to give Elfie a treat as a thank you for all her hard work but, now they were here, he wasn't sure whether he'd overstepped. She'd confided in him, and he'd used that knowledge to plan the evening. Was it too much for a simple thank you?

But first, dinner. There was nothing too much about a simple dinner, surely. They'd eaten together many times now; he often joined her at breakfast or if they were tired after a long day they would order room service and eat together in front of a film, Walter snoring companionably at their feet—or at his side. He'd lost the battle of the sofa weeks ago.

But they always had a small, hairy companion to remind them why they were together. Without him the air felt charged, the evening full of intent.

Elfie looked a little puzzled as he held the restaurant door open, and he smiled as he saw her surreptitiously check the heavy man's watch she usually wore.

'It is a little early for dinner, but there's a reason,' he said, and her colour rose as she smiled.

'An early dinner just makes sure there's time for supper.'

The maître d' greeted them and showed them to a cosy table tucked away in a corner, so it felt almost unbearably intimate. Xander swallowed as he took his seat, all too aware that if Elfie, bare-faced and practical in her day-to-day clothing of battered jeans, was vibrant and attractive, this Elfie, made-up to showcase her remarkable eyes, a slick of red coating the curves of her mouth, hair up, emphasising the slenderness of her neck, was a force he didn't quite know how to deal with. Every exposed millimetre of skin made his pulse speed up, every smile or glance from those long-lashed eyes burnt through him. He'd never physically desired any woman so primally, so totally before.

Desired her, liked her, was challenged by her, interested by her, intrigued by her. More, she understood his work, and increasingly she seemed to understand him. The irony wasn't lost on him that in many ways she was his perfect woman personified—except that Elfie had dreams and aspirations of her own far beyond his world. And surely she deserved more than he was capable of giving.

She perused the menu with the enthusiasm she used for all food that Xander found so endearing. 'I never understand soup as a starter. I mean, in olden days to fill you before a scrag end of mutton fat and turnip absolutely, but soup is a meal in its own right. With bread, of course. Ooh, arancini and salad. That could be tempting. But will it leave enough room for pudding?'

'There's a pudding break scheduled later this evening, so enjoy your arancini.'

'Pudding break? Intriguing. And right, every night should have a pudding break scheduled in, don't you think?'

'Your evenings usually do, don't they?' He'd never met anyone with as sweet a tooth as Elfie. She was, he'd learned, a big fan of elevenses, afternoon tea and supper, in addition to the more usual three meals, and each of those involved cake or biscuits or some kind of chocolate.

'Guilty as charged. I think the chicken for a main. You? No, let me guess. The steak.'

'I'm that predictable?'

'No, but you did tell me once that steak was your go-to meal when you ate somewhere new. Unless this is the place where you bring all the girls?' Her dimples flashed as she shot him a teasing grin.

Xander's reply was interrupted by the waiter bringing bread before taking their order and by the time they were alone again Elfie had moved onto a different topic. Maybe it was a good thing. What would he say? That he usually wined and dined his dates at one of his hotel restaurants, that this little trattoria with its reputation for simple and plentiful food would be dismissed by the kind of women he dated, women who went out to see and be seen. That here with Elfie he was more at ease than he ever had been with any of them—and that he had no idea what to do with that information. No, it was a good thing she was back to discussing the dog show. Safer by far.

Five minutes later, with the wine poured, Xander found himself relaxing into the evening, the stress of the day finally falling away. 'This is better,' he said, almost to himself and Elfie looked up at him.

'You barely ate all day; you must be starving. Here, don't let me hog all the bread; it's ridiculously moreish.'

The bread did smell heavenly and Xander realised how hungry he actually was as he took a slice and dipped it into the rich olive oil. 'You're right, this is lovely, but I wasn't talking about food. More the absence of people.'

'I'm a person,' she pointed out.

'But you're restful to be around, you make it easy.' He paused, surprised by the words, by the truth in them.

'I'm not sure anyone has called me restful before.' Elfie took a sip of wine, her eyes fixed on him. 'Didn't you enjoy today? It must be odd seeing your hotel invaded like that. I guess it's usually a low hum of activity, not such a hubbub. The marquee was absolutely crammed at one point; it's a good thing we asked people to register, otherwise we could have been overwhelmed.'

For a moment Xander was tempted to do what he always did, to gloss over the truth. But in the last couple of weeks he had come to appreciate Elfie's directness, her honesty, and he realised he owed her the same. 'It's the hardest part of my role, working crowds like that, being on display,' he said deliberately and as he said the words out loud it was as if a weight lifted, the sharing of the secret easing some of the self-loathing he could never quite conquer. 'I find crowds, strangers overwhelming; at least I used to. Now I have taught myself to cope but I still don't enjoy them.' His laugh was humourless. 'I've learned to deal with hosting tables and entertaining guests, to play a part, I suppose, but I would never choose to put myself in that position. It's funny, I have no problem with management, with being in charge, with hiring and firing. I can address a conference or give a lecture, but small talk in situations like today can be like an endurance task.'

'It doesn't sound funny; it sounds difficult,' she said softly. 'Especially for a man in your position, where there *is* so much entertaining. If it's any consolation I would never have known you found it difficult; no one would. You looked completely at ease all afternoon. Like you were born to rule, which I suppose you were.'

'Apparently so. Being on display like that is part of who I am supposed to be. My father, my grandfather, they revelled in it. All of it. The title, the guests, the pomp and pageantry. But I always struggled. As a small boy I'd hide in the library, under a table, somewhere quiet with a book. My father said I was his biggest mistake. That I had no Montague in me.' He shrugged, as if the words no longer bit. But they did. Maybe they always would. 'That he had no idea how he'd fathered such a dull son.'

'He had no right to say that.' She was all fire now, grey eyes blazing. 'Besides, you're one of the cleverest people I know. Watching you at work is almost daunting; your brain works so fast. In that conference with the States last week you were so far ahead they were like dachshunds trying to keep up with an Irish wolfhound! I almost felt sorry for them.'

Xander couldn't help smiling at the analogy. 'Ah, but being interested in the figures, in the actual managing of the hotels was never seen as crucial. The ability to hold a crowd with a story, to work a room, to flirt, were considered more important than doing the accounts; after all, we employed people to do that. Being rugby captain, riding to hounds, being at the front and taking every fence was more important than winning academic prizes. We got into Oxford through family legacy, not brains. My father wanted an heir in his own image, not a quiet, shy, bookish boy who grew up to prefer solitary sports like climbing to rugby, a few intimate friends to a large party, books to going out and getting hammered.'

'That shy boy sounds a lot nicer than the alternative. In my line of work I come across a lot of entitled men who absolutely love to go out, get hammered and then harass the help. Your father should have been careful what he wished for—and been proud of you regardless.'

'I don't know; maybe my father and grandfather were right. How they would shake their heads if they could see me now, needing a consultancy to brush up my image. To hear that the guests see me as remote. To see me fail, the way they always knew I would.' He took a gulp of wine, trying to swallow the bitterness. 'I'm sorry,' he said more levelly. 'This is supposed to be a fun night out. Let's talk about something more cheerful.'

'Okay, agreed.' Elfie nodded but her eyes still flashed stormy fire. 'But let me say something first. Okay, yes, you can seem a little aloof at first, but you know who else is aloof at first glance? Mr Darcy. And he is pretty much every woman's ideal man. You're a baron. No one expects you to be just like us; that isn't what anyone pays for. They want the whole smouldering, proud vibe. Take it from me, I've heard guests talk. I say embrace your Mr Darcy image.'

Xander set his glass down, almost choking on his wine. 'Getting a dog is one thing; there is no way I am swimming in a lake for any social media so you can put that thought right out of your mind.'

'That's the TV series, not the book, although never say never. And, secondly, there is no set way to do something, to be someone. No one who came today would have any idea you weren't enjoying it. You were the perfect host. I saw you talking to small children as if you cared about every sticky word, greeting every dog you passed and asking about its age and pedigree as if you were actually fascinated in the lineage of an ancient pug. You may not enjoy it but you have learned how to do small talk and you do it well. More importantly, your staff love you. Actually, they adore you, and I don't get the impression they adored your father in the same way. So you will be a different owner, a different baron? That's fine. You don't have to be a carbon copy of what came before.'

Xander stared at her, absorbing her fierce words. No one had ever said it was okay to do things his way before, had ever suggested there was another way. As much as he wanted to believe her, the idea was too new, too strange to absorb straight away. But, either way, her fierce defence of him warmed him through in a way he had never felt before.

Xander knew he was no coward, no matter what his father said, that facing down a crowd took more courage than clearing the largest fence. That getting his adrenaline rush climbing, not hunting was okay, having a small group of friends rather than a social whirl a valid choice. But how many of his choices, from the women he dated but had little in common with, to his decision to study business rather than pure maths had been done in a fruitless attempt to win his father's approval?

No one had ever told him it was okay just to be him before.

Tonight, he had planned a special surprise for Elfie as a thank you for all her hard work, but she had just given him something priceless in return. Validation.

It was a gift he would never forget.

CHAPTER SEVEN

By the time they finished eating and left the restaurant, Elfie was consumed by curiosity. It was only just after seven and she knew they weren't returning to Thornham House because she had been very clearly promised pudding later, which suggested there was more to the evening. The absence of a car to take them back confirmed her suspicions. Instead, Xander took her arm as they walked up a narrow road leading into Covent Garden. The gesture was almost old-fashioned, yet the light touch set every nerve ablaze, her body instantly springing to attention, hyperaware of his proximity, his breadth, his scent.

It was more than physical attraction. She knew attraction, desire. She enjoyed flirting, enjoyed a bit of romance, that sensation of realising she liked someone and that they liked her back, but it was always a fleeting feeling. She'd never felt comfortable talking about her past or her deepest insecurities before—and she sensed that Xander was the same. Which was why knowing he'd chosen her to open up to felt more intimate than any kind of touch or act. He'd entrusted her with his deepest, darkest secrets. And with that knowledge she felt some of her resolve to keep Xander at a safe distance ebbing way. They were already way past friend zone, but how far this intimacy would—and should—go was still unknown.

One thing she did know was that if she could summon the ghost of Xander's father she would have a few choice words to say to him. Imagine having a brave, intelligent son and trying to change him into the kind of Hooray Henry who gave polo shirts a bad name!

'What's the plan?' she asked as they emerged into the famous square, now blazing with Christmas lights and thronged with evening shoppers and revellers. A huge Christmas tree dominated the space, colourfully festive. The lights, the excited chatter and the sounds of the brass band from the far corner gave her an unexpectedly Christmassy feeling, something that even the snowiest season in the Alps hadn't given her. And, to her surprise, even though she had spent the last fifteen years downplaying Christmas, finding this time of year too hard, she couldn't help but get that old anticipatory flutter.

'You'll see.' Xander was grinning now, his hand warm on her elbow, his steps brisk. 'In fact, we're here.'

'Covent Garden?' Maybe he had some late-night shopping to do?

'There.' He nodded to the huge building dominating one corner and Elfie blinked. She didn't really know London that well—a few shopping trips in her teens, some layovers—this year was the first time she'd actually worked in the city and she spent most of her time in Mayfair and Hyde Park. She scanned the shops, wondering which of them Xander meant, before her gaze alighted on a corner door with a sign over it.

'Is that…?' She turned and looked up at Xander,

her heart suddenly so full she couldn't speak, eyes hot with tears.

He nodded. 'Our destination? Yes.'

'Really?'

'It's the Saturday before Christmas,' he said, smiling down at her. 'And you told me that Christmas isn't Christmas without *The Nutcracker*. I wanted to put that theory to the test.'

'I don't know what to say.' She actually couldn't have said more, her throat too tight, her emotions suddenly raw and exposed and painful.

'You don't have to say anything. This is a thank you. For all your help, for your ideas.'

'No,' she said softly. 'I'm the one saying thank you. This is the nicest thing anyone has ever done for me. You have no idea what it means.' She stood on tiptoe and pressed a light kiss of thanks to his cheek, feeling him quiver under the caress. 'I'll never forget this.'

The next couple of hours passed by in a whirl of music and enchantment. Xander had secured sensational seats, facing straight onto the stage. Elfie was too overcome to really take in her surroundings or the other theatre-goers as they walked into the foyer and up the stairs, sitting in a daze until the conductor entered to applause and the familiar music began instantly transporting her back to childhood. She'd never seen this version before and sat wide-eyed as the party began and Clara received her Nutcracker doll before finding herself in a magical world of toy soldiers. As the first act came to an end, glittery snow falling down onto the stage, a choir's song soaring above the orchestra and what seemed like dozens of snowflakes pirouetted around the stage, the long-suppressed tears finally fell. How she'd missed this. How she'd needed this beauty.

Xander had pre-ordered champagne for the interval and they took their glasses up to the outside terrace overlooking Covent Garden and the lights of the city. Neither really spoke. Elfie was still too full of emotions she couldn't quite disentangle and the beauty of the ballet, whilst Xander seemed as brooding as the Austen hero she had compared him to earlier, his only comment that he was enjoying it much more than he had expected.

The second half was as wonderful as the first, with virtuoso dancing from the Sugar Plum Fairy and her Prince, both of whom fully deserved all the cheers and applause. Elfie held herself together during most of this half, absorbed in the dancing, but when Clara fell asleep, to be returned home, her tears started again, regret that the ballet was coming to an end mixed with grief for the naïve young girl she too had once been, a girl who, like Clara, found herself lost, in her case with no family waiting for her, no happy ending. But within the grief and regret was the realisation that she had been seen and heard. That right now, for the first time in a long, long time, she wasn't alone.

As the tears fell once more, Xander reached over and took her hand, his fingers closing over hers as if they fitted together perfectly, and Elfie held on tight, anchored by his touch as the curtains finally closed before opening again for the dancers to take their bows. Elfie reluctantly let go of Xander's hand to clap as hard as she could, the tears still flowing until the curtain closed for the final time, the lights came back on and people around them started to stand up and move. Elfie couldn't move, still watching the stage, the tears drying on her cheeks.

'Here…' Xander spoke softly, as if he knew she was still caught up in the magic of the music and dance. Elfie looked over and he leaned forward, gently wiping away the tears with a handkerchief, the tender gesture almost setting her off again.

'I must look a fright,' she said with a last gulp, her skin tingling where he had touched her, and he smiled.

'You look beautiful.'

Reaching out, she took his hand and brought it to her cheek. 'Thank you. That was beyond magical. I don't think you could have done anything nicer for me if you'd spent a hundred years trying. I don't think anyone could. I've spent the last sixteen years running from Christmas and you have made it special again. Thank you.' She leaned into his hand, turning towards him as she did so, and almost forgot how to breathe as she saw the heat in his eyes. Heat and desire. Desire for her.

Just a few hours ago she had told herself that this was not a date and reminded herself that Xander was not the kind of man she could walk away from with her heart unscathed. The second of these things was still true but Elfie realised that she no longer cared. Whatever happened now, she was falling, had fallen, for him. Whatever happened now, she would have to deal with those consequences.

Elfie couldn't have said who leant in first, but one minute she was looking into Xander's eyes, still holding his hand to her cheek, the next his mouth was on hers, soft and sweet and intoxicating and perfect for a few precious seconds until someone exited the row behind them, the noise recalling her to their surroundings. She drew back, almost shaking with the emotion swirling through her.

'Thank you,' she said again, almost idiotically, not sure whether she was thanking him for the evening or for the kiss.

'The evening's not over yet.' Xander's eyes were no longer dark chocolate, his expression back to unreadable. Did he regret the kiss? Did he think she did? 'There's pudding, remember?'

The teasing note in his voice reassured her as she realised that any next step had to be down to her. That Xander was not the kind of man to take advantage of an emotional moment, that he wouldn't want her to feel that there was a price to pay for the evening. She could demand pudding right now and act as if the kiss had never happened and he would abide by that choice absolutely.

But that wasn't what she wanted. She knew that with every aching pulse. 'We could skip pudding.'

'No pudding? Are you okay?'

'I'm more than okay.' Slowly, deliberately she reached out and took his hand again, threading her fingers through his. 'I love pudding, as you know. But there are other ways to finish an evening.' To her relief the heat flared in his eyes once again although his voice was even.

'I don't expect payment, Elfie.'

'And I'm not offering it. But I do want you. And I think that you want me. And for all the reasons that it's probably a bad idea...'

'Like the fact that I'm your boss.'

'Like the fact that you employ me, yes. Like the fact that I am out of here in the New Year, and the very important reason that we have a developing friendship that

I am starting to value very much and don't want to ruin. But, even considering all of those things, I would still very much like to see you naked.'

She could hardly breathe as she spoke as boldly as she could. It wasn't the first time she'd made the first move. But somehow this mattered more. For a man like Xander, a man who valued his privacy, his personal space, any misstep could change things between them for ever.

But what else could she have done? She couldn't ignore the simmering tension between them any longer, how she felt. How she was sure he felt.

It mattered. He mattered.

The silence stretched on and on, almost unbearable. Xander's face was still bland, unreadable, but his eyes had darkened almost to black, his jaw granite still.

Then, finally, just as she thought she might scream with tension, he spoke. 'Then what are we waiting for?'

The traffic was light and the cab whisked them back to Mayfair in record time, but every second felt like an hour. Xander hadn't touched Elfie since her proposition, but there was an awareness, almost physical, like lightning crackling between them.

Anticipation—or was she regretting her decision, trying to figure out a way to tell him she'd changed her mind? Maybe it would be for the best, Xander told himself firmly, even as every sinew in his body cried out in protest. He could kiss her now, take her hand, caress it, find that sweet spot behind her ear, on her throat, use every tool in his arsenal to seduce her, but Xander needed to know that if this happened—if they happened—then Elfie was with him because she wanted to be, not because he'd kissed all thought from her mind.

Not that *he* was thinking clearly. His whole mind, his body, every nerve and muscle were straining with the desire to touch her, to hold her, to explore and learn her. He'd never hungered like this before, and it was as terrifying as it was intoxicating. But he needed to remember two things. The first was that here she had to have all the power; his position as her employer made that essential. And the second was that she was leaving. Elfie was a wanderer and she had already stayed in London longer than she'd meant to. She didn't want to be tied down. It should be easy—he wasn't one for ties himself. But nothing was normal where Elfie and his response to her was concerned.

Maybe he should do the sensible thing and defuse the situation. But for once Xander didn't want to be sensible. For once he just wanted to feel.

Finally, the taxi drew up outside the hotel, one of the doormen hastening to open the door and settle the fare, as they walked through the hotel and travelled up in the lift, along the corridor to their door where, with not quite steady hands, Xander unlocked it and stepped back, allowing Elfie to precede him inside. The maid had been in to turn down, the curtains were drawn, lights dimmed and the champagne and chocolates he had pre-ordered awaited them on the coffee table. As Elfie took off her old battered coat and sat to unlace her boots, still not meeting his gaze, Xander opened the champagne and poured them both a glass, offering her one. She took it and downed it in one gulp and then finally looked directly at him, challenge in her eyes.

'So...'

'So,' he echoed, shrugging off his jacket and sitting down opposite her.

'You're a long way away.' Her dimple flashed and with her half smile the atmosphere lightened. They were friends after all, friends with an undeniable spark. This, whatever *this* was, was just a natural evolution.

'I just want to make sure that *you* are sure.' It took all his control not to stride over to the other sofa and pull her into his arms. But he'd just surprised her with the kind of highly charged emotional experience bound to weaken anyone's defences. She'd said this wasn't a thank you proposition but that didn't mean it was a fully consensual one, not if she was overcome by the evening and all it had stirred.

'Me sure? This was my idea, remember.'

'Oh, I remember,' he said slowly, deliberately and watched her pupils dilate.

'Well, then…' She took off her cardigan, watching him as she did so, and his breath caught at the curve of her arms, the exposed length of her neck. He'd never seen anything so alluring as the unveiling of her skin. 'My point remains. You're a long way away.' Her smile widened, eyes alight with mischief and something deeper, darker, more potent. Something he recognised and thrilled to even as he was aware that his control, usually ironclad, was fast slipping away.

'Maybe we should do something about that.' Xander stood, every movement careful, almost languid, enjoying this anticipation. Elfie's grey eyes were still fixed on him, luminous and wide, her mouth parted, her breath coming a little faster and the knowledge that her desire was for him awoke all his most primal instincts. This girl was his, for tonight anyway, and he wanted, needed to make every moment count.

He held out a hand and after a moment she took it and he drew her to her feet, her skin warm against his. She was petite, her head barely his shoulder height, and a fierce protectiveness enveloped him. She deserved happiness, for all her dreams to come true.

Xander couldn't give her the home she longed for, but he could give her tonight. Not that there was any degree of altruism in his mind. He wanted, he needed this, her, more than he could admit to himself.

Her gaze was fearless as he took his time drinking her in. The proud tilt of her chin, the tendrils of hair emphasising her heart-shaped face, the curve of her full, lush mouth, until finally he dipped his head and kissed her. Light, exploratory, teasing; this kiss was just a taste. Their hands entwined, mouths barely touching, each testing out boundaries, seeing what the other was responsive to. Yet, for all its almost chasteness, it was the most intoxicating kiss of Xander's life. Elfie consumed him. The taste of her, wine and a sweet warmth that was all her, her hand in his, their fingers entwined in a caress which shot bolts of desire through him, the scent of her, delicate and spicy, like a Christmas treat.

She stepped closer, her other hand cupping his neck, and Xander could feel the warmth of her breasts against his chest, her hip against his, the line of her long legs. He curled an arm around her waist to pull her tighter still, the kiss intensifying as he did so, an all-in embrace as she opened up to him. Time stood still and all he knew was Elfie, the way her hand clutched at the nape of his neck, almost desperate, as if she were anchoring herself to him, the delicious feel of her warm body as his hand began a slow exploration, taking in the curve of her hip, the roundness of her bottom, before leisurely trailing up to the softness of her breast. She gasped against his mouth as his hand continued to wander, tracing the outline of her breast, grazing her taut nipple as he skimmed kisses along her jaw to the sensitive skin at her neck.

Step by step, kiss by kiss, he slowly manoeuvred her across the sitting room towards his bedroom door. He found the zip of her dress, easing it down until the dress slithered to the floor and she stepped out of it, bold and beautiful in just her underwear while she pulled at his shirt, undoing buttons with impatient fingers until she finally pushed it over his shoulders. Xander stilled for a moment as she explored the lines of his chest with her light delicate touch, her hands everywhere, each finger burning through him. Now it was his turn to unhook her bra, leaving that too on the sitting room floor as they finally reached the bedroom door and he pushed it open, his mouth still on hers, his hands taking their time to get to know every exposed, silky inch.

Finally, finally, they reached the bed and fell, in a tangle of limbs, onto the firm mattress. Elfie's hands had reached his belt and Xander hissed at the almost unbearable sensation as she eased his trousers down, kicking them off impatiently until mere scraps of material separated them. He sucked in a breath and pulled away, looking down at her. Her hair had come undone in their long journey to the bedroom and splayed out on the pillow, her eyes half closed, mouth swollen and lush. She was perfection from her small pert breasts to the swell of her stomach to her slim, long legs. He wanted to touch every part of her, taste every inch, hear her gasp and know that he was responsible for every moan.

'What are you doing?' she asked, eyes fluttering open, one hand reaching out to him.

'I'm just wondering where to start,' he said, allowing his gaze to roam over her, not hiding the hunger in his eyes. 'Here?' He kissed her neck, a light touch that made her quiver. 'Here?' The top of her breast. 'Here?' Her navel. 'Here?' The inside of her thigh. 'Any preference?'

She murmured something and he grinned.

'What was that?'

'All of it,' she said as his grin widened.

'As you wish.'

Elfie woke up with a start, stretching sore yet sated limbs, each ache a memory of the evening and night before. She'd never experienced anything approaching the intensity of last night in her life, had never felt so wanted, so desired, so seen, had never been so bold in articulating her desires or in searching out his. She turned and studied the still sleeping Xander. He looked different asleep, less guarded, more at ease with his hair tousled and long lashes veiling his cheeks. He seemed so innocent lying there, incapable of the deliciously wicked things he had done to her and with her. She shivered at the memory. Not just at the way he had touched and kissed her but the way he had looked at her, as if they had connected in every way, physically, emotionally spiritually.

There had been no discussion about what happened next but how could she go back to her bedroom on the other side of the suite and sleep there chastely, knowing what she knew? Knowing how he could make her feel, and how she reciprocated. She smiled smugly. The austere, aloof Baron Thornham falling apart at her touch, taking her apart in spectacular ways. A side of him hidden to the world that only she was privy to.

'Why are you looking so pleased with yourself?'

She hadn't noticed him wake and gasped as he flipped her over, pinioning her with his strong body.

'Good morning,' he added, his mouth grazing her neck.

'I was just thinking about last night.'

'No regrets?'

'Not an ounce.'

'Good.' His mouth moved lower, and all thought disappeared for a long, long time.

An hour later Elfie had finally made it out of bed to shower and dress, curling up on the sofa with a cafetière of the hotel's delectable coffee.

She took a refreshing sip, reliving the night—and morning—as she did so. Who would have thought that Xander would have been such a practised lover? But, then again, why was she so surprised? He was rich, handsome, titled, successful, with that whole detached vibe that so often made women want to dismantle defences. He must have had potential lovers queuing up. With a quick, guilty glance behind her, she quickly searched on her phone. Xander Montague. Girlfriend.

A string of images flashed up. Xander, that cold look in his eyes which she now recognised as discomfort rather than arrogance, standing with an arm around an array of young women. He didn't seem to have a physical type beyond the kind of elegance that only money could buy. Some of the women were tall, some medium-height, blonde or brunette but they all shared the same type of double-barrelled surname, some with a Lady or Honourable tacked on. Interestingly, he didn't seem to have had any kind of long-term relationship.

'You look absorbed.'

She jumped guiltily as Xander walked into the room, his hair still wet from the shower but in all other ways back to the formidable Baron, suited and formal.

'Just doing some research.'

'Anything interesting?'

'Kind of. Actually,' she admitted, never happy with subterfuge, 'I was looking you up. Well, your romantic history.'

'Found anything interesting?'

She glanced quickly at him, relieved to see his mouth quirked with amusement rather than annoyance.

'Only that you usually date women called things like Figgy Fortescue-Delaney, with pedigrees listed as if they were racehorses. And never for very long.'

Xander poured himself some coffee and sat next to her. Elfie leaned in, glad of his proximity. 'Is this a *where is this going* conversation?'

'No, because we both know exactly where it is going. I am heading off after New Year.'

'I know.'

Elfie tried to repress a small stab of rejection at Xander's easy acceptance of the short-termness of their fledgling relationship although she knew how silly she was being. But for once it would be nice for someone to want her to stay. 'In the interest of transparency, my dating history is equally fleeting, although without so many convoluted surnames. I'm not judging or prying, just interested.'

'You have a right to be interested, Elfie. If you and

I are going to keep sharing a bed, then you should feel free to ask anything you want to about where we stand and about my dating history.' He paused. 'Are we?'

'Are we what?'

'Going to keep sharing a bed?'

'Well...' she pretended to think about it '...I don't want to confuse Walter.'

'Obviously.'

'But if we explain it to him then I'm sure it will be fine.'

'Good.' He dropped a light kiss on her head, the brief gesture warming her through. 'Because I for one am very much looking forward to a repeat. Last night was spectacular.'

'Yes, it was.'

'But I also remember what you said yesterday. We *are* friends, and I really value that. You're independent and brave and kind and I can talk to you in a way that I have never really talked to anyone before. I don't want that to change.' He took a strand of her hair and wound it around his finger. 'I don't want you to feel that I have used you or lied to you, that this is some last wild fling before I settle down. I respect you far too much for that. I can't help thinking that if we were different people this could be the start of something really special.'

'Well, we are navigating co-dog-parenting together,' she said, wanting to provoke a smile, the intensity in his eyes unsettling her. She understood short-term and fun; she'd never had a problem leaving before. She couldn't allow this time to be different, not when her dream was in sight. Not when she knew how much it hurt to lose something—someone—she cared about. She wasn't a for ever kind of person. It was safer that way. 'But I value my independence, my freedom. I don't want to find it compromised by anyone. And you have a Baroness to find.' Xander might like her, value her, desire her, but he didn't want to marry her. 'Any contenders for that position?' Friends should be able to discuss these matters, even if they were friends with benefits, even if unwanted, unaccustomed jealousy clawed at her as she affected an easy tone and a smile.

Xander took a sip of his coffee. 'As you know, I see marriage has to be a practical decision. Things haven't changed that much since debutante balls and Seasons. People like me date, try each other on for size, look at what each partner brings to a marriage and if we're compatible we marry.'

'So that's what you've been doing? Trying these women on for size.'

'And they were trying me, along with other men in our social circle. We all know the score. Fun in our twenties, and now we're all approaching or in our thirties there will be a flurry of weddings. It's the way it's always been.'

'And you don't have a frontrunner?' She tried to sound light, interested, as if she wasn't jealous at the thought of some other woman sharing his bed, his life. Because that would be ridiculous.

'I wouldn't be here if there was. Elfie, what we shared last night was special. My marriage will be practical and that's fine, but I will always be very grateful I got to spend this time with you. Always.'

'It's not over yet.' She reached up and caressed his cheek, revelling in the feel of stubble under her fingers, trying not to dwell on his words, the unexpected disquiet rumbling through her. This was exactly what she wanted, a no-strings fling full of passion and mutual respect which left her free for her next adventure. So why did the thought of Xander marrying some unknown woman he didn't even love make her feel as if she couldn't breathe?

With an effort she pushed all thought away, pulling Xander close, letting her lips find his, losing herself in the sensation of his kiss. The here and now was all that mattered. Tomorrow could take care of itself.

CHAPTER EIGHT

XANDER WALKED INTO the Orangery to see Elfie surrounded by envelopes, laptop open, unusual frown lines creasing her forehead. 'What's all this?'

He wanted to pull her close, kiss her, but they were keeping their fling secret and this space was all too public. It was getting harder not to touch her, to tell everyone, *She is mine*, but Elfie didn't want their relationship to affect the other members of staff, especially when it was going to be so short-lived.

Too short-lived. January was less than a fortnight away. If Elfie hadn't planned to be going away then what would happen? Would they see where this went? Part of him could see it, properly dating, getting to know each other away from this festive bubble. But the rest of him, the sensible part of him, knew that Elfie was a free spirit, that the life of duty he led would eventually feel like a prison. Maybe it was better to have an end date after all.

She looked up, barely mustering a smile. 'These are all the letters and emails from people purporting to be Walter's owner.'

'What?'

She nodded. 'Over three hundred. There were several

features about him over the last few days and so some enterprising con artists have decided that this is the way to make money. Some have asked for money in return for not claiming him, others have sob stories about why they had to give him up and have suggested that a sum of money ranging from several thousand to fifty thousand pounds would enable them to be reunited and keep him.'

'Fifty thousand *pounds*? His pedigree must be a lot more special than we realised.'

'It's more that they know you're a baron and that you own all this. I guess that ups the stakes.'

Picking up one of the letters, Xander scanned the long paragraphs full of woe. 'But what if one of them is genuine?'

'They're not; none have mentioned the squirrel toy left with him and that detail wasn't mentioned to any of the journalists. But I feel like I should check each one, just in case.' She laid a hand on Walter's head. 'For your sake anyway.'

Xander slid into a chair next to her. 'Pass me a pile of these. I'll help.'

'I thought you were busy?'

'I am, but this is important.' Although the thought of actually finding Walter's owner and possibly giving the dog back was far less welcome than it would have been a few weeks ago. He was getting used to his presence, to his sighs and snores, the way he bounded to the door at the word 'walk' to the way he sometimes pressed close to Xander for comfort. It had turned out that Walter was surprisingly good company and walking him was now Xander's favourite time of day. He'd even met several people with the same routine and would stand and make small talk while the dogs played. He had no idea of their names or anything about them other than the name and breed of their dog. It was refreshingly anonymous to be known simply as Walter's owner.

But, at the same time, the letter that had accompanied Walter had made it clear his previous owner had felt he or she had no choice and the small dog had clearly been well looked after and well trained. If his owner did get in touch then surely Xander was duty bound to try and help reunite them, no matter what the personal cost?

But this December had been the best month of his life. A January without Elfie and Walter seemed bleak indeed.

He opened the first envelope and started reading, pushing it aside with a snort at the demand for money. No wonder Elfie looked so miserable. The next half hour was no better and he could feel indignation rising at the depths people would go to in order to make an easy buck, when an exclamation from Elfie made him look up.

'Read this,' she said, handing him a lined sheet of notepaper. He quickly scanned the shaky lines.

Dear Lord Thornham,
Thank you for taking in my Walter. Leaving him as I did was the hardest thing, but the local shelter had no room for him, I have no family locally and I was worried he'd end up in the pound when they took me to the hospice.

I'm sure I don't need to tell you how special he is. Since my Barbara died, I've found it hard to find the joy in life. We were never blessed with children and she was the one for making friends.

And then my neighbours got a puppy they couldn't manage, and I found myself with a dog.

Maybe I was selfish, taking him in at my age, but he's brought me such joy. I hope he brings you as much. Please tell him I'm sorry and that I love him. I hope he still has the blanket and squirrel. They were always his favourites.

Thank you again.

Dennis Barnes

Xander blinked, his chest full with sorrow at the short note. 'There is no demand for money.'

'No.' Elfie's eyes were bright with tears. 'All he wants is for Walter to have a good home.'

Turning over the envelope, Xander noticed an address sticker. 'Dennis is quite nearby…the hospice is just a few miles away.'

'There's no happy reunion for Walter; it's just us,' Elfie said softly. 'At least, it's just you, I suppose. Although I'll visit when I can.' Her voice broke. 'Xander. We have to take him to visit his old owner. He should say a proper goodbye.'

There were at least fifty unread emails in his inbox, half marked urgent, a pile of contracts and other correspondence on his desk. Tomorrow was Christmas Eve, which meant a move to Thornham Park, the festive season and all its calls on his time was in full swing. But there was something about the wonky lines on the tattered paper that touched him. The writer was alone in a hospice and Walter was his only family. Xander knew what it was like to feel alone in the world, and he knew Elfie did too. 'I'll order the car.'

Any doubts over their decision disappeared the

minute a nurse ushered them into a cheerful but unmistakably medical room, hung with tinsel and other decorations, where an elderly man lay in bed, hooked up to tubes, his breathing laboured.

'Dennis talks about Walter a lot; he'll be so glad to see him,' she said quietly as she showed them in. The hospice, for all its comfortable, home-like air, still smelt of boiled food and antiseptic, just like the home where Xander's father had spent his last few months, and Xander inhaled shakily, memories of long days and nights spent at the side of the man he could never please, not even at the end, filling his mind. There had been no deathbed affection or confession of love, just demands for business updates and admonitions and orders. To keep the estate together and profitable, to marry soon and wisely and father an heir. To stop hiding behind his desk and to get out there. To be a Montague, to be worthy of the name. To not let them down. To be a man. He swallowed. Now he could never show his father he had what it took. That maybe he always had.

Walter whined softly, recalling Xander to the reason they were here, and Xander scooped him up, carrying him over to the hospital bed, Elfie at his side.

'Mr Barnes,' she said in a soft voice. 'Mr Barnes, I am Elfie and this is Xander. We've brought Walter to see you.'

Dennis's eyes fluttered open and he blinked uncertainly before recognition and hope flooded his face, tears welling in his eyes. 'Walter?' he asked as the dog whined again. 'Is that you, boy?'

Elfie set a chair by the bed and they placed Walter on it so that his old owner could reach him, laying a wrinkled hand on the dog's head. Walter whined again, pushing very gently against the hand as if he knew how careful he needed to be.

'I never thought I'd see you again. I knew it was wicked leaving him, but that shelter has such a good reputation. If anyone could find you the home you deserve...' His voice was as laboured as his breathing and he came to a painful-sounding stop.

'You did the right thing,' Elfie said, taking his hand with such natural sympathy Xander ached to see it. 'Walter is loved and cared for and happy. He's going to live in the countryside and have lots of space to play and Xander is going to make sure he's well looked after. We promise, don't we, Xander?'

'Yes, I promise.' But Xander was uneasily aware that the promise wasn't quite as it seemed. Walter would live at Thornham Park and would be well taken care of, but Elfie would be gone and Xander himself an occasional visitor. The dog had already been passed from home to home in his short life; he deserved stability, to be with someone who wanted him, not someone who was paid to take care of him.

Maybe he was over-identifying with the dog. But Xander could remember the first Christmas after he'd been sent to boarding school, arriving back at Thornham Park to find all his family away and no spare bedroom put aside for him. He'd been given a room at the manager's estate house until an au pair had finally shown up to take him back to London for the next few days. He'd heard the other boys talking excitedly about going home, about their families, their houses, their bedrooms, desperate to get back to those familiar places. Whereas Xander had loved the routine of school.

To sleep in the same bed every night, to be cared for by the same people, to know what was expected of him.

Maybe he could keep Walter with him whenever he was in the UK after all. With his mother in France and the American hotels attracting a more transitory experience seeking clientele, he didn't need to spend as much time abroad as his father and grandfather had. And he had already determined to have a wing at Thornham Park or maybe the Dower House as a permanent home once he was married and had children, to ensure no child of his grew up with no sense of home. He could start now, carve out space for Walter and him.

He stole a glance at Elfie as she chatted softly to Dennis, telling him about the day she had first met Walter and known he was the one, making the elderly man laugh a wheezing chuckle as she recounted how the dog had performed tricks to get her attention, how he had adapted to hotel life and always seemed to know who to make eyes at for treats.

'All the hotel staff adore him,' she continued. 'But, most importantly, he's happy. I know he misses you; now I've met you I understand why he gets excited when we see men of your age. But he *is* happy. He has his favourite walk, his favourite corner of the sofa, has made friends with the most soft-hearted chefs and eats better than some of the guests. I hope that's of some comfort.'

'More comfort than you can know.'

Yes, maybe there was a way he could balance his nomadic life and keep Walter. It was a shame he couldn't do the same for Elfie. New Year was just over a week away. A week after that she would be packing and off on her next adventure. It was too soon. Far too soon.

* * *

It was a quiet journey back to the hotel, both of them lost in thought, while Walter was unusually subdued, lying with his head on Elfie's knee. She stroked his ears softly, heart aching for the dog and his owner. She'd promised to return next week and hoped Xander would continue to visit after she had left for as long as it was possible.

'Are you okay?' Xander asked and she nodded.

'Just thinking about Dennis. How hard it must have been to make the choice to leave Walter the way he did, how he must have felt like he was abandoning him, even if his intentions were good. To be that alone in the world when the end comes, so alone that there's no one to visit or take care of your dog…' Her voice trailed off. She had always told herself that it was safest to be alone, that it meant never getting hurt, that you couldn't destroy what and who you loved, that you couldn't be left behind, but there was a downside to it too.

'But it sounds like he had a happy life. Did you see the pictures by his bed, of him and his wife? They were laughing in every single one, not forced smiles but real laughter. I never saw my parents laugh together like that.'

'Mine did. It was one of the things I missed most afterwards. The house was so quiet…' She looked out of the window and realised they were near the park. 'I think Walter should have a walk,' she said. 'Can we stop the car? I'll walk him back to the hotel.'

'Would you mind company?'

'Not at all, but I thought you had a lot to do?'

Xander grimaced. 'So much that another half an hour's skiving won't really make a difference.' He leaned forward to talk to the driver and less than a minute later the car glided to a stop, the driver jumping out to open Elfie's door and help Walter get out.

The afternoon was turning to dusk, the air bitterly cold with a sharp wind, and Elfie pulled her coat around her, shivering. Not that she needed to put up with this for much longer; in a couple of weeks she'd be in the Caribbean for a lucrative charter season and the chance to get some much-needed vitamin D. She waited for the usual feeling of pleasurable anticipation to ripple through her, but instead she felt numb—numb until Xander took her hand and then her whole body warmed up in one almighty whoosh of flame. It was embarrassing how much effect a touch separated by two layers of wool had on her, how instantly she responded to the lightest of caresses.

The lights of the Christmas fair flashed in front of them and by unspoken accord they turned down a quieter path, Walter stopping and sniffing every frosty leaf. 'I admit it. You did a good thing,' Xander said at last.

'Me?' Elfie was genuinely surprised.

'Choosing Walter.'

'I think he chose me, to be honest.' She paused, looking for the right words. 'I was unsure at first. You were so disinterested, not even coming along to choose him, and then I realised that you weren't even intending to keep him, not properly. I nearly walked away.'

'Why didn't you?'

She screwed up her face in embarrassment. 'Money,' she admitted. 'I couldn't run the risk of being sacked before I was due to fly out to my next job, and I knew this job could do wonders for my profile. You wouldn't believe how many people take social media popularity into account when hiring seasonal staff. Not everyone, some of the super-rich will pay a lot more for privacy, but my dog nanny account was getting me some seriously lucrative offers.' She bent down and ruffled Walter's head. 'I'm no better than any of those scam artists, am I? Sorry, Walter.'

'You were willing to work for every penny. You've put Walter's comfort before yours every time—you never mentioned how much he hogs the bed or how loudly he snores.'

'I find his snores soothing. But, I have to admit, I found it uncomfortable lying to Dennis then. He thinks Walter is going to have a happy ever after with us and instead...'

'He is. He stays with me unless I have to travel, and he'll have one carer when I am away. You're right; it's not fair on him otherwise.'

Relief filled her, a weight she hadn't realised she was carrying, a guilt she'd been ashamed to admit to lifting her. 'Really? Oh, I am so pleased.'

'He'll miss you, though. We both will.'

'And I'll miss you too, but this is really the best news. You two are made for each other.' She turned to him, laughing. 'And you thought you wanted some kind of noble hound!'

'I told you, I admit I was wrong. Walter was the right dog for the job, and you were exactly the right person. Are the right person.' His grip on her hand tightened, pulling her towards him, and she leaned in, enjoying the uniqueness of this public embrace—they were alone in the lane, but this was Hyde Park; they could be interrupted at any moment. But as Xander tilted her chin, staring at her with an oddly serious expression she couldn't interpret, she forgot where she was and how cold it was, lost in the darkness of his velvety brown eyes.

'Hey,' she half whispered, a little unnerved by the intensity she sensed in him. By the way she wanted to sink into him. She was consumed by him, by the need to touch him, kiss him. Impatient, she tugged his head down to hers, cursing her lack of height as she reached up and brushed his mouth with hers, then again, harder this time. She didn't want sweet, slow caresses; she wanted hard and demanding, the type that left her mouth swollen and her body reeling with desire. She felt him laugh gently against her mouth.

'There's no rush.'

What was he talking about? Of course there was a rush! Their time here was finite, and the clock was ticking. She was off on her next adventure and he needed to pick a suitable Baroness and settle down to his responsibilities. There could be no repeat of this time. So they had to make the most of every single second.

She nudged closer until she was pressed tight against him, exultant as he groaned and deepened, intensified the kiss. For a moment the world went away, the cold and noise receding as she lost herself in him, until something banged against her leg, causing her to stagger to the side, righting herself as an insistent head butted her again.

'I think it's Walter's dinner time,' she said, aware that she was a little breathless, that her head was spinning.

Xander's mouth curved into a smile so deliciously wolfish her toes curled and she might have actually moaned out loud. 'I was thinking it was time we moved somewhere warmer and more private anyway. Shall we?'

He offered her his arm in that peculiarly old-fashioned, gallant gesture of his and she took it with equal ceremony. 'I'm cold.' She gave an exaggerated shiver and summoned up her most limpidly innocent expression. 'I think I need a long hot shower. Care to join me?'

CHAPTER NINE

ELFIE KNEW THE super-rich. She had nannied for families in the heart of New York's most exclusive areas, whose two-storey penthouses had the kind of iconic views most people only saw in film sets. She had been a maid in chalets the size of hotels, fitted with every luxury money could buy, and crewed on yachts worth the same as a small country's GDP. She wasn't easily impressed.

Or so she thought. But when the car swept up the long driveway leading to Thornham Park she found her mouth falling open in awe, audibly gasping as the graceful—and huge—house finally came into sight, lit up against the winter-dark sky. Built in a gorgeous honey-coloured stone and surrounded by green, flower-filled terraces even in winter, the house rose in tiers, the stonework as lavishly decorated as any wedding cake. It was surrounded by acres of parkland and woodland, the farms which had once fed the great house on the very outskirts of the land.

Dusk had fallen and lights were entwined in the trees nearest the house, creating a magical effect, the tall pine trees which signalled the end of the drive tastefully and seasonally decorated. 'It's beautiful,' she breathed as the car came to a stop and Xander escorted her up the grand stone steps leading to the imposing front door and into the great hall, which doubled as a comfortable sitting room and reception with a roaring fire in the gigantic mantelpiece. Like Thornham House, the decorations were lavish, with greenery on every surface and a huge Christmas tree dominating the hall, presents already laid out underneath.

Xander greeted the reception staff and a few guests who obviously knew him well as one porter collected their cases and another disappeared outdoors discreetly with Walter. Elfie hung back for a moment, unaccountably shy. No one questioned her place in London. She was one of them, a member of staff, and they all knew that her friendship with Xander was part of her job. If anyone suspected the truth about the turn their relationship had taken—and a hotel was a small community, after all—she had heard no gossip. But she knew no one here and her status felt uncertain, neither guest nor staff nor family.

But she did have a job to do, she reminded herself, pulling out her camera and starting to document the festive scene. A place. For now, at least.

For a few moments she lost herself, as she loved to do, focusing on small details in order to bring the scene to life: a stocking hanging on the grand staircase, an exquisite crystal bauble, the heart of the fire. After a while she turned her focus onto people, on Xander talking to a regal-looking woman who seemed to be an old friend, the discreet waiters refilling glasses and offering canapés, the doorman standing to attention, as always trying to set them in their scene, looking for the story behind the pose.

There was something satisfying about seeing the world through a lens, being able to put a barrier between herself and the place and people she was photographing, letting her be a legitimate observer, aside from the action, just as she preferred it. She was only recalled to her surroundings when one of the receptionists offered her a glass of champagne and offered to show her to her room. Xander was still engrossed in conversation and, not wanting to appear needy or to look as if she expected more from him than their situation warranted, Elfie smiled her thanks, collecting Walter from the doorman as she followed the receptionist up the stairs, the dog butting at her heels.

'Here you are, Miss Townsend,' the receptionist said as she opened a heavy oak door. 'The Queen Victoria suite.'

'Please do call me Elfie. I am here to work, after all.' Elfie smiled her thanks as she stepped into the suite, stopping to gaze about herself in awe. 'Wow, this is really something.'

It really was. She'd loved the comfortable suite in London, but these rooms took her breath away. Richly decorated in red and gold, with high ceilings and huge old windows, it was easy to imagine herself back in time as she took in the elegant sitting room, her bedroom with its own seating area as well as bathroom and dressing room and the elegant little breakfast room which led out to its own private terrace. Her bags and Walter's bed were already in her room, her clothes unpacked and put away, her collection of practical layers even more incongruous than usual in the antique wardrobe, more accustomed to couture than hardwearing clothes.

Katya, the receptionist, gave her a quick tour, showing her all the very modern modifications hiding behind the antiques, from a state-of-the-art sound system to a cinema-sized screen. Elfie enjoyed playing with the gadgets, waiting until Katya left before exploring Xander's even more lavish room. After promising herself a long soak in his sunken double bath, she pulled her coat back on and stepped out onto the terrace to take in the view as she finished her champagne.

How things had changed in the last month. She'd been expecting to spend Christmas walking pampered pooches stuffed full of Christmas treats, before heading back to her dorm room. It wouldn't have been entirely joyless; she knew that a good Christmas dinner was always served to any working staff, and there were usually plenty of people in the hostel up for a transitory friendship she could have partied with. Instead, here she was in a room fit for a princess, waiting for the only lover she'd ever had who she couldn't get enough of.

Shouldn't she be getting bored by now? Finding the intimacy too confining? It was the chase she loved, those long looks and unspoken meanings. Possibilities and butterflies. Sometimes Elfie thought she would be happy staying in the flirtation stage for ever. But this time her feet weren't remotely itchy yet, the end looming, closer than she liked.

She looked round as she heard the door click and Walter left her to run, tail wagging enthusiastically, into the sitting room, only to return at Xander's heels.

'How long have you been standing out here? It's freezing.' He slipped an arm around her. The casual caress felt so normal, so comforting, and Elfie leaned in, seeking even closer contact.

'The view is stunning, though, even in the dark, the

way the trees silhouette, thanks to the Christmas lights. No moon, though—look at the sky. It's so heavy. Do you think it will snow?'

'You want a white Christmas?'

'Always. This place is just gorgeous. I can't believe it's your family home.'

'I'm glad you approve. You don't mind sharing it with two hundred strangers?'

'It seems fair. A place this size is probably a bit much for one family to keep up nowadays.'

'It needs an army.' He nodded at her glass. 'Do you want a top-up before you get ready?'

'Sounds lovely.' She handed her glass to him and followed him as he took it into the sitting room, where a chilled bottle was waiting. He extracted the cork seamlessly and filled first her glass and then his own. She raised it in a toast and then paused as his last words sank in. 'Thank you. What did you mean, get ready?'

'For the ball.'

'Me?' She took a sip, confusion washing through her. 'Xander, you never said you wanted me to attend the ball. I assumed I'd be on Walter duty. We were planning room service and a Christmas film, weren't we, Walter? He was trying to convince me that *Die Hard* is a Christmas film, and I was trying to persuade him to give *Love Actually* a go.' Elfie knew she was chattering on, but she couldn't stop herself. She was here to look after the dog, not be Xander's date at the most prestigious night in the hotel's calendar.

The Thornham Park Christmas Eve Ball was legendary, its roots stretching far back into Georgian times, and the reason so many guests returned year after year for the festive season. The great and the good of the local area were also invited, along with Xander's extended family and old family friends—people with pedigrees as long as Xander's—who travelled into Buckinghamshire from London or their own home county homes for the event, just as their grandfathers and great-grandfathers had done. The kind of magazines who concentrated on the world of the aristocracy usually sent a reporter and a photographer to cover the evening, and minor royalty had been known to attend.

If she went to the ball as a guest, not as a member of staff, on Xander's arm, then they would be making the kind of public declaration they had been carefully avoiding, an acknowledgement that she wasn't just staff, and what was the point of arousing that kind of speculation? This thing between them might be the most intoxicating affair she had ever indulged in, but it had just over a week left to run. She turned to Xander, a determinedly light smile on her face. 'Is Walter coming too? He doesn't have a tux!'

'For a couple of photos, but then I've arranged for him to stay with one of the managers and his family for the night.' Xander's forehead creased, and she wanted to reach up and smooth the lines away. 'Don't you want to come?'

'Do I want to be part of the famous Thornham Park ball? Of course.' She was only partly lying. Although she would rather not court notice and gossip, part of her was intrigued by the idea of attending. After all, the ball was the epitome of glamour and for once she would be the one sipping the cocktails, not the one serving them. 'But Xander, you might have noticed that I have a limited and functional wardrobe. I'm not sure my trusty maxi dress and a pair of silver flip-flops will cut it.'

'Then it's lucky that you traditionally get your presents on Christmas Eve, isn't it?' His eyes were alight with laughter and her stomach twisted with a poignant desire. 'Go look in the wardrobe in my room.'

'What?' She set her glass down carefully and walked slowly into Xander's bedroom, aware that both he and Walter were at her heels, and opened the heavy wardrobe door, stepping back in surprise. 'Oh, my goodness! What is this?'

It was like setting foot in an alternate universe, walking into the wardrobe to find an upmarket boutique. She could see at least eight styles of dress hung up, each in a couple of different sizes and colours. Propped on the open shelves were a variety of shoes and accessories. She whirled round to look at Xander, leaning against the wall with a proud grin on his face.

'Are you Prince Charming or the Fairy Godmother in this scenario? This is insane!'

'I didn't want to guess your style or taste and get it wrong. I have too many memories of my mother returning jewellery or clothes my father gave her to take such a risk. Anything you don't choose will go back to the store, but hopefully there will be something you like here.'

Elfie ran her gaze over the assorted dresses in rich shades of red and green, subtle ice blue and silver, and couldn't help a grin spreading over her face. 'I'm sure I can make do. How long have I got? I have some serious work to do.'

Normally Xander dreaded the annual Thornham Park Christmas Eve Ball. As host he needed to personally greet every single guest and dance with as many women as possible, favouring none. It gave him some kind of insight as to how it must have been in Georgian times, adhering to a rigid set of social customs. But tonight he was filled with an unexpected anticipation. Tonight he would have Elfie next to him, in his arms, and that knowledge turned a chore into a treat.

The truth was the last month had been the best in his life and that was all down to Elfie. Not just because of the mind-blowing sex, not just because he had opened up to her in a way he had never opened up before, but because she had blown open his solitary existence and introduced laughter and companionship. He knew his path, one of duty and tradition. He had never expected that sharing that path with someone else would make the journey a light-hearted stroll as opposed to a slog.

Now he knew that, how could he settle for the kind of loveless marriage he had assumed he was destined for? An understanding of the obligations a life with him entailed was important, but surely both he and any future wife deserved happiness and laughter too? It was hard to imagine sharing his life with anyone but Elfie, but she had her own destiny, and her dreams didn't involve an ancient title and the burden of a huge estate.

But tonight was Christmas Eve, and decisions about marriage lay somewhere in the future. Tonight for the first time he felt his duty less a burden and more of an honour with Elfie sparkling at his side. She was the queen of living for now, and he was going to take a leaf from her book and enjoy every moment they had left. He winked at her as they took their place in the formal receiving line by the huge double doors leading into the doorway and Elfie grinned back. 'You've got this,' she said. And she was right; he did.

The first half hour was always spent welcoming the guests into the ballroom. Most of the guests were known to him, and all wanted to express their condolences on the loss of his father, 'So sad, coming so soon after your grandfather's death', before turning their attention to Walter who, far from shying away from the noise and lights and crowds, was quite clearly in his element. It was astonishing how far his fame had spread; most guests had an inkling of his past and it turned out many were fellow dog owners, all with a titbit of advice. The receiving line, usually the most excruciating part of the evening, passed in a flash.

And next to him throughout it all was Elfie, camera in one hand, Walter's lead in the other. If she were to attend, she had told him, it needed to be in an official capacity as dog sitter and chronicler and, as a man whose every social occasion was also work, he had agreed. He knew that having a defined role could help someone face a room full of curious strangers. But although she might consider herself on duty she looked like the belle of the ball and he could hear several people asking who the woman with the extraordinary eyes was.

In the end she had chosen the simplest of the dresses he'd ordered, a soft dove grey, almost purple in some lights, blue in others, with a straight satin skirt and a soft georgette bodice. Sleeveless, it had a high modest neckline, dropping low at the back, revealing her delicate shoulder blades. She'd teamed it with teardrop earrings and a matching bracelet, her hair twisted into a low loose bun, tendrils framing her face. The colour accentuated the stormy grey of her eyes; the simplicity of the dress suited her petite frame. She was the most stunning woman in the room and seemingly neither knew it nor cared, happy for Walter to get hairs on her dress or walk on her hem. All Xander wanted to do was sweep her into his arms and dance the night away with her but he had hosting duties to fulfil.

Christmas Eve always followed the same pattern. A tantalisingly delicious array of canapés circulated the room along with champagne, festive cocktails and soft drinks, and a light buffet was laid out in the supper room for anyone who wanted anything more substantial. Transport was available to take anyone who wished into the village for Midnight Mass and when they returned mulled wine and mince pies were served, the traditional end of the ball.

A chamber orchestra provided accompaniment for traditional waltzes and foxtrots, alternating with a cover band who played a selection of tunes from the last fifty years. As a child Xander had found the evening stuffy and boring, as a young man a chore, but tonight he could see the charm in the festive ballroom with its holly and mistletoe themed decorations, in the gorgeous colours of the women's dresses and the elegance of the men's tuxedos. Children skidded across the dance floor and played hide and seek amongst the columns while the few teens in attendance posed for selfies.

The evening passed quickly. After anyone who wanted to had posed with Walter for a picture and he had been fed a carefully regulated amount of treats, one of the hotel managers took him back to the estate cottage where he lived with his family to settle the dog for the night. Xander had introduced Elfie to two of his closest friends, both of whom were here with their wives, and he was relieved to see that they took Elfie under their wing, ensuring she wasn't alone unless busy with her camera. Meanwhile he fulfilled his duty, moving around the ballroom and engaging each group in conversation, taking his father's place and asking some of the older ladies to dance when the orchestra played a waltz or foxtrot. Both his father and grandfather had been accomplished ballroom dancers and being asked by them had been considered something of a privilege. Xander had been brought up to know the difference between a waltz and a Viennese waltz and so he did his best to fill in, his reward the pleasure on the face of a woman who had been a close friend of his grandmother's when he led her onto the floor—and the approval in Elfie's eyes as she raised her camera to capture the opening dance.

It took a couple of hours to work his way around the room, but finally Xander found himself right where he wanted to be, next to Elfie, just as the orchestra started to play a slow waltz. He held out a hand. 'Dance with me?'

'I'm not sure I know how.' She took his hand, and he closed his fingers around hers. 'I've seen you out there tonight and you are good. How didn't I know you had moves?'

'I keep my talents close.'

'What else are you hiding from me?'

'Stick around a little longer and who knows what you'll find out?' It was a light-hearted exchange, but Xander realised with a jolt how much he wanted the words to be true, for Elfie to stick around, to discover more about her as she did about him. For this not to be a month-long friendship, a two-week fling, but something more, something worth exploring.

Maybe there was a way. Could he ask her to stay here

for longer, to see how they worked not as friends with benefits but as partners? Would she feel constrained and confined? And how could he ask her to give up her dreams for his duty?

There were no easy answers and so instead he pulled her close, leading her through a simple waltz. With one arm around her waist, her hand in his, feeling her hand splayed on his back it was easy to see how this old-fashioned dance had once been considered scandalous. He could feel every breath she took, see every expression that flitted across her face tilted up towards him, her lush mouth within kissing distance. How he wanted to whisk her behind a pillar and kiss her until all they could see were stars.

But the room was full of people who knew him and would be speculating about him; there were women here who he had dated, journalists and friends of his father. He couldn't, wouldn't expose Elfie to any gossip so instead he kept her close as they moved in perfect time.

'Are you sure you have never learned to waltz?' he asked, and she shook her head, her eyes dreamy as he twirled her through a turn.

'I always thought I had two left feet. You must be a very good teacher.'

'You make it easy.' And she did. She made everything easy, everything full of colour and light and possibility, and in a week she would be walking away and his life would be dull and dutiful once more.

Unless he figured out some way they could both get what they wanted and enticed her to stay.

'You always have that master of all you survey thing going on,' she said as the music stopped and he reluctantly stepped back, applauding with the rest of the couples as the orchestra bowed before making way for the band. 'But you have something else tonight. I can't quite work it out.'

Xander snagged two smoked salmon canapés from a passing waitress and handed one to Elfie. 'Debonair handsomeness and a devilish air?'

'Of course. Always. But it's something more. You looked absolutely genuinely fine out there, especially when you were charming those women. I thought one might swoon when you danced with her! I'd promised myself to check in with you regularly, knowing how much you find these occasions a strain, but you looked okay. I know you cover it well, but either you're such an exceptional actor we need to get you on the stage right now or you are actually having a good time.'

'I was having a good time. I am.' He didn't know what surprised him most, the truth of the statement or the knowledge that Elfie had been keeping a watchful eye on him. That she knew him well enough to anticipate his fears and cared enough to look out for him. 'I'll be honest; I was dreading tonight, acting as the main and only host, knowing everyone is watching and comparing me to my father. Worried that I wouldn't know what to say and how to be and that everyone would be thinking I was arrogant. But you know what? I'm surprised by what a good evening I'm having. I hope you have been okay. I'm sorry I had to leave you so much.'

'Your friends have taken very good care of me. Are you allowed to dance twice with the same unmarried lady or will that cause a scandal? Because I may not know how to waltz but this song is a particular favourite of mine.'

'In that case, how can I resist?' He took her hand and

headed back to the dance floor, now full of enthusiastic groups and couples dancing along to the famous disco tune. But as he joined in, watching Elfie laugh and twirl to the music, the question lingered in his mind. How could he resist her? More, how could he allow her to walk away when he wanted more, much more?

CHAPTER TEN

SONG FOLDED INTO song and Elfie lost herself in the music. Xander's friends had joined them on the dance floor and so on the occasions he excused himself to speak to someone he had missed earlier, or to wave off an early departure, she stayed where she was, allowing her body to move to the beat and enjoy the sheer unadulterated pleasure of dancing. She might not have had lessons in ballroom dancing, but she enjoyed the chance to let go when she could and the excellent band and the festive atmosphere along with the unexpected connection with Xander's friends gave her the confidence to dance to every tune. Xander was such a cat that walked alone that she hadn't been sure what to expect from his close friends, but she had found herself drawn to them and their wives, all four unpretentious with a warm sense of humour.

The music finally slowed and the groups separated into swaying couples. Elfie retreated, glad of the break, aware that she was both thirsty and a little dishevelled. She helped herself to a glass of refreshing water garnished with mint and elderflower before searching for the restrooms, deciding against going upstairs to her suite.

The cloakrooms were as opulent as the rest of the hotel with a spacious seating area, a discreet screen shielding the entrance to the sinks and toilets. Several women around Elfie's age were lounging on the sofas, scrolling through their phones and gossiping. Elfie was aware of their stares as she walked through the room and headed to the sink, where she wanted to cool her flushed face before repairing her hair and make-up.

The water was deliciously refreshing as she patted her cheeks dry, searching through her bag for powder and lipstick and a comb to tackle her hair, which was beginning to collapse out of its bun after a few too many enthusiastic dances. Engrossed in her task, she tuned out the carrying voices from next door until she heard Xander mentioned.

'Xander looks hot tonight, don't you think?'

The answering voice had the kind of long drawn-out drawl that provoked the same instinctive wince in Elfie as fingernails on a chalkboard. 'Xander always looks hot. That was never the issue. He has the looks, he has the money, he has all this…'

'So, what was the problem?'

'He was just no good at having fun. Even a weekend away was about scouting out the opposition. He never switches off. It's exhausting. And as for conversation? I swear he never heard a word I said.'

'He looked like he was having fun tonight,' a third voice said slyly, and a peal of laughter rang out. Elfie thought she heard someone ask, 'Who is that woman anyway?' and did her best to block out the voices. Eavesdroppers never heard any good of themselves; she'd learned that the hard way, sitting on the stairs and listening to her mother tell her stepfather that she was just going through a difficult phase. The old betrayal ran deep, and she felt her nails cut into her palms as she tried to stuff the hurt back into the past where it belonged, her ears ringing with memories. By the time her hearing had cleared and she had regained control, the laughter had died down.

'I heard a rumour he's ready to settle down,' the woman with the sly voice said.

'Of course he is; he's thirty now and he needs an heir. What about it, Cressie? Fancy being a baroness?'

'I'm considering it,' Cressie drawled. Elfie ran the name through her mind, through the research she had done on Xander. This must be Lady Cressida Wallington-Evans, a tall slender blonde who worked in banking. Brains, beauty and pedigree, she would be a perfect baroness, the kind of woman who would provide an heir and a spare whilst helping run the hotels and estate without breaking a sweat, no hair out of place and nails perfectly manicured as she did so.

'Well, if you don't want him let me know; I wouldn't mind owning all this. And I've always wondered what was under that forbidding exterior of his. I'd like to find out if still waters really do run deep.'

'If you do then let me know,' Cressie said with a laugh as annoying as her drawl. 'I never got anywhere, but luckily one doesn't need one's husband for all one's entertainment. I'd quite happily stay here while he travels around all the time. If I say yes.'

'If he asks you, you mean!'

'Darling, if I want him to then he'll ask me. That's not a worry.'

And with that they were gone, leaving Elfie leaning against the sink feeling a little like Cinderella watching the coach turn back into a pumpkin. She wasn't quite sure what she made of the conversation she'd inadvertently overheard but she did know three things. One, Lady Cressida Wallington-Evans would be looking elsewhere for a husband; Elfie would put a spoke in that particular young woman's wheel before she left if it was the last thing she did. No way was that woman going to have charge of Walter; she sounded like the kind of woman who made dogs sleep downstairs and would never share the last piece of cheese. Two, Xander should only marry someone he loved and respected and who loved and respected him, heir or no heir. Because he was worth more than his title and the estate he had inherited, worth more than the continuation of a family name, and he deserved someone who knew that. Someone who wanted the man, not the trappings.

And three, she had had a timely reminder that, fun as tonight had been, this wasn't her world, and this wasn't her life. She was getting too close to forgetting who she was, why she was here, getting in way too deep, behaving as if they really were a couple, as if this time didn't have an end date. Living in the moment was all very well but she was in danger of thinking the moment was reality.

She had to be careful, rein in her emotions, remember her mantra of moving on while it was still fun. Before she outstayed her welcome. Before she found herself outside looking in once again. Because she had a feeling that this time finding herself rejected would hurt more than it ever had before. And last time had been unbearable.

She took another look in the mirror, chin tilted defiantly, eyes flashing. She was a survivor. An independent woman. She had been on her own for the last decade and that was the way she liked it. A romantic fairy tale fling couldn't, wouldn't change that. No matter how much part of her wanted it to. The part of her that still believed in happy ever afters despite all the evidence to the contrary, the part of her that still yearned to be loved, wanted to be loved no matter the cost.

It was Elfie's job to protect that part of her, to keep the armour polished, to mend all chinks. She and Xander were about a bit of festive fun. She needed to remember that and walk away without a backwards glance, just like she always did.

It was late by the time the last car had driven away, the last guest had gone to bed and Xander was free to return to their suite. He hadn't seen Elfie for an hour or so; she had slipped away pleading tiredness and he thought she would probably be asleep. So it was a surprise when he walked into the suite to find the lamps on and Elfie curled up on the sofa staring into the distance, a wistfulness in her eyes that made his heart ache. He knew she found this time of year hard.

'Hey,' he said softly, and she looked up slowly, her smile not reaching her eyes.

'Are you done now?'

He shrugged off his suit jacket and undid his bow tie in relief. It was ridiculous how constricting he found formal clothes, considering how much time he spent in them. 'Until the morning. This time of year is always intense.'

'Next year you should take a year off. Come and find me on a beach. We can swim and eat ice cream for Christmas dinner.'

'Sounds like heaven.' He felt a piercing ache at the thought that he would never see her bathed in sun, never watch her emerge from the sea, hair wet and plastered back, bikini-clad and glowing. He'd never really cared before, when a relationship neared its end, never wanted to take the moment and hold it tight, to escape time.

'My friends liked you.' He perched on the sofa arm and Elfie shifted so her head was in his lap, her hair spilling out. He took a tendril and wound it gently around his fingers.

'I liked them. Where did you meet them?'

'Prep school. Most people think it's barbaric to send kids away to school at seven, and it's not something I would do, but the truth is I loved school. Loved the security, the routine. I shared a room with Tim and Leo and although we were all so different we became close, like brothers, I suppose. The nearest thing I have, anyway. We all went on to the same senior school and our friendship endured.' He smoothed her hair out, selecting another tendril. 'My parents loved Tim; he was exactly the kind of sports mad daredevil they wished I was, and Leo was always throwing himself behind one cause or another; I guess politics was an inevitable career path for him.'

Her eyes were half closed. 'They're very fond of you. I get the feeling they worry about you. We all need people to look out for us. I'm glad you have them.'

His hands stilled. 'Has someone been telling tales out of school?'

She sat up, turning to face him, taking his hands in hers. 'Not at all. They were just talking about your university days and one of them mentioned that your teachers had tried to encourage you to choose maths. Apparently, you were a bit of a child prodigy.'

That was the problem with friends who had known him since he was small. Friends who'd always tried to invite him home for holidays because they knew he might be heading back to an anonymous hotel room and another temporary nanny. Friends who knew how much he relished the rituals of tradition, of knowing where things were, and hated change. Friends who'd watched him attend every pure maths lecture he could, even as he'd pushed himself to engage with the degree he had chosen.

'I don't believe in looking back, in regrets. Besides, I never had that genius spark needed to pursue maths,' he said, and it was true. He just would have liked the journey.

Her eyelids flickered but she didn't speak and Xander wondered just what had been said during his absence. His friends had very determined views, not just on his career path but on the relationships he pursued and his plans for his future marriage as well.

'You looked very beautiful tonight. The most beautiful woman there.'

The pensive, almost fragile look left her eyes as she smiled and cupped his face with her hands. 'You don't need to flatter me. I already intended you would get lucky tonight.'

He raised his eyebrows. 'Did you? Then lucky is indeed the word.'

Shifting forward, Elfie leaned in and kissed him. It was a sweet, almost poignant kiss, her lips soft on his, her hands still on his cheeks. He pulled her closer, one hand tangling in her hair, the other skimming over the exposed skin of her back.

'I'm glad you chose this dress,' he murmured against her mouth and felt her smile.

'You like?'

He traced her shoulder blade and felt her quiver. 'Very much.'

Now it was Xander's turn to kiss her, deeper, passionate, but still with a hint of wistfulness, as if they were both keeping an eye on the clock and watching their time together run out. Her arms wound around his neck, clutching his nape, pressing so close he could feel her imprinted on him. Slowly, still kissing her, he stood up, bringing her with him.

'Lovely as this sofa is, I am ready to retire for the night. You?'

'I think I could be persuaded.' She took his hand, but Xander resisted as she tugged him towards the bedroom door.

'Aren't you forgetting something?'

She stopped, hand still in his, biting her bottom lip in query. 'I thought Walter was staying away tonight?'

'It's Christmas Eve,' he reminded her and looked deliberately down at her feet, covered by the hem of her dress. 'Shouldn't you be leaving shoes out?'

'I'm a little old for that.' She attempted a smile, but her mouth wobbled and he knew she was thinking about the last Christmas she'd attempted to do so. 'I'm sure Father Christmas is busy with the children tonight.'

'It doesn't hurt to try.'

'I guess not.' She slipped off first one and then the other of the high heeled silver shoes she'd chosen to wear with the dress. 'I can't believe I haven't got blisters; I never wear heels. But then I've never been able to afford this brand before.' Gathering up her shoes, Elfie placed them by the Christmas tree that dominated the far corner of the room and then grinned at Xander. 'Go on; you too.'

'Me?'

'I can't imagine Father Christmas coming here just for me.' Her tone was teasing and Xander laughed as he removed his shoes and placed them next to hers before turning to look at her, mouth swollen, hair tumbling over her shoulders, dimly aware that he had laughed more in the last month than the last decade. But as her eyes darkened with desire, her chest moving with each breath, and his own body heated in response, amusement fled, replaced with a primal need. *Mine* every sinew, every beat of his heart, every nerve, every drop of blood claimed. *Mine*.

He stepped towards her and stood looking at her for one eternal second while the blood thundered around his body before scooping her up, his mouth fastening on hers as he carried her through the sitting room and into the lamplit bedroom.

It was like going back in time, living out her Mr Darcy fantasies as she was ruthlessly swept off her feet and thoroughly kissed before being deposited onto a four-poster bed older than most people's houses. Excitement lit every nerve as Elfie scooted up the blessedly modern mattress to support herself against the pillows and watch as Xander undid every button on his shirt before shrugging it off, moving with that same deliberate haste onto his belt, until his trousers slid to the floor, stepping out of them with careless grace. The breath whooshed from her body as Elfie took him in, greedily exploring every inch of him with her eyes, capturing him in detail so that in a week, a month, a year she would be able to recall just how the lamplight moved over honed muscle, how the shadows emphasised the sharpness of his cheekbones, the darkness of his eyes. He was magnificent and he was hers.

The silk of the dress felt almost unbearable on her heated skin, but when she went to unzip it Xander held up a hand. 'Wait. I want to undress you.'

Her stomach jolted at the words, her breasts heavy and yearning for his touch as she mutely nodded. But he didn't join her, not yet. Instead he stood at the bottom of the bed, clad only in his boxer shorts, examining every inch of her in turn. She could physically feel the journey of his gaze sliding up her legs, along her stomach, moving slowly over the curve of her breast. How could he turn her on so much without even touching her? Finally, he nodded in satisfaction, sitting on the side of the bed, only to torture her further by retracing the path of his gaze with his fingers, gliding along the satin on a torturous, almost unendurable journey. She shifted restlessly and his hands stilled, a wolfish smile playing on his mouth. 'Patience.'

Eyes, fingers and then mouth following that same heated trail, the sensation of touch on satin shooting through her until at last she felt the zip give way as Xander eased it down her trembling body, before repeating the same slow undressing with her underwear, the same slow intense exploration of her body, this time skin to skin. By the time he came to her she was mindless with need, reaching for him, needing his body heavy on hers, his mouth crushing hers, to be enveloped by him, gasping at the rightness of him, of them together. She'd been expecting lovemaking as dark and intense as the foreplay, but it was unexpectedly tender and sweet, their gazes locked together, their bodies as one.

It had been so long since she'd felt so wanted, so cherished, so needed. How could she just walk away in a week with a breezy goodbye as if this hadn't been the most meaningful, intimate experience in her life? But Xander had plans that didn't involve her—and she had to keep her heart safe. Difficult as leaving would be, staying would be infinitely more dangerous. So she needed to hold onto this moment, this night, this week and let its warmth sustain her over the months ahead. Memories were all she could allow herself; she needed to make sure they were perfect.

CHAPTER ELEVEN

IT TOOK ELFIE a couple of moments to name the tingle of anticipation in the air when she woke up. Christmas! She turned, burying herself into Xander's side, smiling to herself at the ludicrousness of a grown woman feeling this excited on Christmas morning. But then she hadn't shared Christmas with anyone for a very long time.

She allowed herself a few minutes to enjoy the feeling. Xander was still asleep, warm and solid to her touch and all hers. She wrapped herself around him, her breathing slowing to match his, drifting back into a contented doze, when she felt him shift, pulling her even closer.

'Good morning—or should I say Merry Christmas?'

'Merry Christmas to you too.' She reached up to press a kiss on his cheek. 'Do you think Father Christmas has visited?' She couldn't quite hide her smug smile. It had taken some stealth to sneak out of bed, retrieve his gifts and put them under the tree while he slept, but she had managed it.

Xander checked his watch. 'Plenty of time before breakfast. Shall we go and see?'

He rolled out of bed and she watched him with shameless approval as he crossed the bedroom naked, only to reappear from the bathroom in a hotel robe, another one slung over his arm which he handed to Elfie. She put it on, fastening the cord around her waist, and ran her fingers through her hair before following Xander into the suite's sitting room, only to pause and gasp at the door.

While they had slept some elf had sneaked in and transformed the room. The tree was lit up, an enticing heap of presents set beneath it; more lights were strung across the mantelpiece. The small table in the corner had been laid, a pot of steaming coffee, jugs of fruit juice and a plate of cinnamon rolls placed there. Walter lay on his bed, thumping his tail, stretching to his feet as she walked in. 'How did you get here?' she asked him as he butted her hand in greeting.

'Christmas magic,' Xander said. 'Coffee?'

'Please.' She took the cup he proffered and wandered over to the sofa and sat down, Walter jumping up to curl up beside her. 'I can't believe someone brought us breakfast and Walter and I didn't even hear.'

'I told you, Christmas magic. Have you checked your shoes yet?'

'Not yet; have you?'

They stayed still for a moment, smiling at each other, and Elfie wanted to take this second and freeze it, this feeling of affection and happiness, silly giddiness and anticipation before the present-opening began and Christmas started. She committed every detail to memory, the aromatic coffee scent mixed with pine and cinnamon, Xander with his morning stubble shadowing his chin and sleep-tousled hair, Walter's tail wagging furiously, the festive lights, the feeling of complete contentment. She didn't need presents; she just needed this.

'Okay,' she said at last, taking her coffee over to the tree. 'Let's take a look. Walter, there are several here with your name on; I wonder what they could be? Hey, Xander, looks like you've been a good boy; your shoes are nice and full.' She slid them towards him and he took them.

'How about you? Have you been a good girl?'

'Looks like Father Christmas thinks so.'

'He's not the only one.' Their eyes met, the atmosphere charged, before Walter jumped off the sofa, breaking the tension and, laughing, Elfie investigated the content of her shoes. Chocolate, some expensive-looking perfume, a pretty pair of silver earrings. She put the earrings on, watching Xander open his own gifts, also chocolate, a book on how to teach your dog tricks, some new gloves—she'd noticed he was always losing his—and some handmade soaps, small bottles of artisan liqueur and fudge she had bought at the craft fair held alongside the dog show.

Most of the presents under the tree were for Walter; not only had both Elfie and Xander bought him gifts but so, it seemed, had half the staff and by the time they'd finished helping him unwrap them he had quite the pile of toys and balls, treats and chews and a couple of smart coats and jumpers. Elfie took several photographs, most for his accounts, but one to send to Dennis so he could see how Walter was being spoiled and loved.

There had also been a few presents for Xander. A shirt from his mother, expensive malt whisky from one of his friends, a book from another. Usually, he explained, he would open them after Christmas dinner, downstairs with the guests, but this time he had wanted to enjoy a private Christmas for once. Elfie, on the other hand, wasn't expecting anything. She hadn't given her mother an address; normally money was deposited in her account on birthdays and Christmas, and she didn't have friends she exchanged gifts with. So she was more than a little surprised when Xander handed her a large brightly wrapped gift.

'For me?' She read the tag. 'Oh, Walter, you shouldn't have!' Once she would have torn the paper off, but she wanted to savour the moment, carefully peeling back the tape, teasing open the paper to reveal a huge rucksack from a brand she had always coveted but never been able to justify buying. 'Wow! Thank you, Walter.' She kissed the top of his head and then leaned over to kiss Xander as well. 'You have been generous with his pocket money.'

'He noticed that your bags were looking a little battered. Someone who is always on the move needs the right equipment.'

'He is very wise.'

There were just two gifts left now and, feeling more than a little nervous, Elfie picked up a flat package and handed it to Xander, her cheeks heating as he read the tag.

'To Xander, love Elfie and Walter.' She was embarrassed to think how long it had taken her to write the brief message, her pen hovering over the word love for what felt like hours.

'You didn't need to get me anything,' he said as he opened it and she shrugged.

'We wanted to, didn't we, Walter?'

She watched anxiously as he slid the picture out of its wrapping, his forehead crinkling as he looked at it. It was a simple pen and ink drawing of a scruffy dog she'd had framed, the initials AT in the corner, dated twenty years earlier.

'It's one of my dad's,' she explained. 'He often drew simple pictures like this to amuse me, and I realised how much this one looked like Walter.'

'It really does,' he said slowly. 'Of course, your father was Albert Townsend. Why didn't I make the connection? Elfie, this is way too valuable, both in sentimental and actual value. I can't accept this.'

'You know my dad's work?'

He nodded. 'Figgy worked at an art gallery; they had a display of your father's pictures while we were dating, and I went to the opening party. I was absolutely blown away by his use of colour and line. I promised myself I'd treat myself to one of his paintings one day.'

Elfie swallowed. 'My dad would have been so happy to hear that; I wish you could have met him. And of course you should keep it; he did me a lot of these little scribbles, mostly of animals, and I have them all safely stored with some of my childhood belongings. I'll never sell them. They weren't meant to be sold, they were just for me, but this one belongs to you.'

'You're sure?'

She nodded.

'Then I am honoured to accept it.' He leaned over to kiss her. 'Thank you. And this is for you.' He handed her the last present, labelled simply *For Elfie. X* in Xander's distinctive handwriting.

'But you gave me my gift last night.'

'That was to celebrate French Christmas; this one is for the English Christmas.'

She glanced at him uncertainly as she took the present and began to open it, her heart beating fast. The paper fell away to reveal an antique powder compact, delicately painted with a picture of a ballerina. She pressed the catch and as the lid sprung up a tune started to play. 'The Dance of the Sugar Plum Fairy,' she said in surprise. 'Oh, this is beautiful. I've never seen anything so exquisite.'

'It was my great-grandmother's. It seemed fitting to pass it onto you, considering the tune. Apparently, these musical compacts were quite the thing in the nineteen-forties. Do you like it?'

'I love it…it's absolutely perfect. Thank you.' She leaned in to kiss him, her heart hammering. These gifts weren't generic presents, chosen for passing ships, they were meaningful and personal for the giver as well as the receiver. And what that meant was more than she could process.

The rest of the day was mercifully busy, allowing her little time to dwell on the intimacy of the gifts. The hotel served a festive breakfast to the guests, followed by a series of activities ranging from walks to board games in the library, leading up to Christmas dinner itself. After dinner more gifts were exchanged and it was touching to see how many people clearly returned year after year, even buying presents for other guests. Xander and Walter both received plenty and the hotel, on Xander's behalf, had presents for every guest, handing out hampers full of homemade delicacies and blankets made from the Glen Thorne tartan.

But, for all the festivity and generosity, the care of the staff and the good humour of the guests, the day seemed to lack something and it wasn't until she took a photo of the whole group that Elfie realised what seemed strange—there were no children this year and, as no one commented on it, it clearly wasn't unusual. Elfie's heart ached to think of Xander spending so many childhood Christmases alone amongst strangers and adults.

For all his private fears of not living up to the family tradition, Xander was the consummate host, making sure no guest was excluded, as if this really were the private house party the hotel modelled itself on. It wasn't until presents had been exchanged, a vigorous game of charades concluded and guests had drifted off to read or nap that Elfie had him to herself once more.

'Let's take Walter for a walk,' she suggested. 'I could do with the exercise if I am going to have any chance of tackling the supper buffet.'

'Sounds like a plan.' He looked out of the window at the low heavy sky. 'Better wrap up warm; it looks like snow to me. You might get a white Christmas after all.'

Elfie dressed Walter in one of his new coats, snapping and posting a picture as she did so, then met Xander at the back door. He was wearing his new gloves and held up his hands to her with a grin. 'Very cosy. Thank you.'

'Try not to lose them,' she said, and he shook his head.

'These came from you. I'll guard them well.' His tone was teasing but his expression was intense and the same heaviness that had hit her that morning pressed down on her. This was supposed to be fun, not serious. Somewhere along the way she'd taken her eyes off the road and things had accelerated without her even noticing. But it wasn't too late. She just needed to step back. Step back and head off like she always did.

And tell herself this time was no different.

But the conversation she'd overheard the night before

was still churning through her brain. She couldn't walk away and leave Xander thinking he deserved a loveless sensible marriage when he deserved all the happiness in the world. She knew it; she just needed to make sure he did too. And then she could leave, her conscience clear.

By the time she reached the Caribbean this would all just be another adventure. She was almost sure of it.

Elfie was unusually quiet as they left the hotel, gripping Xander's hand so tightly he could feel the pressure through their gloves. It was dark now, but fairy lights lit a path through the gardens and they followed it. There were no stars tonight, the clouds full and almost luminous. As they reached the rose garden the first snowflakes began to fall, dancing in the slight breeze. Elfie lifted her face up to the sky, eyes half closed.

'Making a wish?' Xander asked and she nodded.

'First snow of the season.'

He wanted to ask what she was wishing for, but something held him back. The cord that bound them felt so gossamer-thin, and although that was what they had both signed up for he was all too aware of its fragility, that he wanted to strengthen it, reinforce it, bind them together.

'Can I ask you to do something for me?' Elfie said abruptly and, surprised, he stopped, her hand still in his.

'Anything.'

'Promise me not to rush into marriage. Don't marry the kind of woman who you wouldn't trust to take good care of Walter if you weren't there.'

'The kind of woman who *what*?' Xander stared at Elfie in confusion.

She bit her lip, eyes lowered. 'I just think it will be

a mistake if you choose someone to marry because of her family credentials or her CV. Don't pick someone who sees only the title and the estates and the money. Marry someone who sees you, Xander. Who wants to marry the man, not the Baron.'

Gently he reached out and touched her cheek and Elfie leaned into the caress. 'Hey, what brought this on?'

'I know you think that a quasi-arranged practical marriage is the sensible thing to do, but it isn't. It'll just drive you inside yourself and you deserve so much more than that. Don't marry someone who doesn't want *you*, Xander Montague, as opposed to Baron Thornham. Who you don't actually want and respect and love. Don't marry for heirs or because it's expected. So the title goes to a distant cousin? Does it really matter? Do you think Henry VIII's search for an heir was worth the lives of all those women, the disruption to the country—and in the end his great-nephew got the throne anyway and then his line died out. It's all meaningless when all is said and done.'

'I've never really thought of myself as Henry VIII before and I wasn't planning on executing my future wife if no heir appeared but...'

'I know! I just mean you can marry someone because she has the right name and credentials and be unhappy, but it won't necessarily give you the outcome you want. So why not be happy and see where it takes you?'

Her eyes, dark and intense, fixed on him as if she was willing her words into him. Words not dissimilar to his own thoughts over the last few weeks. Thoughts that had only started since he'd met her.

His world had rules for men like him: marry someone with the same background and ensure discretion if one looked for passion elsewhere. Xander had spent his whole life in that world and never met anyone he had wanted to invite in, to bare his soul to, to grow old with. The only woman to ever touch him in that way was Elfie.

But now he knew what it was like to hunger, to want, to need, to feel, to burn. Now he knew what happiness felt like. So how could he go back to merely existing? The truth was that confiding in Elfie didn't feel like weakness but like sanctuary and in return she had confided in him and he had taken her burdens willingly and gladly. How could he swap what they had for a loveless arrangement?

Loveless... It wasn't that he *loved* Elfie exactly; how could he? It was still so early, and he wasn't sure that he even knew what love was. But he liked her, desired her, wanted her to be happy. Surely that was close?

The snow had intensified, now falling thick and heavy, carpeting the ground in soft white, and Xander realised how cold it had become. Walter pressed close to his legs. 'Let's walk before we both get turned into icicles,' he said, tugging her hand. 'You're right. I've been thinking about my future too.'

'Well, that's good.'

'Elfie, I was raised to put duty first, to think that choosing any path for personal reasons was selfish, and I've always lived that way, not even knowing that something essential was missing as a result. But then I met you and everything changed. You're right. I do deserve more. We both do.'

He felt her stiffen, retreat. 'This isn't about me.'

'No? Shouldn't it be?' Every doubt, every question

he'd had about their next steps faded away. They were good together, really good. How could they turn away from something so rare, so special? 'You said yourself that I should be with someone who sees me, not the title. You do, Elfie, you see me.'

'Xander, what are you saying?'

'I'm saying stay. Don't go to the Caribbean. Stay with me. Let's see where this goes. We made the rules, Elfie; we can change them. We're good together. Let's not throw this away.'

Elfie dropped Xander's hand and backed away. 'No,' she said numbly. How could she have got it so wrong? 'I didn't mean me.'

'Why not?'

'Because I'm not the settling-down type. I don't want marriage and babies and all that.'

'I'm not talking about marriage, Elfie, at least not yet.' The excitement in Xander's face had faded, to be replaced by confusion, and it hurt her to realise she had caused it. 'And I know you want to fulfil your father's dream. But there's no reason you need to be alone to do that. Or that you can't do that from here.'

'It's not about the retreat. At least it's not just that. It's just this, us, right now, is perfect, Xander. How we are is perfect. I don't want to ruin that.' Although she had an awful feeling it was too late to worry about ruining anything; the damage had been done. Why had she said anything? Why hadn't she saved her advice for the last day they were together?

'How will seeing where we go ruin what we have? Sure, we might not work out…but, Elfie, we might… we really might.'

'We won't!' She didn't mean to speak so loudly and heard the echoes of the words reverberate throughout the night. Lowering her voice, she half whispered, 'We won't. I'm sorry, Xander.'

The look of shock on his face cut her straight through to her heart. 'No, I'm the one who should apologise. I misread the situation, got carried away. Forget I said anything.' The snow was falling faster and faster, blanketing the ground, the trees, and she wished she could blanket her heart, her feelings, with the same numbing cold.

'It's not you.' Part of Elfie wanted to stay quiet, to shut the conversation down, but she couldn't let Xander think any part of her refusal was to do with him. Because it really wasn't. The way he had made her feel over the last few weeks, the way he took her seriously and yet made her feel like the most desirable woman alive. It was like magic, like living in a movie. Of course she was tempted to stay for a little longer. But it was because she was beginning to care so much for him that she had to make sure she wouldn't be tempted to push her luck any further.

Some men would shrug the rejection off, move onto the next woman in a matter of weeks, but Xander might see this as proof that he had been right to pursue his dutiful idea of a suitable marriage and she didn't want that for him. She wanted him to have it all, happiness and love and a house filled full of children with his eyes and puppies and kittens, like some kind of fifties bucolic fantasy. Just because she couldn't figure in that fantasy didn't mean he didn't deserve it.

'It's not you, Xander, it's all me.'

'Elfie…' He rubbed his gloved hand over his forehead. 'Honestly. You don't need to say anything, explain anything. Let's move on. I'm getting cold; shall we head back in for the buffet?'

She'd never felt less like eating in her life as he started back to the house, Walter looking back at her as she stood irresolute before breaking into a jog over the soft snow to catch up with him.

'Xander, I drive people away. That's what I do. I don't mean to, but it happens anyway, and I don't want that for you, for us. I want to remember us like we were this morning, not the moment you leave me.'

'So you'll leave me instead?'

'It's safer that way. I promise. For both of us.'

He stopped then and took hold of her shoulders. 'Who hurt you, Elfie? Who made you feel this way? I know your relationship with your mother is complicated, but...'

'Complicated? I wish. It's broken, Xander, and it's all my fault.'

'Elfie,' he said gently. 'Whatever happened, you were a child. No one can hold you responsible for anything. You certainly shouldn't allow it to dictate your whole life. I want you to stay, I want to see if this is just a passing attraction or something stronger. If you don't want to stay, if you know in your heart you don't have the right kind of feelings for me then that's fine. It has to be. But if you are walking away because you're scared or because of something that happened a long time ago then you are doing both of us a huge disservice.'

How she wanted to believe him, to take hold of his words and let them into her soul, but she had spent too many years hardening herself against everyone and everything to weaken now.

'I killed my father,' she said, holding his gaze. 'I killed my father and broke my mother's heart. Now do you see why you're better off without me, why I should always be alone?'

Elfie wasn't sure what she was expecting Xander to say, but she knew what she would see. Dawning disgust, revulsion, for him to step away. But, instead, he drew her closer, his eyes warm with a sympathy she knew she didn't deserve.

'You were twelve when your father died. He got run over. How could that be your fault?'

'Because he wouldn't have been out if it weren't for me,' she burst out, twisting out of his arms and walking as fast as she could through the swirling snow towards the hotel.

'Elfie, that doesn't make the accident your fault.'

She'd heard those words before, and she hadn't believed them then either. 'Who else was to blame? It was absolutely torrential rain, but he preferred to be outside rather than with me. I drove him out because I was bored and difficult.' The words were coming fast now, tumbling out as Xander grabbed her hand.

'Slow down, Elfie. It's okay.'

'It's not okay. It will never be okay.' She took a deep breath, glad of the numbing cold. 'His picture wasn't working but because of the weather he had to paint inside. I knew he needed space and quiet, but I'd been promised a trip out and I was grumpy, kept needling at him to play. I wouldn't leave him alone, no matter how many times he told me to, until he grabbed a coat and left because walking in the torrential rain was better than being inside with me. If I had just shut up, if I had just stepped away, then he wouldn't have been on that bend in that weather and he would be here now. Mum wouldn't have been left a widow and found herself a new family that didn't include me. I deserved it, though; I deserve to be alone.'

'That's the most ridiculous thing I have ever heard.'

Shocked, she stopped and turned to face him. *'What?'*

'Your father's death was an accident, a terrible, tragic, life-changing accident. And of course you can't help but wish you had done things differently, could go back and stop him, but that doesn't make any of it your fault. I'm sure your mother would say the same.'

But Elfie shook her head. 'I didn't want her to marry James. I begged her not to, told him I would never live in his house, and she was so angry. "Haven't you done enough?" she said. "Must you ruin everything?"' She stopped, horrified at the words, at the truths she had kept buried for so long. 'And she was right. I do ruin everything eventually, and I don't want to ruin us. I want to look back at these weeks and remember how happy we were. So can we go back and pretend all this never happened?' But, even as she said the words, she realised their futility. You could never go back; she knew that all too well.

Why had she spoken up? Why now? Because she was incapable of not self-sabotaging. She couldn't even get to the end of a fling without driving the other person away. Elfie blinked back hot, painful tears. She didn't cry, didn't regret, didn't look back.

'Let's talk about this inside.'

'No, I've already said too much; let's not talk about this again. But just because I'm not the right woman for you, Xander, doesn't mean that there isn't someone out there who is. Don't settle because we didn't work

out, or because you think you should. I really want you
to be happy.'

'But you can't want that for yourself?'

'I've learned not to,' she said so quietly she wasn't
sure he'd heard her. But the words were true for all that.
Fleeting happiness was all she deserved, and she knew
not to hope for more. It was so much safer that way.

CHAPTER TWELVE

IT WAS EARLY, still dark out, when Elfie awoke to find herself alone. Xander had obviously decided to take Walter out on a morning walk without her. She couldn't blame him because, although they had done their best to carry on as normal, their conversation in the snow and the secrets revealed had remained hanging over them, an almost tangible dark cloud. They'd somehow managed to put on a front during supper and the after-dinner games, as if they were the same people who had gone out on the walk, before returning to their suite to make love with an intensity she had never experienced before. But they weren't the same people. The innocence and fun had left their relationship.

She rolled over, pressing her hands over her face, wishing yet again that she had stayed quiet, that she could turn back the clock, could have stayed laughing, fun Elfie and not showed Xander the darkness and bitterness within. But the damage was done and one thing was clear; she couldn't spend another week pretending nothing had changed. Elfie didn't know what would be worse, knowing that Xander still hoped she'd stay or knowing he'd changed his mind. Either way, staying wasn't an option.

She'd learned a long time ago to numb her emotions, but it took everything she had to stay focused as she swiftly packed. She hesitated for a while about using the new rucksack she'd been given but in the end she decided that leaving it would look petty, although she did reluctantly opt not to take the grey dress and shoes. There wasn't much use for them in a transient worker's life. She lingered for a long time over the compact, but in the end she couldn't bear to leave what it meant behind—the knowledge that someone had seen her, heard her, thought about her. Finally, she was done. She looked around at Walter's bed and toys, at Xander's possessions, at the picture she had given him and swallowed. Onto the next adventure, just a little earlier than planned.

She'd called a taxi before commencing packing and an alert told her it was here. Grabbing her bags, Elfie took a last longing look around. She would see such luxury again and soon, but she'd be on the other side of the metaphorical baize door, unpacking the bags, serving the meals, bringing the drinks. That was fine; she'd never been afraid of hard work. Hard emotions, however; they were another thing entirely. Which was why she was being such a coward and leaving without saying goodbye. She swallowed, trying not to think about Walter, already separated from one beloved caregiver. He had Xander; they would be fine. But what would they think when they returned and she wasn't here? She hesitated, irresolute, and it wasn't Walter's soulful eyes she was picturing, it was Xander's, full of hurt she would be responsible for.

Maybe he wouldn't be hurt, maybe he would be angry—or relieved that she had made parting so painless. Besides, it wasn't as if she had chosen to sneak away; she had no idea when Xander would return and every second she delayed was another tick on the taxi meter.

However, it wasn't until she was in the taxi that it dawned on Elfie that she didn't actually have anywhere to go. Her flight wasn't for a week, she'd given up her room at the hostel and as it was Boxing Day all transport was shut down and most hotels would be both expensive and booked up. She hadn't really thought out her departure. But then she hadn't thought any of this out very well.

'Whereabouts in London?' the taxi driver asked, and Elfie swallowed painfully. There was only one possible destination.

'Actually, I've changed my mind. Can we go to Surrey instead?'

She gave the taxi driver the address and then pulled out her phone, trying to think of anything to say to Xander that might make her actions look a little less pathetic. The right words wouldn't come, probably because there was nothing she could say. Finally, she simply texted.

I'm sorry. I truly believe this is for the best—and so do you now, probably. I really hope you find someone who makes you really happy. Love to Walter. X

And then she switched her phone off and sat back, eyes closed, wishing she could sleep the next week, next few months away. If her actions yesterday hadn't destroyed any illusions Xander had held about her then her decision to run away this morning would definitely have done so. Self-protection or self-sabotage? Elfie wasn't sure she even knew the difference any more. All she did know was that she would keep on working, saving, dreaming of a place she could call home and keep on protecting herself. And if that meant feeling so unbearably lonely she could barely face the next minute let alone the next hour then that was how it would be.

It seemed both no time at all and yet an eternity until the taxi drew up outside a large nineteen-thirties detached home on a quiet tree-lined road of similar houses. Elfie paid, turning down the driver's offer to carry her bags to the door, only belatedly realising that she was turning up without gifts. She had sent one, of course, like she did every year, a hamper for everyone, easy to order and hard to get wrong. But she should still have brought something for her siblings to open. Not that she had the faintest idea what to get for a twelve-year-old boy and ten-year-old girl she had barely spent any time with.

Swinging the rucksack onto her back, she picked up the other bag and started along the curved driveway. How she had hated this house when they'd moved here, with its ivy-covered red brick, but she had to admit it looked festive with the wreath on the front door and the lights entwined in the trees. She could see the Christmas tree in the bay window and her chest tightened as she recognised one of the baubles as one from her childhood. She'd always thought her past had been subsumed into her mother's new family. Had she misremembered, too caught up in her pain and anger to see where there was partnership rather than a takeover?

Elfie stood by the front door, irresolute, for a long, long minute, trying to think of the right things to say, before she finally pressed the chiming doorbell. She heard footsteps thudding, a high-pitched voice yelling that they would get it and then the door was flung open and she found herself face to face with her half-brother.

'You're as tall as me,' she said stupidly, trying to think when she had last seen him. 'Hi, Polly,' she added to the smaller girl who had appeared at his side.

'Mum! Mummy! Guess what, Elfie's here! It's Elfie!'

'Who is it, Oliver? Polly, step away from the door and let me through.' Elfie's mother bustled up to the front door and stopped, her hand over her mouth. 'Oh, Elfie,' she said, her face crumpling. 'You came home for Christmas after all.'

'I forgot that you always go out on Boxing Day; I'm sorry to have ruined your plans.' Elfie felt more than a little awkward as she walked along the snow-covered river path alongside her mother. Despite that awkwardness, she was relieved that her mother had suggested the walk; it was always easier to spend time together when they weren't facing each other, when there was something else to do or talk about other than all the many, many things they so carefully didn't say.

Her mother squeezed her arm, a quick, almost careful touch. When had they become so careful around each other, stopped being so tactile? Her childhood had been full of easy hugs, hand holding, kisses. But now she barely touched her mother, a dutiful kiss on the cheek, the occasional quick awkward hug. When had they shifted? When her father died? After the move? Once James and his family were in the picture? 'You haven't ruined my plans at all; it's such a treat to see you. I can pop over later on; you should come too. It's

Juliet's first time hosting and she's a little nervous, I think. She'd be glad to see you.'

'Did she come over yesterday?'

'Oh, yes, she and Aaron were with us all day and Portia, Mark and the baby came for dinner, along with your grandparents and James's parents.'

'Quite the crowd.'

'As always, but we had room for one more. There's always room, Elfie.'

Elfie didn't know what to say so she didn't say anything at all. They continued in silence for a while until her mother spoke.

'When did you say your flight was?'

'The second of January. But I can find a hostel tomorrow...'

'Nonsense, of course you'll stay with us. We would love to have you.'

Elfie's instinctive reaction was to refuse but she managed to bite it back. It was one thing to stay away for work reasons, but when her mother knew full well that she wasn't working, to choose to pay to stay elsewhere was the kind of snub their already brittle relationship might never recover from. 'Thank you; that will be nice.' And maybe it really would. Her half siblings had seemed pleased to see her, even James had muttered something about the prodigal returning before handing her a coffee and offering to make her French toast.

She still felt prickly, out of shape and place in the house that had never felt like home in the four years she had lived there, but there had been no time to dwell on the past or her discomfort when Oliver decided to show her some game he had received yesterday and insisted on talking her through it in excruciating detail and Polly had brought down her sketchbook and new watercolour pencils. Elfie had found herself raising her eyebrows at her mother in some astonishment as she looked through the book. Her small sister had some talent.

The silence returned and stretched on as they walked, Elfie barely taking in the scenery, trying to think of something to say, relieved when once again her mother spoke up first.

'And where are you off to next?'

'The Caribbean again. I have a second stew post lined up, with another one starting straight after. The second stew doesn't pay as well as the Chief Steward-ess role but it's half the hassle and the tips are just as good. After that, who knows?' She tried to sound as devil-may-care as she usually did, as she usually was, but for once her itinerant future didn't sound so be-guiling. Didn't feel so exciting. Instead, it felt lonely. Weeks of drudgery. Yachting was a young person's game. She was getting too old for the long hours and nonstop partying.

'The Caribbean does sound appealing right now, but it's a shame your other job has come to an end. Your posts are so clever; you have a real eye—and a way with words.'

'You follow my account?' Elfie stared at her mother in astonishment.

'Your dog nanny account? Yes. For a few months now. It was Juliet who showed it to me; she's been want-ing a dog for ages and has been using your pictures to persuade Aaron.' Her mother paused and when she spoke again her voice was very carefully casual. 'You know that Juliet is our Head of Marketing now? She says you are full of flair, that you should work in social media full-time. We could do with someone with your skills.'

'I'm not going to move home and work for the family firm, Mum.' Not her home, not her family, but for once she kept that part to herself and the unsaid words weren't bitter on her tongue.

'No. I suppose not.' Another pause. 'It's your life, darling...'

'But?' Here it came. But, at the same time, Elfie couldn't help but acknowledge that she reverted to angry teenager the second she saw her mother, her skin paper-thin, every nerve on edge, every word perceived as an implied criticism.

'Not a but, more of a what. How long do you think the travelling and the short-term jobs will make you happy? I'm not criticising,' she said hurriedly, and Elfie's heart constricted. She wasn't the only one walking on eggshells here. 'You have been all round the world, seen so much, had adventures. It's just...where does it lead? Do you want to be doing this at thirty? At thirty-five?'

'Actually, I do have a plan. I was hoping I could buy the French house from you.' Elfie hadn't meant to ask so abruptly, or yet, but really, what was she waiting for? Her savings were healthy, she had a good social media presence of her own, thanks to some strategic tagging and cross posts; she could put some steady months in on charter and then head to France at the end of the season and get started. She waited for the anticipatory excitement that always filled her when she thought about owning her childhood home, but it didn't come. Instead, all she felt was the same numbness that had consumed her since last night.

'The French house? You don't have to buy it, silly girl; it's yours.'

'Mine?' It wasn't the answer she was expecting and it took Elfie a few moments to absorb it. If the house was hers then there was nothing stopping her from living her dream, nothing at all. She just needed to push away the memory of dark eyes, clever hands and a reluctantly charming smile. 'I had no idea. How, when?' Not the most articulate of responses but it wasn't every day that she found out she was a homeowner.

'As soon as I get the documents drawn up and transfer ownership. I always planned to sign it over to you. I don't visit any more, too many memories, I suppose, and it didn't seem right to take James there. But I also didn't want to burden you with any debt, so I have been renting it out as a holiday home to pay off the rest of the mortgage and it finally happened earlier this year. Don't get too excited, though. The place is a money pit. Honestly, we barely make enough on it for the repairs once the cleaning and letting costs are taken into consideration...'

'I don't want to let it. I want to live there. I want to open it as a retreat, like Papa wanted. He didn't get the chance to make his dreams come true, thanks to me. So I want to make them come true for him.'

Elfie couldn't help but see the concern in her mother's eyes. 'Like I said, Elfie, the house is yours whenever you need it, whatever you want to do with it, but are you sure it's the right place for a retreat? It's small, remember? Only three bedrooms and one of those is a boxroom. And it still gets cut off from the village whenever it floods, and the range is as temperamental as ever. As for the water pressure... I market it as bijou and rustic and price it accordingly because, no matter how charmingly I decorate it and the quality of the welcome hamper, people still like hot water upstairs and to be able to cook their meals evenly.'

'I could replace the range.'

'You could. It's cast iron and practically weighs as much as the house itself. But you'd still only be able to have two guests, even if you take the boxroom.'

'I was thinking of pods, you know, glamping pods and shepherd's huts. They're very popular.'

'You'd need a bigger cesspit,' her mother said. Her voice softened. 'How you remind me of your father.'

'What do you mean?'

'You're a dreamer too.'

'There's nothing wrong with having dreams,' she said defensively.

'Of course there isn't. I loved that about him, his ability to ignore practicalities, to conjure up his version of reality so enticingly I found myself convinced, despite my misgivings. I certainly never meant to be married and pregnant at twenty-two, living in a rundown cottage in the middle of nowhere in a different country, but he made every moment exciting, anything possible. Of course, it wasn't all roses around the door. There were plenty of times when it snowed and the range went out and we had no hot water and I couldn't cook, when we were cut off by floods and running out of food—then he turned to me for practical solutions. And you know how terrible he was to live with when his painting wasn't working the way he wanted. It's a good thing I wasn't the same way. Can you imagine how it would have been if we'd both stamped around swearing?'

Elfie heard her mother's reminiscent laugh, the fondness in her voice with some surprise. 'You still miss him.'

'Of course I do!'

'But James is so different.'

'Elfie, it's quite possible to love two very different people. When your father was alive I could ignore all the impracticalities in our life, but once he was gone it all seemed impossible, especially with a child to take care of. I wasn't looking to replace your father, his place in my heart is his alone, but I love James just as much. I needed someone solid, someone settled, and he gave me that. I know you never took to him and I know how much my marrying him hurt you, but he has made me happy.'

'I want you to be happy,' Elfie mumbled. How had they never had this conversation before? At first she had been too young, too raw, too angry. Too guilty. And then she'd made sure she was never available for any kind of conversation, often thousands of miles away and keeping up her defences on her rare visits. 'I'm sorry.' The words were almost choked out.

'You don't have to be sorry for anything. I should apologise to you, Elfie, and I have been searching for the right moment for quite some time.' Her mother took a deep breath. 'I know how much upheaval you went through, losing your father, leaving your home, and my marriage to James must have felt very sudden. And I know that I was so busy trying to be the perfect stepmother to Juliet and Portia, to help them through the transition, that you felt neglected. I guess I thought that we were such a tight unit nothing would come between us. I was wrong and I have had to live with the consequences of that ever since. I miss you, Elfie, every day. And I am sorry for letting you down.'

'But you didn't. I let you down. Papa died because of me. That's why I have to build his retreat, to make his dreams come true. And that's why I am so, so sorry. Can you ever forgive me?' The words tumbled out, held inside for so long.

Her mother stopped, turning to Elfie with shock on her face. 'Elfie, I don't need to forgive you; what happened was not your fault. Have you really thought that all this time? But why?'

'Because...' The whole world was swaying around her. 'I wouldn't leave him alone, even though I knew better. He went out to get away from me. I was responsible. You know this. You were right when you said I ruined everything.'

'When?' Her mother's eyes were full of shock.

'Before you married James. When you wanted me to come shopping for bridesmaids' dresses...' Elfie could remember every second of that day. How had her mother forgotten?

'That was wicked of me, but Elfie, I was talking about the times we spent with James and the girls, your refusal to be at the wedding, not your father. I should never have said it at all, but I had no idea you thought... that all this time.' And then her mother was crying, huge sobs racking the petite frame she had bequeathed to her daughter, and as Elfie allowed herself to be drawn into her mother's arms she felt the cold sting of tears on her face and realised that she, who hardly ever allowed herself to show weakness, was crying too.

CHAPTER THIRTEEN

'So this is Scotland…what do you think?'

Xander wasn't really expecting Walter to answer, which was a good thing as Walter just cocked his head to one side and looked enquiringly up at him. They'd arrived at Glen Thorne that morning, after taking the sleeper train up from London, and were both in need of some fresh air and exercise.

The snow had melted in Buckinghamshire and London but was still thick in this corner of the Highlands. The view from the hotel grounds was stunning, with white mountains dominating the horizon in two directions, the blue of the loch ahead. Usually, Xander looked forward to his visits to the castle, found a certain amount of peace in the beautiful landscape, but his heart was heavy as he looked around.

It was four days since Elfie had sneaked out of the hotel in his absence, leaving him just a terse text. At first he had been angry, too angry to reply. If she was going to treat him with such a lack of courtesy, to act like a coward then he had misjudged her and was better off without her. Or at least that was what he tried to tell himself. Then he decided that with less than a week to go of their friendship, what did it matter when she left and threw himself into work, barely emerging from his office for forty-eight hours. But at night he could see the anguish in her stormy grey eyes as she'd told him she was doomed to ruin everything she touched, heard the urgency in her voice as she'd begged him to marry for love and he would replay the conversation, wondering where it had gone wrong, what he could have said or done to turn the direction, to convince her.

Convince her of what? That she was entitled to a happy life of her own? Allowed to love and be loved? Needed to forgive herself? Needed to find her own path rather than obsessively follow a dead man's dream? How could he convince her of those facts if he had never lived that way himself? The irony was that she'd urged the same on him. Two people who wanted more for the other than for themselves.

It was ridiculous. 'Ridiculous,' he told Walter, who was more interested in eating snow than listening to Xander. And who could blame him?

What was also ridiculous was that four days in he was missing her more than ever and being here without her just intensified the ache of loss. He'd wanted to share the journey with her, see the moment she first set foot in the castle, have her by his side when he hosted the Hogmanay party. He wanted stolen kisses in corners and walks in the snow and long, heated nights in bed. He wanted to run ideas past her and see her frown of concentration as she decided on the caption for a picture, her utter focus as she set up a photo, her laughter when she played with Walter. Her desire when their gazes locked. He had never had this connection before. Had never wanted anyone so much, enjoyed anyone's company so much. He loved everything about her. He…

Hang on. He *what*? 'People don't fall in love in just four weeks,' he told Walter and the dog grunted dismissively as if to say: *What do you know?*

'Of course they don't.' He stomped on through the snow. 'Okay, Leo always said the second he set eyes on Kate he knew that she was the one and they were married within a few months, but that is just Leo. He's impulsive; he was just lucky they worked out.'

They carried on into the woods, forging a path as they did. Xander welcomed the cold, the distraction. But, try as he might, he couldn't shut out the word spinning through his mind.

Love.

'I can't love her. Because if I did I would have known what to say, I would have been able to make it all right. Wouldn't I?'

Was that what love was? Knowing what to say, how to make things right? Was it this hollow feeling that an essential part of him was missing? Or was it the desire to know that Elfie was safe and well, even if she was a thousand miles away, that her happiness was paramount? One thing he knew for sure was that she wasn't happy, that she'd been running away for over a decade now and her early-morning departure was just another stage in her escape from feeling anything for anyone. Including herself.

He looked at Walter. 'I think…' he said slowly. 'I think that if I thought she was genuinely happy then I could live with missing her. But she's not, is she? She doesn't know how to be. That's why I think she should know that someone is on her side. That, no matter what she says or does, she's loved unconditionally. Because she is. I do.'

Suddenly aware that Walter had wandered off and that he was standing talking to himself, he called Walter to heel and made his way back to the hotel, an imposing granite castle that had stood in this spot, repelling invaders for hundreds of years. Inside, the décor was traditional, with plenty of the family tartan, comfortable tweed and leather furniture and the odd stag's head on the wall. He'd looked into modernising it a couple of times, but the feedback had always convinced him that the guests loved it just as it was, loved stepping into a Highland fantasy.

As always, they were booked up for New Year, but the castle had plenty of public spaces and Xander had the smaller library to himself as he settled into a comfortable chair by the fire, Walter at his feet and a whisky in his hand. He stared into the flames, mind whirling. It seemed that, much as he tried to, he couldn't escape two indubitable facts. One, he loved Elfie. No matter that it seemed too soon, that he had never meant this to happen, he loved her. And, despite everything that meant, despite her absence, the knowledge warmed him through as thoroughly as the whisky. He hadn't thought love was for him, assumed himself incapable. Turned out his friends had been right all along. All he needed was the right woman. Which led him to point two. The right woman wasn't here. He had let her down and let her go. He didn't even know where she was.

He looked down at his phone. That wasn't entirely true. He could call her or text her, or he could show her how he felt. Go back to the beginning.

He looked down at Walter. 'I think I need your help.'

Walter looked up sleepily, his tail half wagging.

'If all else fails, we could make a dramatic journey

to the airport, I suppose. But let's see if she responds to you.'

One thing was certain. No matter what happened with Elfie, Xander knew he couldn't allow his life to be so narrowly defined again. He was allowed to combine personal happiness along with his duty. Doing so didn't make him weak or selfish; it just made him human.

He just hoped the realisation hadn't come too late.

Elfie sat at her mother's kitchen table, only half listening to the busy chatter around her. What a different life her half siblings, no, her brother and sister, she corrected herself, lived. They had grown up in a busy home with extended family all around, so different from her isolated childhood several miles from the nearest village. She'd gone to school, of course, had friends, but she'd often been absent when her father had decided he needed a road trip, and she'd been too far out for anything but play dates scheduled in advance. She'd been a happy but solitary child, content with her own company. She'd never lost that sense of isolation even when crammed with roommates and other staff into small crew quarters on a yacht or the tiny service living space in New York penthouses, keeping something essential of herself back. But she hadn't kept anything back from Xander in the end.

Not that it had done any good. She had left and he hadn't contacted her since. She didn't blame him in the least, but she had to admit that a part of her had wished for a huge dramatic gesture, some sign that he missed her, wanted her to return. It was ridiculous; he didn't even know where she was. And surely it was better this way; she had to sort herself out before she was by any means ready to be in any kind of relationship.

Xander deserved someone without baggage or hesitations, not a half-formed girl. She repressed a sigh. She couldn't expect him to wait for her, especially after that cowardly exit and text goodbye. The best-case scenario was that he would fall in love with someone wonderful and live happily ever after. The most likely scenario was that he would marry Cressida within the year and revert to the remote Baron, striding through his estate, suppressing all emotion for duty.

Either way, she wouldn't be there, and even if it was through choice it still hurt almost unbearably. She found it hard to sleep and when she did finally drift off it was with Xander's face before her, sometimes the brown eyes soft with empathy, sometimes alight with desire, but in her nightmares they were always hard with contempt. She had been right when she'd told him that she destroyed everything; the irony was that it was a self-fulfilling prophecy. She did it to herself. And now it was too late.

The buzz of her phone interrupted her thoughts and she glanced over at the screen, noting that she had an email and a social media message notification. She hadn't posted anything over the last week, sending all the sign-in details for Walter's and the Dog Nanny accounts to the Baron Thornham marketing people, and kept away from her personal account, unable to fake a life she no longer understood. She opened the email, expecting to see a marketing message, only to let out a surprised cry as she took in the contents.

'What is it?' Her mother looked up from the other

end of the table where she was giving Polly a drawing lesson. 'Is everything okay?'

'Not really. The ship I was employed on has been in an accident and needs some major repairs, so the first charter season has been cancelled and the second's in doubt. They've said if I fly over they'll see if they can get me some cover work, but…' she shrugged '…it's not easy fitting in with a crew halfway through a season and financially it's not as stable.'

'How much do you make?' James, her stepfather, asked.

'The salary isn't bad. Around two thousand pounds, sometimes more, for the six weeks, but it's the tips that make it worthwhile. I can clear three thousand pounds a week.'

James whistled. 'Nice.'

'And with very few expenses. With two seasons lined up, I was hoping to take home around forty thousand after costs.'

'For twelve weeks' work?'

She nodded. 'If I was employed the whole time. I should pick up work easily, but every day spent waiting for a vacancy is money not earned and spent on accommodation and food.' It wasn't just the lack of employment giving her pause. It was the knowledge that the thought of the forthcoming season gave her no pleasure at all. She was tired of travelling, tired of being alone. 'But I don't have anything else lined up. It's too late for the ski season now.' And she had thrown away her job at the hotel along with any chance of a future with Xander.

'You don't have to make any decisions now,' her mother said. 'You can stay here as long as you need to. Maybe we could go over to France and see if the cottage is suitable for what you're envisioning.'

'That's kind of you. I'd like that.' And she would. Maybe visiting France with her mother would help lay some ghosts. And the thought of staying here didn't feel as painful as it usually did. She and James seemed to be getting on better and she was enjoying getting to know Polly and Oliver. Her stepsisters both lived nearby and had suggested meeting for a drink, which was an unexpected and not unwelcome olive branch—and she knew she still had a long way to go repairing her relationship with her mother. None of it was easy; heading off was by far the easiest option, postponing all this family reconciliation for another time. But it was time to stop running.

And if she was staying in Surrey then maybe she could try and see Xander. Apologise. Try and explain, if she could figure out what to say.

'What are you planning to do tomorrow?' her mother asked.

'Tomorrow?'

'It's New Year's Eve.'

'Of course. I was supposed to be in Scotland.' Which meant Xander was already there. Was he missing her? For a second the realisation of all she had thrown away overwhelmed her, a physical pain. Xander had listened to her, understood her, tried to repair her and she had walked away because she was scared.

Was it too late to tell him she was sorry? That she missed him? That she wished she had made different choices?

Her phone buzzed again, a second notification. She picked it up and realised it was from the same account as the first, one she didn't recognise, and she frowned as she cautiously opened it. Unknown accounts could often mean trouble, spam if she was lucky, unwanted pictures if not. The account was named Future Adventures and she grimaced. If this was some wellbeing site trying to persuade her to buy their visualisation techniques then it would be an instant block.

Instead of a hard sell or a picture of some male anatomy she saw Walter, wearing a bow tie made of an attractive grey and purple tartan. The caption merely said 'Missing you'. Tears welled up as she looked at the small dog, knowing Xander must have taken the photo, set up the account to send it to her.

She swiped onto the next picture. Walter again, this time next to a photo of Xander, looking absurdly young in formal dress, black tie and a kilt. 'He misses you too'. Elfie repressed a smile as her phone pinged again with a third notification. She opened it, butterflies fluttering madly. This time Walter was outside, panting by a message carved into the snow. 'We love you, Elfie'.

Elfie sat and stared at the picture, reading the words over and over. Love? After everything? As in platonic love? It was a word that could be tossed around so carelessly; she saw it all the time. Or romantic love, hearts and flowers, sweet but possibly insubstantial? Or real love, strong and deep and enduring? The kind of love that grew with time, anchoring and supportive. Because, with no surprise but more a growing awareness, she knew that she loved Xander in all three of those ways. He was her friend, he was her lover and he was her oak. Did he feel the same way?

There was only one way to find out.

'I think...' she said, still staring at the phone '...that I will be going to Scotland for New Year's Eve after all. I'd better book my train.'

* * *

It had been over twenty-four hours since Xander had sent Elfie the messages, and over twenty-four hours since she had opened them, but he hadn't heard a peep from her in all that time. Had he misjudged the situation? Did she not want to hear from him; had their time together been just a fling after all? Or had he scared her? She already found it hard to trust; had the messages sent her fleeing?

Or was she thinking about the best way to respond?

No matter which it was, the ball was in her court now. All he could do was wait and hope.

Luckily, he would be busy tonight at the annual Hogmanay party. Guests would be treated to drinks followed by a lavish five-course meal, before a ceilidh took them into the New Year. The night was packed with traditions, with Auld Lang Syne sung at midnight before one of the villagers arrived as the first footer, armed with gifts of shortbread and cake for all the guests. Like Christmas at Thornham Park, the New Year celebrations involved many return guests and the ceilidh was open to anyone from the village who wished to attend, making it a long and festive night.

As was customary, Xander was in black tie complete with kilt as he received his guests, Walter by his side, dapper in his bow tie. The ballroom was resplendent, decorated with plenty of greenery and sparkling lights, cosy seating areas in the alcoves along one side for those who would prefer not to dance. A local band played traditional folk songs as the guests mingled, champagne circulating, the villagers as dressed up as the guests, many of whom they knew from years gone by, and the two groups chatted easily as they caught up on a year's worth of news.

Xander found himself relaxing as the last of the guests entered the ballroom. He was nearly done. He had hosted a festive season on his own. The guests were happy, repeat bookings already being taken for next year, the PR and reviews positive and the staff seemed pleased. He would never have his father's hearty presence or his grandfather's easy charm, but he could be himself. He just wished he had realised that a long time ago.

He was about to step into the ballroom when he saw a last guest come hastily through the reception and turned to greet her when Walter, who had sat patiently by his side throughout the whole receiving line, gave a little high-pitched whine before hurtling along the passageway to throw himself on the distant figure. Xander was about to call him back when the figure came into view and he froze, heart thumping wildly.

Elfie. Cheeks flushed, wrapped up in her big coat, hair ruffled.

'I'm sorry I'm late.'

'What kept you?' He could feel a smile curving his mouth as she responded in kind, her smile lighting up her eyes.

'My train was late and so I missed my connection. I ended up getting changed in the loos at Edinburgh. I wasn't the only one, though.' She shrugged off her coat to reveal a black lace cocktail dress, cut low at the front, the straps encircling her arms, leaving her creamy shoulders bare. 'It was quite the party. I was almost sorry to leave.'

'Nice outfit.'

'It's my stepsister's.'

He raised his eyebrows and she laughed. 'I have a lot to tell you, but first…' Her eyes grew serious and he took her hand, not wanting anything to spoil this perfect moment.

'But first we dance.'

'In there?' She sounded a little daunted and, looking around, Xander realised that the folk music had given way to ceilidh music and the guests had started an enthusiastic Dashing White Sergeant.

'No, in here.' He pulled her into the small antechamber beside the ballroom, closing the door, although the music was still clearly audible. 'In here and like this.'

'The dancing doesn't seem to match the music,' she said as he enfolded her in his arms, swaying gently.

'We'll just have to make do. Elfie, I can't believe you're here.'

She looked up, her heart in her eyes. 'Xander, I am so sorry. I panicked and I did what I always do when I am overwhelmed; I ran.'

'My life can be a bit much. I'm often overwhelmed myself.'

'No, not by your life. That's part of you, the duty and obligation you bear. And you do it so well; that's one of the things that drew me to you. No, I was overwhelmed by you. By the way I feel for you. I had convinced myself that the only way to keep myself safe was to keep myself away from any connections. I told myself I was happier that way. And then you came along and I tore up the rule book. I let you into my life, my bed, my confidence and then I realised that I had let you into my heart and that was terrifying. Leaving you like that was wrong and I am so sorry, but I honestly thought I was doing the right thing for both of us.'

'You let me into your heart?' He needed to hear her say it and she nodded.

'I love you, Xander. I tried not to, but I just couldn't help it. I love how much you care. How you make me laugh. How you make me feel. And if it's all right with you, I would like to agree to your suggestion that we see where this thing goes. Because with you by my side I'm not afraid. Not any more.'

There. She had said it. She'd laid her heart on the line and it was up to Xander now. And even if he said he had changed his mind, even if he sent her away, she wouldn't regret any of it. Not the long journey north, not the words, not the long hard look at her life she'd used the journey to do. Because she was better for knowing him, for loving him, and how could she regret that?

'I love you too Elfie.' It had been one thing seeing the words written down; it was another to hear them, spoken low and intimate, his voice full of sincerity and passion. 'I think I loved you from the moment I first saw you. You make me want to be better, to do better. My life isn't easy and it's not conventional, but if you could bring yourself to share it with me I would be the luckiest man alive.'

'I'm not afraid of unconventional or hard work. I would want a base, though; I've not had one for a very long time. Here or Buckinghamshire, a place to hang our pictures, to put our books, a bed only we sleep in.'

'Don't forget Walter.'

'How could I?' She could feel a small head butting

her knee and leaned down to caress the silky curls. 'He's our matchmaker.'

'Yes to the base. Yes to anything you want. Just as long as you'll stay.'

'For as long as you want me,' she promised, and his eyes were tender.

'Then prepare yourself for forever.' And with that he kissed her, sweet and welcoming, a pledge of the days—and the nights—to come. Elfie sank into the kiss, into Xander, knowing that whatever happened she was no longer alone. That where Xander was, she was meant to be.

She'd spent her whole life searching for a home, yet running from any kind of commitment. But how could she regret any of it when her search had brought her here, to Xander? To a man who miraculously seemed to need her, to want her, to love her as much as she needed and wanted and loved him.

It had been a long, lonely road, but Xander's kiss promised a brighter future filled with love, happiness and laughter.

'I love you,' she whispered against his mouth and felt his answering smile.

'And I you.'

He held her tight as they moved to the music, Walter close by their sides, and as the clock struck twelve and ushered in a New Year, Elfie knew her journey had ended at last.

* * * * *

SNOWBOUND WITH THE BROODING BILLIONAIRE

KATE HARDY

MILLS & BOON

With much love to Gerard, Chris and Chloe,
who indulged me with that research trip to the Dolomites!

CHAPTER ONE

'I LOVE YOU, HAN,' Sophie said, 'and I really appreciate the offer, but we both know I can't *really* stay as long as I like. Your spare room's going to be your nursery.' She indicated the bump under Hannah's maternity sweater. 'Which you're going to need in three months' time. So it's time for me to help you decorate it—and move out.'

Hannah folded her arms and glared at her. 'You're my best friend, Soph. I am *not* letting you be homeless.'

'I won't be homeless,' Sophie said, hoping she sounded a lot more sure than she felt. 'As soon as I get a job, landlords will see me as a viable tenant and I'll be able to rent somewhere.' Through the tricky bit, she thought with an inward shiver, was going to be getting a job in the first place. 'Hopefully the temp agency will find me something.'

'You've applied for forty positions, Soph. Surely *one* of them will give you an interview.' Hannah shook her head. 'You cook like an angel. Look at all the reviews your restaurant got. People love your food.'

Sophie believed in her own professional capabilities. But the black mark against her was so huge that she could see exactly why nobody had even offered her an interview. 'Would you employ someone whose business had crashed? Someone who might bring all that bad luck with her?' she asked.

'It wasn't your fault that you had to sell the restaurant,' Hannah said loyally.

Sophie wrinkled her nose. 'Yes, it was. You know those horror movies where someone goes to investigate strange noises in the basement on their own, and you know they're going to end up in trouble because of it, and you're shouting at the screen, "Don't do it!"? Let's be honest, Han. I'm on a par with *that*.'

'You,' Hannah said, 'were swindled, when you were trying to make the world a better place. Which is not the same as being a too-stupid-to-live horror movie character.'

'The end result's the same,' Sophie said softly. 'The restaurant's gone—along with my flat. And Mum and Dad must be looking down on me, wondering how I could've been so stupid as to let my inheritance fall through my fingers like that.'

'Your mum and dad,' Hannah corrected, 'would've been so proud of you. You put the money they left you into the restaurant, and you've built up the business.'

'And I trusted someone to look after the money side of it for me.'

'Blake swindled you,' Hannah repeated. 'And if he hadn't skipped off to a country that doesn't have an extradition treaty with England, he'd be in court right now for fraudulent appropriation of funds.'

And how stupid had Sophie been? Thinking that Blake wanted her for herself, that he loved her and he'd asked her to marry him because he wanted to settle down and make a family with her. The family she'd lost and missed so much. The family she'd wanted so desperately.

All the time, he'd quietly been planning to empty the restaurant's bank account; as the restaurant's admin manager, he'd been a signatory on the account. Sophie had trusted him to pay the bills, sort out staffing and supplies, and arrange everything so she could concentrate on the main business: making the best possible food for their clients.

She'd been doing well enough to consider expanding the business. Liking the idea of being able to do something in the community and give a chance to people who'd struggled at school, the way she had, she'd found a second premises. She'd even applied for a mortgage and was waiting for the building survey to come back to see if they could move forward.

And then, the day before month-end, Blake had called in sick, saying he'd gone down with the flu and she wasn't to come round with chicken soup or anything because he didn't want her to catch the virus from him. He'd stayed in touch on his mobile all day, texting her to apologise for not being in, and she'd been touched by his dedication.

The following day, her suppliers had started calling to say their bills hadn't been paid. Her staff had all come in, aghast, saying their wages hadn't gone into their bank accounts. And then, most horrible of all, the bank had called to say that she'd gone beyond the level of their agreed overdraft.

An agreed overdraft that was much, much bigger than she'd expected.

It seemed that Blake had stopped all the direct debits the previous day and transferred the money from the account—along with the amount of the overdraft she'd known nothing about—into some offshore account that was completely untouchable.

When she'd called him to find out what was going on, a recorded message told her that the number she was calling was unobtainable.

She'd gone to his flat; it was empty. And none of his neighbours had a clue where he was.

Blake had told her he had no family, but the police managed to trace his parents; it turned out they'd been estranged for years and they had no idea where he was.

He'd vanished.

Along with the money.

She'd had to sell the restaurant to repay the overdraft, settle the wages and pay the outstanding supplier bills. She hadn't even been able to sell her engagement ring to go towards the bills; when she'd had it valued, the solitaire diamond in its platinum setting had turned out to be cubic zirconia set in silver, with a resale value of practically nothing.

Luckily the business had been sold as a going concern, so her staff still had their jobs. She couldn't have lived with herself if they'd all lost out, too. But Sophie had lived in the flat above the restaurant. Selling up to pay her debts had made her officially businessless, jobless and homeless. And, with Blake having left the country, it was pretty clear she was fiancé-less, too.

The one good thing was that she hadn't been declared bankrupt. She could start again without *that* against her name, at least. But who would take a chance on her, after her appalling lack of judgement?

'Which brings us back to our very stupid horror movie heroine,' Sophie said wryly. 'I shouldn't have trusted him in the first place. But we'd been engaged for a year, Han. We'd been together for nearly two. I didn't think a swindler would wait that long?'

'If they were playing a long game, they would,' Hannah said. 'When Blake came into your life, you'd only recently lost your parents in that car crash. You were filling the gap with building up the business, and that meant you were vulnerable. And, instead of seeing the lovely woman with a big heart that you really are, I think he saw your inheritance money. He played you, Soph. I just wish you'd got me to check the agreement you had with your new bank.'

The change of account that Blake had persuaded her to make because she'd get a better rate of interest on her balance.

What she hadn't realised was that he'd applied for a larger overdraft at the same time. And she'd trusted him, as her admin manager, to get the details right.

She wished she'd run it past Hannah, too, but at the time her best friend had been undergoing IVF, and Sophie hadn't wanted to put any extra pressure on her. 'I can't change the past. All I can do is learn from it—and I'll never, ever let anyone be a signatory on my account again.' She sighed. 'Though it could've been worse. OK, so I've lost the business and my flat and I don't have any money, but I've still got Mum's wedding ring and Dad's watch. If I'd been made bankrupt, the court would've made me sell them, too.'

'And I would've bought them and kept them for you until the bankruptcy was discharged. Only you,' Hannah said, 'could see a bright side in this. Six months pregnant or not, if Blake was in front of me right now

I'd punch him really, really hard. Break his nose, and possibly another couple of bits of his anatomy.'

Sophie smiled wryly. She could imagine Hannah—who could be very scary indeed—doing just that. But she'd resigned herself to the situation. 'I admit, I'm hurt and I'm angry and right now I'm feeling very stupid about trusting someone who lied to me, but what's the point in getting worked up over something I can't actually change? I'd rather spend that energy picking myself up, dusting myself down and starting all over again.' She lifted her chin. 'I know nobody's given me an interview so far. But I can kind of understand it. I'm either stupid or unlucky, depending on your point of view, and nobody wants their business tainted with that.'

Hannah coughed. 'If it had happened to someone else, *you* would've given them a chance.'

True. But Sophie knew that not everyone saw the world the way she did. 'Nobody's going to give me a junior position,' she continued, 'because I'm overqualified and they'll think I'm not likely to stay any longer than it'd take to find something more suited to my skills. So that rules out the permanent jobs. But, if I'm a temp, that takes out any potential recruitment or bad luck issues because I won't be there for long enough to have an impact. And Christmas is coming; everyone needs extra staff to cope with the office parties from around mid-November. The temp agency's my best chance. Then, once I've got some up-to-date references, I can start to find something permanent.'

And, as if on cue, her phone rang.

She glanced at the screen. 'It's the agency. Fingers crossed they're ringing with an interview.'

'Take the call,' Hannah said. 'I'll go and make us a cup of tea. Good luck!'

By the time Hannah came back with two mugs of tea, it was a done deal.

'You're looking at a proper chef again,' Sophie said, beaming.

'Fantastic!' Hannah, clearly delighted, hugged Sophie. 'Where is it and when do you start?'

'Ah. That might be the catch,' Sophie said. 'It's at a ski resort in the Dolomites. And they're flying me out the day after tomorrow—apparently the season won't really start until the end of November, but they like staff to settle in and do the training, and be there to look after the people who come just before it starts getting busy.'

'The day after tomorrow?' Hannah stared at her, looking shocked. 'You're never going to have time to arrange that!'

'Most of my stuff's in storage already, and it won't take me long to sort out the rest,' Sophie said. 'My passport's in date. It's Italy, so I don't need any extra vaccinations. All I really need are snow boots and a coat—and ten minutes in a sports shop will sort that for me.'

'But you can't ski,' Hannah said.

'I'm not going to be skiing. I'm going to be the chef in a posh chalet,' Sophie said. 'Absolutely no skis required.'

'And you hate snow.'

'Because I'm clumsy and I fall over all the time.' Sophie shrugged. 'But I guess at least there the snow'll be deep enough that if I fall over I won't hurt anything more than my dignity.'

'You—and snow?' Hannah looked anxious. 'Soph, are you *sure* about this?'

'No,' Sophie admitted, 'but I think it's the best chance I've got. And maybe challenging myself a bit might help me to get my self-esteem back. I need a fresh start, somewhere nobody knows me.' And then maybe she'd stop feeling quite so useless and stupid. But the one thing she was clear on: no more relationships. No more putting her trust into someone who'd let her down.

How could one single day suck all the light out of the world? Josh wondered.

But today would always be his dark day of the year. The anniversary of the day his life had unravelled. He'd lost the championship and Annabel in very swift succession. Gone from being on top of the world to the bottom of a very deep and very dark hole: sixty miles an hour to zero in what felt like a nanosecond.

In the following months he'd focused on his physio. Worked on his knee every single day. Forced himself through the pain. Blocked out the unfair and untrue media stories and tried to persuade his family—and the friends who'd stuck by him—that he was completely fine. He'd almost persuaded *himself* that he was completely fine.

And then, last month, his surgeon had sat down with him to discuss his future.

'It's up to you, Josh,' the consultant surgeon had said, leaning his elbows on his desk and steepling his fingers. 'The surgery was a success. You've done well with your rehab. But, if you go back to skiing competitively, it's not a question of *if* you're going to have another knee injury, it's a question of *when*. Next time you might do even more damage; I might not be able to repair it if you damage your patella tendon as well as your anterior cruciate ligament and meniscus. So you need to make a decision. What would you rather do: go back to competitive skiing now, or still be able to walk unaided in twenty years' time?'

What kind of choice was that? Josh had been horrified. 'Competitive skiing's what I do. It's who I am.'

And if he couldn't ski...

He was privileged, he knew. Born into a seriously rich family so he'd been able to indulge his love of skiing—and his talent. For years Josh's father had wanted him to give up what he considered a seriously dangerous sport and join the family firm, with the aim of becoming CEO of the family software business. All Josh had to do was smile and agree.

Though, if he did that, Josh knew it would crush his big sister's dreams. Lauren had worked her way up through the company to become head of development. She'd be the perfect person to be CEO of Cavendish Software. She'd proved herself and she *deserved* the position. He absolutely wasn't going to shove his sister out of the way.

At the same time, Josh knew that the surgeon was right. He'd seen so many injuries happen on the slopes. He knew a few people who'd given up while they could still walk away; and he knew a few more who'd carried on until they'd had one injury too many and there was no way back.

The sensible decision would be to give up competing.

But the idea of never, ever having that rush again: it made the world seem flat and lifeless.

And, if he gave up skiing competitively, what would he *do*? Who was he without his skis?

'Think about it,' the surgeon had said quietly. 'It's your choice.'

'What would you do, if say you had an accident which meant you couldn't operate any more?' Josh had asked.

'Teach,' had been the prompt answer. 'Because then I'd still be working in medicine, still be making a difference. It'd be second best, but that would still be better than losing medicine from my life completely.'

Josh had thought about it.

And thought some more.

He could become a coach. Teach the next generation of elite athletes.

Or he could take a different path. Still teach, but bring the thrill of skiing to people who'd never done it before. Take them from rookie to…well, not reckless, but from being barely able to stand upright on their skis to enjoying something more challenging.

He'd ended up talking over the situation with his own coach.

'Don't rush into anything,' Angelo advised. 'Take some time out and think about what you really want to do. Moving from competing to coaching worked for me, because I still get the fun of being at a championship but without my wife worrying about me and without the risk to my middle-aged knees.'

He'd said it lightly, but that was the point. Josh wasn't middle-aged. At thirty, he'd thought he still had another five or so years left in competitive skiing.

'If you want to do a bit of teaching, to see if it's for

you, you could work alongside me for a while,' Angelo suggested.

It was a generous offer, Josh thought, and one he appreciated: but he wasn't sure he could handle being at a championship on the non-competing side. Not yet.

Angelo raised an eyebrow. 'Or, if you want to try something different, there's my family's ski resort.'

Pendio di Cristallo, a private resort in the Dolomites. A luxury family resort, rather than the kind of place competitive skiers and their glamorous set hung out, which meant it wouldn't be full of people who knew or recognised him. Josh had stayed there plenty of times with Angelo's family, who'd always treated him as if he was one of them. There, he could be practically anonymous.

As if Angelo guessed at Josh's fears, he added, 'It's for families, not ski-heads. You could maybe spend a few months there. Get away from the pressure, teach for a couple of days a week, and build your strength up. Ski for fun instead of trying to beat the clock.'

'Stop and smell the roses?' Josh asked.

'Not on a ski slope,' Angelo said with a grin. 'But you know that poem. "What is this life if, full of care, we have no time to stand and stare?" There's an awful lot of truth in that.'

'I guess.'

And so Josh had done his teaching qualifications. He'd met people on his course who planned to work with disabled skiers, and in the back of his head a kind of lightbulb had flickered. He wasn't disabled—but he did know exactly what it felt like to have restricted movement, and to undergo surgery and painful physiotherapy. Maybe that was something he could explore:

helping people with restrictions to ski and feel the thrill of hurtling down a slope. Assistive ski instructing.

At Pendio di Cristallo, there was enough snow even this early in the season that he'd been able to spend a couple of weeks skiing; though it had been on slopes that were kind to his knee but didn't make his heart beat fast, the way the freestyle aerial and mogul stuff always had. Giovanni, Angelo's older brother and the resort manager, had offered to help him sort out a small list of very select clients, and Josh was hoping that teaching would hold different pleasures. If he could give complete novices their confidence, and teach them how to handle themselves on a slope to the point where they could ski downhill and feel the magic for themselves, then it might remind him of his own first forays into skiing and bring back some of the joy he'd lost over the last year.

And if teaching meant that he didn't lose skiing completely, then he'd take the vicarious pleasure. His surgeon had been right about that. Having the snow in his life was better than cutting the snow out of his life completely; he'd already tried doing without the snow during rehab and it had just made him miserable.

He was still thinking about working with assistive skiing. Maybe that would be the answer to wiping out these lingering traces of restlessness. He couldn't go back to his old life. But he could make a better future: for others as well as himself. He'd give it until the end of the season, and then he'd decide where he went next.

It was snowing.

Big, fat, fluffy flakes, which floated down softly as a feather.

Here in the Dolomites, it wasn't like the tiny snow-flakes in London which either melted swiftly or turned into grey sludge; here, the snow lay thickly and was a white so brilliant that Sophie could understand exactly why she'd been advised to pack sunglasses. She'd fallen in love with Pendio di Cristallo, with the jagged mountains and the pine trees and the amazingly blue skies. She'd fallen in love with the posh chalet she was working in—she still couldn't quite believe she actually had her own room in it—with its pitched roof, wooden flooring, log fire, mood lighting and the wall of pure glass with a stunning view over the mountains. Not to mention the spa pool, which she and Kitty, the chalet maid, were allowed to use when the guests were out and was utterly blissful. A good book, a mug of tea, the bubbling water and the view: it didn't get better than that.

And she'd really fallen in love with the sparkly, bright snow.

How had she ever thought she hated the stuff?

When it was falling like this, it was so pretty and she itched to be out in it; it was like being in a real-life snow-globe. And when it stopped snowing and the sun came out, the light glinted on the surface and made it look as if the ground was made of bright, sparkling diamonds.

Her guests wouldn't be up for another hour, and she'd already prepped everything. There was something she needed from the shop, so she might as well multi-task and enjoy the snow at the same time. Sophie grabbed the snow boots she'd bought back in England—boots with a thick rubber sole, fleece-lined and made of bright pink waterproof material to keep her feet warm and dry—and the matching padded jacket. She put on her sunglasses, pulled up the hood of her jacket and slipped on a pair of mittens, then headed out of the chalet. It was so quiet here. There was no traffic, and the snow dampened any noise. Walking in it was magical. But she wanted something else. She stopped where she was and lifted her face up to the sky; the flakes drifted down in spirals, brilliant white against a flatter white sky. Utterly, utterly perfect. She opened her mouth to let the snow fall in; it tasted crisp and clean and fresh.

Her new beginning.

Starting now.

Smiling, she started to walk across the snow again—and let out a scream as a man on a snowboard materialised out of nowhere and zoomed across the path just in front of her. A skier screeched to a halt next to her and demanded, 'Are you *insane*?'

What the…?

When Josh had stayed here for weekends before, he'd seen tourists not looking where they were going in the resort, but was this one completely crazy? Thankfully the fuchsia-pink jacket had made her visible. But she'd just wandered onto the edge of the piste and stopped dead; she was standing there without a care in the world, sticking her head up and staring at the sky.

OK, so it was early morning and there weren't that many people about, but surely she'd seen the skiers and snowboarders coming down the slope? He planned to drill into his pupils about rights of way for skiers and that joining a piste was like joining traffic on a road—but the woman wasn't skiing. She was looking at the sky. He was heading straight for her; a snowboarder just about missed her and whizzed in front of her, but he was at the edge of the piste and there was already someone skiing on his other side, so he couldn't simply turn to avoid her.

She was lucky he knew how to stop on a sixpence, otherwise he would've crashed into her and both of them could've been hurt. As it was, his knee protested at the sharp turn that brought him to a halt. He'd need to work on that later. And he just hoped this wasn't going to mean a setback. He'd worked so hard to get this far, and the worry made him snap with irritation at her.

'Are you *insane*?' he demanded.

She stared at him, one mittened hand clutched to her chest, breathing hard. 'Oh, my God! You nearly crashed into me. You *frightened* me!'

Good. Hopefully he'd frightened her enough so she wouldn't do this ever again. '*You* frightened *me*. And, for the record, I didn't nearly crash into you. You're lucky I have the experience to be able to stop.' Exasperated, he glared at her. 'What the hell are you doing on the piste?'

'Oh, my God—I didn't realise I'd wandered this way!' She looked shocked. 'I was looking up at the snow.'

'Which is *incredibly* dangerous.' He could barely believe someone could be this clueless. 'You need to keep more of an eye on where you're going. Is this your first time skiing here?'

'I haven't actually been skiing yet,' she admitted.

It sounded as if it was her first day in the resort, then. 'If you want to make it to the end of the week in one piece, or without putting someone else in hospital, take my advice and always check uphill before you walk anywhere,' he said dryly. 'Yes, it's early in the season and early in the day, but there are still some diehard skiers out.'

Her face—the bit he could see between her hood and the oversized glasses—turned a dull, embarrassed shade of red. 'Sorry. I just…' She gestured around her. 'The snow. It's pretty.'

'And it's *dangerous*,' he repeated, wanting to hammer the point home. 'You could've caused a serious accident.' And he knew all about the fallout from serious skiing accidents. It had taken long, miserable months to recover. 'Let me escort you safely to the side before someone crashes into you and ends up in hospital.'

'Thank you. And I'm sorry,' she said again.

He glanced uphill. Thankfully there was a gap in the skiers, and he was able to take her to the side of the piste without any further incident. 'Look where you're going in future, no matter how pretty the snow looks.' He gave a sharp nod, then disappeared down the hill.

So much for her new start, Sophie thought. She might as well have 'call me stupid' tattooed across her forehead.

She'd been so entranced by the snow that she hadn't been paying proper attention to where she was going. She'd thought she was heading away from the piste. Instead, she'd completely missed the fact that the fresh snow had covered the edge of the piste and she'd nearly caused an accident.

Maybe she ought to call off her skiing lesson this afternoon; but then she'd fail before she even started. This was meant to be challenging herself, forcing herself past the pain barriers and getting all of her courage and self-esteem back so she could make that new start properly.

This time double-checking her surroundings before she walked on, she headed into the town to pick up the blueberries she wanted from the supermarket. The teenage girl in her chalet's family had admitted to loving blueberries, and Sophie wanted to make some blueberry and lemon muffins for her. Particularly as tomorrow was their last day in the resort before changeover; it would be a nice way of saying goodbye.

She loved her new job. Every single detail: from calling the guests beforehand to check their dietary requirements, and whether there were any birthdays or anniversaries during their stay, through to planning the menus and discussing them with the guests. The plan was to prepare a full cooked breakfast six days a week and continental breakfast for her day off, to prep afternoon tea every day, and to make canapés and a three-course evening meal six days a week.

It was everything she enjoyed most at work: cooking, chatting about food, and delighting her customers. Here, she was essentially working as a private chef, providing a truly personal service rather than sticking to someone else's menus and recipes. It was almost as good as running her own business.

Plus sorting out the business side of things might make up for that huge black mark on her CV, because here she was responsible for purchasing supplies, budgeting, accounting, management and stock control.

And this time she didn't have someone like Blake to guide her through the numbers—or bring her crashing down.

Thankfully the supermarket had the blueberries she wanted, and she headed back to the chalet to start baking. She took a selfie in the middle of town to reassure

Hannah, and sent it with a message saying she was loving every second out here.

I'm taking my first skiing lesson this afternoon. Will report back later. xx

Even though the idea of hurtling down a slope terrified her, she knew she needed to challenge herself. Prove that she could do it. And then maybe it'd give her the confidence to go back to England with her head held high and start all over again.

CHAPTER TWO

ONCE SOPHIE HAD made the muffins, double-checked the contents of her backpack, and drunk a mug of coffee to sharpen her mind, she headed out to meet her skiing instructor.

The snow had stopped, and the sunlight made everything sparkle.

Her heart was thumping as she made her way to the beginners' area where they'd agreed to meet. The skis were surprisingly heavy, her boots weighed a ton, all the ski stuff she was wearing was extremely bulky, and she was carrying poles as well as her backpack. Had she maybe overreached herself? What if her habitual clumsiness kicked in and she fell over and made a fool out of herself?

But she wasn't going to back out now.

Apart from the fact that she'd promised herself she'd get past the fear, the private skiing lessons she'd booked were expensive. An indulgence she probably should've reined back, given the state of her finances. Although she was determined to try something new, she'd made enough of a fool of herself over Blake to feel that a beginners' class was still too much to handle. Thinking that it might help her pick up the skills more quickly if the instructor was focused on just her, she'd talked to Giovanni Rendini, the resort manager, and asked his advice. He'd been swift to recommend Josh Cavendish. 'He's not listed with the rest of the instructors,' Giovanni said, 'because he doesn't take many clients. This is kind of a trial season for him.' Sophie's doubts must've shown on her face, because he added quickly, 'But I can vouch for him. I've known him for more than a decade. He's a close friend of the family.'

That had reassured Sophie—a bit. But it would've been nice to be able to look him up and see his profile along with those of the other instructors, and know what to expect from him.

Josh Cavendish was a mystery.

She just hoped he would be kind.

Because meeting him in five minutes' time would be make-or-break for this whole skiing thing.

Josh recognised that coat. In-your-face fuchsia-pink. Teamed with oversized sunglasses that he also recognised, and with fluorescent yellow ski pants that clashed spectacularly with her coat.

Surely the clueless tourist he'd rescued this morning wasn't his new student? He couldn't imagine anything more horrifying. Introducing novices to the joy of skiing was one thing, but he really wasn't up for babysitting a walking disaster.

But she seemed to be making a beeline for him: as if following his directions to his new student to meet him under the clock, and she'd find him easily because he'd be wearing an orange-and-purple-striped beanie.

He saw the second that she recognised him from

this morning, because her face bloomed with colour to match her coat.

'I'm...um...Sophie Harris.' She held one gloved hand out to shake his. 'You must be Josh Cavendish. And I apologise again for this morning.' She bit her lip. 'I feel very stupid.'

He knew he ought to be kind, even though he was still a bit annoyed with her for the near-accident this morning. And he really didn't want to have to babysit her on the slopes. It would be incredibly frustrating, working with someone so clueless.

But then Sophie pushed the sunglasses up on top of her head to reveal the fact that she had the most stunning blue eyes: a deep, cobalt blue, like the sky on a perfect skiing day. And a heart-shaped face. And the most perfect rosebud mouth.

His tongue felt as if it had been glued to the roof of his mouth. And all of a sudden there weren't any words in his head.

Not good.

Really not good.

He hadn't felt that zing of attraction towards anyone since Annabel—and that had gone so badly wrong that he didn't trust his judgement any more.

Gorgeous or not, Sophie Harris was his student. He needed to be professional, not gawking at her. What was wrong with him?

'Ms Harris,' he said, shaking her hand. And he was glad they were both wearing gloves. He didn't want to know how badly skin-to-skin contact with her might be able to distract him.

She looked nervous; he wasn't sure whether it was learning to ski that worried her, or the fact that he was going to be her teacher after their last encounter—when she'd done something unbelievably ignorant—had been awkward.

'I assume the ski hire place fitted your boots?'

She nodded.

'Good, but I prefer to check things myself.' And focusing on a checklist might stop him being distracted by the shape of her mouth. What the hell was wrong with him? He never let himself get distracted at work.

Well. He had. Once. When Annabel had announced that she was pregnant, then straight away given him that ultimatum: marry me or I'll have a termination. He'd let it distract him from what he should've been concentrating on, and the end result had been a disaster. Never, ever again. That had been too hard a lesson to forget. He shook himself mentally and went through his mental checklist.

'Can you wiggle your toes?' he asked.

'Yes.'

'Good, otherwise your feet will be cold. Can you move your foot around in the boot?'

'Only a tiny bit,' she said. 'Does that mean they're too tight?'

'No—if your foot moves too much you won't be able to control your skis,' he said. 'And your heels are flat on the sole of your boot?'

'Yes.'

'That's a great start—but if your feet hurt at the end of your lesson, you need to go back to the ski hire and change the boots, OK?'

'OK.'

'And those ski pants are waterproof, yes?'

'Ye-es.' She grimaced. 'I know they don't go with my coat.'

'You're not here to be a fashion icon.' As soon as he heard them, he knew his words were too sharp. It wasn't her fault that his ex *had* been a fashion icon. 'Wearing bright colours is a good idea because it helps other skiers spot you on the mountain,' he said, trying to be kind. 'This is your first time skiing, right?'

'Yes.'

'You're in exactly the right place,' he reassured her. 'So. Gloves, helmet and goggles?'

She nodded.

'Perfect. We're going over to the beginners' area now, and we'll put your skis on.'

Sophie started to panic inwardly. She hadn't expected her skiing instructor to be so gorgeous. Tall, dark and handsome, with amazing grey eyes and the most beautiful mouth.

Thanks to their encounter this morning, he already thought she was completely ditzy and hopeless. She needed to get a grip. Right now. Prove to him that she was more than that. Especially because he clearly didn't like her.

You're not here to be a fashion icon.

He'd covered it up with another comment, but he was obviously impatient with her.

Which was yet another reason why she should make herself concentrate. What was wrong with her? Her mind kept wandering off and coming up with scenarios that involved softly falling snow, fairy lights, and Josh Cavendish in very close proximity—something that absolutely wasn't going to happen.

If she kept this up, she was going to make a total fool of herself and fall flat on her face.

'Everybody falls over,' he said.

Mountain, please open and swallow me now, she begged silently. 'I didn't mean to say that out loud.' And she really hoped she hadn't said the rest of it aloud, too.

'You didn't have to say it. It was written all over your face,' he said. 'But your ski pants are padded and waterproof, the snow's soft, we're not going on a steep slope and we're not going fast. When you fall over—and it's a when, not an if—you're not going to hurt yourself or slide off the edge of a mountain. You'll just land in a pile of snow. What you do then is get back up again, smile and shake it off.'

And now she had Taylor Swift singing in her head.

For pity's sake. Why was she letting herself get so flustered? She wasn't the sort to moon over handsome actors or pop stars, and she'd always managed to be polite and friendly to her customers and colleagues, whatever they looked like.

Well, except for Blake. She'd fallen for him like a ton of bricks. But that had been the biggest mistake of her life, and she needed to remember the lesson she'd learned. A very, very hard lesson.

To her relief, if Josh had even noticed her reaction to him, he simply ignored it. He talked her through putting her skis on, and helped her adjust her goggles. 'You'll find these useful today,' he said. 'We're protected from the storms here and get more sunshine than anywhere else in the Alpine region—and sunlight reflects on the slope, making it hard for you to see. Your goggles have pink tints, which means they'll let the light in but enhance the contrast, so you can see any irregularities in the snow.'

'Right.'

'So this is your first time on skis. How about ice skates?' he asked.

'No. I haven't been on roller skates, either.' Which made her feel even more foolish. What had she been thinking, challenging herself to ski when she'd never done anything remotely like it?

His expression was carefully neutral. 'That's fine. I just wanted to know what your experience was, so I know where to start. Everyone starts somewhere. And it's absolutely normal to feel wobbly and a bit awkward, the first few times.'

She gestured to the small children whizzing down the slopes further along. 'They don't look wobbly.'

'They probably ski all year. Ignore them. This isn't about them. It's all about *you.*'

She noticed then how intense his grey eyes were. And it made her knees feel even more wobbly.

She'd barely even finished thinking it when she fell over.

'That's good—just what I wanted to happen,' Josh said.

'What?' She didn't understand. He was meant to be her teacher. Why did he want her to fall over? 'Why?'

'Firstly, now you'll know from experience that falling over isn't going to hurt, so you'll relax, making you less likely to fall again,' he said. 'And, secondly, so I can teach you how to get up.' He smiled. 'Ironically, it's easier to get up when you're on a steeper slope. The boots stop you flexing your ankles, so on the flat it's hard to get your legs underneath you. But what I want you to do is to get your feet downhill from you parallel to the mountain, use the poles and push yourself up in a squatting position.'

She tried a couple of times and failed dismally.

'Frustration is your enemy,' he said, 'so I'm going to help you up this time. But, by the end of this afternoon, you'll be able to do it yourself.'

Sophie wasn't so sure. But she really wanted to do this. It would help her in her real life, too. Prove that she could do something. That she wasn't the useless idiot she'd felt herself to be ever since she'd discovered how badly Blake had scammed her. That she could try something new and difficult, and she'd *succeed*.

Even though Josh was wearing gloves and her jacket was padded, she was sure she could feel the warmth of his hand as he helped her up. Again, it made her feel all quivery and weird.

She hadn't felt like this about anyone since Blake.

And that in itself should be a warning. She had terrible judgement when it came to men. Blake was absolute proof of that. Plus Josh was her teacher. She didn't want to come across like some kind of ski groupie. Be cool, calm and collected, she reminded herself. The Sophie you've promised yourself you'll be. *New* Sophie. Competent, confident Sophie who knew her own value.

'Thank you,' she said, proud of the way her voice didn't betray her attraction to Josh. Or the fact that his deep, gorgeous voice put butterflies in her stomach.

'We're going to walk sideways at first, so you get used to the feel of the skis,' he told her.

She followed his instructions, taking side steps along the snow. The incline barely even counted as a slope, it was that shallow. The more they stepped, the more confident she felt.

'You've got the hang of it. Good. Ready to try going forward?' he asked.

No. But New Sophie answered for her. 'Yes.'

'I'm going to teach you the snowplough.'

She'd read up on that. 'You point the front of your skis towards each other, right?'

'Not quite,' he said, 'because what happens then is your skis will cross at the tips, you'll get tangled up and you'll fall over. Think of your skis as being like the outside of a boat. Tilt them and keep pushing your knees together and your feet apart. The wider the plough and the more you tilt, the easier you'll stop.' He demonstrated, and stopped a little way away from her.

'Now you do it. Come towards me,' he said.

'What if I crash into you?'

'You won't. You're not going to crash and you're not going to fall. You've got this.'

It was maybe six or seven metres. Barely even a slope. She could do this.

She assumed the position he'd shown her, and went down the slope towards him. She was actually going slower than walking pace. Possibly even slower than a snail about to hibernate—did snails hibernate?

But she'd done it. Skied forwards.

He gave her a high-five, and that smile made her heart do a backflip. 'See? Now you're going to do it all over again.'

He walked back to their starting point. Feeling like a very ungainly and very ugly duckling, she waddled after him.

And then she repeated the slide, over and over again, until he was satisfied.

'Now we're going to add a tiny, tiny thing,' he said. 'You're going to turn.'

'Turn.' Was that really just a tiny thing, or was he jollying her on?

'What you do is shift your weight to your outside foot, face the way you want to turn, and lean your body in the opposite direction,' he told her.

Huh? He expected her to do *three* things at once? No way. Absolutely no way was she going to be able to do this. Tiny thing, indeed. It was huge. Scary. Out of her abilities.

But he talked her through it. He was kind, patient—and absolutely implacable.

Three things at once.

And, to her surprise, she managed it.

'I did it!' And her voice *would* have to squeak.

But there wasn't a hint of scorn in his face. He was just kind and encouraging. As well as gorgeous, though she'd have to stop thinking about that or she'd fall over again.

'See? You can do this,' he said.

They practised a bit more.

'I think you're ready for the magic carpet, now,' he said.

'Magic carpet?'

'It's a kind of conveyor belt—a quick way of getting you to the top of the nursery slope,' he said, taking her over to it. 'It works like the travelator you see in airports. Hold your poles in one hand, shuffle forward onto the magic carpet, and it will take you up and push you off at the landing area at the top,' he directed. 'And I'll be right behind you, ready to take you to the slope and guide you down.'

Adrenalin fizzed through her veins, and she wasn't sure whether it was from his nearness or from doing something unfamiliar.

But, to her surprise, everything happened exactly as he'd explained it.

'Ready? Remember—knees together, feet apart, and tilt. If I call "snowplough", that's what I want you to do.'

This slope was longer. And it felt as if she was flying, even though technically she knew she could walk faster than she was skiing.

'That was amazing,' she said. And then it occurred to her how naive and starry-eyed she must sound. How over the top.

But he was smiling. 'That,' he said, 'is precisely how it's meant to feel. Want to do it again?'

He sounded as enthusiastic as she'd felt. Not jaded or bored or supercilious. And it felt as if a weight had fallen off her shoulders.

He got what it felt like, to fly.

Of course he would. As an instructor, he'd be able to ski much more difficult things than this.

But, as he'd said, everyone started somewhere. Just as she'd started at the bottom at catering school, learning to make a simple *mirepoix* base for a soup and working her way up to producing something much more complex, complete with timing plans.

She nodded.

They went down half a dozen times more—and, on the last run, he didn't have to remind her with a gentle, 'Snowplough.'

'I think you're ready for the next stage,' he said. 'Green slope.'

She looked at the slope he was indicating with one hand. 'That's terrifyingly steep,' she said.

'I promise you it's not,' he said. 'The point of this is for you to have fun, not be terrified out of your wits. I won't take you on anything that's outside your capabilities.'

Which meant she had to trust him.

The last time she'd trusted a man, it had gone very badly wrong.

But Josh had been good with her so far. Honest. So maybe she should take that little leap of faith. 'Green slope,' she said. 'So is there another magic carpet to take us to the top?'

'No, this time there's a button lift—which is a bit like the zip wire you'd see in a playground.'

The sort of thing she'd never go near because she'd fall off and hurt herself. Like when she'd fallen off a slide and a swing; or when she'd fallen off the beam in a gym lesson, one time, because the supply teacher had refused to let her have someone holding her hand for balance. As a child, she'd always had scabs on her knees and elbows.

And it was moving.

'You've got plenty of time to manage it,' he said. 'Hold your poles in the hand that's away from the lift, grab the lift-pole with your other hand and grip the pole between your legs. When you get to the flat bit at the top, just squat slightly and push the seat away.'

She watched six people get on the lift before she could summon up the courage to try it for herself.

'You've got this, Sophie,' he said. 'If I didn't think you were ready, I wouldn't suggest it.'

And this was his job. If he wasn't any good, he wouldn't have any clients, would he? Even though Giovanni Rendini had said something about this being a trial season as a coach.

She didn't want to let herself down. She wanted to feel capable again. The woman who'd built a career and had run a successful restaurant. Her parents had always encouraged her, telling her she could do anything she wanted if she tried. And she wanted that confidence back. Challenging herself to do something way out of her comfort zone was the best way she could think to do that.

She took a deep breath, braced herself, and went for it.

To her relief, she didn't miss or fall. And then she was at the top of the slope.

The views were amazing. The sun glinted off the mountains as far as she could see; the contrast between the brilliant white of snowy peaks, the dark pine trees and the wide cerulean sky was magical.

But there was a steep slope in front of her. A long slope. Much bigger than the one she'd skied down before. Intimidating didn't even *begin* to describe it.

'You've got this,' Josh said. 'And I'll be right by your side all the way down. If you're going too fast, simply tilt your skis and the resistance will slow you down. You've practised and you know how to do it.'

Learning to ski was the challenge she'd set herself, to prove to herself that she could move past the mess she'd made of her life.

'You're right. I've got this,' she said. She shuffled

forwards. And then somehow she was going down the slope. Fast. Too fast. *Way* too fast. She was going to fall. She was going to crash. She was going to—

'Snowplough!' Josh called beside her.

Knees together, feet apart, tilt.

And all of a sudden she was back in control. Still going a bit too fast for her liking, but in control. She'd never felt an adrenalin rush like it: to the point where, when she came to a halt, she was actually crying.

She'd done it. Faced the challenge and proved to herself that she *could* do it. She was still standing upright. She hadn't made a fool of herself; she'd faced that terrifying slope and *done it*.

Thanks to Josh's guidance. He'd helped her rather than sticking obstacles in her way. His direction had finally helped her to move forward, away from the fear and the self-pity. She wasn't sure whether she was more grateful, relieved or excited. Maybe all three, in a weird kind of cocktail, but the end result was that tears were running down her face.

At the bottom of the slope she pushed up her goggles before they started misting up, and scrubbed at her face. 'Sorry.'

'Don't apologise. It's your first proper run,' he said. 'I remember how it felt. You're so thrilled you've actually done it, you don't quite know what to do with yourself once you've stopped.'

She mopped her tears. 'Are you telling me you cried your eyes out?'

'No. I was young enough to whoop my head off—as I couldn't exactly jump up and down when I was wearing skis. So I just stood there, feeling a bit lost and a bit ridiculous.'

Which was how she was feeling right at this moment, now the euphoria of achievement was wearing off.

'You're good at this,' she said.

'What?'

'Being empathetic. Teaching.'

He inclined his head. 'Thank you. Ready to go again?'

Yes, because she needed to prove to herself that this wasn't a one-off. She took a deep breath and nodded. 'Ready.'

All too soon, the lesson was over.

'So I'll see you the day after tomorrow,' he said.

And she could hardly wait.

Though she reminded herself that it was because she'd discovered that she liked skiing. It had nothing to do with the fact that Josh's smile made her heart skip a beat.

'In the meantime, I want you to practise a ski sit.' He talked her through the manoeuvre. 'If you want to practise skiing on your own tomorrow,' he said, 'stick to the nursery slope or the green slope.'

'How would I know I've got the right slope?' she asked.

'Because you won't need a chairlift to get to the top,' he said. 'You're not going to be quite ready for that on your next lesson, but I'm pretty sure I'll get you safely on a blue slope before the end of your holiday.'

'I'm not on holiday,' she said.

Josh stared at Sophie, not understanding. 'You're not on holiday?' he repeated.

'I work here. I'm a chef in one of the chalets. I came here a few days ago.' She gave him a rueful smile. 'I'm rather better with a sharp knife than I am with skis.'

'A chef?' He looked at her. 'Forgive me for being nosey, but I don't understand why on earth you'd come to a ski resort to work as a chef when you've never skied before. This is the sort of job you'd take because you want to spend as much time as possible on the slopes when you're off duty.'

She wrinkled her nose. 'It's a long story and much too boring to take up your time. And, I hate to be rude, but I do need to get back because it's my family's last full day today.'

Which explained why she hadn't booked a lesson for tomorrow: with it being changeover day, she'd have no free time to go on the slopes. 'You're not being rude. Just practical,' he said. 'Well, practise that ski sit against the wall, and I'll see you the day after tomorrow.'

And funny how he was looking forward to it already.

CHAPTER THREE

SOPHIE WAS SAD to say goodbye to her chalet family, the next morning: parents, grandparents, aunt, two teenagers and a cute ten-year-old. She'd really enjoyed cooking for them, and they in turn had adored her. She and Kitty were too busy getting everything ready for Sophie to give Josh more than a passing thought. But then the new guests arrived: a group of ten guys in their late twenties who clearly had too much money and not enough sense of responsibility, and who thought that booking the chalet meant they could do and say whatever they wanted. Including groping Kitty, the chalet maid, and indulging in the kind of 'banter' that bordered on bullying.

Anyone who'd behaved like that to her staff in her restaurant would've been asked to leave. Immediately. Politely, but very firmly, because she'd had a zero-tolerance policy and she always stood up for her staff.

Here, she was powerless. But this group had only booked for a week. Surely she could put up with them for a week? She'd do her job, be polite, and resist the urge to 'accidentally' drop iced water in their laps.

'We're only here to feed you and keep the chalet clean,' she said with a smile. 'I'm afraid anything else is completely off the menu.'

'Jealous because you're not as young and pretty as Kitz, you're flat-chested and we don't fancy you?' one of them, who seemed to be the leader of the group, sneered.

No, you pudgy-faced idiot, and if you touch me inappropriately I'll 'accidentally' stand on your foot in spike heels.

But she didn't say it. She simply smiled. 'More coffee and cake to soak up some of that booze, lads?'

'God, they're awful,' Kitty whispered to her in the kitchen. 'My mum used to work in a bar when she was a student. She said that's how people behaved towards the bar staff back then. Though they're not allowed to do it now—the bouncers would throw them out. It's the only reason she let me take a gap year to do this.'

'You'd think even *they* would've heard of #*metoo*,' Sophie said dryly. 'Don't worry. I'll make sure you're not alone with any of them. And I'm going to have a word with the resort manager so he's aware of the situation and can step in if we need him to. It's not OK for them to behave towards you like that.'

'Can I spit in their coffee?' Kitty asked.

Sophie grinned. 'That's very tempting—but no. We'll smile sweetly and we won't give them the satisfaction of a reaction. Then, like any other bullies, they'll get bored and stop.'

She hoped.

The guests needled her all through the evening. Obviously their boredom threshold wasn't quite as low as their manners. But she did her job, and she did it well—even if they didn't really appreciate the food she made for them.

The next morning, Sophie was up early to prepare

breakfast. Part of her was tempted to make as much noise as possible and cook things with scents that would make anyone with a hangover feel super-queasy; but then again she loved this time of day, and what was the point of spoiling her few moments of peace just to score a few petty points against people who didn't actually matter? So, instead, she made the batter for the waffles and then a mug of coffee for herself so she could sit by the glass wall overlooking the mountain.

Even though the sun hadn't yet risen, it was still bright outside because of the snow. She could see the smooth whiteness of the snow on the ground, the dark spiky pine trees spreading up the mountain, and then the peak itself; the vertical nature of the cliffs meant the jagged peak wasn't covered in snow, and the stone turned bright pink as it caught the first rays of the sun. The sky behind the mountain shimmered from deep pink through peach up to the palest blue.

It didn't get any better than this, she thought, and the sight went a long way to restoring her temper.

But the lads were brash and braying all through breakfast, boasting about how fast they were going to ski all the black runs, commenting about Kitty's very demure outfit and how she should be wearing a skimpy black mini-dress and a frilly white apron instead, and generally being obnoxious.

When they finally left, Sophie made a chocolate and orange cake for the afternoon and prepped the veg for the evening meal; but even baking and the scent of chocolate didn't help. She was still in a thoroughly bad mood when she met Josh for her skiing lesson.

'If looks could kill,' he said, 'you'd be in the dock on a murder charge. What's up?'

She grimaced. 'The new guests. I wish the old ones were still here; they were so nice.'

'What's wrong with the new ones?'

'Rich boys,' she said. 'The sort who've never really had to work for anything. Let's just say they have a strong sense of entitlement. And it wasn't helped by the amount of booze they tipped down their throats last night.'

Josh winced inwardly. Rich and entitled. That was precisely his background; and, although he hoped he no longer behaved like a spoiled brat, he knew there were definitely times in the past when he had.

'Is it worth having a word with Giovanni Rendini?' he asked.

'Already done,' she said. 'I'm not bothered for myself, but I worry about the way they talk to Kitty. She's only eighteen.' She grimaced again. 'She's vulnerable.'

'If you're in any doubts,' Josh said, 'both of you lock yourself in your rooms and call Giovanni. You don't have to tolerate that sort of behaviour. There's a zero-tolerance policy at the resort.'

She nodded. 'I just don't want any trouble.'

'Your safety comes first,' he said. 'For now, they're not here and they're not worth the headspace. So forget about them and ski it out. I'm going to take you to a different ski run.'

'A steeper one?' She looked anxious.

'No. Just a different green run,' he said. 'You'll manage it just fine.'

And he was careful to stay right beside her on the piste, reminding her when to turn and when to slow down. He enjoyed seeing the way her expression changed from cross and anxious to peacefulness.

'Thank you,' she said at the end of the lesson. 'I needed that.'

Her eyes had cleared, and again Josh realised just how pretty she was. Weirdly, she didn't seem to know how lovely she was. 'The mountains always make it better,' he said, and realised that it was true: even though he hadn't been doing any of the elite skiing that had been his life before the accident, just being on the slopes in the snow was enough to soothe his soul.

'I think you might be right,' she said.

'Have you had a chance to try any of the après-ski yet?'

She wrinkled her nose. 'I'm not really one for partying.'

He smiled. 'This is more of a family resort than a party place, as the guys in your chalet might find out—and also skiing with a hangover isn't fun, so if they were hitting the booze last night they'll have found that out the hard way and they might not drink so much tonight. Which means they might behave better.'

'I hope you're right,' she said. 'They were going on about improving their times on the Val di Lungo today, whatever that is.'

'One of the black runs,' he said. 'Which means they're experienced skiers. Listen, I know somewhere that does the best hot chocolate in the Dolomites. Would you like to join me, to celebrate doing that green run?' he asked before he could stop himself.

'Sadly, I can't because I need to be back for afternoon tea,' she said. 'I'm hoping that good cake might sweeten their mood a bit.'

'You weren't tempted to stick salt or some super-hot chillies in the cake?'

'No, because that would be a waste of good food. I'm still hoping a charm offensive will work. If I treat them the way I want them to treat me, with courtesy, maybe it'll rub off. I've always found that if you're nice to people, they're usually nice back.' She wrinkled her nose. 'Or at least this lot will get bored if I don't react to their stupid comments.'

Sophie Harris wasn't a pushover, Josh thought. She was determined. He'd already seen that by the way she'd tackled the skiing lessons. And he approved. 'See you tomorrow, then,' he said.

'See you tomorrow.'

And funny how her smile seemed to make the snow sparkle that little bit more in the sunlight.

Josh couldn't get Sophie out of his head.

She wasn't his only student—but she was the one he looked forward to teaching most. Which probably meant he ought to let her work with a different instructor, or at least keep his distance.

Though his mouth clearly wasn't listening to instructions, because the next day after her lesson he found himself asking her to join him for hot chocolate again. This time, she accepted.

Better still, Sophie actually chose a slice of strudel from the display of cakes. So very different from Annabel, who would've insisted on consuming minimal calories, opting for green tea rather than hot chocolate and looking disapprovingly at the cakes. Sophie took absolute pleasure in hers, closing her eyes so she could concentrate on the taste of the very first mouthful; watching her as she tasted the strudel was the sexiest thing Josh had seen in years.

'Good?' he asked.

'Very. That buttery apple hit, with just the right amount of cinnamon,' she said. 'The pastry's perfectly flaky. Did you know that if you've rolled out strudel pastry properly, you should be able to read a newspaper through it?'

No, he didn't. And Sophie seemed to be unfurling. Instead of the clueless, shy student he'd first taken onto the slopes, the day before yesterday, here she was in her element. Knowledgeable, but using that knowledge as a delight to be shared rather than to prove her own superiority.

The more he got to know her, the more he liked her. 'So are you enjoying the skiing?' he asked.

'Yes. The first day was really scary, but I'm getting over that now. I think I'm starting to understand why people love it so much.'

Joy shone from her face. Josh envied her; it was a long time since he'd felt that, and although the vicarious enjoyment was good, it wasn't quite enough.

She looked at him. 'I know I only booked three lessons with you—but do you have space to fit some more in, please?'

'Sure. Do you have your diary on you?'

She nodded. 'It's on my phone.'

'Snap,' he said, and flicked into his diary app.

It didn't take long to book in some more lessons. And Josh was surprised to discover how pleased and relieved he was that he still had a good excuse to see Sophie and get to know her better.

'Did you come to Pendio di Cristallo specifically to learn to ski?' he asked.

'No.'

'Then what made you come here?'

She wrinkled her nose. 'It's a long and boring story.'

She'd said that before. But this time, maybe, she'd talk to him. 'I have time.'

'I...' She sighed. 'I don't really want to dwell on it. The short version is that I trusted someone I really shouldn't have trusted—someone who let me down pretty badly.' She shrugged. 'So this is my new start.'

'In a ski resort. When you've never skied before.' He still didn't quite get that.

She nodded. 'I wanted to do something completely out of my experience. The idea was to challenge myself. Push myself past—well, the *past*. So I'd come out stronger on the other side.'

He knew exactly how that felt. Not that he was going to tell her. With her not being a skier, she clearly didn't know who he was. And he didn't want that to change; if she knew who he was and what had happened to him, she'd no doubt do the same as his family and friends and see him differently. Pity him, perhaps. He'd already pitied himself way too much over the last year. 'Sometimes,' he said carefully, 'you need a complete change.'

'Get out of your comfort zone,' she agreed. 'But it does mean that now I'm at a bit of a crossroads. What do I do when my job ends here?'

That was his dilemma, too. When the season had ended here, would he go back home to work for his dad? Maybe helping her talk through her own choices might help him get his own situation straight in his head. 'What are your options?' he asked.

'I'm still trying to work it out. I guess I need to find myself another chef job, back in London.'

'What made you decide to be a chef?' he asked.

'I'm dyslexic, so I struggle a bit with paperwork, and I knew I wasn't going to get great exam grades, no matter how hard I worked. But I discovered I liked cooking, and I made it through catering school. Since then, I've worked my way up from prepping to being the one who makes all the decisions.' She gave him a rueful smile. 'They say never trust a scrawny chef, but I assure you I do eat. I have a fast metabolism.'

'You're not scrawny. You're petite,' he said. A pocket Venus, though he didn't think she'd accept the compliment and he wasn't going to make her feel awkward by saying it. 'And you don't come across as one of these scary TV chefs who scream at their staff.'

'Because I'm not,' she said. 'That's not how you get the best out of people. You get the best out of them if they love what they do, and they won't do that if they're unhappy at work. In the best kitchens, you let your team share their ideas and you give them the chance to shine. I know this is going to sound a bit ditsy and flaky, but food made with love always tastes better than food made with fear.'

She still hadn't actually told him what had gone wrong, just that she'd trusted someone who'd let her down. And Josh didn't quite get why that meant she'd had to leave her job. Had she maybe fallen in love with whoever owned the restaurant where she'd worked, and he'd cheated on her? Obviously working together would be horrendous, after that, and it would be understandable why she'd left. Though there wasn't a way of asking that without either prying or stamping all over her feelings.

'Finding another job and working for someone else is one option,' he said. 'Have you thought about maybe working for yourself?'

Pain darkened her eyes.

He reached over to take her hand, but he didn't have a chance to apologise for treading on what was clearly a sore spot because the door banged open and a group of men who looked to be a couple of years younger than him came in, shoving each other and laughing uproariously.

'Oh, look, there she is! Sophie the chef!' one of them called.

'Having a cosy little drinkie-poos with the boyf?' Another of them made kissing noises.

'Your guests, I presume?' Josh asked.

She closed her eyes briefly. 'Unfortunately.'

'Love the skimpy top, Cheffy Soph. Been getting all hot and sweaty, have you?' another of them said.

'Watch you don't have too much cake. It'll make you fat,' another called.

'Mind you, she could do with a bit more up top,' another said, mimicking squeezing breasts.

'That's enough,' Josh said. 'Leave her alone.'

'Ooh! The boyfriend's getting all protective.'

Josh ignored the sing-song voice, knowing the man was looking for a reaction. He wasn't sure whether this lot were on their way to getting drunk, or whether they were just hyping each other up and acting like a pack of hyenas. Either way, the best way to shut this down was to ignore them.

Sophie clearly thought the same, but Josh noticed

that she hunched over her hot chocolate and she'd quietly slid another layer over her strappy top.

When the group finally realised Sophie and Josh weren't going to engage, they went over to the counter to order drinks.

'Do you mind if we go?' Sophie asked, her voice low. 'I'm sorry for wasting the drink and the cake.'

'It's fine,' he said. 'Let's slip out now while their attention's on ordering their drinks.'

But, when she was safely outside the door, he said, 'I'll walk you back to your chalet, but I've just realised I left my wallet on the table.' It wasn't true, but she didn't need to know why he really intended to go back. 'Wait for me here?'

She nodded, her face pinched, and huddled into her jacket.

Josh walked back into the café. Sophie's guests had finished ordering and had claimed a table, where they were busy throwing sugar sachets at each other.

'Afternoon, lads,' he said. He wasn't smiling, and maybe something in the way he carried himself made them stop the raucousness and shut up.

'What do you want?' asked a pudgy, whey-faced, sandy-haired man—the one who seemed to be the leader.

'I want you to treat Sophie and Kitty with respect.'

'It's none of your business, *mate*,' the pudgy one said. 'We'll do what we want. We paid a lot of money for this holiday.'

'That's right, Gaz,' one of the others chipped in.

'Paying for a holiday doesn't give you the right to harass the staff in your accommodation. There's a zero-tolerance policy in Pendio di Cristallo.'

'What, you're going to throw us out?' Gaz scoffed. 'Are you the manager or something?'

'No,' Josh said. 'But, if you're looking to be asked to leave for unacceptable behaviour, it can be arranged.'

'It's not going to happen. Piss off and mind your own business,' Gaz said.

'Yeah. We're not interested,' one of his friends said. 'We're busy sorting out our black run for tomorrow.'

It was obvious Josh wasn't going to be able to get through to them by appealing to their better nature. And they clearly weren't serious ski-heads or they would've recognised him. But they were talking about black runs: so maybe he could teach them a lesson in another way.

'You're all experienced skiers, right?' he checked.

'Yeah,' Gaz drawled. 'We did Val di Lungo today.' He named a time that was respectable enough for Josh to know they really were experienced skiers, rather than boasting, but slow enough that the plan forming in the back of Josh's head was likely to work.

'Here's the deal. Tomorrow morning, seven o'clock, we'll have a race.' And now to dangle the bait. Josh named the course.

Gaz's eyes widened. 'Hang on. That's the ski championship course.'

Josh inclined his head. 'Which means it's all set up for automatic timing and there will be no margin for error. The board will be very clear about who's the fastest. Who wins.'

'But you can't get lift passes to ski there,' one of the others said.

'*You* might not be able to,' Josh said softly, 'but *I* can.'

'At seven o'clock in the morning?' Gaz asked.

'It's half an hour before sunrise, so it'll be light

enough,' Josh said. 'If it's clear, the skies will be stunning.'

They just gaped at him. Which wasn't what he wanted; he wanted to teach them a lesson so they'd leave Sophie alone. Time to add some seasoning. 'Or aren't you man enough to compete with me?'

The goading had exactly the effect he wanted. 'So what are the stakes?' Gaz demanded.

'If I win,' Josh said, knowing there wouldn't be an 'if' about it, 'you leave Sophie and Kitty alone.'

They looked at each other and laughed.

'Plus each of you pays ten thousand pounds to a charity of my choice.'

That got their attention. Sophie had been right in her assessment: rich and entitled. This lot were heavily motivated by money.

'What if one of us wins?' Gaz demanded.

Josh shrugged. 'Then I'll match the payment to a charity of your choice.'

'There are ten of us.' Gaz's eyes narrowed. 'You'll match ten thousand pounds for each of us?'

'To a charity of your choice, for each one of you who beats me.' He shrugged again. 'Or for all of you. As you wish.'

Gaz blinked. 'You're serious?'

'Serious enough that the manager of the resort will be there to ensure it's a fair race.'

'How do we know you're good for the money?' Gaz asked.

'Have a little think about it. This wager means that either I'm very good at skiing,' Josh said, 'or I'm very rich.' Actually, he was both, but they didn't need to know that. 'In the meantime, I suggest you treat Sophie and Kitty with respect.'

There was a ripple of uncertainty from all of them now.

'And this,' he added, 'is strictly between us. Not a word to Sophie. I'll send a driver for you in the morning. Six-fifteen. Make sure you're ready.' Wanting to make absolutely sure they turned up, he added, 'If you're late, I'll consider it a forfeit because you're too chicken to face me.'

'All right,' Gaz said. 'You're on.'

'Good. See you tomorrow, *gentlemen*,' Josh said, making it very clear he didn't think there was anything gentlemanly about them, and left the café.

Sophie's face still looked pinched when he joined her. 'They didn't give you any trouble, did they?'

He'd taken too long about it. Of course she would've looked through the window and seen him talking to them. 'It's fine,' he said. The championship course wasn't easy. He'd skied it several times before and knew that some of the turns were seriously tight. If it was icy... He'd just have to hope his knee held up to the strain, or he might have made things worse for Sophie rather than better.

Once he'd walked her back to the chalet, he went to see Giovanni.

'Josh! What can I do for you?'

'I need a favour, Gio,' Josh said. 'Quite a big one. I need an escort for a party of ten to the championship course, for a seven a.m. start tomorrow—and I need you to be there.'

Giovanni raised his eyebrows. 'Why?'

Josh explained as succinctly as he could.

Giovanni winced. 'Sophie told me her guests were difficult, but she said she was dealing with them. Perhaps I should put her and Kitty in a different chalet and give this lot a male chef and a butler for the rest of the week.'

Josh shook his head. 'Then she'll guess I've said something to you as well. I think she needs to feel that she's handling this.'

'If she finds out what you've done,' Giovanni warned, 'it's going to blow up in your face.'

'She won't,' Josh said, 'because they're not going to admit they've lost the race, and particularly to losing all that money. But hopefully it will be enough of a shock for them to listen to what I say to them afterwards, and they'll learn to treat people better in future.'

'What about your knee?' Giovanni asked. 'Will it stand up to the run? Have you talked to your consultant about this—or to Angelo?'

Josh smiled. 'It'll be fine.'

'In other words, you haven't spoken to either of them.' Giovanni folded his arms and gave Josh a hard stare.

'What they don't know can't hurt them.'

Giovanni compressed his mouth. 'Angelo's my favourite brother.'

'And I've practically been your youngest brother for the last decade or so, since I started working with Angelo,' Josh said.

'Of course you count as family. That's why we put up with you.' Giovanni rolled his eyes. 'As the nearest you have to a big brother, I can tell you I'm not happy about this, Josh. At all.'

'The situation needs sorting,' Josh said, 'and sometimes you need an unorthodox solution to solve a problem effectively.'

Giovanni sighed. 'This is just a downhill race, right, not freestyle? And absolutely no moguls or aerials?'

'Promise,' Josh said. 'I'm not completely reckless. I know what the consultant said and I want to be able to walk unaided in twenty years' time.'

'OK. I would've come with you even if you hadn't asked. I'll drive you to the slope myself.' Giovanni frowned. 'Have you secured access to the course?'

'No, but I don't think it'll be a problem,' Josh said with a smile.

'If it is, let me know and I'll get Babbo involved.'

Vincenzo Rendini—Giovanni and Angelo's father, and the owner of the resort—was a former world champion skier himself. 'If you tell your dad, he'll suggest taking my place,' Josh said. 'And then your mum would kill me. You and your dad, I'm not scared of. Your mum, on the other hand...'

'Everyone's scared of Mamma.' Giovanni grinned. 'Perhaps we should introduce her to Sophie's guests instead. She'd sort them out within seconds.'

'But then Sophie would definitely know I've interfered. This way, she won't.' Josh clapped his friend's shoulder. 'Thanks, Gio. I really appreciate this.'

'You're insane,' Giovanni grumbled, but he was smiling.

CHAPTER FOUR

Sophie was dreading the return of their guests. No doubt there would be more comments about her curves—or lack of them—and smutty suggestions. Maybe they'd all be bearable on their own, but together they were a pack who egged each other on. They'd made her feel so horrible in the café that she'd left instead of spending time with Josh.

Not that she should be thinking about Josh in that way. She wasn't looking for another relationship. Not after Blake. They might become friends, possibly, but that was the outer limit of any possible relationship between them. And she'd be back in England again in a couple of months, so what was the point of even starting something? Besides, for all she knew, Josh could be committed elsewhere. He'd held her hand today, admittedly; but that just confused things. Had he actually wanted to hold her hand, or had it just been a gesture of kindness and sympathy?

When they returned, her guests treated her as if she was invisible. Which suited her just fine. She was clearing up after dinner, when Pete, one of the quieter and nicer ones in the group, came into the kitchen. 'We're going skiing really early tomorrow. Can we have an early breakfast?'

'How early?' she asked.

'We're being picked up from here at quarter-past six.'

If they'd been like her last guests, Sophie would've offered to get up early to make them bacon sandwiches—and she would've made them granola bars to take with them. But with this lot she was playing strictly by the rules.

'I can leave you a cold spread,' she said. 'Cereals, rolls and fruit. You'll have to make your own coffee.'

'Cheers.'

While she was setting the table for breakfast, she could hear Gaz saying something about a bet and how he was going to win. She tuned him out and wrote a quick note to advise her guests that there was a platter of cheese and cold meat in the fridge, along with yoghurt and juice. Then she headed to her room for a shower and an early night with a good book.

At the championship course, the next morning, Josh had checked everything with the staff and was sitting in the car with Giovanni and Vincenzo, waiting for Gaz and his friends to turn up.

'It's a crazy idea,' Vincenzo said. 'But it's an elegant solution. Are you sure your knee will hold up?'

'No,' Josh admitted, 'so this could go spectacularly wrong.'

'It won't.' Vincenzo looked at him. 'So, Sophie's special.'

Yes. But Josh wasn't quite prepared to admit this. 'She's a nice woman and I don't like bullies.'

'She's special,' Vincenzo repeated, 'or you wouldn't take a risk like this.'

Oh, help. Josh had forgotten how perceptive Giovanni's father was. 'I barely know her. We only met a few days ago.'

'So?' Vincenzo shrugged. 'I knew the very second I met Maria that she was the one for me.'

Josh thought back to his very first meeting with Sophie. He'd been aghast at her cluelessness. But then he'd met her for her first ski lesson. The second he'd seen her blue eyes properly...

No, no and absolutely no. He wasn't looking for a relationship. He was still tending his wounds from the fallout of what had happened with Annabel, literally as well as figuratively. He didn't *think* Sophie was anything like his ex—she would never have given him such a shocking ultimatum in the first place, let alone dropped a bombshell with such vicious timing—but could he trust his judgement any more?

He didn't want to think about that right now. Thinking instead of focusing on the slope was what had wrecked his life. If he hadn't been distracted, he wouldn't have fallen and damaged his knee to the point where he'd had to give up the career he'd loved so much.

'It's not the case with me and Sophie,' he said.

'Hmm,' was Vincenzo's only comment.

A couple of minutes later, the minibus turned up and Gaz and his friends came to meet them.

Josh introduced them swiftly. 'This is Giovanni Rendini, the resort manager, and Vincenzo Rendini, who owns the resort.'

'You've got friends in high places, then,' Gaz said, raising an eyebrow.

'I have friends in a lot of places.' Josh shrugged. 'I learned long ago that you should treat people properly on your way up. It doesn't matter what level they are: treat people with kindness and respect and they'll do the same for you.' Even though what he was planning wasn't particularly kind, he could still be pleasant about it.

Gaz looked at his friends and scoffed.

'The staff here have come in early to sort out the lifts and the timers for us,' Josh said. 'Do you want a practice run, first?'

Gaz shook his head. 'Bring it on.'

Josh really hoped he'd never been as arrogant as that. 'As you wish. But watch the middle section of the course. It's tricky and the turns are tighter than you'd expect on a normal downhill course.'

'Listen to him.' Gaz addressed his friends and waved a dismissive hand at Josh. 'Anyone would think he's a world champion who's skied this a million times.'

Josh forbore to mention that the last time he'd skied here, he'd come away with two gold medals—for downhill as well as freestyle—and a world championship. They were clearly recreational skiers rather than the sort who followed the sport, because they hadn't recognised him. 'Did you bring energy drinks and bars?' he asked.

'Whatevs.' Gaz rolled his eyes.

'And Josh is right about the course,' Vincenzo added. 'Watch the turns.'

'So you're an expert, are you, old man?' Gaz demanded.

'If by "expert" you mean world champion three times running, then, yes, that would be my dad,' Giovanni said. 'Look him up. Vincenzo Rendini.'

Josh gave the tiniest shake of his head to warn his

friend not to blurt out who *he* was, and Giovanni gave an equally tiny nod of acknowledgement.

'World champion?' Gaz suddenly looked a bit less sure of himself.

Good. About time, Josh thought. 'Want to toss for who's going first?' he asked. 'I'm happy to go last.'

'I'll go first,' Gaz said.

His time was good for an amateur; the next couple from the group did well, too. Then Gaz was back from the chairlift. 'Ha. *Knew* I'd be top,' he crowed, pointing at the board. The next member of the group knocked Gaz off the top spot, leaving Josh feeling pleased.

And finally it was Josh's turn.

He thought of Sophie. Hopefully what he was about to do would make life better for her. For her sake, he needed to get this right.

He stood at the top of the slope and looked down. Today was the first time he'd skied here since his accident; but at least the accident hadn't been on this course, so he didn't have memories to flood into his mind and put him off.

But this was a championship course. He hadn't skied anything as difficult as this in the past year, because he knew his knee wouldn't stand up to it. Was he just about to make the second-biggest mistake of his life?

'You've got this,' Vincenzo said, standing beside him. 'Focus. Remember to look ahead. And their timings are way off what you can do, even without practice. You don't need to take any risks. Just enjoy the run and do what you know you do best.'

'Yeah. Thanks, Vincenzo.'

Josh took a deep breath. He closed his eyes for a moment; and then he was away, his body tucked in tightly for the aerodynamics. As he hurtled down the slope, he felt the adrenalin flood his body, and then the sheer joy of skiing and being at one with the mountain. He made a sharp turn, leaning forward. Another turn. And he was smiling, really smiling, as he looked ahead on the course, judging his speed and his angles.

This was what he was made for.

This was what he'd missed for the last year.

This.

He skied over the finish line, feeling at peace with the world, and took the chairlift back up to the top. As soon as he glanced at the board, he saw that he'd skied much, much more slowly than the last time he'd been on this course. But it was still twenty seconds faster than Gaz.

Guilt pricked his conscience. It was massively unfair for a professional to take on amateurs like this. What he'd just done made him almost as bad as Gaz. Maybe he shouldn't take the money; even though it was for charity, it felt wrong. The fact he'd beaten them so soundly should be enough to make his point and keep them from bullying Sophie—or anyone else—in future.

Gaz was waiting for him with narrowed eyes. 'How the hell did you *do* that?'

Josh shrugged. 'It's all in the turns.'

'Well, you've won.' Gaz looked furious.

'I'm not going to make you pay a penny,' Josh said. 'I simply wanted to make a point. The most important part of the terms of our bet was that you'll treat Sophie and Kitty with respect, and I'll hold you to that.'

Gaz shook his head. 'I'll pay the money we agreed. Nobody says I don't pay my bets.'

'That isn't what I'm saying,' Josh said tiredly. 'And

it wasn't the point of this. Just maybe you can start to think before you act. Treat people decently. Because you never know who they are or what they're going through. Kindness costs nothing and it makes the world a lot better.'

'He's got a point,' Pete, one of the quieter members of the group, said.

'I guess.' Gaz's voice was tight with resentment.

'You're a ski instructor, right? Can we book a coaching session with you?' Pete asked.

Josh shook his head. 'Sorry. I'm fully booked for the next month.'

'Can we at least buy you breakfast?' Pete asked. 'Because—I mean, even though we all lost, skiing here was *amazing*. And we'll pay for the booking fees.'

'No cost. I called in a favour to get the slot,' Josh said.

'The people who opened up, who did the ski lift and the timer—the least we can do is pay them for their time,' Pete said.

'You're right, Pete,' one of the others agreed. 'And we owe you an apology.'

'No, you owe Sophie and Kitty an apology,' Josh corrected.

Pete nodded. 'You're right. We'll apologise.' He looked at Gaz.

Gaz's expression was murderous, but eventually he nodded. 'Yeah.'

Maybe he could make a token gesture so their apology wouldn't stick in their throat and they'd be more encouraged to be nice to Sophie, Josh thought. 'It's not every day you get to ski at a run like this. Why don't we do it again—this time *without* the timers, so we can focus on enjoying the run?'

'Great idea,' Pete said.

Some of the others had dropped the aggressiveness of their stance, too, Josh noticed. Maybe they'd start standing up to their leader and it would make the rest of the week bearable for Sophie. He hoped. 'Let's go.'

Sophie had just finished making the lemon drizzle cake and scones when the chalet door opened and she heard their guests coming in.

Oh, no.

She'd been hoping they'd be out all day on the slopes, as they had yesterday. Or maybe she could sneak out the back way, so they wouldn't notice her...

Too late.

Gaz walked into the kitchen, carrying a box of chocolates. 'These are for you and Kitty.'

'For us?' She felt her eyes widen. 'Why?'

'To say sorry.' He stopped, clearly waiting for her to fill in the rest. *For being obnoxious.*

She didn't have a clue what to say. It was so out of character, given the entitled and boorish way they'd behaved since their arrival. From Pete, the quietest one, she might've understood it. But from Gaz—'gas-bag', as she and Kitty had dubbed him—it didn't ring true. 'Why?' she asked again.

'Let's just say your boyfriend showed us the error of our ways.'

'Boyfriend?'

'The skiing coach. The one you were holding hands in the café with yesterday,' Gaz clarified.

Definitely Josh. Who was definitely not her boyfriend. What had he done?

'We'll, um, watch what we say in future,' Gaz said.

'Thank you,' Sophie said, feeling utterly clueless. Josh was going to have a lot of explaining to do at her ski lesson, this afternoon.

He was already at their meeting place when she arrived.

'Had a good morning?' she asked sweetly.

'Fine, thanks.' He smiled at her. 'You?'

'Preparing dinner for my guests. Who just paid me a visit, when I thought they'd be out skiing all day.'

'Uh-huh.'

'What did you do, Josh?'

He gave her an innocent look. 'I don't know what you mean.'

Oh, yes, he did. She narrowed her eyes at him. 'They apologised. And they bought chocolates for Kitty and me.' She raised her eyebrows at him. 'You told them you were my boyfriend.'

'Actually, I didn't. They assumed it and I didn't correct them.'

'Which is the same thing. It's still a lie.' And she'd had more than enough of lies. Blake had trashed her life with his lies. She'd been lucky to be able to save her staff's jobs and stave off bankruptcy. Dishonesty was a huge red flag for her. She'd started to like Josh, to trust him and the way he was helping her to face her fears. But had she been as hopeless and naive about him as she'd been about Blake? Was he another man like Blake, a habitual liar who treated others cavalierly, using a veneer of charm and saying what he thought people wanted to hear so he could get his own way, and not caring about the effects his actions had on others?

'Sophie, you were upset and I wanted to make things better.'

'By letting them think you're my boyfriend? I'm not even looking to date anyone.' She glared at him. 'And I'm perfectly capable of managing my own problems, thank you very much.'

'They were giving you a hard time. I was trying to make them back off. And it worked.'

'It wasn't just talking, was it?' Because she'd already tried that, and her efforts had been in vain. 'They said you showed them the error of their ways. What did you do?'

He winced. 'I took them down a black run, this morning.'

'Which I assume is the really difficult sort of ski slope?'

'Yes.'

So *that* was why they'd gone out so early. And hadn't she heard them saying something about a bet? 'There's more to it than that, isn't there?'

He blew out a breath. 'OK. I challenged them to a race. If I won, they had to apologise to you and behave better in future.'

She gasped. 'Do you have any idea how insulting that is?'

'It wasn't meant to be insulting.'

'You made me part of a bet!'

'I wanted to get through to them, and it seemed as if the only way to make them think twice about what they were doing was to challenge them.'

'To a *race*.' She shook her head with annoyance. 'Like a teenage boy boasting with his first car.'

'That wasn't the intention. I was honestly trying to help.'

'I didn't ask for your help,' she pointed out quietly.

'OK. I interfered. I apologise.'

But that wasn't what was really getting to her. It was the fact he hadn't been honest. 'How did you even know they could all ski well enough? How did you know they weren't just boasting to make themselves sound good, when they were really just as much of a novice as me?'

'They told me their times skiing Val di Lungo. That's something you can't fake. I knew from that they'd be able to cope with the run.'

'What if one of them had fallen and hurt himself?'

He flinched, suddenly looking haunted. 'Fortunately, they didn't.'

'You *hustled* them, Josh.'

'They deserved it.'

Part of her had to agree. 'Even so, it wasn't your place to step in. I wasn't looking for a knight on a white charger. Or a hero on skis.'

'I got it wrong,' Josh said. 'I won't do it again.'

'Too right, you won't.'

He coughed. 'It's possibly not a good idea to go skiing when you're angry. I don't want you to lose focus and fall.'

'What I want to do right now,' she said, 'is to smack you round the head with my skis.'

'I'm sorry, Sophie. I really did just want to help, but in future I'll trust your judgement and your client management skills.'

'Thank you.'

'So can we start today again? Plan for this afternoon: ski lesson, plus hot chocolate and strudel?'

Part of her wanted to say yes; but part of her was wary of getting too close. 'I'm still cross that you let them think you're my boyfriend.' Another lie, and it really grated. If Josh had asked her out before this had happened, she would've been tempted to say yes. More than tempted. But now he'd shown that lies came easily to him. Even though his intentions had been good, he'd still not been honest: and that wasn't something Sophie could overlook.

'How about,' Josh said, 'we drop the "boy" and I'm just your friend?'

Drop the 'boy'? There was nothing boyish about Josh, except perhaps for his smile. He was all man. Even as she thought it, she found it suddenly hard to breathe. 'You're my skiing teacher,' she said, more to remind herself than to tell him.

'Which puts me nicely in my place,' he said. 'But it doesn't change my offer of friendship. I like you, Sophie. Particularly because you're honest.'

'Which you weren't. You should have told them you're a ski coach and given them, I don't know, some kind of time advantage.'

'Then I wouldn't have been able to take them down a peg or two,' he pointed out.

'And who's going to take *you* down a peg or two?' she retorted.

He grinned. 'Are you offering?'

Part of her enjoyed the flirting; but his lack of honesty still worried her.

When she didn't reply, he looked serious again. 'I also realise now I'm in the wrong. But I'd like to make it up to you. And I'd like to be friends with you, Sophie.'

'Friends.'

'As you said, I know the area. You're new here. Maybe on your days off—or in the middle-of-day bit, when you're not looking after your guests and you have some free time—I could show you a few places.'

'You're my skiing teacher,' she said again, needing to put that little bit of distance between them.

'So we'll operate with two sets of rules,' he said. 'When I'm teaching you, we'll have a professional relationship only. And when I'm not, we'll be friends.'

Sophie thought about it.

Friends with Josh Cavendish.

Defining their relationship would make him safe. She wouldn't be tempted to act on the attraction she felt towards him—and, more importantly, she wouldn't make the same mistakes she'd made with Blake. She wouldn't fall for someone who had such a cavalier disregard for the truth—though, to be fair, Josh had seemed penitent once she'd pointed out what damage his lies could've done.

'All right,' she said. 'We'll be friends.'

'Good.'

She ignored the fact that his smile made her heart give a funny little flip.

Even though she was still a bit cross with him, she enjoyed every second on the slopes—and she enjoyed going to the café with him afterwards, when he bought them both hot chocolate and strudel. If Gaz and his crew came in today, it would be very different; she could stay relaxed and enjoy her cake.

'So, tomorrow,' Josh said, 'would you like to go to the Christmas market? It's in the next valley along and it's very pretty. If we switch your lesson to the morning, we could have lunch there.'

He'd offered her friendship; weirdly, this felt more as if they were planning a date.

She damped down the little flutter of adrenalin. It *wasn't* a date. And Blake had taught her that she was a rubbish judge of men. Friendship was the sensible option. 'Don't you have other students?'

'I do, but none of them are booked in for tomorrow,' he said.

'All right. A trip to the Christmas market sounds really nice. Provided I buy you lunch,' she said.

'OK. We'll drop your skis back at my place after the lesson,' he said, 'and then I'll make sure we've collected them and you're back at your chalet before afternoon tea.'

'Sounds like a good plan,' she said with a smile.

His answering smile made her heart feel as if it had done an acrobatic—and anatomically impossible—ski jump...

CHAPTER FIVE

THE CHALET GUESTS weren't obnoxious that evening and, when Sophie served the cheeseboard with her home-made rosemary crackers and ran them through the local specialty cheeses, they actually asked her and Kitty to join them for a glass of wine and to share the cheese.

'Whatever your Josh said to them, it worked,' Kitty said to Sophie in the kitchen afterwards.

'He's not *my* Josh,' Sophie said with a smile. And she didn't have the heart to disillusion the younger woman by telling her about the downhill ski race and how Josh had hustled them.

'A guy only does something like that if he likes you,' Kitty said. 'And I mean *like* like.'

'We're friends,' Sophie said.

'Hmm,' Kitty said.

Sophie decided not to mention the trip to the Christmas market, not wanting Kitty to misinterpret it. But she was awake ridiculously early, the next morning, full of anticipation. Only because she'd be seeing more of the area, she tried to convince herself. Though, if she let herself face the truth, it was actually because she'd be spending more time with Josh.

She enjoyed her skiing lesson. 'I think I'm starting

to get my ski legs, now,' she told Josh as they headed back to his chalet.

'Good. We'll get you on a blue run, next week,' he said.

'One of the ones where I have to take a chairlift to get to the top?' The idea was daunting. And what if she fell off the chairlift? At least the button lift meant she was close to the ground...

Maybe her fear had shown in her voice, because Josh said, 'Remember how you felt, the very first time you were on the nursery slope? But you managed that. When you went up to the green slope, that felt scary—but look how much you enjoyed it today. The first time you do a blue run, you'll worry because it's the unknown. But then you'll get to the bottom, realise you're OK, and then you'll be ready to do it all over again,' he told her. 'Trust me. I wouldn't let you do it if you weren't able to. I hate it when experienced skiers drag their novice friends into something they're not ready to cope with and scare them. I'd never do that to anyone.'

She could see the sincerity on his face. But, even so, could she take the risk of really trusting him with herself? What was the saying? Fool me once, shame on you; fool me twice, shame on me. Blake had fooled her. What if Josh turned out to be another Blake?

Or maybe she was being unfair. Paranoid. Apart from Blake, most people lived up to her theory that people were nice if you gave them the chance to be. Was she going to let Blake take her ability to trust from her, as well?

'I guess. Sorry.' She took a deep breath. 'Just being ridiculous.'

'Actually,' he said, 'I admire you. You were clearly

terrified of the idea of skiing, but you've made yourself do it.'

To prove to herself that she could. To get her confidence and self-esteem back. It was that, or find herself inhabiting a smaller and smaller comfort zone every day. 'I'm trying,' she said.

When they got to his chalet, Sophie was surprised by how small it seemed. Did he live alone or did he share his space with another instructor? Though it felt rude to ask. He didn't offer to show her round; he simply propped her skis and poles in the rack next to his in the hallway.

'Christmas market, here we come,' he said with a smile, and drove her to the next valley.

'I'm not sure I'd be brave enough to drive, out here,' she said. 'It's not just because it means driving on the other side of the road. There's the snow piled up on the side, the fact the roads are so steep and with hairpin bends, and that sheer drop on one side.'

'You'd be surprised how quickly you get used to it,' Josh said. 'And they're used to dealing with snow here. It's not like England, where a couple of centimetres of snow makes everything grind to a halt.'

Maybe driving the roads here was a challenge she'd set herself before she went back to England. Once she'd conquered a blue ski run.

She caught her breath as they skirted the mountain and she saw the view of the valleys. 'That's amazing,' she said. 'I don't think I've ever seen anything so beautiful.'

'It's pretty spectacular,' he said. 'With any luck we'll catch the sunset on the way back to Pendio di Cristallo; the mountains and the snow turn pink.'

'That sounds wonderful,' she said. 'It was definitely a good idea to come here.'

'The mountains are a good place to think,' he said.

Once he'd parked, they walked together through the streets. Evergreen wreaths were strung across the cobbled streets between the houses and the shops, twinkling with brilliant white lights; some of the streets to the side had strings of icicle lights rather than the evergreen swags, with white wicker hearts suspended every so often along the string.

'This is so pretty,' she said. 'I love the Christmas lights in London, but our snow turns to grey slush. Here—it's just what I imagined Christmas would be like in the Alps. It looks like a real-life winter wonderland.'

Just as she said it, she could feel her feet going from beneath her. Oh, no. She was going to make a fool of herself by falling over—and the snow wasn't as deep here as it was on the piste. This was going to hurt…

'Hey.' Josh caught her before she fell, and drew her close against him, anchoring her.

And it felt as if all her breath had suddenly left her lungs.

Josh had supported her before, on the slopes. But that was different. That was him acting as her skiing instructor. This felt like something else. Something that made her heart beat faster, her breathing shallow, and what felt like pure adrenalin fizz through her veins.

At the same time as thrilling her, it worried her.

Josh had suggested being friends. But what she was feeling right now was nothing like friendship. It was sheer, heady attraction. Not just physical; she liked him, too. Instinctively. He felt like the sort of man you could rely on.

Then again, hadn't she made that mistake with Blake? A mistake that had cost her her business, her self-respect and her confidence. She knew she'd never get her money back, but she wanted the rest of it back.

'OK?' he asked.

'Yes,' she fibbed. 'Sorry. It's a bit slippery underfoot.'

He didn't release her; instead, he kept her arm tucked through his. 'Hang on to me. If you feel your feet sliding, hang on more tightly.'

What if she pulled him over?

Either it was written all over her face or she'd said it aloud, because he reassured her, 'You won't pull me over.'

And oh, that smile.

It actually took her breath away.

She needed a large dose of common sense. Fast. To stop herself thinking how close he was, how easy it would be to reach up and touch her mouth to his...

Please don't let any of this show in her expression.

And she was really glad of her oversized sunglasses. Hopefully they'd go a long way to hiding her thoughts. The last thing she wanted was for Josh to realise how attracted to him she was. He'd made it very clear that this was friendship only.

'Thank you,' she just about managed to mumble, and walked with him into the village; every fibre of her being was aware of his closeness. His strength.

Josh had noticed that, even though Sophie worried about things, she still just got on with it and did it—like the skiing. It had clearly been daunting for her, but she'd pushed herself out of her comfort zone. He liked that.

He liked *her*.

She was really easy to be with. And the way she saw things, the way she found delight in things he'd taken for granted, made him feel different. Alive. Connected.

He'd always liked the Christmas season in the Dolomites, but he'd been so jaded since his accident that last year had been a blur. This year, he was seeing things through Sophie's eyes. Instead of it being the commercial Christmas crush, with everything all lumped together, everything seemed bright and sparkly, with tiny details jumping out at him. It was all fresh and new, as if he was seeing it for the very first time.

'Oh, wow, just look at this!' she said as they rounded the corner into the town's main square, where the Christmas market was being held. The area was packed with wooden stalls, all festooned with strings of fairy lights.

'Even in the middle of the day, it's stunning. After dark, this place must really be a winter wonderland,' she said.

There were Christmas trees scattered about the market, and there was a particularly large one in the centre of the square, decorated with lights and huge red baubles. But the thing that seemed to draw Sophie most was the snow on the branches.

'Imagine that. Christmas trees decorated by nature with real snow.' Her face was full of delight. 'I've never seen anything so gorgeous. I mean, the wreaths at the Christmas markets and shops in London are pretty— but here it's so much more natural.'

Next to the enormous Christmas tree was a large reindeer made of lights with a red bauble on its nose.

'Do you mind if we stop so I can take a picture of this?' she asked. 'My best friend would love it.'

'Better than that, why don't I take a picture of you next to the reindeer?' he suggested.

'Thank you.' She beamed and handed him her phone.

He took the snap, enjoying her enthusiasm. Without her, he probably wouldn't have even bothered visiting the Christmas market. With her, he was seeing a lot more than he would usually notice. Shapes and colours and light: things that had always merged into the background for him. Through Sophie's eyes, they weren't just commonplace, everyday things. She noticed them, enjoyed them to the full, and drew them to his attention so he could enjoy them, too.

'This is wonderful,' she said. 'Look, there's a nativity scene over there.' They went over to take a closer look, and she oohed and aahed over the delicate work.

'You get that in most Italian towns,' he said. 'And there will be something like this in the windows of most of the shops. It's a tradition over here.'

'It's so perfect. The snow-globes, and the wooden ornaments, the gingerbread and the candles. And those wreaths over there, made from dried oranges and cinnamon sticks: they smell of Christmas, too.' She sniffed. 'Freshly baked cookies, roasted chestnuts…this feels like Christmas. Everything. The sights, the smells, the sounds…'

All the senses. The taste of Christmas foods and spiced hot chocolate. The soft feel of the Christmas textiles. The cool crispness of the air. Put together, they magnified the experience for him, too. Instead of being just another tourist attraction, the market felt *special*.

A guitarist, a singer, a keyboard-player and a drummer were set up in one part of the square, singing carols and Christmas pop songs in a variety of languages.

'Do you mind if I buy some Christmas presents?' she asked.

'Sure. I'll carry your bags for you,' he offered.

'Thanks.' She dawdled over the delicate lacy shawls, and the beautifully knitted scarves, hats and gloves.

The food stalls attracted her, too, particularly the one with all the Christmas cookies.

'I can't decide which ones to try,' she said. 'Maybe the glazed ones with rainbow sprinkles?'

'Those ones are usually flavoured with anise,' he said, 'which people either love or hate.'

'True. And look at those ones with layers: orange, white and chocolate. I need to get some of those, too.' She ended up buying a selection of cookies.

'You're seriously going to eat all these?' he asked.

She laughed. 'No, but I do want to try a bit of everything and see which ones I'd like to make or do my own twist on for afternoon tea for our guests. I know I could do traditional English mince pies, or American sugar and cinnamon cookies, but I want to do something local. You're probably right about anise not being the most guest-friendly choice, but I want to see what the texture's like. I could maybe do a vanilla version. Or cinnamon.'

'Let me take the bag for you,' he said, 'so you've got your hands free.'

'Thanks. That's lovely of you.' She rewarded him with a smile that made his heart feel as if it had done a backflip.

He tried to remind himself of the lines they'd drawn, but her enthusiasm was infectious and irresistible. And it was so good to *feel* something again, instead of being in an insulated box.

She was entranced by the stall selling panettone, and another with all kinds of flavoured oils, and one with various traditional sauces and jams.

And then they came to the stall selling *zelten*.

'What's this?' she asked, pointing to the words on the board. 'Obviously it's some kind of cake. But my Italian's too basic to translate.'

'I don't know what *zelten* is, either,' he admitted. 'Though it sounds German; in this part of the Dolomites we're on the border with Austria, so the people here speak German as well as Italian. Some speak Ladin, which is the original language of this area.'

'Latin?' she asked.

'Ladin,' he corrected with a smile. 'Some of the resort staff speak it, so the Rendinis all speak it, as well as Italian, German, English and French. They taught me a little; you'd say *bun dé* instead of *buon giorno* or *Guten Morgen*.'

She looked at him with her head tipped slightly to one side. 'How many languages do you speak, Josh?'

'Four,' he said, 'simply because of my job. I did French and German at school, but I picked up Italian as I went along, and a smattering of a few others. It's nice to speak to people in their own language, even if I only know a few words; it puts them at ease.'

'In that case,' she said, 'would you mind acting as a translator for me, please, and ask the stall-keeper what *zelten* is for me?'

'Sure.' Josh spoke in rapid Italian, but the stall-keeper replied in English.

'It's a traditional sweet bread, made with yeast and dried fruits soaked in rum or brandy.'

'So a bit like a boozy English hot cross bun,' she said thoughtfully.

Josh stood by as she and the stall-keeper traded recipes and suggestions. Although the foodie talk mostly went over his head, he was fascinated by Sophie. By her intense focus and concentration, the way she'd switched so seamlessly from tourist to professional.

What would it be like if she focused on him? Touching, tasting, learning what made him groan with pleasure...

He shook himself.

No.

He was absolutely not going to have a fling with Sophie Harris, whatever his body might be urging him to do. This was about...

Actually, he didn't know what it was about. At all.

But it had been so long since he'd wanted to let anyone else into his life, he was beginning to think that he should go with his feelings. Sophie had talked about challenging herself, about pushing past her boundaries to get her confidence back. Maybe he needed to do the same.

Could he take a risk with her?

Annabel had left him feeling used. Miserable. And he'd realised that his ex had seen him as a way of providing the lifestyle she wanted. For her, he'd been a celebrity boyfriend—a trophy boyfriend, even—so she'd be invited to the right parties: the son of a billionaire, to whom money was no object. She hadn't seen him for himself, or wanted him for himself.

That realisation had hurt even more than the physical pain of his damaged knee. And, when it was clear that his future was going to be very different from the way things had been before the accident, Annabel had been quick to dump him—and to get her story out there first. By the time he'd realised what was happening, any denials would've been too little and too late.

So he'd melted quietly into the background, knowing that the best way to kill a story was to deny it oxygen. Yes, it hurt that people thought he'd be the kind of heartless bastard who'd dump his fiancée after a miscarriage; but sticking Annabel with a defamation suit would've made the situation even worse. People would've murmured about him trying to cover up the truth, buying his way out of a situation, and acting like a bully. None of which was true.

He was trying not to dwell on it. Trying not to let the hurt shape who he was. And he was beginning to think that maybe Sophie was the one who could help him move on from the past, because with her he felt different. With her, he could see the joy again. And maybe he could help her move on from the guy who'd let her down, too.

Sophie was talking rapidly into her phone, now; he tuned back in and realised that she was dictating a recipe from the stall-keeper, who was adding little bits here and there when she stopped, clearly enjoying sharing. She was lit up from the inside, shining just as brightly as the fairy lights draped over all the little stalls.

And she bought every single variation the shopkeeper was selling. 'This will be afternoon tea for my guests tomorrow,' she said. 'But Ruggiero's given me a recipe and some of his favourite tweaks, so I'm going to try making them myself as well.'

Josh smiled. 'I know you're a chef, but you're *such* a foodie.'

'Busted,' she said with a grin. 'I love my job. I love making food for people. And I want to extend my repertoire a bit while I'm here.' She looked at him. 'It's my day off tomorrow, so I'm thinking about trialling some recipes. If you're free, do you fancy being my guinea pig?' Then she added swiftly, 'As a friend.'

Of course. A stark reminder of the boundary he'd set and was starting to wish he hadn't.

'Your day off, and you're spending it cooking?' he asked.

'I love what I do,' she said. 'For me it isn't just my job.'

He knew how that felt—or how it had used to feel. It was something he missed dreadfully. Teaching novices had its own reward, but it wasn't the same as competing. He needed more.

'Your day off,' he said again. 'So does that mean you're free in the evening as well?'

'Yes.'

He looked at her. 'OK, how about tomorrow I'm your guinea pig, I do the washing up, and then I take you out to dinner?'

Her blue eyes looked huge. 'As friends?' she checked.

No. As a date. The idea made him feel hot all over, anticipation and excitement bursting through his veins, but the wariness in her expression meant he needed to hold back. For now. He'd spend tomorrow trying to get her to see him as something else. 'As friends,' he confirmed.

'That'd be nice,' she said. 'Thank you.'

They wandered through the market, and she insisted on buying them lunch at one of the food stalls.

'Porchetta paninis are good and they're traditional here around Christmastime,' he said. 'Pork, stuffed with garlic and herbs, then slow-roasted.'

'Gorgeous,' she said after her first taste. 'Fennel, sage and rosemary.'

'It amazes me that you can work out what's in something so quickly,' he said.

'Practice,' she said simply. 'Just as I suppose you can look at a ski slope and know exactly what the snow's going to be like and how it'll affect the way you ski.'

'I guess,' he said.

'And I want to try these cookies,' she said when they'd finished their paninis, and nibbled a corner from one of the tri-coloured amaretto ones. 'Oh, now this is excellent. Try this.'

Before he realised what was happening, she was holding the cookie to his mouth in just the way that a lover would offer a taste.

His libido practically sat up and begged.

And he couldn't help watching her mouth. He noticed that her mouth parted slightly just as he opened his lips: almost as if she were offering a kiss.

He didn't have a clue what the cookie tasted like, and mumbled something anodyne. All he could think about was how *she* might taste…

He just about stopped himself from wrapping his arms round her, drawing her close and kissing her properly. And to his relief she didn't seem to notice anything. 'Lovely,' he managed, putting on his brightest smile.

'I'm definitely going to find a recipe for these,' she said. 'Oh—and I want to stop here.'

It was a stall selling filigree cones that looked like stylised Christmas trees, decorated with various Christmassy shapes; underneath the cone, there was space for a tea-light, and the heat of the candle made the Christmas tree twirl round. 'I love this sort of thing,' she said. 'So pretty and Christmassy.' She chose a reindeer one, which the stall-holder wrapped for her.

Normally, Josh would barely have even noticed the stall; but now he could see the romance of it. A room lit by candles, looking out on snow. And the fantasy blooming in his head had Sophie firmly at the centre.

This was dangerous.

He'd told himself he didn't want to get involved with anyone after Annabel. And yet Sophie drew him. The more time he spent with her, the more irresistible she became.

At another stall, where they sold musical boxes, he couldn't resist one that played the Sugar Plum Fairy's dance from *The Nutcracker*. 'For my niece,' he said. 'Willow's three. She's just started ballet lessons. She'll love this.'

And Sophie found a wooden crib mobile which played 'Twinkle Twinkle Little Star', with a moon and stars hanging down.

'This is so lovely! I want to get this for Hannah's baby—my godson-to-be,' she said. 'Her due date's the end of January, so I'll be back in England just in time for the birth.'

'You're not staying for the whole of the season?' he asked, surprised.

'I have a three-month contract,' she said.

He was still processing that she'd be leaving sooner than he'd expected. But it also meant she'd be here on December the twenty-fifth. And Sophie loved Christmas. Something didn't quite feel right. Why would she spend Christmas miles away from her friends and her family? 'Given that you clearly love Christmas, won't it be hard for you, not seeing your family for Christmas?' he asked.

'Actually, it'll be the fourth Christmas I haven't seen my family,' she said quietly. 'My parents were killed in a car crash.'

He sucked in a breath. 'I'm so sorry.'

She gave him a sad little smile of acknowledgement. 'Me, too. They were the best parents I could've asked for. I loved them so much. And I have to admit I was raging for a while, afterwards; the way I saw it, if someone had to die, why couldn't it have been someone mean and horrible, rather than them?'

'That's understandable,' he said. 'Tell me about them—if it doesn't hurt,' he added swiftly.

'Mum worked in a museum,' Sophie said. 'I loved all the stories she could tell me about the exhibits. The people who wore the clothes or cooked with the pots, and what their lives were like. She made it all come alive for me.' She smiled. 'She used to take me for a proper afternoon tea, too, with sandwiches and cakes and scones.'

Josh had a pretty good idea where Sophie's love of food had started. 'She sounds lovely.'

'She was.'

'What about your dad?'

'He worked in insurance. My gran died from a heart attack, so he used to fundraise for a heart charity in his spare time. Everything from doing a ten k run to organising a bake sale in the office. But, even though they both had busy jobs and busy lives, they always made time for me.'

Just as his parents had, too. He'd grown up knowing he was loved.

'What about your aunts and uncles? Grandparents?'

She shrugged. 'Mum and Dad were both only children, born late, so I don't really have any family: but I'm lucky that I have good friends. Hannah always invites me to spend Christmas with her family.'

I don't really have any family.

That momentary bleakness in her face.

And Josh was guiltily aware that he took his family for granted, all their love and support. He made a mental note to ring his parents and his sister that evening, and tell them he loved them. Because he *did* love them. And he realised now he didn't say it enough.

'I'm sorry,' he said again. 'I really didn't mean to bring up difficult memories for you.'

'It's fine.' She took his hand and squeezed it briefly. 'You weren't to know. And I have only happy memories of my parents. I'm so much luckier than many people.'

She was amazing. Most people in her position would still have dwelt on the unfairness of the loss. Yet Sophie seemed to take it in her stride.

It made him wonder just what had happened to make her come here to Pendio di Cristallo, so far out of her comfort zone.

'Come on. I have more shopping to do,' she said lightly. 'I saw a knitted hat back there that would look so cute on Kitty.'

What could he do but go along with her?

On the way back to Pendio di Cristallo, he stopped at another village.

'I think you'll like this,' he said. 'Every year, there's a snow sculpture exhibition here. The artists get a three-metre cube of pressed snow; they're allowed to use water, a saw, a shovel, and their imagination.'

And he loved the fact that she was so entranced by the exhibition: everything from Santa in his sleigh with his reindeer, through to a Christmas tree, a dazzling shooting star, penguins, a rose, and a dramatic lion with a huge mane.

'I assume this one's a Greek—well, Roman—god?' she asked by a winged statue. 'Who's the Roman god of winter?'

'I have no idea.' He looked it up on his phone. 'Apparently Boreas was the purple-winged Greek god of the north wind and winter. His Roman name was Aquilo.'

'We've both learned something new today.' She paused before a beautifully detailed geometric snowflake. 'This is gorgeous. I'd love a small version of this in a snow-globe, or as a pendant.' She looked thoughtful. 'That'd be a good theme for an afternoon tea. Snowflakes. Coconut's the obvious thing there—some kind of mousse cake made into the shape of a ball. Or a feathery glaze on a pastry, or a tiny snowflake decoration made from white chocolate.'

'I love the fact you see things in terms of food,' he said.

She shrugged. 'A dress designer would see things in terms of fabric, and someone who makes jewellery would see things in terms of shapes, stones and metal.'

'True. But I think I've seen the Christmas market through different eyes today, thanks to you.'

'When you're showing someone round,' she said, 'you notice things all over again instead of taking them for granted.'

'I guess,' he said. 'But thank you anyway.'

When they went back to his car, the sun was beginning to set.

'I know you told me, but I still can't believe the mountains really do turn pink at sunset,' she said. 'They look so beautiful.'

'And sunrise. It's called *enrosadira*,' he said. 'There's a very elaborate story about it being because the king of the dwarfs kidnapped a princess and hid her in his rose garden; although he had an invisible cloak to hide him, the movement of the roses as he walked through them gave his position away to the guards who were looking for her. When they captured him, he cursed the roses for giving him away, saying they'd never be seen again by day or night—but he forgot to mention sunset and sunrise, and that's when the roses appear on the mountain.'

'Interesting story. What happened to the princess?' she asked.

'No idea.' He looked at her. 'What would you want to happen?'

'Justice for the princess,' she said promptly. 'I'd want her to be queen in her own right so she could order the king to do something to make up for kidnapping her.'

'Something to make the world a better place.'

'Exactly,' she said. 'The problem with most fairy stories is that the heroine is always feeble and has to be rescued by the prince.'

'So you'd want the heroine to rescue the prince?'

'No. I'd want them to rescue each other,' she said.

Rescue each other? That had never occurred to him before, and he rather liked the idea.

Rescuing her from Gaz and his friends had definitely made Josh feel better. But Sophie couldn't rescue him. Not unless she changed careers completely and invented a new system for fixing knees. And that wasn't going to happen.

'So what's the real reason why the mountains look pink at sunrise and sunset?' she asked.

'The composition of the stone—calcium carbonate and magnesium—and the way it reflects the light.' He glanced at her. 'Maybe on one of your days off, weather permitting, I can take you skiing at dawn. Or at least somewhere you'll be able to enjoy watching the sun rising over the slopes.'

'I'd like that,' she said.

They picked up her skis and poles from his chalet, and he dropped her back at her chalet.

'Thank you for today. I've really enjoyed it,' she said. She leaned forward to kiss his cheek, but somehow her lips ended up brushing the corner of his mouth.

In response, his mouth tingled and his skin suddenly felt too tight. Josh was shocked to realise just how much he wanted to kiss Sophie properly; she was the first woman he'd wanted to kiss since Annabel.

Though he also knew Sophie was wary; if he did what he really wanted to do, hauling her into his arms and kissing her until they were both dizzy, she'd run a mile. He was pretty sure that she felt some kind of attraction towards him, because her pupils were huge and there was a bloom of colour in her cheeks, but he knew he needed to take this more slowly.

Please let his voice sound normal so it didn't make her back away.

'You're very welcome,' he said, relieved to hear that he sounded normal. 'I'll see you for your ski lesson at half-past nine, and then I'll be your kitchen assistant, and then we'll go somewhere for dinner?'

The whole day with her.

If anyone had suggested to him even a month ago that he'd look forward to spending the whole day with someone, he would've laughed.

But he was really looking forward to it. Getting to know her better. Finding out what made her tick. And maybe, just maybe, she'd start to let him closer.

'See you at half-past nine,' she said. 'And thank you again. Today's been utterly lovely. A proper winter wonderland.'

'My pleasure,' he said.

And with any luck he could talk a certain restaurant into squeezing in a table for him: because he really, really wanted her to love having dinner out with him tomorrow night. To the point where she'd agree to change the terms of their friendship into something else.

CHAPTER SIX

'GET THE LETTERS in the right order,' Sophie told herself in the mirror. 'S-K-I-S, not K-I-S-S.'

But she couldn't stop thinking about last night.

What she'd intended as a friendly kiss on the cheek to say thank you had turned into something else entirely. She'd ended up kissing the corner of Josh's mouth, instead. And, for a moment, she'd thought that he was going to kiss her back.

But he'd drawn very strict lines, not to be crossed. They'd agreed that while he was teaching her, he was her ski instructor; and when he wasn't, he would be her friend.

Nowhere had either of them said anything about being lovers.

He hadn't mentioned a partner. But surely he wouldn't have taken her out yesterday if he'd had one? Because there had been definite moments when it had felt like a date. When he'd told her to hang on to him. When she'd fed him the cookie. When he'd taken her to the snow sculpture exhibition. When he'd pointed out the pink mountain peaks and told her that crazy story about the roses.

When she'd accidentally kissed the corner of his mouth in the car.

She really was going to have to get a grip.

If she didn't stop mooning about, she'd fall over and make a complete idiot of herself during the lesson.

They were absolutely *not* dating. She wasn't looking for any kind of romance. Josh was a nice guy—but Blake had seemed like a nice guy, too. And he'd let her down so badly. She didn't want to put herself in that position ever again. Her time here was meant to be about picking herself up and dusting herself off and getting her confidence back.

Even so, there were butterflies in her stomach and her pulse kicked up several notches when she saw him. Her mouth was tingling, too. What would it be like to kiss Josh properly? In the snow, with huge fluffy flakes falling gently around them? The idea made a shiver of pure desire ripple down her spine.

To make things worse, Josh was strictly professional with her throughout the entire lesson. He could hardly make it any clearer that he wasn't interested in her as anything other than a student and a friend.

'So do you still need me for kitchen assistant duties this morning?' he asked.

'If you're still free,' she said carefully, wanting to ask if anyone would actually mind him spending time with her—but holding herself back, because if she asked that it would be obvious that she was starting to have feelings for him. If those feelings weren't reciprocated, it would make everything super-awkward.

'I'm looking forward to it.'

As her friend. Nothing more than friends, she reminded herself as they walked back to her chalet.

* * *

Josh had kept himself under iron control during the lesson and hadn't let himself think of Sophie as anything other than a pupil.

Now they were back off that professional footing, supposedly in the friend zone. But he couldn't stop thinking of that kiss and wondering what it would take to make Sophie truly kiss him.

She'd seen him in his element, on skis; he was finally going to see her in hers. And he couldn't wait.

Everything was laid out neatly in the kitchen.

'So what can I do?' he asked.

'Make coffee?' she suggested. 'I like mine with a dash of milk, no sugar.'

'Got it.' And everything was in an obvious place—for the guests, he presumed—so it was easy for him to make them both a coffee. 'So what are you making?'

'*Zelten* and three types of cookie. Kitty, bless her, nipped to the supermarket this morning for the bits I needed.'

'Right.' He watched her measure things into a mixing bowl. 'No scales?'

'I measure by volume,' she said. 'It's not quite as accurate, but it's easier for me.'

'Because of your dyslexia?' he guessed.

'I'm OK with numbers, unless it's a tricky font,' she said. 'It's really certain letters. And you don't want to see my handwriting.' She smiled. 'Which is why I dictate to my phone rather than write. There's less chance of me getting it wrong.'

'I noticed you doing that yesterday, when the guy at the *zelten* stall was talking to you.'

'It just makes life easier.' She smiled at him, and his pulse ratcheted up a notch. 'Thanks for the coffee.'

'Pleasure. What else can I do?'

'Sit and chat to me.'

'You can talk to someone while you're making something for the first time? You don't have to concentrate?'

She grinned. 'I have two X chromosomes. It means I can multi-task.'

'You sound like my sister,' he said. And funny how he suddenly missed Lauren. He had a feeling she'd like Sophie, whereas he knew Lauren had never really liked Annabel.

'Willow's mum?'

She'd remembered that? He was impressed. 'Yes. Her name's Lauren.'

'Is she younger or older than you?' Sophie asked.

'Two years older,' he said.

'It must've been nice, growing up with a sibling.' She looked slightly wistful. 'Mum couldn't have any more kids after me, and she always said she felt guilty about me being an only one. But I had Hannah.'

'Yeah, it was nice. We've always got on well and Lauren looked out for me when I was little.' Not just then: she still did. She'd flown straight out to his hospital bedside after the accident to support him. And, when the surgeon had broken the bad news a few months ago, she'd sat him down and told him that if he wanted to work at Cavendish Software, she'd do whatever it took to help him be happy there—including stepping aside so he could run the place. He'd hugged her and told her he loved her, and no way was he shoving her out of the way because in his view she was the best one to take over from their dad. As for him: he just needed to work out what he wanted to do with his time, now he couldn't do his dream job any more.

He watched Sophie's hands as she measured and mixed. It was the first time he'd seen her at work, and he noticed that she shone from the inside out. This wasn't Sophie the student, who was scared of the snow but was absolutely determined to push herself past her fear; this was Sophie the professional, in her element, confident and secure in her knowledge. Strong.

An anchor.

He'd felt adrift, this past year. Was Sophie the one who could be his anchor, help him find out who he was, now he couldn't be a champion skier any more? And could he, in turn, help her push past what was holding her back?

He remembered what she'd said about fairy tales when they'd watched the mountains turn pink in the sunset. *I'd want them to rescue each other.*

Could they do that?

He looked at her. She was glowing. He wanted to be the reason why she glowed like that, too. And he really, really wanted to kiss her. To find out how it would feel if she held him close, matched him kiss for kiss. To find out how those beautiful, capable hands would feel against his skin.

To distract himself, he asked, 'So how did you end up working here?'

'I signed up with a temp agency,' she said.

'OK,' he said, 'but how does that fit in with what you said before about someone letting you down?'

She sighed. 'All right. You might as well know the depths of my stupidity, though please don't judge me for it. I despise myself enough.' She rolled her eyes.

'When Mum and Dad died, they left everything to me. The owners of the restaurant where I was working as head chef wanted to retire and sell the restaurant. I loved the restaurant, and I got on well with all the staff, so I decided to take the leap and buy it. I tweaked things a little bit, so I could put my own stamp on it, but I was still the head chef, and my team had stability.' She beat the cookie batter a little bit harder. 'I had been thinking about expanding. It wasn't just empire-building. At catering college, one of the tutors noticed I was struggling with the paperwork side and she was the one who taught me a few workarounds. She made a real difference to me. Just like the owners of the restaurant who took me on, going by my references rather than by my exam results. I wanted to pay it forward and give other people a chance, too.'

He liked that. And maybe she was the one who could help him with the idea he'd been mulling over, about helping people with disabilities learn to ski. She might have an interesting take on how it could work.

Though right now wasn't about him. It was about her.

'So you were going to open a second restaurant?'

She nodded. 'I'd actually found premises I liked. But it didn't happen, because everything went wrong.'

'Someone gazumped you? The building had problems you only found out about when you started renovations—it turned out to be a money pit?' he guessed.

'No,' she said. 'As I said, it was my own stupid fault.' She took a deep breath. 'I didn't date that much at college. Nothing serious. I was focused on getting through my exams and getting my career off the ground. And then, after my parents died, I kind of buried myself in the business. It's how I met Blake. He was the restaurant's admin manager. We started dating after I bought the restaurant. I loved him and I thought he loved me. When he asked me to marry him, I said yes.' She looked away. 'A few months later, he got me to change bank accounts, to one that would pay me interest on my balance.'

Josh had a nasty feeling he knew where this was going. She'd said she'd trusted someone who'd let her down. He'd thought that maybe the guy had been unfaithful, but it was starting to sound as if it was a different sort of cheating.

'Blake was engaged to me. He'd been the restaurant's admin manager for a couple of years. Of course I trusted him,' Sophie said. 'You don't agree to marry someone you don't trust, do you?'

'No.' But clearly her trust had been misplaced.

She shrugged. 'He was a signatory on the restaurant's account because he sorted out the payments to suppliers and the wages. I hadn't realised there was an overdraft facility on the account—at least, not the size of the overdraft.'

'He emptied your account?'

'The day before the wages came out—and the day before all the suppliers should've been paid.' She blew out a breath. 'And that's when I found out about the overdraft. Because he took that to the max, too.'

'But—if he emptied your account and ran up an overdraft without your knowledge, that was fraud. You can get the money back.'

'The money bounced around a bit and ended up in an offshore account that can't be touched. And Blake himself has left the country. The police traced him to Spain, but then the trail went cold. Hannah thinks he went somewhere that doesn't have an extradition treaty with England, so I can kiss the money goodbye.'

'That's terrible. There must be something you can do.'

She shook her head. 'Believe me, if there was a way to get the money back, Hannah would know—she's a lawyer—or one of her colleagues would know and be able to help. The only way I could pay all the money I owed and wipe out the overdraft was to sell the restaurant. And who's going to employ someone who made such a huge mistake? Who's going to lend money to someone to start up another business when their last one crashed so spectacularly? The only job I could get after I sold up was a temporary one. *This* one.' She shrugged. 'So there you have it. I made a bad judgement and I'm paying for it now.'

Just as he'd made a bad judgement: letting his fight with Annabel distract his concentration. A few seconds had changed his entire life. 'I know what it's like to make a really bad mistake,' he said. 'I'm sorry your ex cheated you like that.'

'So am I.'

'Are you sure you were liable with the bank, though? You didn't know about the extent of the overdraft, and you weren't the one who emptied the account.'

'I signed the contract, he was a signatory, and nobody coerced me,' she pointed out.

'Who read the contract over for you?' he asked. 'I know you said your best friend's a lawyer, so she would know about contracts, surely?'

She winced. 'At the time, I couldn't really ask her.'

Josh thought about it. Sophie had said the baby was due at the end of January. He made a rapid calculation.

Maybe when this had all happened, Hannah was at the early stages of pregnancy and things were complicated. 'So who read the contract over for you?' he asked again, his voice soft.

'Blake.'

'And he read out what you wanted to hear instead of what was actually in the contract?'

She narrowed her eyes at him. 'I'm dyslexic, not incapable.'

'Of course you're not incapable.' He frowned. 'But you said yourself that certain letters give you trouble. I'm assuming you didn't get an electronic copy of the thing that you could run through your text-to-speech reader yourself?'

'No.'

'Then in your shoes I would've wanted someone else to double-check the paperwork for me. Someone I trusted.'

'Which is precisely what I did,' she pointed out. 'I trusted Blake. He'd worked with me for a couple of years. We'd dated for a year and we'd been engaged for another. Why would he ask me to marry him and then scam me?'

'Because some people aren't very nice?' Josh suggested. 'Think about how many people think they've fallen in love with someone they've met on the internet, help them out with money—and then discover it was all a con.'

'When I look back, I remember he didn't push me to set a date for the wedding. I thought he was being kind, being flexible and not putting any pressure on me when I was trying to expand the business. But now I can see it wasn't that at all. He never had any intention of marrying me, did he?' She shook her head. 'I *hate* this. Before Blake, I used to think everyone was nice until proven otherwise. It was the way I was brought up. Give someone a chance to be their best, and they will—but it's been hard to believe that since Blake. And I hate that he's taken that away from me. That I can't trust people, the way I did in the past. I suspect everyone's motives, and that's not a good way to live. It's not who I am.' She grimaced. 'As well as my inheritance, he took my belief in myself and my confidence. And I want them back.'

Now Josh realised why she pushed herself so hard on the slopes. To prove to herself that she could do something she'd thought herself incapable of doing. To give her back her self-confidence.

But one thing he didn't understand. Before she'd bought the restaurant, she'd been its head chef. 'Why didn't the new owners keep you on as chef?' he asked.

'They wanted to do their own thing. And, really, do you want the ex-owner hanging about your kitchens? I understand where they were coming from,' she said. 'They wanted a fresh start.'

'Couldn't you have got a loan to buy the other restaurant?'

'Not without a deposit. Besides, if you were a bank manager, would *you* lend money to someone who'd just lost her business because she trusted the wrong person?'

'Everyone deserves a second chance,' he said.

'It wasn't happening. And I was just lucky that Hannah had room for me to stay with her. But she's going to need her nursery back in a couple of months. Taking this job means I have somewhere to live and a bit of a breathing space. When I go back to England, at least there'll be something else on my CV that will push the stuff before into the background—and hopefully that means someone might give me a chance in their kitchen.'

His heart ached for her. 'What if someone was prepared to go after Blake for you?'

'You, you mean?' She shook her head. 'I know you mean well, and I appreciate the offer, but you're a ski instructor, not a lawyer. What could you do that Hannah and her colleagues couldn't?' Before he could answer that, she added, 'I can look after myself and I'm not looking to be rescued. I don't need rescuing.'

'But Blake cheated you.'

'It's not so much the money,' she said. 'It's how he made me feel: that the only thing that was worth anything about me was the money I inherited from my parents.'

That really struck a chord with Josh. It was how he'd discovered Annabel had seen him: not for himself, but as a billionaire's son and a media darling. She hadn't wanted him for his own sake; she'd wanted him for the money and the lifestyle he could give her. Which was why she'd given him that terrible ultimatum.

He knew exactly how it felt to be wanted for your money, and he hated to think that was how Sophie saw herself.

'No. That's not true at all,' he said. 'You've come out here, to a country where you don't speak the language, to hold down a demanding job—the level of cuisine the chalet clients expect is way above the level of even a really skilled amateur—and you're challenging yourself to do something that scares you. You're worth way, way more than any money.'

'Thank you,' she said. 'That's what I've been telling myself. What I need now is to stand on my own two feet again—and to know I'm capable of picking myself up and I don't have to rely on anyone else to do it for me. Life isn't a fairy tale and I'm not a princess.'

Josh could respect her point of view, even though he knew all he had to do was pick up the phone and make a few calls; a good private detective would be able to find Blake, having the time and resources that Sophie and her friends didn't have.

But Sophie had made it very clear that this wasn't Josh's fight—and he'd already got it wrong by stepping in with Gaz and his friends. So, much as he wanted to charge in and rescue her, he had to do the harder thing: stand down and wait for her to ask for his help.

'So what about you?' she asked. 'How did you get to be a ski instructor?'

If he told her the truth, how would she react? As Josh the ski instructor, she'd taken him at face value. But he remembered what she'd said about the chalet boys, the other week.

Rich boys. The sort who've never really had to work for anything.

That was true of him, too. He'd had to train hard to get where he had in the world of skiing, but someone from a more modest background wouldn't even have had the chance to do that. He'd never had to earn a living. If she knew he was from a very wealthy family indeed, would she see him differently—as privileged and whiny, a 'poor little rich boy' who was sulking because his plans hadn't worked out and he didn't really know what to do with his life now?

Especially given that she'd worked so hard and she'd lost everything.

Maybe he could tell her part of the truth: just without telling her what his old job was or who he'd once been. The truth, and nothing but the truth: just not the *whole* truth.

'I've been friends with the Rendini family for years,' he said. 'When my last job didn't work out, they offered me the chance to work here as a ski instructor. So I did my qualifications and came here. This is my trial season.'

'And are you enjoying teaching?'

'Yes,' he said. 'I like seeing my students blossom. You, for example: that first day, you were terrified of falling over and you could only see the danger and not the fun of skiing. And you've said yourself that now you're getting your ski legs you're enjoying it. And that's what makes the job feel worthwhile. Because I'm giving people the chance to know that joy.'

'Would you want to make it your career?'

He blew out a breath. 'Good question. Maybe.'

'What's your alternative?'

Sophie definitely had a business mind, he thought. She cut straight to the point. 'I've been offered an office job.'

'Would you be happy doing that job?'

'Honestly? I don't know,' he said. 'Very probably not.'

'So if you don't teach and you don't do the office job, what do you want to do instead?'

'That's the thing,' he said. 'I'm at a bit of a cross-roads. Do I take a complete change of direction, or do

I keep teaching?' Which in itself was a change of direction, too.

'For what it's worth,' she said, 'you're good at teaching. If it makes you happy, then think about where it can take you in five years. Is it somewhere you'd want to be, or would your complete change of direction—even if you didn't enjoy the job at first—give you other opportunities that would make you happier?'

'I honestly don't know,' he said.

'Could you go back to your old job, but working for someone else?'

If only. 'No,' he said. 'My bridges are a bit on the burned side.' Crashed and burned, thanks to his knee.

'Maybe,' she said, 'you need a challenge. Something to make you pull yourself out of the hole you're in, so you can move on.'

'Like you and the skiing.'

She nodded. 'What are you most afraid of?'

Wrecking his knee again so he wouldn't even be able to walk, let alone ski. Having to rely on other people and losing his independence. Feeling trapped. 'Making the wrong choice,' he said.

'There's a theory that if you toss a coin, it'll help you focus. But that only works if you have two choices,' she said.

'How does it work?'

'If you're pleased or relieved at the result, then you know you've made the right choice. If you're disappointed, then you know that what you really wanted was the other option.'

'It's a good theory.' But he didn't have two choices. 'So, given the choice of doing absolutely anything you wanted in the world, what would you do?'

'Open another restaurant,' she said promptly. 'It'd be me giving myself a second chance—and I'd want to do that with my staff, too.'

Which might just fit in with his own ideas of what he could do in the future, with assistive skiing instruction. He knew first-hand what it was like to have reconstructive surgery and a gruelling programme of physiotherapy, so that would help him to understand the needs of his disabled skiing students. He almost asked Sophie there and then what she thought about the idea: but then he'd have to explain about his knee. About his past. And he wasn't quite ready to open up about that. The more he got to know Sophie, the more he thought he could trust her. She was a million miles away from Annabel.

But what if his judgement was still off? What if he got it wrong again?

So instead, he focused on her. 'That bet I had with Gaz and the lads,' he said carefully, 'involved a donation to charity.' A sizeable one. And he could add to that money. 'It'd be enough to get you a lease, stock and a few months of staffing, if you want to open that restaurant when you go back to England.'

'No,' she said. 'The offer's kind, but no. Apart from the fact that this would be a business, not a charity—so taking the money would feel dishonest and wrong, for me—I need to stand on my own two feet.

'Understood. But think about it before you reject it out of hand,' he said. 'The offer's there. Should you wish to take it.'

It was oh, so tempting to accept his offer.

But it would mean letting someone else rescue her. With money that hadn't been obtained honestly, in her view. Plus she wouldn't be setting up a charity. It wouldn't be honest. And honesty was important, especially after what had happened to her. Her integrity wasn't for sale.

At the same time, she was relieved that Josh didn't seem to think any less of her now he finally knew the truth about the huge mistake she'd made.

And it seemed that he, too, was at a point where his life had to change.

Maybe they could help each other.

Though she had the feeling that he was holding something back. He'd been very cagey about his previous job. Or maybe he'd worked in financial services and didn't want to tell her, given the way she'd lost all her own assets.

By mutual unspoken consent they didn't talk any more about their jobs or their past. Sophie enjoyed working with him in the kitchen, getting him to try different flavours and textures.

'I've got a teaching session in half an hour,' Josh said when he'd finished doing the washing up, 'so I really need to go. But I'll pick you up for dinner at half-past six.'

'What's the dress code?' she asked.

'Smart,' he said.

She was glad that Hannah had persuaded her to pack a little black dress. But there was one teensy problem. 'I'm not sure I'll manage heels in the snow,' she said.

'Wear your snow boots outside, and whatever you like inside,' he said. 'Bring a bag for your boots. I'll carry it for you.'

'All right. Half-past six it is,' she said.

He kissed her on the cheek, and it felt as if little fires were dancing underneath her skin. 'See you later.'

'Have a good lesson,' she said.

Kitty came back from the slopes and fell on the goodies Sophie had made. 'These are so good,' she said.

'Thanks. I thought I'd start doing a couple of Christmas-based afternoon tea things each week for our guests,' Sophie said.

'Great idea.' Kitty smiled at her. 'So what are you up to, this evening?'

'I'm going out for dinner.'

'With Mr Sexy Ski Instructor?'

'He's just a friend,' Sophie reminded her.

'If you say so,' Kitty said with a grin. 'What are you wearing?'

'A dress.'

'Show me.'

Sophie did so, and Kitty nodded her approval. 'What about jewellery?'

'I don't really wear much,' Sophie said. 'Just my mum's rings.'

'You need jewellery with that dress. Pearls would be good. Come with me,' Kitty said, and ushered Sophie into her room. 'Put the dress on.' She rummaged in her jewellery box. 'Right. Borrow these.' She handed Sophie a choker of creamy pearls. 'And I think you should wear your hair up.'

'I don't—' Sophie began.

'You do tonight. I'll do your hair and make-up.' Kitty grinned. 'I've already worked out that you don't wear much, so don't worry; I'm not going to make you look orange or put huge false eyelashes on you. Just a bit of foundation, mascara and lippy.'

At twenty-five past six, Sophie barely recognised herself in the mirror. Kitty had put her hair into a sophisticated updo with tiny curls at the sides, and the make-up was subtle but made her eyes look huge and her mouth look beautiful.

'You look amazing, Soph,' Kitty said with satisfaction. 'Almost as amazing as you are inside.'

Sophie felt tears prick her eyelids. 'That's such a nice thing to say.'

'It's all true. The cook here before you was a bit snooty and I didn't get on with her; you've already taught me loads and my mum's going to love you for ever because it means I'll be able to cook proper food at uni and won't just live on pizza.'

'You'll live on pizza because that's what students do,' Sophie said with a grin, 'but knowing how to cook means that if you decide to eat together in your flat, you'll get the fun of cooking and everyone else will do the washing up.'

'Perfect,' Kitty said. 'Now go and have fun with Mr Sexy Ski Instructor.'

'We're *friends*,' Sophie protested.

'He's taking you out to dinner somewhere dressy. That means more than friends,' Sophie said. 'And, from what I hear, he hasn't dated anyone for months.'

That answered one question; better still, she hadn't had to ask it.

The doorbell rang.

'All yours,' Kitty said. 'Have fun!'

Josh stared as Sophie answered the door while shrugging into her pink padded coat. He'd asked her to dress up, but he hadn't expected her to look this stunning. He remembered that kiss last night and felt as if his tongue was glued to the roof of his mouth.

But it was obvious that she expected him to say at least hello.

'You look…exquisite,' were the words that burst out of him.

She went very pink and her eyes glittered. 'Thank you. But it's all down to Kitty. She did my make-up and hair.'

'You're beautiful—it's *you*, not the way you're dressed. I'm not quite that shallow.' Well, he was, but he wasn't going to admit that.

She went even pinker, and changed the subject. 'Where are we going?'

'A place where the food is seriously good—because I wouldn't dare take you anywhere else,' he said with a smile.

'The food is always more important than the surroundings,' she said. 'Antique furniture, the best linen and porcelain, and crystal glassware aren't enough.'

'Isn't presentation important?'

'Yes, but if it looks beautiful and the food doesn't live up to expectation, then it's a disappointment rather than a delight,' she said.

He thought about it. It was also true of people. Annabel was confident and beautiful outside, but hadn't lived up to the beauty inside; whereas Sophie… Sophie was beautiful inside and didn't have the confidence she deserved. He'd rather have one Sophie than a hundred Annabels.

Not that he could tell her that without a lot of awkward explanations.

So he simply drove her to the restaurant, getting her to glance out at the sky.

'The stars don't look like this in London,' she said.

'You're lucky if you can see half a dozen constellations. Here, without the streetlights, there's a whole sky full of stars I've never seen before.'

That was how she made him feel. As if a filter had been stripped away and everything was clearer. Brighter.

He parked outside the restaurant. The path had been cleared to the front door, so she changed from her snow boots to heels, but he tucked her arm through his so she wouldn't worry about slipping.

'This is lovely,' she said, gesturing to the wooden chalet with its pitched roof covered in snow. There were fairy lights draped around the edge of the roof and twined through the branches of the small spruce trees in pots either side of the door.

Inside, the tables were covered in starched white linen, and the plain silver cutlery was set very precisely; the table setting was simple, with a glass vase containing white hellebores and a plain white candle in an elegant silver holder.

The waiter showed them to a quiet corner table with a view over the mountains, and Josh made sure that Sophie was the one to get the view.

'This is lovely,' Sophie said. 'Elegant and simple.'

He wondered what her restaurant had been like, but he didn't want to hurt her by asking. Given what she'd said about presentation, earlier, he was pretty sure she'd gone for simple rather than fussy.

She took one look at the menu and then raised her eyebrows at him. 'How many stars does this place have, then?'

He blinked. 'You can tell just from the menu?'

She nodded. 'The fact there's a tasting menu pretty much gives it away.'

'Shall we go for that?' he asked.

'I'd love to,' she said, 'provided we go halves on the bill.'

He frowned. 'I'm taking you out to dinner.'

'Josh, I don't mean to be rude, but you're a part-time ski instructor. Paying the bill for both of us is going to put a bit of a hole in your budget.'

This was his cue to tell her who he was. Who his family was. Why he wasn't worried about the bill to-night.

But it stuck in his throat.

He didn't think Sophie was a gold-digger in the way Annabel had been, but he did think that telling her the truth about his background would change the way she saw him. He didn't want that. He wanted her to keep seeing him for himself. Just Josh.

'I have savings from my last job,' he said. As well as a trust fund that he'd come into when he was twenty-seven: old enough, in his grandparents' view, to be sen-sible. He'd invested some in property and the rest in a fund that was doing very nicely indeed, thank you.

'Even so,' she said. 'I don't want you to blow your savings on taking me to dinner.'

'Let me treat you,' he said softly. 'You can buy me hot chocolate and strudel tomorrow after your ski les-son.'

She shook her head. 'There's a big difference be-tween buying a snack in a café and picking up the bill for a tasting menu in a place like this.'

'Humour me. I wouldn't have brought you here if I couldn't afford it,' he said. 'This isn't about trying to impress you by taking you somewhere posh. It's about sharing some seriously good food with you—something I like and that I hope you're going to enjoy.'

'Then thank you, Josh,' she said. 'This looks amazing.'

The food was excellent, each course beautifully presented.

'This is perfect,' she said. 'There's one main ingredient that's clearly the star of each dish. The way it's put together, the colours and the textures…and for me the beetroot gnocchi is standout.'

'Good.' He smiled. 'It's lovely to share dinner with someone who enjoys it rather than picking at it.'

'It's impossible not to enjoy this.' She smiled back. 'Thank you so much.'

'My pleasure,' he said, meaning it.

She was relaxed with him, now, chatting easily. It was a long time since he'd enjoyed dinner out as much as this. If he could freeze time, he'd make tonight last for ever.

Well, if he could intercut it with that light kiss goodnight. The anticipation. The way desire had bubbled through his veins.

'I love the fact there's a pre-dessert,' she said when the waiter brought out a tiny moulded creamy dome on a plate, garnished with a crystallised violet and with a scribble of dark chocolate on the plate next to it. 'And if this is what I think it is…'. She took one tiny spoonful and closed her eyes in bliss. 'Oh, yes.'

Her voice was as sexy as hell. Josh could imagine her saying those words as he touched her, caressed her. For a moment, he almost forgot where they were and leaned over the table to kiss her. But he held himself back. Just.

'Violet panna cotta,' she said, sounding delighted. 'This is sublime.'

She was sublime. And he really wanted her. But she'd notice if he didn't eat his pre-dessert. 'This is possibly a little too floral for me,' he said when he'd tried his.

'Violet creams—posh ones—are my favourite sweets in the entire world,' she said.

He stored that little nugget away for future use, and let her finish his panna cotta.

But the dessert, when it came, was more to his taste. 'Deconstructed apple strudel in a glass,' she said happily. 'I love the way they've done this. A sharp apple parfait, sweet zabaglione, spiced raisins and a cinnamon tuille.'

Even though they lingered over coffee and petit fours—a tiny lemon tart, a lush raspberry jelly and rich, dark gianduja—they reached the point where Josh knew he needed to take Sophie home. She'd need to be up early for her guests and it wasn't fair of him to keep her out late.

But he stopped at a viewpoint on the way back to Pendio di Cristallo. 'There's something I want to show you. You'll need your coat,' he said, and climbed out of the car. When he opened her door, she was wearing her coat and snow boots.

'Look up,' he said.

'That's amazing,' she said. 'I don't think I've ever seen so many stars in one place before.'

'New moon and dark skies,' he said. 'In summer it's even better because you can see the Milky Way. This time of year, sadly, you can't.'

'I'm going to add that to my bucket list,' she said. And then she pointed. 'Look! A shooting star.'

It was visible for only a few seconds, but he saw it streaking across the sky, a trail of silver and turquoise like a lone and silent firework. 'They're meant to be lucky. And you're supposed to make a wish when you see one,' he said.

'A wish.' She looked wistful.

Whatever she was wishing for, he'd make it come true. If she'd tell him what she wanted.

He knew what he wished for.

He wanted her to kiss him.

She looked up at him, and he felt his heart stop for a moment.

And then, at last, her mouth was touching the corner of his. Every nerve-end zinged with awareness of her.

'Sophie,' he said softly, and rubbed the pad of his thumb against her lower lip. 'Sophie.'

Those beautiful blue eyes were huge in the starlight.

And he couldn't resist her any more.

He dipped his head, and brushed his mouth against hers. Once, twice. The lightest touch, but it made his whole body ache with need.

And at last she was kissing him back, her arms wrapped round his neck and his wrapped round her waist.

That falling star had definitely done its work.

And he loved every second of it. The softness of her body against his. The warmth of her skin. The scent she wore. The silence of the snow at the deserted viewpoint. Just the two of them underneath the stars, surrounded by the snow…

Then, shockingly, she pulled away. 'I shouldn't have done that,' she said, not meeting his gaze.

It was his own fault. He'd been the one to set the parameters. He'd put himself in the friend zone.

'I'll drive you back,' he said.

It felt beyond awkward, in the car. He didn't know what to say. She clearly didn't, either. And the silence grew more and more awkward with every passing mile.

Eventually they reached her chalet. 'Thank you for this evening, Josh,' she said politely. 'I had a lovely time.'

So had he. He'd really enjoyed her company. 'Pleasure,' he said.

He needed to regroup, because she was clearly spooked by that kiss.

He'd have to stay stuck in the friend zone until he'd worked out how to change her mind. How to ask her to take a chance on him. 'I'll see you tomorrow for your lesson.'

'Tomorrow,' she agreed.

He waited until she was safely inside, then drove back to his own chalet.

That kiss had awoken so many things he'd thought were dormant. Desire. Need. Attraction.

The more he got to know her, the more he liked her. And that liking was tipping over into something else. It wasn't something he was ready to name: something that had let them both down in the past and made them both wary. But could it be different for them, this time round? And, if so, how was he going to get her to change her mind—and take a chance on them?

CHAPTER SEVEN

THE NEXT MORNING, it was snowing lightly.

Just like the morning when she'd first met Josh when she'd stood outside, catching snowflakes on her tongue, not realising she'd wandered onto the bottom of a piste.

Today, Sophie thought, she was a little less clueless.

Though she felt just as wary about meeting him. Last night—well, Josh wasn't the sort of man to assume that taking her out to dinner meant that she owed him sex. But she'd enjoyed sharing the posh, luxurious dinner with someone who appreciated good food as much as she did. She'd enjoyed his company. She'd loved the fact he'd stopped to show her the stars on a crisp Alpine night, the starlight reflecting on the snow-covered trees.

And that moment when she'd kissed him under the stars, when he'd brushed the pad of his thumb along her lower lip, making every nerve-end tingle, and then he'd kissed her…she'd wanted more. She'd wanted him to sweep her back to his chalet and make love with her.

But they'd agreed to be friends.

And she was a failure at relationships.

So she'd chickened out. Pulled back.

And how she regretted it. She wished she'd taken the

chance. She could've said something in the car, instead of sitting in awkward silence. She could've leaned forward and kissed him goodnight when he'd parked outside her chalet, let him know without words that she wanted to be more than just friends.

But she hadn't.

And he hadn't made a move, either. He hadn't brought up the subject or said that he wanted to rethink their agreement. When he'd kissed her under the stars, she'd thought that maybe it was the first step to something else.

The fact he hadn't taken it further... Clearly he'd changed his mind and she needed to be sensible and stick to what they'd agreed instead of wanting more. They were friends. Strictly friends.

Josh was waiting for her by the lift to the blue run. 'Good morning.'

His smile made her heart skip a beat. 'Good morning. Can we actually ski in the snow or do we need to reschedule?'

'We can ski in the snow unless it's a blizzard. The weather forecast says it's going to stop soon—and fresh powder's lovely to ski on.' He smiled. 'Though it's also tiring. It's easy to catch an edge so your skis stop dead and you fall over.'

'And if I fall over, I pick myself up, smile and shake it off,' she said.

He grinned. 'Oh, good. A student who actually listens to what I say. Yes. Let's go.'

The snow seemed to muffle the usual noise on the slope. And it felt almost like skiing on a duvet. If she fell, it would be all cushiony and—

Yup. It was cushiony, she discovered when she fell.

And it was really, really difficult to get up. She tried once, twice, and just couldn't do it.

'Here.' He took her hand and pulled her to her feet. Except he was stooping, and pulling her up meant pulling her into him, and they ended up face to face. Just like last night. Except, instead of being surrounded by starlight, they were surrounded by soft, fluffy snow-flakes.

As slowly as the huge flakes drifted down past them, his face lowered to hers. His lips brushed hers once, twice. Sweet and gentle and promising. Enticing. Asking, not demanding. Persuading. Everything she'd wanted since last night.

What could she do but drop her ski poles and slide her arms round his neck, just as she had last night?

He'd dropped his ski poles, too, and his arms were tightly wrapped round her.

And all she could think of was the heat and sweet-ness of his mouth against hers, the softness and cool-ness of the snow. She closed her eyes, kissing him back, luxuriating in his closeness.

And then, shockingly, he broke the kiss.

'Sorry. I, um, crossed a line there.'

More than one. From teacher to friend to…some-thing else.

But the snow had stopped as suddenly as it began, and all the glittering possibilities vanished with it.

'I'm sorry.' He rubbed a hand across his face. 'Actu-ally, no, I'm not sorry for kissing you. I'm glad I kissed you. But I'm sorry for making things complicated. For not checking with you first.'

Oh.

And that made all the difference.

She leaned forward, holding on to him for balance, and kissed him.

When she broke the kiss, he pushed his goggles up.

She did the same, so she could look him properly in the eye.

'So what now?' he asked.

'I don't know,' she said.

'You're still getting over your ex.'

'No. I've had enough time to think about it. I'm not in love with him any more. But I don't quite trust my judgement in men now,' she admitted.

'I know how that feels,' he said. 'My last relationship went wrong. Badly.' He took a deep breath. 'But maybe we could take a risk. Together. See where this goes.'

'I don't know what I'm going to be doing when my contract ends,' she warned.

'I don't know what I'm going to be doing in a few months' time, either,' he said. 'Maybe we could treat this as just time for us and not worry about the future. We'll deal with it when the time comes.'

Which felt as scary as standing at the top of a steep slope, knowing that the only way you could reach the safety at the bottom was to conquer your fear and push yourself over the edge. 'So we're redrawing the lines?'

'When I'm teaching you,' he said, 'I'm your ski instructor.'

She coughed. 'That would be the ski instructor who just kissed me and crossed said line.'

'The ski instructor who is going to keep himself under strict control from now on and stick to teaching during a lesson. But, the second that the lesson ends,' he said, 'we cross back over the line.'

The line that they'd originally agreed was friendship. 'Except we're not going to be just friends?' she checked.

'Definitely not just friends.' His voice was slightly husky, sexy as hell. 'And I'm looking forward to being your lover. Finding out what pleases you, what takes your breath away, what turns you to flame.'

What could she do but reach up again and kiss him?

'That,' he said when she broke the kiss, 'was serious line-crossing, Sophie Harris. So we're going to ski down the slope now. And then we're going back to the top and practising it all over again. Without kissing.' He glanced at his watch. 'For another twenty-five minutes. And then...' He raised his ski goggles so she could see the intensity burning in his grey eyes. 'And then we're crossing that line. Together.'

She wasn't sure whether the anticipation was more delicious, scary or exciting. 'One more condition,' she said.

'Which is?'

He'd said his last relationship had gone badly wrong. 'We've both been hurt. So we should agree to be kind to each other.'

'Kind isn't quite how I'm feeling right now,' he said. 'It's more...troglodyte.'

'Troglodyte?'

'As in I'd like to carry you off somewhere warm and private.'

She got it, now, and grinned. 'Your cave. That would be acceptable.'

He kissed the tip of her nose. 'Good. And I agree. We'll be kind. We won't hurt each other.'

The anticipation grew with every trip they took back to the top of the run and down to the bottom.

At the end of one more run, Josh glanced at his watch. 'Lesson over,' he decreed.

Sophie's stomach swooped. 'Time to cross that line.' And suddenly it was really, really scary.

As if she'd spoken that last bit aloud, he said quietly, 'It doesn't mean we have to cross the line *quickly*. And I kind of liked the tradition we were setting of having hot chocolate and strudel after a lesson.'

'I need to be back at my chalet by four,' she reminded him.

'And I have a lesson at two. So we're not going to rush into anything today,' he said. 'We're going for a mini-date: hot chocolate and strudel in my favourite café. And we'll make a list of all the things you want to do while you're here in the Dolomites.' He raised his ski goggles again and his grey eyes were suddenly hot. '*All* the things,' he said softly, 'not just the places you want to visit.'

She was very glad of the ski poles she was hanging on to, because her knees had just gone seriously weak. 'All the things,' she croaked. His earlier words were burned into her brain.

I'm looking forward to being your lover. Finding out what pleases you, what takes your breath away, what turns you to flame.

She wanted that, too. She'd never wanted anyone so much in her entire life.

He stole a kiss, leaving her breathless. 'Strudel, first. We have all the time in the world.'

Actually, they didn't. She was due to leave Pendio di Cristallo at the end of January, only a few short weeks away.

But for now it was nice to pretend.

She insisted on picking up the bill for hot chocolate and strudel. 'You bought dinner last night,' she
reminded him.

'And you're not a fairy tale princess,' he said. 'No
rescuing, unless it's mutual.'

'I'm glad that's sorted.'

But she enjoyed sitting in the café with him, their
legs entwined under the table and their fingers entwined
above the table. Cute and cosy and fun. All the things
she'd been missing and trying to tell herself that she
could do without. Except she'd been so very, very lonely
since Blake had duped her and left her without even
saying goodbye.

'I know hardly anything about the area, really,' she
said. 'The only thing I can think of that I'd really like
to do is visit the Christmas market again when it's dark,
so I can see the lights at their best.'

'We can do that on your next day off, so you don't
have to rush back to make dinner for your guests,' he
said.

'Thank you. What else would you suggest?'

'Walking round the lakes,' he said. 'Obviously it'll
be too cold to swim in them—and some of them you're
not allowed to swim in, anyway—but the views will
be amazing. The colour of the water has to be seen to
be believed.'

'Sounds good,' she said.

'We can have a look at some of the villages, because
they're really pretty. I'm happy to drive you,' he said.
'And maybe we can take a sleigh ride through the forest.'

'Drawn by reindeer?' she asked.

'By horse,' he said.

She smiled. 'I'd love that.'

With his free hand, he made notes on his phone. 'OK. I'll text this to you. We can pick something from it each day, depending on the weather and how we feel. And maybe we can look up some touristy things online.' He smiled. 'If you like museums, we can go and see Ötzi the Ice Man. He was found by hikers in a glacier, and he's the oldest man ever found intact—he's more than five thousand years old.'

'Older than Egyptian mummies?' she asked, surprised.

'There are older mummies, but they'd had their organs removed during mummification. Ötzi didn't—he was preserved by the glacier.'

'How come you know all this stuff?'

'The Rendinis,' he said. 'Vincenzo's very proud of his heritage.'

'Then let's add visiting Ötzi to our list,' she said.

They wandered round the village together, hand in hand.

'There are plenty of other winter sports apart from skiing. We could go ice skating,' Josh suggested.

Sophie shook her head. 'Ice skates have sharp blades. And I need my hands for work. That's a risk too far, for me.'

'How about snow-shoeing?' he asked.

'Maybe. How likely am I to fall over?'

'You're not. Unless I get you to do a snow angel— and that doesn't count because it's deliberate falling-over.'

'Got it,' she said. 'All right. Let's add it to our list.'

He walked her back to her chalet. 'Our list,' he said. 'We're not going to set a time for it. But the one thing

I really want to do is make love with you. Touch you and taste you and explore you until I really know you.' He held her gaze. 'And for you to do the same with me.'

His goodbye kiss was scorching.

And Sophie was tingling all over as she walked into the chalet, with the simmering undercurrent of knowing that very, very soon they'd make love. Be skin to skin. Trust each other with themselves...

Over the next week, Sophie enjoyed going out with Josh after their lessons. As he'd suggested, they went for a walk round one of the lakes, their arms wrapped round each other.

'This is amazing,' she said. 'Even though there's ice on the surface of the lake and snow on the edges, you can see the water properly in the middle—and the reflections.' The snow-capped peaks and the forests surrounding the lake were reflected perfectly in the clear emerald water. 'And you were right about the colour. It's stunning.'

'There are others that are almost a milky turquoise, and others that are the same blue as the sky,' he said.

He took her to pretty Alpine villages with ancient churches covered with frescoes, cobbled streets and beautiful fountains in the central squares; everywhere looked incredibly gorgeous, dusted with snow.

He took her out on a morning when there was fresh snow everywhere, and taught her how to make a snow angel; and then he kissed her to the point where she forgot that she was cold because his mouth made her feel hot all over.

And, best of all, one afternoon, he took her for a sleigh ride.

'It's just like a real Father Christmas sleigh,' Sophie said with delight when he took her over to their sleigh.

It was drawn by a large black horse—a Noriker, Josh told her—who had tinkling bells on his harness. The driver helped them onto the seat and wrapped a fleecy blanket round them both, then sat on the front of the sleigh and gently urged the horse on.

All she could hear was the crisp sound of the sleigh sliding through the snow as they drove through the forest, and the tinkling of the harness bells. The air was so fresh and clear; but even more heady was the warmth of Josh beside her, his arm round her shoulders and his thigh pressed against hers.

'It's really like living in the middle of a Christmas song,' she said.

To her delight, Josh broke into an impromptu rendition of 'Sleigh Ride', his voice deep and clear and tuneful; and she found herself singing along with him and laughing.

This was so perfect, she thought. Life didn't get any better than this.

They drove round a lake similar to the one Josh had taken her to before, except this time the water was the same bright cerulean as the sky. The mountains and the forests were reflected in the lake, and Sophie had never seen anything so beautiful.

'This is utterly magical,' she whispered to Josh.

'I know,' he whispered back, and kissed her.

On her next day off, he took her to the Christmas market after sunset, and from the top of the Ferris wheel the whole village looked like a winter wonderland, full of fairy lights. Best of all, second time round,

Josh kissed her all the way up the Ferris wheel, and all the way down again.

'Stay with me tonight?' he asked. 'I'll drive you back to the chalet before you need to get breakfast ready.'

Crossing their final line: from friendship to dating to being lovers.

Part of Sophie wanted to. *Really* wanted to. And part of her was terrified that this was where it would all go wrong.

'Or,' he said, 'you can just come back for a glass of wine. And I'll get you home before midnight.'

He meant it.

She could set the pace.

He wasn't going to push her into anything she wasn't ready to do.

'You don't have to decide now,' he said. 'We'll have dinner first.'

He took her to a tiny hut in the mountains, where the food was amazing: simple traditional recipes, freshly made and locally sourced.

When he pulled up outside his chalet, she said, 'I've decided.'

He kept his expression carefully neutral. 'Uh-huh.'

'I'll stay,' she said.

And the heat in his eyes was scorching as he scooped her out of the car and carried her through his front door and into his bedroom.

They worked their way through their list: the museum, snow-shoeing, and a scary afternoon where he took her tobogganing. And on Sophie's next day off Josh collected her well before dawn; he drove her into the mountains, and together they watched the sun come up.

'The roses on the rocks again,' she said. 'And I can't believe that even the snow is pink. This is amazing, Josh.'

'I hoped you'd like it. But I haven't finished yet,' he said. 'I have plans with a capital P.'

'What sort of plans?'

'Ones I hope you'll like.' He refused to be drawn on any of the details.

They spent the day skiing, and then he drove her to a small cottage in the mountains.

'What's this?' she asked.

'I borrowed a cottage to make you dinner,' he said.

'You borrowed a cottage?' she echoed.

'From the Rendinis. I wanted to have a kind of early Christmas with you because we'll both be working on the day.'

'That's such a lovely idea,' she said. 'So are you telling me there's a full Christmas dinner sitting in a cool-box in the back of your car?'

'No. I put dinner in the fridge here, yesterday,' he said. 'It's an Italian take on a traditional English Christmas dinner. It's kind of worrying, cooking for a trained chef, so I cheated a tiny bit and enlisted a bit of help; most of it, I just need to put in the oven. But I hope you'll like it.'

She smiled. 'Don't be intimidated, cooking for me. I appreciate you making a fuss of me and I'm not going to be all picky and score you on presentation or whatever. But if you need a sous-chef, let me know.'

He unlocked the cottage and they put their boots and skis on the rack in the hallway. She could smell spruce, cinnamon and orange. 'Whatever you've done,' she said, 'it definitely smells like Christmas.'

'I set most of it up last night, but I need to do a couple more things. Maybe you can boil the kettle for us and make coffee?'

'Sure,' she said, and let him usher her into the kitchen.

When she took the milk out of the fridge door, she tried very hard not to look at the rest of the contents, not wanting to spoil his surprise. Once she'd finished making coffee, she called, 'Let me know when you're ready for me to bring it through.'

'Now's fine,' he said.

She sucked in a breath when she followed his voice and walked into the living room. There was a real Christmas tree in the corner, decorated with twinkling lights and red baubles and gold stars; there was an evergreen wreath along the mantelpiece, studded with orange slices and bundles of cinnamon sticks; the room was lit by what must've been twenty or thirty candles; and there was a crackling log fire in the hearth.

It was the most romantic thing she'd ever seen in her life.

'This is absolutely lovely,' she said. 'The perfect Christmas.'

He looked pleased. 'That was what I was trying to do. Right. I'll be five minutes in the kitchen.' He handed his phone to her with a streaming app already open. 'Have a look through here and find some Christmas music you like,' he said.

She found a list of Christmas music for solo piano and had just set it playing when he returned.

'This is lovely,' he said. 'Dance with me?'

'I'd love to.' She glanced up. 'But where's the mistletoe?'

'You'll have to imagine it,' he said with a grin. 'Pretend it's right there above us.'

'Promises, promises,' she teased.

'I deliver on my promises,' he said, and kissed her.

And it was wonderful, dancing with him in a candlelit room, just the two of them, with beautiful music and Christmassy scents.

It would be oh, so easy to get used to this.

To fall in love with Josh.

She was more than halfway there already. She liked his warmth, his sense of fun, the way her blood fizzed whenever he kissed her.

And things had gone wrong for both of them, before. Which meant that this time maybe they could get it right...

His phone alarm chimed.

'Kitchen duties,' he said, and kissed her. 'Whatever you're thinking, hold on to that thought.'

'Can I help at all?'

'Nope. The idea is to spoil you,' he said.

Dinner was chicken fillet wrapped in prosciutto, with roast potatoes that were crispy outside and perfectly fluffy inside, tiny Chantenay carrots, and Brussels sprouts shredded and stir fried in butter, garlic and chilli, served with a creamy marsala sauce. He'd opened a bottle of champagne, too.

'I'll stick to one glass,' he said, 'because I'm driving. But I think tonight deserves proper bubbles.'

'This is all perfect,' she said. 'Thank you so much for spoiling me.'

She particularly liked the chocolate panettone he served for dessert with a large spoonful of mascarpone.

'I'm going to get some of this shipped to Hannah,' she said. 'It's fabulous.'

He smiled. 'I'll give you the name of my supplier.

Tell them that I sent you, and they might throw in some of their lemon cookies—which are pretty spectacular.'

'I will,' she promised.

But when he went to make coffee, she heard him say, 'Uh-oh.'

'What's wrong?' she asked.

'Go and look out of the window,' he said.

Outside, she couldn't see anything but white. It was snow, but not like she'd seen it before. 'Is that a blizzard?'

'It's a whiteout,' he said. 'Visibility's not good enough to risk driving. We'll have to wait it out for a bit.' He grabbed his phone and checked the weather report. 'Ah. It seems the road to Pendio di Cristallo is closed for the foreseeable future.'

'So how are we going to get back to the resort?' She looked at him, aghast. 'I know I'm off tonight, but I need to be back there to make breakfast for the guests in the morning.'

'I think Kitty will have to do the kitchen duties for you,' he said. 'With conditions like these, and according to this weather report, we're going nowhere tonight.' He shook his head. 'I'm really sorry, Sophie. This wasn't on the weather forecast yesterday. I know how quickly weather can change in the mountains and I should've double-checked. Text Kitty to let her know where you are, and I'll call Gio and let him know we're snowed in here tonight.'

Sophie bit her lip. 'I feel terrible about letting everyone down.'

'It's not your fault. The blame's completely mine for not keeping an eye on the forecast.'

'You can't change the weather.' She sighed. 'Can I

speak to Giovanni when you call him, please? I'd like to apologise.'

He nodded, and while she texted Kitty he called Giovanni; he spoke in rapid Italian, then handed the phone to her.

'I'm so sorry, Mr Rendini,' she said.

'It's not your fault, *bella*. These things happen. I'll arrange to get someone to help Kitty in the morning,' Giovanni said.

'Thank you. I'll swap my next day off for tomorrow, to make up for it,' Sophie added.

'Really, it's not necessary,' Giovanni said. 'Take care.'

She handed the phone back to Josh. 'I really hate letting people down.'

'It was my mistake, not yours,' he told her. 'There's nothing we can do about it until tomorrow. So either we can do this the English way and keep worrying about things we can't change, or we can remember where we are and do it the Italian way—make the best of the situation.'

'I guess.'

'Right now, I think you need a hug.' He wrapped his arms round her.

She leaned into him, enjoying his warmth and his strength.

They ended up dancing together again, and curled up on the sofa together in front of the fire. The combination of champagne, skiing and mountain air meant that Sophie ended up falling asleep in Josh's arms. He woke her gently. 'Let's go and get some proper sleep.'

It didn't matter that they had no nightclothes; the cottage was warm and the bed was comfortable. And Josh made love to her so tenderly that she almost cried.

In the morning, she woke in his arms, warm and comfortable and happier than she'd felt in a long while.

'I think,' he said softly, 'for once I'm glad the weather got in the way. Because waking up with you is the best thing that's happened to me since I don't know when.'

'Me, too,' she admitted.

It had stopped snowing during the night; Josh checked the weather report and drove her back to Pendio di Cristallo after a breakfast of coffee and leftover panettone.

'I'll see you later for your lesson,' he said when he dropped her at her chalet.

'Perfect,' she said, and kissed him.

CHAPTER EIGHT

THE NIGHT OF the whiteout marked a sea-change in their relationship; after that, Josh and Sophie snatched every moment together that they could. Sophie felt more settled and happy than she had in months. Provided she could take time out to see Hannah and the baby at the end of January, she'd be happy to stay in Pendio di Cristallo for the rest of the season.

She didn't even mind that she took a hard tumble on the slopes, one particular morning, because Josh helped her to her feet and whispered to her that he'd kiss her better later.

And he did.

Life, she thought, was finally on the up again.

This Christmas, Sophie had secretly expected to be miserable: hundreds of miles away from London, in a temporary job, trying to get her confidence back.

Instead, it was turning out to be wonderful. Christmas in a winter wonderland. Yes, she'd be working—cooking a proper Christmas dinner for her guests of a smoked salmon mousse with crème fraîche, turkey with all the trimmings, Christmas pudding flambé, cheese, and petit fours—but she loved what she did out here. Better still, there would be time to see Josh. To make a snow angel with him, kiss him and make love. She could watch him unwrap the present she'd chosen specially for him; she'd secretly gone back to the Christmas market without him, and bought him a watercolour by a local artist showing the mountains at sunrise that she'd noticed had caught his eye. She'd made a proper English Christmas cake for her guests each week, and the last couple were maturing and waiting to be iced.

Everywhere she looked, there were Christmas trees. Everywhere she walked, she heard Christmas songs. And all the menus in the cafés and bars were distinctly Christmassy, offering eggnog lattes and stollen.

This was going to be the best Christmas since the last one she'd spent with her parents.

She wasn't quite ready to say it out loud, but she'd fallen in love with Josh Cavendish. With the man who'd helped her get her self-confidence back. With the man who was teaching her to trust again. Josh was definitely a good man. One who wouldn't let her down. One who could make her heart beat faster with a smile or a sidelong look.

Love.

Something Sophie hadn't thought she'd find again, after Blake.

And that made it all the sweeter.

How life could change in a heartbeat, Josh thought. A few short weeks ago, he'd been miserable and lost. And then Sophie Harris had walked in front of him and stood there, in her bright pink coat and gaudy sunglasses, and a moment of intense irritation at her cluelessness had dissolved into something warmer and fresher.

He actually looked forward to waking up in the

morning, because most of the time she'd be waking in his arms. He looked forward to their lessons, seeing her gain in confidence and skills every single day. And most of all he looked forward to picking her up at her chalet after her guests had finished dinner, because that meant he could carry her to his bed and they could both lose themselves in each other. In pleasure.

The warmth and sweetness she'd brought into his life had melted every block of ice he'd stacked round his heart. And he was more than halfway to falling in love with her. Much more than halfway; because he knew he'd found the person he wanted to spend the rest of his life with.

Though what did she really want?

Would she stay here with him in the Dolomites, if he asked her?

Because he was beginning to work out what he wanted, now. To have his own resort, one which catered for skiers of all abilities and disabilities. And if he ran the ski school, maybe she could run the food side of the business. He was more than happy for her to hire people who needed a second chance, the way she'd wanted to do in London.

And he thought he knew the perfect time to ask her: under a sprig of mistletoe, on Christmas Eve. It was only a couple of weeks away. Maybe it was rushing it; but now he knew what he wanted from life, he wanted it to start as soon as possible.

But, a couple of days later, Josh woke to his mobile phone ringing. He looked at the screen, frowned and answered swiftly. 'Gio? Is everything all right?'

'No, it's not.'

'What's happened?' He went cold. 'Is Vincenzo ill? Angelo?'

'No, everybody in the family's well.'

'Then what's wrong?' Josh asked, knowing that his friend wouldn't normally call at such a crazy time of the morning.

'There's a story about you in the press.'

'Me?' Josh had kept a low profile for months. The world championships weren't for a few weeks yet, so there wouldn't be anything about past winners. 'What sort of story?'

'I think you'd better see for yourself. I'll text you the link. Call me back when you've read it.'

Josh's frown deepened when he clicked on the link to a gossip magazine. There was a photograph of him helping Sophie up from a tumble, captioned *World Champion to Novice?*

What?

He didn't understand. The only people who really knew who he was in Pendio di Cristallo were the Rendinis, and they treated him as part of their family. None of them would ever sell him out.

Then he skim-read the story and saw the name of the source.

Annabel Smethurst.

Oh, for pity's sake. Hadn't she made enough trouble in his life? Thanks to her bombshell news and that ultimatum blowing a hole in his concentration before the championship race, his career had literally crashed. She'd wiped out his reputation straight after, with her sob story in the media—a story which had been completely untrue, but he'd been in no fit state to protest until it was too late. Now he was starting to put his life back together again, and she was cutting the ground away from beneath his feet.

Scowling, he went back to the beginning and read the article properly, this time, knowing that whatever she'd written was going to annoy him, but wanting to know exactly what she'd said.

It was full of artfully composed photographs. Amazing scenery, a bottle of top-label champagne and fairy lights, big fat fluffy snowflakes falling in front of pine trees. Everything about it screamed luxury and aspiration.

And it was all embellished by little snippets of text with a giggly, confessional tone.

A weekend skiing in Pendio di Cristallo

What had Annabel been doing here? He'd thought this place would be way too quiet for her tastes. He'd always taken her to her favourite glitzy—and super-expensive—resorts: St Moritz, Gstaad and Courchevel. Places where the rich and famous mingled freely. Pendio was quieter and more family-oriented; it catered for all levels of budgets and experience, from the luxury chalet where Sophie worked through to a budget hostel. The rich skied here, too, but it tended to be the super-rich who didn't want publicity and parties and fuss.

Yet Annabel had clearly visited.

The idea of her staying in Sophie's chalet, being demanding and over-picky…

No. He would've known if she'd stayed at Sophie's chalet. If she'd been a guest, Giovanni would've known and given him a warning.

He was also surprised that Annabel had been any-

where near a blue run. Annabel had always liked to
show off her skills. Or maybe she'd got up late one
morning and ended up stuck with the less confident
skiers in her party. If she'd been thoroughly bored by
the lack of challenge, she would've started looking
around—and maybe that was why she'd noticed him.

*Guess who I saw on the slopes? AJ Cavendish.
How the mighty have fallen—from champion skier
to coaching novices!*

It sounded gloating, and it left a nasty taste in his
mouth.

*Has super-rich playboy—son of billionaire IT
mogul Alexander Cavendish—gone from flying
high to barfly?*

There was a picture of him from his championship
days and another of him sitting at a bar with two drinks
in front of him—the implication being that he was using
alcohol as a crutch. Nothing could be further from the
truth. He knew exactly which bar that was, and had a
pretty good idea which day it was, too. He'd actually
been having a quiet drink with Giovanni, who at that
point had clearly left their table to go to the bathroom.
But the angle of the photograph made it look as if Josh
was lining up shots to drown his sorrows.

Josh was furious that Annabel had dragged Giovanni
into what felt like a personal vendetta. Gallingly, he
couldn't even slap her with a defamation suit, because
the words were just on the right side of the law—posing
a question instead of making a statement.

Clearly he's not very good at coaching, either.

That little remark was accompanied by a picture of Sophie after she'd taken a tumble and him looking slightly alarmed as he helped her up.

He could just about ignore the comments about himself and treat them with the contempt they deserved. But that little dig at Sophie wasn't on. Sophie was worth a million Annabels. Not in monetary terms, maybe—but Sophie was *real*, not a woman who put on a fake show half the time. She was warm and sweet and lovely. She wouldn't sneer at someone for not wearing designer brands or high-end cosmetics, the way Annabel did. Sophie saw what was really important in life, and she'd shown him that, too. It was why he'd fallen in love with her. No way was he letting Annabel drip her vitriol on Sophie. Not to mention the invasion of Sophie's privacy. He'd set his family lawyers on to this and make Annabel issue a public apology.

He sorted that out first, then rang Gio back.

'That...' Gio swore very colourfully and very inventively. 'Hasn't she done enough to hurt you?'

'Clearly not,' Josh said. 'I don't know what she thinks she's achieved by this piece of spite. It's not going to make me want her back or make anyone else think any better of her.' He sighed. 'I'd better go and see Sophie and warn her, before she finds out about it from someone else.'

'Does she know about Annabel?'

'No.' He hadn't told Sophie about an awful lot of things. Including his background. And he was going to have to tell her now, before she saw that story. 'No.'

'This isn't going to be pretty.'

That was an understatement. Sophie would be furious that he'd kept so much from her. He knew how much she valued honesty, and he knew how much Blake's lies had hurt her.

Josh hadn't actually *lied* to her. He'd simply omitted to tell her his background. But he was all too aware that she might see that as a form of dishonesty.

His gut turned to water. Hopefully she'd give him a chance to explain. He hadn't kept the information from her in order to hurt her; he'd kept his background from her because he'd wanted her to see him for himself, not as a poor little rich boy. And he hadn't told her about Annabel because he'd wanted to put that part of his life behind him.

But this was a conversation they needed to have face to face. 'I'm going to see her now. Thank you for the warning.'

'What do you mean, I'm in a gossip magazine?' Sophie asked, looking up from the waffle batter she was making.

'You're in *Celebrity Life*.' It was Kitty's favourite gossip mag, about the rich and famous; she read it avidly.

'Why on earth would I be in a gossip magazine?' Sophie asked. She wasn't even vaguely famous. She was just a quiet, unassuming chef in a ski lodge. OK, one with a past: but Blake wasn't famous, either.

Unless he'd been caught...

But that wouldn't have made the gossip pages. It probably wouldn't even have made the newspapers. Who cared about a con man who'd skipped the country with someone else's money?

'It might be someone who looks like me,' she said.

'Nope. It's definitely you and Josh.' Kitty handed over her phone.

Sophie stared at the photograph. 'That's when I fell over on the slopes, the other day.' And she hadn't been able to get up. Josh had had to help her.

She wasn't so bothered about being photographed looking a bit foolish—but her name was there, too, and that was enough to set up a little niggle of worry. What if the press dug further into her background? She'd been working so hard to repair her reputation. The last thing she needed was to become famous in the press as the woman so stupid that she let her fiancé empty her bank account and ruin her business. Then she'd never, ever get another job.

'Don't worry too much,' Kitty said. 'It's like that horrible model or whatever who took that picture of the old lady in the gym changing room and made nasty comments—it's just made everyone realise how vile she is.'

'But why me?' Sophie asked, looking at the name of the woman who was credited with the story. 'Annabel Smethurst? I've never even heard of her before. I definitely haven't met her. Why would she put a photo of me in the gossip magazine?'

'It's not you she's after. She's having a bit of a go at Josh,' Kitty said.

Sophie scrolled through the article: *World Champion to Novice?*

But Josh wasn't a champion skier…was he?

She read further. 'AJ Cavendish…that's *Josh*?'

'Seems so,' Kitty said. 'And he was world champion. In the skiing world, that makes him the equivalent of the guy who won a big award for best actor. You've been dating a superstar.'

Sophie brushed it aside. 'But, if he's a world champion, why is he here in Pendio di Cristallo, giving lessons to people like me? And who's this Annabel Smethurst?'

'I don't know,' Kitty said.

Super-rich playboy...

What? The Josh she knew was a part-time ski instructor.

But he'd taken her to a Michelin-starred restaurant. One where, now she thought about it, they'd treated him as if he was a regular customer.

Son of billionaire IT mogul...

Was that true?

And why hadn't he told her?

That picture of Josh in one of the resort bars, lining the drinks up in front of him—that wasn't the Josh that Sophie knew. He might have a glass of wine with dinner, sure, but if he was driving he wouldn't drink any more than that one glass.

Or maybe he was different when he wasn't with her. In the evenings, when she was working and maybe wasn't staying over at his, perhaps he really did sit in a bar and drink heavily. And perhaps Giovanni Rendini was recommending him to clients in the hope that it would give Josh something to do and keep him sober.

Well, that would certainly explain why Josh wasn't a world champion skier right now. If he really did have a drink problem, the way the article implied, then he needed help. She ought to be kind.

But right at that moment she felt numb and cold with fear. Because everything she knew had suddenly been turned upside down. She'd thought she'd been dating an ordinary man. A gorgeous man who turned heads, but still ordinary. A ski instructor. Not someone famous. Not someone from a super-rich, glamorous background that was a million miles away from her own.

'Can I...?' Sophie gestured to the phone.

''Course you can.'

She tapped Josh's and Annabel's surnames into the search engine. And then she wished she hadn't when the stories came up.

Champion skier dumps pregnant fiancée.

The photographs that went with the story were definitely of Josh, though the media called him 'AJ'. He'd changed his name, clearly. To cover his tracks? And maybe he thought the media wouldn't go looking for a world champion in a little family-oriented skiing resort.

There were pictures of Josh and Annabel together at swish parties with people that even Sophie recognised; they had a very, very glamorous social set. Gstaad, where it was hinted that they'd skied with the royal family. And then there were other pictures with Annabel looking distraught, dabbing at her eyes with a handkerchief and with her hand resting protectively over her stomach.

Some of this didn't feel right. The Josh Sophie knew would never abandon his pregnant fiancée. He had integrity.

But then again, was the Josh she knew even real? The Josh she knew was a part-time ski instructor, whose old job had fallen through and he was trying to choose between a future in teaching and an office job.

What he hadn't told her was that his old job was being a world champion skier.

Or that the office job he was thinking about taking was being the CEO of his family's firm. Because AJ was the son of billionaire software developer Alex Cavendish, and some news articles were hinting that AJ was poised to take over from his father when Alex retired.

And to think she'd worried about her part-time ski instructor boyfriend putting a hole in his budget when he'd taken her out. With a family background that wealthy, he could probably buy this entire resort with his spare change.

She felt sick.

She'd been honest with him about the awful mistake she'd made.

In return, he'd kept something huge from her. He'd misled her about who he was. She'd thought they were getting closer, that maybe there was something special between them; but the man she'd believed she was getting to know, the man she'd fallen in love with, didn't really exist.

Had he been using her? Slumming it, to make himself feel better?

And why hadn't he told her the truth about himself?

No wonder he'd lied so easily to Gaz and his friends. His whole life here was a lie. She'd been furious with him for being dishonest with that bet, and he'd promised never to do anything like that again. No doubt he'd been laughing at her the whole time. Stupid Sophie, so easily duped. So easily lied to. And she hadn't learned from what Blake had done. She'd still trusted someone. She'd trusted Josh.

And he'd let her down.

'I can't believe this,' she whispered.

Kitty took the phone from her and skim-read the stories. 'That doesn't sound like the Josh we know. He's *nice*.'

But was he really? Was the Josh they knew the *real* one? He'd lied to her, even though he knew how much she valued honesty and integrity. 'Right now, it feels as if I've just dropped into a parallel universe,' Sophie said. 'Where everything I thought was true isn't.'

The chalet doorbell rang.

Sophie and Kitty stared at each other.

'It's not delivery day,' Kitty said.

'Even if it was, they wouldn't be here at this time of the morning, before our guests are even up,' Sophie said.

'Supposing that's the press?' Kitty's eyes were wide. 'I'll go. If anyone's snooping around, looking for you, I'll tell them you're not here.'

Another lie. This had to stop. 'No,' she said wearily. 'I'll go. If it's the press, I'll face them and tell them there isn't actually a story. Josh is my skiing instructor, and that's all.'

He wouldn't even be that, in a few minutes' time.

Because she was going to call everything off, as soon as she'd dealt with whoever was at the door. And it was nothing to do with the desertion story: it was the fact he hadn't been honest with her. She'd had enough of lies with Blake.

Never, ever again.

Steeling herself—all she knew about the paparazzi was what she'd seen in the movies, with camera flashes going off everywhere and a horde of journalists all talking at once so you couldn't make out a single word—she opened the front door.

There was no babbling horde, and no flashes.

Just Josh.

Except he wasn't *just* Josh, was he? He was famous, he was wealthy, and he'd been playing games with her to amuse himself.

'What do you want?' she asked.

'To talk to you.'

She shook her head. 'There's nothing to say. You lied to me—and you know how I feel about dishonesty.' Even though it hurt to say it, and it meant her dreams were shattering all over again, this was the only course of action she could take. 'We're through.'

Oh, no.

It looked as if she already knew about the article.

'Sophie, please. We need to talk.'

'There's nothing to say,' she repeated.

The warm, lovely girl he'd fallen in love with wasn't standing in the doorway. Instead there was a stranger with cold eyes and a stony expression.

'The article. I'm sorry. You shouldn't have been involved, and my lawyers are going to make her issue an apology.'

'I'm not interested,' she said. 'I don't care what it said about me. You *lied* to me, Josh. Or should I call you AJ?'

'My name's Josh,' he said. 'Officially it's Alexander,

after my dad, but everyone's always called me by my middle name. I used my initials for work—for skiing.'

'Yes.' Her expression cooled even further. 'World champion. You knew I wouldn't have a clue who you are. So the article was right about that, wasn't it? You're a rich kid, slumming it and pretending to be someone you're not.'

'Sophie, I didn't lie to you.'

'A lie of omission is still a lie. You bent the truth to suit yourself, and that's as dishonest as what Blake did. It's not OK, Josh. Not OK at all.'

'Sophie—'

'No,' she said. 'I deserve better than this.'

'You do, and I'm sorry.'

'Too late,' she said. 'I told you everything about me. And you didn't even have the courtesy to tell me your real name, let alone who you are.'

Because he hadn't wanted her to see him as a poor little rich boy. He hadn't wanted her to pity him. He'd wanted her to see who he truly was, not through the filter of the media.

How had it all gone so badly wrong?

'I don't want to see you any more, Mr Cavendish,' she said. The formality in her voice felt as if she'd flayed him. 'I've had more than enough lies to last me a lifetime. No more. Goodbye.'

And then, to his shock, without even giving him the chance to explain, she closed the door in his face.

He stared at the closed door, wanting to hammer it down with his bare fists, but knowing that it would alienate Sophie even further. She'd made her position perfectly clear: she didn't want to see him again. She wasn't even going to give him the chance to explain.

He'd lost her.

And this felt worse than that terrible meeting with his consultant, the one that had forced him to face reality and see that his career was over. Everything he'd defined himself as was over.

Josh had managed to scrape himself back together since then. But this...this felt worse.

Because he'd lost *her*.

Just when he thought he'd found someone special. Someone who made him feel different. Someone he wanted to spend the rest of his life with.

She'd said it was over.

And all the sunshine seemed to have vanished from the world.

Everything around him felt cold and sterile. Unwelcoming.

He didn't know how he could even begin to fix this. Where to start. How to persuade her to give him five minutes of her time so he could tell her what really happened.

But for now everything felt so bad that the only thing he could do was pick up his skis and head for a black run. He'd once told her that the mountains made everything better; and he hoped to hell he was right.

Even though he didn't want to see anyone or talk to anyone, he knew that the first rule of the mountains was that you told someone where you were going—especially if you were heading out on your own. So he sent Giovanni a private message saying which run he was going on, and then turned his phone to silent so he could ignore any reply.

Gio would probably give him a hard time later for doing a black run and putting his knee at risk, but Josh knew that nothing less would sort his head out. He needed something where he'd get the buzz of skiing at high speed, whizzing down a mountain with just his skill to guide him. Something steep and scary to conquer.

He brooded all the way up on the chairlift.

He brooded as he double-checked the bindings of his skis.

He brooded as he got to the edge.

And then he pushed himself off, tucked himself in, and waited for the rush of skiing to clear his mind, the way it usually did.

Except he misjudged a turn, caught the edge of his ski, and tipped over.

At speed.

Christ.

He knew the drill of falls. Distribute your weight as evenly as possible. Land with a straight arm by your side and a straight leg, to avoid hitting your head or your hip. Then turn and dig your arms into the snow to reduce your speed. The last thing he needed now was to slide uncontrollably towards a drop and fall again.

But his knee caught something.

When he finally stopped, he couldn't put any weight on his knee when he tried to get up.

This was bad.

Really bad.

A skier came to a halt beside him. 'You OK, man?'

'No. My knee's…' Josh shook his head, unable to articulate his fears. Terror put a huge lump in his throat and blocked the words.

'Is anyone with you?'

'I'm on my own.'

'OK. Give me a second and I'll sort out help.' The other skier collected Josh's skis and stuck them, crossed, in the snow above Josh to warn other skiers there was an obstacle. 'Did you hit your head or black out at all?'

'No.'

'Well, that's something.' The other skier called the emergency services, giving all the details to help them locate him and Josh.

Was history repeating itself?

The last time he'd had a bad fall, it had been after his relationship had imploded. When Annabel had given him the news that she was pregnant—and then, before he'd even had time to absorb the fact that he was going to be a dad, she'd casually told him she would have a termination unless he married her.

He'd known at that moment how much he didn't want to marry her.

This time, his relationship had fallen apart for a different reason. He hadn't trusted Sophie with the truth. But he'd forgotten the hard lesson he'd learned from Annabel, and he was so angry at himself for not connecting it.

Don't ski when your head's in the wrong place.

He should've found a different way—a safer way— to clear his head.

But no.

He'd gone for the adrenalin rush to wipe out the pain and misery. Instead, he'd wiped out his knee. What if he'd done the rest of the damage his surgeon had warned him about? What if he wasn't able to ski ever again? That would mean he'd lost everything. He'd lost Sophie, he'd lost his new dream of opening an inclusive ski re-sort, and although adaptive skiing was a good alterna-tive it would never give him the same rush as the kind of skiing that he really loved.

It would all be bearable if Sophie was there.

But he'd ruined that by not telling her the whole truth.

It seemed like for ever before the rescue team got there. And even longer while Josh was stuck in the am-bulance. He hated having to be dependent, but he had no choice other than to text Giovanni to say that he'd fallen on the slope and was going to hospital.

By the time Giovanni met him at the hospital, the doctor had already told Josh the news wasn't quite as bad as he feared—he hadn't snapped his ACL again or damaged his meniscus—but he'd need more physio. More work to reduce inflammation and swelling, more exercises to restore full knee extension, and a repetition of all the work he'd done last year.

The worst bit was the doctor's unbreakable rule: no more skiing for the rest of the season.

'So are you going back to England?' Giovanni asked.

'Even if I can't ski—'

'There's no "if" about it,' the doctor cut in.

Josh acknowledged that with a wry smile. 'I'd still rather be here in the mountains.'

'No skiing, no snowboarding, no snow-shoeing, no ice skating, no tobogganing, and no other winter sport I haven't mentioned yet or haven't heard of,' the doc-tor warned. 'You don't even *walk* anywhere if there's the slightest chance you might slip on the ice and jar your knee.'

'I'll make sure he behaves,' Giovanni said. 'You're coming to stay with us, Josh.'

Josh shook his head. 'I don't want to be a burden on you.'

'You'll be more of a burden if you're on your own, because I'll be worried sick about you,' Giovanni pointed out.

'I'd rather be on my own,' Josh said.

'Wallowing in self-pity?' Giovanni demanded. 'Get over yourself!'

It stung, but Josh knew he deserved the rebuke. 'I'm not good company right now, so I'm really better off on my own,' he said. 'But I promise I'll check in with you every morning and every evening.'

'And every lunchtime.' Giovanni folded his arms. 'I'm tempted to let Mamma deal with you.'

Josh gave him a tired smile. 'I know my limits. And I'm not going to do anything stupid. Just work on my physio.' And work out what the hell he was going to do with his life, if he couldn't ski a black run ever again.

'All right. And I'll let Sophie know.'

Sophie.

What Josh would do right now to have Sophie's arms round him. To have her calm common sense whispered into his ear. To feel her warmth and sweetness.

But it wasn't going to happen. He'd ruined that.

'No need. Sophie and I are over.'

'But surely if she knows you're hurt, she'll—?'

'No,' Josh cut in. She'd already rejected him. He wasn't going to let that happen a second time. Or, worse, that she'd be with him out of pity. 'I have my pride.'

'And pride is a very cold bedfellow,' Giovanni said. Right then, Josh didn't think he'd ever feel warm again. 'It's all I have, right now,' he said. 'Would you mind giving me a lift back to Pendio?'

'Only,' Giovanni said, 'if your doctor agrees.'

'Provided you stick to the conditions,' the doctor said.

'No winter sports of any kind,' Josh said dryly. 'I've got the message loud and clear.'

And he had a lot of thinking time coming up. The minutes stretched out emptily before him. Minutes, hours, days, weeks.

And it was all his own stupid fault.

It was a beautiful day. The sun was shining, the sky was impossibly blue, and it was the perfect day for skiing.

Though Sophie didn't plan to ski any more. She missed it—much more than she'd expected to—but no way was she risking going anywhere she might bump into Josh. She'd even asked Kitty to return her skis, poles and helmet to the ski hire place for her, to make doubly sure she didn't accidentally see Josh; and if she wanted any shopping outside their weekly delivery, she asked Kitty to pick it up for her.

She'd resolutely ignored *Celebrity Life*. Kitty had started to tell her something about Josh that had happened a year ago, but Sophie had cut her short. 'I like you, Kitty, but we're going to fall out really badly if you take his side.'

'I'm not taking his side, Soph. But if you'll just li—'

'No ifs. No buts. Josh and I are history. I don't want to hear anything more about him.'

Kitty's shoulders had slumped, but thankfully she'd respected Sophie's feelings and stopped talking about Josh. Sophie had resisted the temptation to look up anything more about Josh's past. He was clearly a rich boy who'd been slumming it and wouldn't know what honesty was if it jumped up in front of him and shouted 'boo'; and she'd had a lucky escape from yet another poor decision.

Luckily Hannah wasn't a fan of the gossip magazines, either, so Sophie could avoid telling her best friend about what had happened and what a fool she'd been.

So much for thinking that this Christmas would be special. That it would mark the start of a new phase of her life.

Josh had tried to call her, but she'd rejected the calls. She'd deleted all his texts unread.

He'd sent her flowers, too. An enormous and hugely expensive display of roses.

She'd given them to Kitty and sent him a note to say thank you for the flowers, but they hadn't changed her mind.

Although she'd made sure the chalet was decorated for the perfect family Christmas for her guests, she knew her smiles were fake and she wasn't even enjoying making Christmassy food for them. Though she had to stick it out and finish her job here in Pendio; she couldn't just leave and go back to England, because she needed the reference as well as the money. She'd get through this. One day at a time. One foot in front of the other.

But never, ever again would she allow herself to trust another man.

Josh didn't answer the video call. Just as he hadn't answered any of them since the day after the accident.

He'd holed up in his chalet and spent all his time on physio and brooding, keeping everyone at a distance.

A few seconds later, a message flashed up on the screen.

Joshie, if you don't answer my call, I'll be forced to fly over to visit you. You wouldn't make me do that with morning sickness, would you?

He stared at the screen. Wait, what? Morning sickness? He was going to be an uncle again?

He called her back. 'Lauren? Are you all right?'

'Yes. Though I'm not using the Tube again until this phase passes. Rush hour crush and questionable personal hygiene isn't a good mix with morning sickness.'

'It's not a good mix, full stop.' He smiled at her. 'Congratulations!'

'It's still early days, so it's not public knowledge,' she warned.

'Got it. Mum and Dad know?'

'Yes. So does Willow. She's thrilled at the prospect of having a baby sister to play with and she's already picked out her favourite teddy as a present.' She laughed. 'She's been such a sweetie. I was throwing up yesterday, and she actually asked if I wanted Daddy to bring me some of the pink medicine to make the baby better.'

'That's lovely.' And suddenly Josh missed his family. His mum. His dad. His sister. His brother-in-law. His beyond cute three-year-old niece.

'So how are *you*?'

'I'm fine,' he fibbed.

'You don't look it,' she said, not pulling her punches.

'And you're in pushing-everyone-away mode, just like when you crashed in the race, so does that mean your knee's worse than last time?'

'We're not talking surgery—at least, not yet. Just intense physio.'

'Right.' She paused. 'So what actually happened?'

He gave her a condensed version of Annabel's article, Sophie's reaction and his fall.

Lauren rolled her eyes. 'That bloody woman. I wish she'd just leave you alone.'

Yeah. So did he.

'What are you going to do about Sophie?' Lauren asked.

'At the moment, there's nothing I can do. She won't talk to me.' And he wasn't brilliantly mobile, so he couldn't exactly chase after her to try and make her change her mind. She'd rejected his calls and ignored his texts; although she'd been polite and sent him a text to thank him for the flowers, she'd made it clear he was wasting his time because she wasn't going to forgive him.

'You should've been honest with her.'

'I would've been, if she'd given me the chance,' he pointed out.

'But you had plenty of opportunities to tell her before Annabel stuck her oar in,' Lauren said dryly. 'So what now? Are you just going to sit there stewing in self-pity?'

'Probably,' he agreed.

'Men!' She groaned. 'Josh, it's Christmas in a couple of days. I'll give you until Christmas Day to sulk, and then I'm pulling rank as your older sister. Either you find something you want to do with your life, or you're coming to work for me. And if you thought *you* were a slavedriver to yourself when you were training for the world championship, you'll find that I take it to the next level.'

His sister was the sweetest person he knew, besides Sophie. No way was she a slavedriver. Everyone in the company loved her. He couldn't help smiling.

'That's better,' Lauren said. 'Seriously, Josh, everything you've told me about Sophie makes it clear she meant a lot to you. Why don't you ask her to give you a chance to explain? And this time tell her everything. Including what Annabel did. I still think you should've sued that woman for libel.'

'I just wanted the whole mess to die down. Putting my side of the story out would only have raked it all up again, and some people would still have believed her anyway because she got her story in first,' he said. 'As for Sophie, I've blown it. I know dishonesty's a big thing with her.' He told Lauren what had happened with Blake.

'That's awful,' Lauren said, looking shocked. 'But you can do something to help her, Josh. We can pay a private detective to track the guy down. Even if he's spent all the money and she doesn't get a single penny back, at least we can find him and that'll give her closure.'

'She explicitly told me not to interfere.' He explained what he'd done about Gaz and his friends.

'Hmm. You should've handled that a wee bit differently.'

'Tell me about it.'

'So she told you not to interfere. She didn't tell *me*

not to interfere, though,' Lauren said sweetly. 'And I don't like cheats and liars, either.'

He winced. 'I get the point. I screwed up. Big time.'

'And you're suffering for it.' She sighed. 'So what are you going to do, Josh?'

'Right now, I don't know. Work out how to get her to talk to me. And then work out what I'm going to do with my life.' He shook his head. 'Much as I love you, I don't want to work for you.'

'You're right. It'd be a disaster. We'd drive each other potty,' she said. 'And I don't think you'll settle for being a ski instructor. Not long term.'

'I have,' he said, 'been thinking about something else. Making the world a better place.' Taking his cue from Sophie.

'That sounds good. What are you thinking?'

'I love skiing,' he said. 'It makes me feel free. Alive.' She nodded.

'And I know I'm one bad fall away from disaster with my knee. Right now, and with what happened last year, I've got some understanding of how it feels to be restricted in what you can do physically.' He took a deep breath. 'So I've been thinking about adaptive skiing. Maybe I could set up a place where the whole family can ski together, regardless of injury or ability. We'd have trained instructors and the right equipment. Somewhere that makes the world a bit brighter for people with disabilities who've already had to struggle enough. Somewhere with a spa and massage therapy, and rooms that work for everyone.'

'That,' Lauren said, 'sounds brilliant.'

'But?' He could see the wariness in her face.

'But please tell me it's not going to be somewhere

miles away from the family, so we never see you. You've spent the last ten years or so travelling the world. We miss you.'

'There's room for compromise,' he said. 'I want to set up a resort here—but in the summer months I'd be happy for someone else to manage it as a spa retreat, and I'll come back to England.'

'You *could* get snow machines and build a resort here, near Mum and Dad,' she said.

'It wouldn't be the same. There aren't any mountains near London,' Josh pointed out. 'And dry slopes just aren't like real mountains.'

Lauren sighed. 'Then your compromise sounds about the best thing. Dad's handing Cavendish Software over to me properly next month. As the new CEO, I'd be happy to offer some serious sponsorship. Not just helping you set up the place, but making it affordable for your clients. Assisted places.'

'That,' he said, 'would be amazing.'

'What's the point of being rich if all you're going to do is spend it on fancy clothes and partying?' she asked.

Which was what he'd done with Annabel. Wasted all that time and resources when he could've done something better: the complete opposite of what he knew Sophie would have done in the same circumstances.

'Sophie,' he said, 'would absolutely love you. And you'd love her.'

'Then you'd better fix things between you, little brother.' She smiled at him. 'Right. Nagging over. I'm going over to see our parents and reassure them that you're still just about in one piece. And you're going to talk to Sophie. In her shoes, I would ignore your calls and texts, too. You need to do this properly, face to face.'

'I will,' he promised. 'Not this evening, because she's working and it wouldn't be fair of me to go and demand attention. But tomorrow. I'll talk to her tomorrow after I've done my morning physio.'

'Good luck,' she said.

'Thanks. I'm going to need it,' he admitted.

CHAPTER NINE

THE COFFEE SMELLED REVOLTING, and Sophie nearly gagged. No way could she drink this.

No way could she serve this to her chalet guests, either. It would be the worst Christmas Eve breakfast drink ever.

Except...the coffee had been fine when she'd opened it yesterday, and she'd stored it in an airtight container in the fridge: so it wouldn't have suddenly gone off.

Maybe she'd done something stupid. She couldn't think what, but then again she was finding it hard to think rationally at the moment. Worrying about the future. Worrying about what was going to happen when she left here in just over a month's time. Would she be able to find a new job, and quickly? Could she afford a room in a shared house in London?

Josh had been a distraction from that.

But Josh had lied to her. Toyed with her.

She tipped the coffee down the sink and made a fresh batch.

Only the new batch smelled vile, too.

Hannah had been like that six months ago, unable to bear the smell of—

She stopped mid-thought, breath frozen in horror.

Of course she wasn't pregnant.

OK, so she'd missed a period, but stress always did that to her. She'd missed three in a row after her parents' accident, and two when she'd lost the restaurant. This was just stress, she reminded herself. She'd be fine.

But the suggestion was in her head and it wouldn't go away.

Pregnant.

She and Josh had used protection when they'd made love, but condoms could fail. The chance was infinitesimally small, but it was still there. And it only took one sperm to fertilise an egg. Sophie knew from Hannah's infertility journey exactly when you could get pregnant: it wasn't just that little window during ovulation. Sperm could live for up to five days in fertile pre-ovulation cervical mucus. And...

No. She couldn't be pregnant.

Could she?

She managed to keep in professional mode for her guests, making waffles, eggs Florentine and endless toast, but the cooking scents made her feel slightly ill.

Ill enough for Kitty to notice. 'Are you OK, Sophie?'

'Yes, sure,' Sophie said, brushing it off. She knew she needed to come up with a plausible excuse, so she added the fib. 'Just a bit of a headache. I'll be fine. And you go off skiing early. I'll clear up.'

'Are you sure?'

'Yes.' She wanted to be on her own to think things through.

By the time the kitchen was restored to perfect shining order, she'd come to the conclusion that she was probably being ridiculous, but buying a pregnancy test would reassure her that her missed period was down to stress and nothing more significant.

And please, please don't let her bump into Josh. It would be just her luck.

Thankfully there was no sign of Josh. She didn't know the person on duty in the pharmacy, and was able to buy a pregnancy test and shove it to the bottom of her bag without the risk of any gossip.

The walk back to the chalet seemed to take for ever.

She put her shopping away, then went to her en-suite bathroom. Time to prove that she was worrying about nothing.

'It's stress, Sophie Harris,' she told herself firmly. 'Just stress. Do the test, and your period will probably start tomorrow.'

She didn't bother reading the instructions. Apart from the fact that she knew the stress of the situation would make her struggle more than usual with reading, and the letters of the tiny print would merge together, she'd been there enough times to hold Hannah's hand. All tests worked on the same principle. Pee on the stick, cap it, check the first window for a line to show that the test was working, wait a bit, look at the other window, and then there was either a line to say you were pregnant—or, in Hannah's case, month after month, a window as empty as her womb.

Her heart squeezed. Hannah was going to be such a great mum, yet she'd had such problems conceiving. It would be horribly ironic if Sophie, whose life was currently in a mess and who didn't have a partner, had fallen pregnant without even trying.

And, if she was expecting their baby, how would Josh react to the news?

'Don't overthink it,' she counselled herself aloud. 'It isn't an issue because you're not pregnant. You're just stressed, that's all.'

Just to prove it, she glanced down at the window.

Had she been holding the stick, she would've dropped it in shock. As it was, it lay where she'd set it on the side of the sink.

There was a line in each of the windows.

Meaning she *was* pregnant.

What now?

She'd thought about having children when Blake had asked her to marry him. She'd thought that she'd be able to combine motherhood and a career. That her children would grow up in a happy home, just as she had, safe and secure. She'd so wanted to be part of a family again.

Right now, she had no security. Her job here would end in a few weeks, and she didn't yet have anything lined up for her return to England—despite applying for several jobs online. She had nowhere to live. She'd saved her salary here and most of her tips, but those savings wouldn't last for long.

Her time in the Dolomites was supposed to be a way of getting herself back on her feet. Picking herself up and dusting herself down, just as she would if she fell over in the snow. Working out a plan for her life.

This had turned everything upside down.

A termination felt wrong, when her best friend had struggled so hard to fall pregnant.

And a baby would mean that she had a family again. Someone else in the world who was related to her by blood, instead of her being alone.

Though the baby wasn't just hers. It took two to make a baby. She couldn't just pretend Josh didn't exist. He had the right to know that he was going to be a father, even though she didn't intend to take a penny from him; she wasn't letting him back into her life, because she didn't trust him not to let her down again. Who knew what else he'd lied about?

How was she going to tell him?

Write to him? Even though she was angry with him for keeping her in the dark, for not telling her the truth about himself, she wasn't going to tell him by text or email. This wasn't the sort of conversation she could have on the phone, either. It would have to be face to face.

She grabbed her phone and texted him.

Need to talk to you. When's convenient?

More painkillers weren't the answer. The only way was to push himself through the pain.

Josh gritted his teeth and did the physio. It hurt. It hurt *a lot*. But it was his own stupid fault. Hadn't he learned his lesson, last time? Don't ski when distracted. Especially don't ski a black run.

God only knew how far that tumble had set his progress back.

So much for telling Sophie that the mountains made everything better. This time, they had made things worse.

Maybe he should give up skiing completely.

What was it Sophie had said? Toss a coin and you'll know what you need to do. OK. Heads he battled on; tails he gave up.

He tossed the coin.

Tails.

Give up, then.

She'd said his reaction would make him know if it was the right choice. Be horrified, and he'd know he should carry on. Be relieved, and he'd know giving up was the right thing to do.

But what if you felt…empty?

He didn't feel anything. Anything at all.

It was like being stuck in a snowdrift, everything still and quiet and getting gradually colder, the change so gradual that he was barely aware of it happening. Chilled to the bone, the blood growing sluggish.

Just empty.

Because he'd lost her.

No way could he go to talk to her when he was in this mood. He was likely to say something stupid and make things even worse between them. Somehow he'd have to clear his head. Except what he always did to clear his head wasn't an option. No skiing. He couldn't even drive himself out to a forest somewhere.

Why would Sophie want to bother with such a pathetic specimen?

Well, she'd made it pretty clear she didn't want to bother with him any more.

Happy Christmas.

Not.

This was shaping up to be the most miserable Christmas ever. And he needed to shake off the self-pity. That wasn't who he was.

His phone beeped to signal an incoming text.

Probably a message from Giovanni to remind him that it was Christmas Eve and they were expecting him for dinner tonight. He definitely had to improve his mood before then; but even if he was still feeling this low, he was going to fake some Christmas joy, for their sake. Maybe playing with the kids would help.

But when he looked at the screen, he saw the message was from Sophie.

The person he most wanted to speak to; yet, at the same time, the one person he knew he ought to avoid until his head was straight, so he didn't mess it up.

Need to talk to you. When's convenient?

Straight and to the point, which he expected from her. But, at their last meeting, she'd made it very clear that she wanted nothing more to do with him. What did she want to talk to him about?

Unless Giovanni had told her about the fall and his knee. If Lauren hadn't thought to tell the Rendinis that she'd staged an intervention, maybe Giovanni was under the impression that Sophie could get through to Josh when he was in pushing-everyone-away mode and had asked Sophie to get in touch with him.

He planned to deflect her—but his fingers clearly weren't agreeing with the plan, because he found himself texting back.

Whenever's convenient for you.

Oh, for pity's sake.

Disgusted with himself, he started a new message to say that he had a meeting—she didn't need to know that meeting was with himself to do his physio that afternoon—when his phone beeped again.

Now? Your chalet?

So she knew he wasn't teaching?

Well, duh. He wouldn't have replied to her text if he'd been teaching, would he?

Might as well get it over with.

OK.

On my way

That was her reply.

Then reality snapped in. The chalet was a pigsty. One glance and she'd know what a mess his head was in. So, if she'd been sent by the Rendinis in an attempt to find out what kind of state he was really in, she'd call them straight away.

Why hadn't he been sensible and suggested meeting at her chalet, or better still on neutral ground? Too late, now.

He needed to fix this.

Fast.

If he tidied the living room and kept her out of the kitchen, he might get away with pretending everything was just fine.

He scooped up the magazines and books he'd tried reading and had tossed aside, and dumped them on his bed. The pizza boxes and takeout cartons went in the bin. The empty coffee mugs and stray bits of cutlery went in the dishwasher, out of sight. He dragged the overflowing laundry basket from the bathroom—just in case she asked to use it—to his bedroom.

There was no time to vacuum or dust. But if he opened the kitchen window there would be some fresh air. It'd be cold—seriously cold—but that was a huge improvement on the stale warm air that was there now.

It was snowing, but not hard enough to mean he couldn't leave the window open.

He'd just put the kettle on and shaken ground coffee into a cafetière, hoping that the scent of fresh coffee would mask any lingering smells of pizza remains, when there was a knock at his door.

His knee was hurting, but he wasn't going to admit it. And he wasn't going to let her see him limp, even through the frosted glass of the door. He forced himself to walk normally, even though it hurt like hell, and opened the door to her. 'Come in. Coffee?'

'No, thanks.'

Her face looked pinched, he thought, but he suppressed the urge to wrap his arms round her and hold her close. She'd made it clear she didn't want that from him. 'Can I take your coat?'

'It's a bit...' She gestured to the snowflakes. 'It's OK.'

'So what did you want?' he asked, knowing it sounded a bit abrupt and rude but not knowing what else to say. And scared that his mouth would run away with him and beg her to give him a second chance.

'I, um...you need to know,' she said. 'I missed my period. I did a test this morning. I'm pregnant.'

Pregnant.

There was a roaring in his ears.

He'd been here before.

All he could see was Annabel standing in front of him, that fateful day. The day of the championship competition. The day that had changed his life for ever.

'I'm pregnant, Josh. I'm going to have a termination. Unless you're planning to marry me.'

An ultimatum.

One that had clarified everything for him: yes, of course he had a responsibility to her because she was pregnant—but he didn't want to marry her. He didn't want to spend the rest of his life with her. They'd had fun together, but he'd started to suspect that she'd seen him in terms of his family background. The wealth. The lifestyle she wanted. The fact that he was world champion, so they were invited to all the glittery parties and events.

The way Annabel had told him the news—no discussion, just an ultimatum—had shocked him.

They'd had a huge fight.

And she'd stormed out.

He'd been thinking about it on that mogul run, instead of concentrating on what he was doing. Crashed. Wrecked his knee.

And Annabel had miscarried their baby.

At least, the press had said she'd miscarried. The story had been plastered across social media and the gossip pages. Photographs of Annabel looking wan and tearful. Annabel, who'd claimed he'd dumped her and broken their engagement—when they hadn't even been engaged.

The whole thing had felt staged. Maybe he was being unkind and she really *had* miscarried. But it didn't quite gel with the woman who'd given him the ultimatum *Marry me or I'll terminate the pregnancy.* That sounded like a woman who didn't care about a baby one way or the other.

And she'd certainly been happy enough dating the new world champion, a few weeks later.

Being stuck indoors had left Josh with too much time

to brood. Too much time to wonder what the truth really was.

'You're pregnant,' he said, talking to Sophie but seeing Annabel.

'I thought you had the right to know,' she said. 'But I don't expect anything from you and I won't be claiming any kind of child support. We'll be fine on our own.'

He couldn't quite process this.

She was pregnant.

She wanted nothing from him.

She just thought he should know that he was going to be a father.

His mouth opened and closed, but there weren't any words. His head was as empty as his heart.

Before he could collect himself, she said, 'Clearly you're OK with that. Fine. Goodbye, Josh.'

And she walked out into the snow.

Closing the door quietly behind her.

What?

'Wait!' he called, and this time he hobbled to the door as fast as he could.

But she'd already gone.

Hell.

He couldn't rush after her the way he wanted to. Not when it was so icy and snowy outside. He couldn't risk slipping and doing even more damage to his bad knee. He couldn't drive, either.

What was going to be quicker? Limping to her chalet, or getting a taxi?

He called the local cab.

They were busy, but they could pick him up in twenty minutes.

Twenty minutes?

He couldn't wait that long. He wanted to talk to Sophie properly. Ask her to give him a chance. Ask her to let him explain. And he needed to do it now. The longer he left it, the less likely it was she'd talk to him.

When Sophie had told him her news, he'd been instantly transported back to the past. To Annabel. But Sophie was nothing like Annabel. She was honest. She wasn't going to run to the press and tell them a pack of lies to try and get what she wanted from him. Sophie had even said she expected nothing from him.

That wasn't what he wanted. At all.

What he wanted was Sophie—and their baby.

But first he was going to have to find her. And persuade her to talk to him.

He tried calling her, but the phone went straight to voicemail.

This wasn't something he wanted to do by voicemail message or text. She could ignore a phone call, but she couldn't ignore him standing on her doorstep.

Which left him with a choice. It was either wait twenty minutes for a taxi, or risk his knee on an icy path. And, given that the journeys would take about the same amount of time, this time he'd go for the sensible option.

He booked the taxi.

CHAPTER TEN

IT DIDN'T LOOK as if the guests were in residence, Josh thought as he made his way up the steps to Sophie's chalet. Hopefully Kitty would be out on the slopes. And hopefully Sophie had come back here rather than going to a café in the resort.

He knocked on the door.

There was no answer.

He called through the letterbox, 'Sophie, I'm staying here until someone lets me in—whether it's you, Kitty or your guests. We need to talk. Please.'

Still no answer.

He texted her.

Sitting on the front step of your chalet. Staying here until you talk to me. Even if sitting here turns me into a snowman.

No answer.

He waited three minutes. He didn't care about the cold or the snow, but his knee was really starting to hurt. He texted her again.

OK. Going to borrow a megaphone and hold my side of the conversation very publicly.

That got him an answer.

She opened the door. 'What do you want, Josh?' she snapped.

Doing his best not to wince as he stood up, he said, 'We need to talk. I owe you an apology—and a lot of explanations.'

She shook her head. 'You don't owe me anything. We're done with each other.'

Oh, no, they weren't. 'You're pregnant with my baby, and we need to sort this out.'

'You can't dump me like you dumped Annabel, because I've already broken up with you.'

He winced. 'I guess I deserve that, though for the record there's an awful lot more to that story than what she told the press. But, first off, I want you to know that I'm not deserting you and I never would.'

Her expression was cold. 'I don't want you, Josh.'

He sighed. 'Please, Sophie. Let me explain. And then if you decide you don't want me in your life I'll walk away. But, regardless of anything else, I want you to know that I fully intend to support you and our child.'

'So that would be the son of a billionaire throwing money at a situation to make it go away?'

'No!' Oh, why did this have to be so complicated? 'I mean, yes, my dad's a billionaire, but I'm not trying to buy you off.'

'I thought you were a part-time ski instructor who had a bit of savings but you were thinking about taking another job. You let me believe that.' She shook her head. 'How many other lies have you told me?'

Technically, he hadn't lied. He *was* a part-time ski instructor thinking about his next job. He just hadn't told her that the savings were substantial. Or about his family background.

'I didn't set out to hurt you, Sophie. I know I've made a mess of things, and I'm sorry. But if you'll let me explain—let me be completely honest with you now—then maybe we can work our way through it. Please?'

She was silent for so long that he thought she'd say no, but finally she nodded. 'Come through to the kitchen.'

Then she frowned as he tried to walk normally beside her and failed. 'You're limping.'

'That doesn't matter right now. You're the important one. Are *you* all right? My sister had terrible morning sickness with Willow. How are you feeling?'

She stared at him. 'You're concerned about me?'

'Of course I'm concerned. You've just told me you're pregnant, you're in another country and you don't have family or close friends near—and it's Christmas Eve.'

'There's a thing called the internet. And another thing called a global mobile phone network. I don't have to be physically in the same place as my best friend to be close to her.'

He understood why she was angry with him. Hormones probably weren't helping. But his knee hurt and he was bone-deep tired and miserable. He didn't want to fight any more. 'Just answer the question, Sophie,' he said quietly. 'Are you all right?'

'Yes.'

'Good.' He took a deep breath. 'I'm sorry about the way I reacted when you told me about the baby. I was a bit shocked.'

'That makes two of us,' she said.

'I needed a few moments to process things,' he said quietly. 'I'm not here to fight with you. I'm on your side. Team Sophie.'

Her eyes filled with tears. 'How do I know that's true?'

'You don't,' he admitted. 'I can't prove it. But maybe if we talk it through you might…' He grimaced. 'I would say, start to trust me, but I've already blown that one. You might see it from a different perspective, perhaps.'

Her shoulders finally relaxed. 'OK.' She glanced at the way he was standing. 'You'd better sit down and take the weight off your knee.'

Did she know about either of his crashes?

'What happened?' she asked, gesturing to a stool in the kitchen.

He sat down, grateful for the pressure to be off his knee. 'The quick answer is that it's an aggravation of an old injury. Entirely my fault.'

'And the slow answer?'

'That would be part of my explanation,' he said.

'All right.' She paused. 'Do you want a cup of tea?'

The English answer—or perhaps the chalet host's answer—to everything. 'No. Just to talk,' he said.

She nodded. 'I'm listening.'

'I was never engaged to Annabel,' he said. 'She was one of my set, and her background's similar to mine. I dated her, yes—but I never asked her to marry me. I think deep down I knew we weren't right for each other.'

Sophie said nothing.

'What you said, about your only value to Blake being your money—that, and my position in the media, was precisely my value to Annabel,' he said softly.

Sophie flinched.

'She liked dating a world champion, having access to swish parties and skiing invitations that might not otherwise have come her way. And it suited me at the time to have someone beautiful and glamorous as my partner.' He paused. This might upset Sophie, but then again she already knew some of it from the media stories. 'I don't want to hurt you or give you the wrong idea. I'm just telling you the facts,' he said carefully. 'Annabel told me she was pregnant.'

Sophie still said nothing, but her eyes were huge and full of wariness.

'Not like the way you told me,' he said. 'Annabel told me if I didn't marry her she'd have a termination.'

Shock flittered across Sophie's face. 'That's—' She shook her head. 'I don't know what to say.'

'Her timing wasn't great,' Josh said dryly. 'I told her I didn't have the headspace to think about the situation until after the competition. I was racing that day. Freestyle.'

At Sophie's blank look, Josh explained, 'It's the thing where you do acrobatics. Jumps, turns, spins, that sort of thing. You ski on moguls—the bumps made when people do turns. I loved doing that, more than anything else in the world.' He paused. 'Anyway, I had some time to think before the race. I tried to imagine myself settled down with Annabel and a baby, the way my sister was with her husband and Willow, or my parents had been with Lauren and me. And I just couldn't see it. I couldn't imagine her cuddled up with a toddler and a book, reading a story. She wouldn't tolerate sticky hands on her designer clothes, or risk her hair being mussed or her make-up smudged. She would've had a team of nannies and insisted on boarding school.' He shook his head. 'That wasn't what I wanted. At all. I realised then I didn't want to marry her. I was attracted to her, yes, but in a really superficial way. I didn't love her. Obviously I had responsibilities to her and the baby, and I would never have shirked them. Of course I would've supported them. But I didn't want to marry Annabel and spend the rest of my life with her.' He dragged in a breath. 'Normally, when I raced, my mind would be completely on the course. That day, all I could think about was Annabel and the baby, and her ultimatum. If I married her, we'd all be miserable. If I didn't…she'd terminate the pregnancy. I wasn't paying enough attention to what I was doing and I crashed. Wrecked my knee. My surgeon said I had a choice: I could go back to doing what I loved, but it was highly unlikely I'd still be able to walk in twenty years' time. Or I could be sensible and stop competing.'

Sophie winced. 'So you had to give up what you loved most in the world. I'm sorry.'

'It wasn't your fault. It was mine, for letting myself be distracted at the wrong moment.' He frowned. 'Annabel realised I didn't have a future in professional skiing any more, so she wouldn't get the invites to all the parties and all the things she enjoyed most. She broke it off between us.'

Sophie narrowed her eyes at him. 'The papers said you dumped her.'

'I guess the "heartbroken dumped fiancée" was a better spin for her than "disgruntled girlfriend dumps injured champ who'll never race again while he's still in hospital"—and she broke the story about my knee, too,' he said. 'Which meant all my sponsorship deals were terminated pretty quickly.' He grimaced. 'I understand why they dropped me from their campaigns, but it wasn't her place to tell them.'

'Why didn't you tell everyone the truth—that she was the one who dumped you?'

'At the time, I had other things to think about,' he said. 'I was coming to terms with the end of my career. Plus she got her story in first. If I'd protested a few days later, people wouldn't have believed me. Plus their minds were already made up by then.' He looked away. 'Annabel didn't want to marry me for myself. I'm not sure whether she just wanted the glory of being with a champion skier, or whether she wanted to marry a billionaire's son so she could carry on with the lifestyle she enjoyed. As I clearly wasn't going to be forthcoming on either front, she decided to cash in and sell her story. Even though it wasn't true.' He shrugged. 'It took a few weeks, but the story died down eventually.'

'What happened to the baby?' Sophie asked.

'She told the papers she had a miscarriage. Maybe she did; or maybe she had a termination. Your guess is as good as mine.' He spread his hands. 'Either way, I don't think she was as devastated as she made out to the press. Apart from the fact she'd given me that ultimatum in the first place, it wasn't very long before she was dating the new world champion skier.'

Sophie digested this.

All was becoming horribly clear.

No wonder Josh had reacted with silence when she'd

told him about the baby. He'd been here before and it had turned his life upside down: not in a good way.

'Let me get this straight. You'd had an accident, you'd really hurt yourself, you weren't going to be able to do what you loved most any more—and Annabel not only told everyone lies about you, she did a hatchet job on your career and your reputation as well.' Blake had cheated her and lied to her, but what Annabel had done was on another scale entirely. She'd really rubbed salt in Josh's wounds.

'Looking back, I know I had a lucky escape. We would have made each other seriously unhappy and ended up with a really messy divorce. Though I would've made sure I had custody of the baby so my child could at least grow up feeling loved.'

She believed him; the way he'd talked about his family, he'd grown up loved and he'd do the same for his child.

'So why did she make up this new story?'

'My best guess is that it was because she was unhappy and I'm an easy target for her,' he said. 'I hear on the grapevine that her latest guy dumped her recently. Maybe she was lashing out to make herself feel better. Although Pendio's a family resort rather than the kind of glamorous party place where she'd normally ski, someone had obviously invited her here for a break. Unfortunately she saw me—saw *us*—and it was one of those things where she couldn't stand to think I was happy when she wasn't. I'm sorry she dragged you into it. My family lawyer's arranging that she makes a public apology to you.'

Sophie shook her head. 'It doesn't matter about me. To be honest, I'd rather you left it. I don't want her digging and finding out about Blake. I really don't want the story spread everywhere.'

'Then we'll do it the other way,' he said. 'I'll get my lawyer to tell the gossip magazines I don't have a drink problem and remind them about the laws of defamation. She won't get any more airspace because they won't want to risk having to pay damages.'

It was a good solution. 'I can live with that.' But there was something else worrying her.

'You weren't limping, the last time I saw you,' she said. 'So what happened?'

'After the accident, you mean? I had a lot of physio, before I came here,' he said. 'Racing's completely off the cards for me now. Angelo—my coach, and Giovanni's younger brother—suggested I tried coaching, because at least then I could stay on the slopes. I did my teaching qualification and the idea was to spend this season here, to decide what I want to do. This isn't the sort of place that people who follow skiing championships would come to, even though Vincenzo—Angelo and Giovanni's dad—was a world champion in his day. But, even so, using my name instead of my initials gave me a little bit of anonymity. Space to think.'

'That wasn't what I meant. Why are you limping *now*?'

'Ah. That. Pure stupidity,' he said. 'You know I told you that the mountains make everything better?'

She felt her eyes widen. 'What did you do?'

'Went as fast as I could down a black run,' he said. 'I took a tumble. And I hit my knee when I was trying to come to a halt.' He grimaced. 'It's the second time I've ever been taken off a mountain by the rescue teams. There won't be a third.'

'How bad is it?'

'Not as bad as last time,' he said. 'But, when they found out what I'd done, my coach shouted at me, my surgeon shouted at me, my parents shouted at me, my sister shouted at me, Gio shouted at me...' He moved his hands in rueful circles.

Did he expect her to shout at him, too? For taking a stupid risk? But there was always a reason why someone behaved in a certain way. And she remembered what he'd said about his original accident. It had happened because he wasn't concentrating, because he was thinking about the baby and his fight with Annabel.

This time, had he been thinking about *their* fight?

She needed to know.

'Why did you fall? Was it because...?' Guilt made the words stick in her throat.

'Of the fight I had with you?' he finished, clearly guessing her thoughts. 'No. It was my own fault. I wasn't paying proper attention.'

'Because you were thinking of the fight.'

'I should've had more sense than to go out in the first place,' he said, 'so do *not* blame yourself. This one's all on me.'

'How long will it take to fix?'

'I don't know,' he said. 'I'm doing the physio, even though it hurts like hell. And that's probably another reason why I wasn't as receptive to you as I should've been this morning. Physio always leaves me in a filthy mood.'

'I'm sorry.'

'So am I,' he said. Then he looked her straight in the eye. 'So where does that leave us?'

'I...' She shook her head, not knowing what to say.

Did they have a future? Or had she messed it up? 'I'm sorry I didn't give you the chance to explain about Annabel.'

'I understand why you didn't. I lied to you—mainly by omission,' he said. 'Because I thought you'd see me in terms of my background.'

'You thought I'd be a gold-digger?' It hurt even more that he'd thought she could be like Annabel.

'No. I thought you'd see me as a poor little rich boy. Spoiled and entitled, like Gaz and his friends.'

She frowned. 'You're not like that.'

'But I have been in the past,' he said, 'and you were pretty scathing about rich boys who'd never done a day's work in their lives. I didn't want you to see me as one of them.'

She could understand that.

'Given the damage Blake did to you by lying, it's not surprising you were angry with me when you found out who I was. I knew how you felt about lying, and I should've told you the truth sooner. A lie of omission is still a lie.'

She could sugar-coat it and say everything was OK. But it wasn't. 'Yes, it is, and yes, you should have,' she said. 'It hurts that you didn't trust me.'

'I pretty much lost my trust in relationships and I didn't want to get involved with anyone, after Annabel. The same way as I'm guessing what happened with Blake made you lose your trust in relationships.'

'Yes.' She hadn't wanted to get involved with anyone again, either.

He looked at her, his grey eyes very clear. 'Then I met you. And everything changed. I'd started enjoying working with my students, but you were different. There was something more. You were like sunshine making everything sparkle, and I couldn't wait for our lessons. You gave me a different perspective, and I started seeing the world through your eyes. Seeing the magic of the Christmas market, with the fairy lights: I think that's the moment when I really fell in love with you.'

She stared at him. 'You fell in love with me?'

He nodded. 'I never intended to. And all that stuff I said about just taking things as they come—I think I was trying to convince myself as much as convince you.'

He loved her.

Or did he? Had he changed his mind, since she'd ended things between them?

'So,' he said. 'We're having a baby. And I'm telling you now that I plan to be a hands-on dad. My dad worked ridiculous hours when I was growing up, but he never missed anything at school—from sports days to the awful concerts where Lauren and I played one or two shrieking notes over and over on a recorder. That's the kind of dad I want to be. Not just the fun dad who does afternoons in the park, but the one who changes nappies, gets up in the night when the baby's teething and fractious, reads a bedtime story and coaxes a toddler to eat more veg.'

'That's what my dad was like,' she said.

'And I want to be your partner,' he said. 'Your husband, if you'll marry me, or living with you, if not. I want to support you, Sophie. That dream of having a restaurant that gives other people a second chance—I can make that happen. Anywhere you want it to.'

Her dream. Handed to her on a plate.

It was tempting.

But was it what Josh wanted from life? She'd thought he wanted to stay out here in the Dolomites. Even after his accident, he'd chosen to be in the mountains rather than England. The last thing she wanted was for him to feel trapped and end up resenting her. 'What about you?' she asked. 'What are your dreams?

'Short of getting someone to invent a new kind of knee replacement, I'm not going to get my old job back,' he said wryly. 'I didn't lie to you about that. No more championship skiing.'

'But you love the snow. Surely you want to stay in it as much as possible?'

'I do, and I have ideas of what I want to do here,' he admitted, 'but I love you more. If it's a choice between you and the snow, then you win, hands down.'

'There must,' she said, 'be some room for compromise. Or are you planning to work for your dad, after all?'

He shook his head. 'Lauren's the one who's worked for it and deserves it. She'll be a brilliant CEO—way better than I ever could be. She understands the business and she's great with the staff. I'm not shoving her out of the way. Ever.' He took a deep breath. 'Actually, this last tumble has done me a favour.'

'How?'

'It's focused me,' he said. 'It's made me realise what I want. You know your coin challenge?'

'Ye-es.'

'I tried it. It seems I don't want to be a ski instructor and I don't want to be a world champion skier any more, either. What I want is to make the world a better place.' He looked at her. 'I want my own ski resort.'

His own ski resort. She frowned. 'That means snow. I mean—I know we sometimes get snow in England, but nothing like it is here. You couldn't have a ski season in, say, London.'

'Technically I could, with a snow machine and dry slopes; but it's not the same. It's not the mountains.'

'So what are you thinking?'

'There's a place in the next valley from this one. The owners are looking to sell,' he said. 'Except I'd want to make a few changes. With the injuries I've had over the last year or so, the limitations I've had to face, it's made me realise I want to do something with adaptive skiing.'

'Adaptive skiing?'

'For people with disabilities,' he said. 'And their families. So they can have a break together and all of them can enjoy the thrill of going down a slope. Nobody's left out. I'm thinking a hotel, self-catering chalets for families, a ski slope, specially trained disability instructors and physiotherapists, and a spa.'

Which all sounded amazing: but it didn't fit in with her dream of getting another restaurant in London. They couldn't spread themselves that thinly. She'd have to give it up.

Either it showed in her face or she'd accidentally said it aloud, because he said softly, 'You don't have to give up on your dream. I was thinking maybe we could spend snow season here, and the rest of the time in London with someone else managing the resort. So either you could have a restaurant as part of the resort, or you could have a place in London with a manager during ski season. Whatever works for you. We can do both. Work together. You could work with me at the resort in snow season, and I could work with you at the restaurant in summer. A waiter, perhaps.'

'A billionaire's son—a former world champion skier—working as a waiter in a restaurant?' she asked.

'A husband,' he corrected, 'supporting his wife's business and helping her make a difference.'

'You haven't actually asked me to marry you,' she pointed out.

'Because I'm terrified you'll say no,' he admitted. 'And I'm also terrified you'll say yes, in case I don't live up to what you want from a husband.'

She blinked. 'How could you ever think you wouldn't live up to what I want?'

'I quote,' he said, '"I deserve better than this." And you're right. You do.' He shrugged. 'Plus I'm pretty sure I can't get down on one knee. Though I wish I could, because it's snowing—just like it was the first time I met you.'

'I remember. When I wandered onto the edge of the piste.'

'It was too early for many skiers to be out, and the snow had obscured the edge of the piste,' he said. 'And you were looking up at the snow.'

'Thinking that this year I'd see a proper white Christmas with proper snow, not just a tiny dusting in some corner of London that was miles away from me,' she said. Then she looked at him, her blue eyes piercing. 'It's Christmas Eve.'

'It hasn't felt like it,' he admitted. 'All the magic of Christmas I had with you, from the market and the sleigh ride and the snow angel—and it was gone, wrecked because I didn't tell you the truth about myself soon enough.'

'You've explained now,' she said. 'And I understand why you didn't want to tell me earlier.' She reached out and took his hand. 'It's snowing. Like it was when I first met you.' She took his hand and drew him outside to the deck, where they were sheltered from the wind and the snow was falling in huge, slow, fluffy flakes.

'Look at it,' she said. 'This is pure magic. The mountains and the trees and the snow. And the way you got me to wish upon a falling star, that night... Do you know what I wished for?'

He waited.

'I wanted to fall back in love with life. Leave all the bad bits of the past behind,' she said. 'And I think even then I wanted to feel safe enough to fall in love with you.'

'It's safe,' he said. 'I might have a dodgy knee, but you can always lean on me.'

'You taught me,' she said softly, 'to trust again. To hurl myself down a slope on two tiny bits of wood or whatever skis are made of, and know that I'm not going to fall and hurt myself. You gave me my confidence back. And I've realised now that what I want for Christmas is for you to feel the same.'

'Safe enough to fall in love with you?' he asked. 'Yes. I love you, Sophie. But do you feel safe enough to fall in love with me?'

She pretended to think about it, then dropped down on one knee. 'I love you, Josh Cavendish. With you, I've got my confidence back. I feel safe. I don't care how much you're worth and I really don't care about skiing in posh places or partying with celebrities. I just want to make a family with you and our baby—and to work with you to make the world a better place. Happy Christmas, Josh. Will you marry me?'

'In a heartbeat,' he said, drawing her back up to her feet. 'Happy Christmas, Sophie.'

And then he kissed her as the snow fell softly round them.

EPILOGUE

Christmas Eve, two years later

OPENING DAY.

Josh had worked incredibly hard on setting up the resort, spending his entire trust fund and savings on it, refurbishing all the accommodation so it was suitable for all guests and their families, no matter what their physical abilities. Cavendish Software had given them an extensive sponsorship package to fill in the gaps, and although they'd been up and running properly for a month today was the day that Josh's sister Lauren was going to cut the ribbon and open the resort officially. Christmas Eve: a day special to all of them.

Sophie had worked by Josh's side all the way, creating menus that could be easily adapted to their guests' needs; she worked on training the seasonal chalet staff, too, doing the interviews herself and giving people a chance to turn their lives round.

Today, the resort was in full Christmas mode. A Christmas market, sending out the gorgeous smells of Christmas food; Christmas trees dotted around the resort; Christmas songs being played by a local band;

and Father Christmas in his sleigh, ready to hand out presents to everyone.

'Ready?' Sophie asked.

'Yes. No.' Josh took a deep breath. 'This is scarier than standing at the top of a championship freestyle run. Right, Lex?'

Little Alexandra Louisa—named after Josh's dad and Sophie's mum—who was comfortably sitting on her father's shoulders, pulled her father's hair, kissed him and laughed. 'Dada!'

Josh grinned. 'Just like her mum. Keeping me in line.'

Sophie laughed. 'She loves you to bits. Just like I do. Just like we all do.' She stole a kiss. 'I'm so proud of you. And I'm prouder still that you're not going down the slope as a champ but as an assistive instructor.' And Josh's student Mia—an eight-year-old girl with cerebral palsy—was going to be the star of the show, proving that a girl the doctors had said at birth might not ever be able to walk could beat the odds.

'This isn't about me,' he said. 'It's about making the world a better place. Giving people chances.' He kissed her. 'Just like you've done with me. You rescued me.'

'We rescued each other,' Sophie said. 'Now go and ski.'

'Me ski,' Lex said hopefully.

'Later, princess,' Josh promised.

'Go and make sure Mia's all right,' Sophie said, taking Lex off her father's shoulders and settling her on her own. 'We'll be waiting for you both at the bottom, with Mum and Dad.' Josh's parents had asked her to call them that even before the wedding. Lauren had welcomed her instantly as a little sister. And Sophie had been drawn straight into the heart of the Cavendish family as one of their own.

'The woman I love, our daughter, our family and our community. And doing a job that actually means something and makes a difference to other people's lives,' Josh said. 'It doesn't get any better than this.'

Oh, but it would.

Though Sophie wasn't going to tell him that particular piece of news until he was safely at the bottom of the slope again, with his skis off. He didn't need the distraction of a positive pregnancy test.

So she just smiled. 'I love you.'

'I love you, too,' Josh said.

'Dada ski,' Lex said, patting the top of her mother's head.

'Yes, Dada ski,' Sophie agreed.

She went to stand with the Cavendishes and watched as Josh met Lauren and Mia at the top of the slope, Lauren made a short speech and cut the ribbon, and Josh helped guide Mia down the slope. She made sure all the waiting staff were circulating with drinks and nibbles and had the support they needed in the kitchen, the journalists had all the background they needed, and posed with Josh, Lex and Mia for photos.

And then, when everything was in full swing and Lex was with her grandparents, she whisked Josh off to a balcony for a private moment.

'Happy?' she asked.

'Ecstatic,' he said. 'Today's been perfect.'

She grinned. 'There's always room to add a cherry on top of a Christmas cake.'

'How?' He looked intrigued.

'I have a Christmas present for you.'

Josh looked intrigued. 'A present?'

'Not something to unwrap right now. But your hospitality manager would like to give you advance warning that's she's taking leave in July.'

'July?' He looked confused. 'Are we going on holiday somewhere, Soph?'

She laughed. 'Not quite. It's a particular kind of leave. Which I'll need to take in about—ooh—seven months' time. Hence July. And that's why you can't unwrap your present now. You'll have to wait until July.'

She rested both hands on her stomach and watched as the penny dropped.

'Sophie Cavendish! Are you telling me we're going to be parents again?'

'Yup.'

His face filled with delight. 'That's not just an extra cherry on top of a Christmas cake. It's one of those cake fountains.' He picked her up and whirled her round. 'So when did you find out?'

'This morning,' she said. 'I've been dying to tell you all day. But I'm not giving you news like that before you go down a slope—even if it's not a black run and you're teaching. That's a distraction too far.'

'You're right,' he said. 'But it's the perfect bit of news to end a perfect day. In the perfect place. With the perf—'

'I've got the message—you don't have to say that word again,' she cut in with a grin, and kissed him. 'Happy Christmas, Josh.'

* * * * *

COMING SOON!

MILLS & BOON

THE HEART OF ROMANCE

A ROMANCE FOR EVERY READER

MODERN

Prepare to be swept off your feet by sophisticated, sexy and seductive heroes, in some of the world's most glamourous and romantic locations, where power and passion collide.

HISTORICAL

Escape with historical heroes from time gone by. Whether your passion is for wicked Regency Rakes, muscled Vikings or rugged Highlanders, awaken the romance of the past.

MEDICAL

Set your pulse racing with dedicated, delectable doctors in the high-pressure world of medicine, where emotions run high and passion, comfort and love are the best medicine.

True Love

Celebrate true love with tender stories of heartfelt romance, from the rush of falling in love to the joy a new baby can bring, and a focus on the emotional heart of a relationship.

Desire

Indulge in secrets and scandal, intense drama and plenty of sizzling hot action with powerful and passionate heroes who have it all: wealth, status, good looks…everything but the right woman.

HEROES

Experience all the excitement of a gripping thriller, with an intense romance at its heart. Resourceful, true-to-life women and strong, fearless men face danger and desire - a killer combination!

To see which titles are coming soon, please visit

millsandboon.co.uk/nextmonth

MILLS & BOON

Coming next month

VEGAS WEDDING TO FOREVER
Sophie Pembroke

There was safety in numbers. And Toby was alone.

Or he had been, until he woke up married.

Still, now the time came to actually put his plan to her, the words seemed stuck in his throat. Was this crazy? Probably. But it was still the only plan he had.

"I've been thinking." In between the pounding hangover and the being shouted at. "About this marriage thing. I know it might not have been exactly planned on either side, but you are my wife." The marriage certificate had shown up in the pocket of the trousers he'd been wearing the night before, already creased and crumpled.

"If this is you about to offer me money again—"

"It's not," Toby said, quickly. Now he'd had some more coffee, he could see the flaws in that plan. He'd never paid for sex, he wasn't about to start paying for marriage. Not to mention that scandal it would cause if it came out. His father would be revolving slowing in his grave already, but if anyone else found out what had actually happened here he'd probably go into a full on spin.

"Then what?" Autumn asked, impatiently. "I've got to go and clear out my room after this. And, you know, find another job." She waved her phone at him too fast for him to make out anything more than the vague impression of a text message. "My roommate says the boss is about to throw my stuff out into the street if I don't go and collect it. I mean, I travel lighter than most, but I'd still like to not lose everything I possess, if you don't mind?"

"I think we should stay married." The words flew out unbidden, sending Autumn's eyes wide and her mouth clamped shut. "I meant to build up to that a bit more," he admitted, rubbing a hand across his aching brow. "Explain my reasons and such. But in essence, I think we should stay married, and you should come to Wishcliffe with me. For a time."

Continue reading
VEGAS WEDDING TO FOREVER
Sophie Pembroke

Available next month
www.millsandboon.co.uk

MILLS & BOON
MEDICAL
Pulse-Racing Passion

Set your pulse racing with dedicated, delectable doctors in the high-pressure world of medicine, where emotions run high and passion, comfort and love are the best medicine.

MILLS & BOON

HEROES

At Your Service

Experience all the excitement of a gripping thriller, with an intense romance at its heart. Resourceful, true-to-life women and strong, fearless men face danger and desire - a killer combination!

Inc... ...ilmore
is l... ...known
theatres. Married with one daughter, one fluffy dog and
two dog-loathing cats, she can usually be found with her
nose in a book. Jessica writes emotional romance with
a hint of humour, a splash of sunshine, delicious food—
and equally delicious heroes!

Kate Hardy has been a bookworm since she was a
toddler. When she isn't writing Kate enjoys reading,
theatre, live music, ballet and the gym. She lives with
her husband, student children and their spaniel in
Norwich, England. You can contact her via her website:
katehardy.com.